PARSIFAL

Peter Vansittart

PARSIFAL

A Novel

PETER OWEN · LONDON

U.S. DISTRIBUTOR
DUFOUR EDITIONS
CHESTER SPRINGS,
PA 19425-0449
(215) 458-5005

ISBN 0 7206 0711 6

PETER OWEN PUBLISHERS
73 Kenway Road London SW5 0RE

First published in Great Britain 1988
© Peter Vansittart 1988

Photoset by Photo·graphics Honiton Devon
Printed in Great Britain by A. Wheaton & Co. Ltd Exeter

To Paul and Diana Tory

Do the stripped boughs grapple
above the troubled streams
    when he dream-fights
his nine-day's fight
    which he fought alone
with the hog in the wilderness
    when the eighteen twilights
    and the ten midnights
and the equal light of the nine mid-mornings
were equally lost
    with the light of the saviour's jury
and the dark fires of the hog's eye
which encounter availed him nothing.

        David Jones, from *The Sleeping Lord*

What's real and what's true ain't necessarily the same.

Salman Rushdie

Archer had always been inclined to think that chance and circumstance played a small part in shaping people's lot compared with their innate tendency to have things happen to them.

Edith Wharton

There are certain limited beings of dazzling but shallow beauty whom, to be frank, we should be quite justified in despising if it were not for the fact that they present us with the spectacle of a flawless adaptation to existence, a miraculous equivilance between their desires and the things within their reach, between their words and the questions they are asked, between their abilities and the professions they exercise. They are born, live and die as if the world were made for them and they for the world, and the rest – the doubters, the troubled, the curious, Étienne, I – watch them go by and wonder at their 'naturalness', their unexpected spontaneity and ease.

Michel Tournier

One

When I first met Richard Wagner, in an overcrowded tavern, I thought I might arouse his interest by telling him that I had known Parsifal with some intimacy. With my experience of people, I should not have been surprised by his immediate irritation. He asked me no questions, indeed did no more than growl out some imprecation about idle witness, and though we were several times fellow-guests at court, he always avoided me, with obvious suspicion and dislike.

Two

1

Once upon a time there was a mighty warrior who sired seven sons and loved to exclaim to himself, 'Far away and over the hills'. It is not surprising that he was often far from home and at last was killed in battle, together with six of his sons. Naked, the bards sang, they came to the field, and naked they left it.

The widow, to preserve her youngest, fled with him to the damp woods. With her went other women and children, together with bards, slaves, old men, and those who with fine words and loud voices had shrunk from riding to battle. In her grief, a bard declaimed in cracked, fleeting tones, the sun was for her but a dreary mist, she forswore the world's delights: day and night were one, her heart a bag of sorrow.

Now she possessed this one boy, together with many pigs and a cauldron engraved with snakes and rivers. On the boy all her love and hopes were now set. Before his birth she had listened much to solemn flutes and grave song, gazed at runes cut on trees, and pictures scrawled in dust by the wind. She had sat with experienced women and knowing Oak Priests, undeterred by her own aunt who had done likewise but proved deaf to the wisdom of music and words and indeed, much later, angered by both, had hanged her daughter.

The youngest son was born in spring under favoured skies and trees. With his stalwart ancestry he was fated to perish by violence or commit wilful injury, so, to outwit yet appease the fate goddess, daughter or mother of the Great Queen, very probably both, he was given a wren to squeeze so that it died. This, the Oak Priests swore, would relieve him of all raging ambition, though not all thought it enviable. Women decided, without having been asked, that his blood-brother was a deer or swan, beloved by gentle gods. The mother constantly washed his hands in dew. Why? It scarcely needs explaining. This would prevent his becoming a thief: dew, perpetually fresh, not quite rain or stream, neither cloud nor pool, but partaking of all, was a border between mortals and gods, thus peculiarly powerful.

She taught him all she knew – not very much – of the Other World. Also, how to kindle a fire, recite verse, pluck a harp. But of weapons and fights she said nothing, and forbade all talk of smiths, forays, dragons, victories. Instead, she told him tales of lovers, seals, boars, birds that bore daughters to the east wind. She would remind him that he was ugly, not because it was true, but to make him shy of women and prevent him boasting, which offends all in the Other World, notably the Great Queen. The boy, not yet named, known only as the Widow's son, was now some four years old. Within the dark-green shades of groves, never soundless, he stored memories of chattering, striding people; wild music, clash of metal, thud of horses, about which he was forbidden to ask. In these safe woods weapons were concealed, horses were lacking.

Life had certainly changed for all who had kept their memories polished. Brilliant lamps were extinguished, much treasure was lost, the old stir and clamour of her husband's day might never have been. All was now hushed, quiet as the moon. Thick trees and hedges protected yet besieged them, dense with presences furtive yet live. At dusk, in the hushed, mysterious embrace of light and dark, willows might follow you down the path, speaking in low, thin tones like the dead, which perhaps they were. Night was magician's territory: walls were higher, straining at flimsy, drifting shades. Towards midnight the dead certainly approached, creeping through shadows, expecting to find the inhabitants sleeping, the fires still warm, ready to be aggrieved, even malevolent, if disappointed. Most of the dead, however, clustered on mountains, the readiest paths to the Other World.

In darkness the Widow listened, very powerful, daughter of gods, but fearful, for within the apparent stillness was much fidgeting. Cross-paths clasped each other, then hurried on, handmaids of the Great Queen, proceeding from the unseen, departing to the unimaginable, or to the Great Queen herself, even less imaginable. Rites were often held at crossways, invisible watchers gathering behind the air and feeding on spirits of

10

transgressors buried beneath. Here too the dead were placated with blood from severed heads.

The Great Queen? Who she was could not be uttered, save as Mother of the Lake, Protector of Horses, Lady of Three. To speculate was dangerous, to inquire was worse. Secretly the Widow's son wondered whether she was moonlight, even the moon herself, who certainly had three masks – the curve, the circle and the black mask. He did know that she lived in the Other World, and when mortals approached her there they must avert their heads. To look upon her would blind you, as it had done Diall the Unsmiling, or even turn you to stone, as was proved by the tall boulder at the forest edge.

Roads, bridges, edges, summits are dense with presences. Walls and gates cannot exclude the unseen or withstand the unpredictable. Everything has power, its glow faint or strong – twig, knife, pig, story. Once, in a blessed well, he saw a head, recently cut, to strengthen the water. It stared at him from beneath the green surface, and he ran away when it smiled. At a ford he met another head, gazing from a pole, bald and wrinkled, still dripping. At fords, in the dark time, an old chief was said to fight a youth.

Limits were perilous, damming up life which might then explode, drenching the world with flame. One old man, crossing a water boundary, always so trembled that he could go no farther. He had once been a warrior, collector of heads, though forbidden by the Widow to reveal his exploits. Perhaps these, hoarded within him, had rotted his spirit.

Somewhere deep in the woods lived not only the small Forest People but the Alder King, the Bird Man, the Wood King, seen by none but priests, who could describe them only under the circular moon. It was whispered that the Great Queen herself haunted some region both far away and very near. Undeniably, on an island forbidden to all, hung a wooden goddess.

Wherever he went, trees, hedges, waters moved too, passing him, circling him, twisting away to nothing. He would halt to see if they did too, and usually they did.

Moving from the hall into the trees he held his breath, not always knowing he did so. Under branches, different airs covered him, different sounds warned or preyed from the loftiest branches. Out of a mound of holly and briar might issue high, prolonged keenings, to repel ghosts from parts of the forest occupied by them alone. Sometimes a tree murmured 'Distance' or even 'Forward'. He knew that ahead, always a little ahead, was where 'the Beloved', the great white boar, chose to leave his dung, a holy place, for boars are honoured by gods and chiefs. Somewhere, too, in the exact centre of the forest, a vast oak was watched by

11

a stone hedge. It was like the earth itself, fixed in the very centre of the sky, so that the two were directly linked. If the oak were reached, the venturer could pluck shining gifts. It hovered, a promise, a dream of an isle of apples, the white boar leading you to lands beneath the earth.

Occasionally you could feel, indeed see, another's thoughts: mother's fear of metal, a girl desiring an apple, an old woman scared of wolves. It was probably at this oak that, every ninth year, chosen ones had their throats cut, as they hung over a cauldron dedicated to the god Teutates. Strangers could thus vanish, abandoned, the priests said, by the Great Queen, having been proved neither gods nor messengers. Messengers had queerness; protected, they could yet die unexpectedly, though an axe had lately been drowned for wounding a messenger. Other sacrifices were due every seventh year. There were whispers of children being eaten by wild goats, not seen again until that night between Cutting Time and Midwinter when mortals mingled with the dead. When the chosen is stabbed or beheaded, from his way of falling, from his last posture, Oak Priests and Alder Kings can foretell the future. Occasionally in winter, as the boy listened, pondered, half slept before the steaming cauldron, life seemed but a grudging pardon from the Great Queen.

Lines existed, unseen but powerful ripples. Sometimes, on these secret lines, the Oak Priests ordered dances to strengthen the earth, and also the dead or, as some old fellow muttered, stamp them down deeper, for though some of the dead were welcome, others were feared.

Girls, he was learning, had always to be careful, for ghosts could enter even fish, nuts, beans, which, if eaten at certain periods, might emerge as babies, children of a god, the priests believed.

For whatever reasons, mother debarred girls from the hall, so that they seemed to exist only amongst the poor. He knew little more about them save that they sometimes flew out of their bodies to spy upon men. Older girls might be glimpsed crouching by fords, and because souls originated in water, theirs might be very strong. Certainly a woman kneeling or weaving by water had to be avoided, though it was not always known why. The Great Queen was known to wash herself at fords.

2

Once this Widow's son accidentally killed a white bird by throwing a flint in the air. Its body, twisted and oozing, a mass of stained feathers, made him weep, for birds delighted him.

12

Their swoops, their songs. From his alarmed mother he learnt a new word: 'cruelty'.

Always his thoughts, drifting away from him, would alight on a wing, a root, a bud, giving them fresh colour. He learnt to beware of eyes, the eyes of man and animal. They seemed to burn into his skin, or noosed him with vague threats which paralysed him.

Days were passing. He was ugly, he was nameless and, save for his mother, he was alone. She continued to deny him a name, to bind him closer to her. Names could be bestowed or inherited, they could also be won and, never forgetting the deaths of her husband and sons, she blamed them on their need to claim new names. Names were usually ancestral; to assume an ancestor's name risked inheriting his soul, here inadmissible. Seeking a name meant much ruin. Grieving for her lost ones she defied life, its deceptions and temptations, and was determined to thrust off the day when it would more fully claim her last-born. To him she spoke more often of the Other World, to distract him from mortal ambitions.

Some folk knew of the Lady Arianrod, far away and over the seas, was it three score years ago, was it three thousand? Arianrod, Silver Circle, had cursed her son for some fault and refused him a name, leaving him disgraced and weak. When you are nameless, you drift unarmed against the restless caprice of star, earth, fate. You are dedicated to no god, no hero, no ancestor, who would protect you. Names had powers, so that people dreaded uttering those of chiefs, the dead, the unlucky, lest an evil eye be attracted. The fierce wolf king was called 'Friendly Uncle', a savage eagle 'Loving Brother'. Some gave their children such menial names as 'Dust', 'Platter', 'Mouse', to hoodwink the evil eye. Unwanted daughters might be awarded such resplendent names as 'Whiter than the Sacred Boar', 'Most Beautiful under the Sky', presumptions certain to arouse the ire of demons or the Great Queen. Secretly you were free to choose your own name – 'Bear Brave', 'Bird Swift' – pressing beyond yourself, exploring mysterious corners, seeking what was elusive but perhaps within reach. Occasionally the Widow's son called himself 'Nasty Face', 'Nothing in Particular', or 'Nix Naught Nothing'.

Secretly? Yes. For others to know your real name would be risky, exposing it to vile spells that could injure your body as violently as a poisoned dart thrust through your footprint. To address a ghost or Other World prince by name would offend them.

Wise folk, therefore, had two names, one concealed from all but blood-brothers. The Widow said to herself, 'My son has no name, he is protected by my own. Therefore he is safe.'

Her son, though not indeed ugly, was not yet handsome. No

13

goddess had kissed his brow and left it shining. From pools and polished surfaces he knew that his hair was shapeless, his ears too large, his eyes too shy: he did not realize that his movements were light and that his eager smile might one day bring ruin even to the beautiful. Believing he was unfavoured, even deformed, affected by his dead brothers, themselves more real by never being mentioned, and whose ghosts he saw, or thought he saw, he remained awkward and diffident. His mother forbade him to show friendliness not only to girls but to other boys, save Badly Fed, who will be mentioned again. They are, she said, ill-destined. His own destiny she did not reveal, so that he imagined himself dedicated early to the Other World, even to the god Teutates.

So, like a charcoal burner cherishing his secrets, he strove to escape his mother's anxious care and roam the woods, his wondering blue eyes increasingly alert. A grey wall, too distant, never seen again, set his mind leaping. Keeping abreast of him on hills above the forest, towers loomed on the edge of the world. One tower would turn with the sun as if on a wheel, moving even when he was motionless though, even on a bright day, it might shine so fiercely that only the blinding fire showed where it stood.

He moved carefully, for everyone knew that crossing a bridge, path, threshold, or any place blasted by lightning, without whispering a password, might wither you, or worse. He avoided noise, quarrels, questions as he did snakes, and withdrew when obscene rhymes were exchanged to ward off vengeful imps. But those blue eyes and wide ears were more than ever vigilant. At sundown, when rasping querns were stilled and kiln fires sank, the trees quivered, satyrs flitted between shadows, people dissolved under leaves, though most would return with the light. Often a voice sounded, high and uneven, from blackness, to coax the moon back to life. Certain trees expected to receive gifts: wine, nuts, garlands, blood. Blood might come from an animal, and animals, especially stags, had been known to speak. Priests too sometimes dressed as wolves and occasionally changed into them, though few knew why. Pigs never spoke, which was a loss, for they, like birds, snakes, birds, were intimate with the secrets of Above and Below, and swineherds, like smiths, were honoured by all, and could be sought as mates even by queens. The sacred pigs' unwillingness to speak, meant that the Other World could be revealed only in sleep. Calm people, always young, moved in radiant garments, their voices just too soft to be understood. When a bard intoned 'Long ago . . . ' you felt something of the Other World.

He began to trace paths which, twitching and turning, were

14

said to have been made by the dead seeking their birthplace. Here he looked for white birds, which promised fair fortune. Crows and ravens did not. All around were further promises and warnings. Pools quivered with hidden lives. On a bridge at noon gods and mortals could throw off their shadows and partake of each other naked, but this the boy was afraid to contemplate, his mother ordering him to fear nakedness and avoid swimmers. Also, if ambushed by demons, you had only to count them and they would flee howling.

His mother tried to keep him within the hall, but he disobeyed her, for outside, interesting events always occurred. A fellow and his sling were summoned by the bards for slaying Red Deer, the baker. The man was forgiven, the sling was whipped, then used to kill a deer for the Midsummer Feast. Somehow he saw, swarthy above flames, Gonfan the limping smith, who had once put the wind in a bag.

This boy, call him Nix Naught Nothing, saw still more heads, skulls, horse masks tied to trees, to stakes, appeasing plague, famine, the Great Queen. Once, seeing one stake bare, he sensed that it was reserved for his own head, but was afraid to ask questions. To ask questions, his mother said, challenged fate and caused trouble. In a cleft of a hill he saw folk standing in green, glistening robes and holding silver goblets while shrill pipes sounded. He at once fled when they held out the cups to him, for gifts from the Other World were dangerous. One boy, 'long ago', accepted a trinket, fell asleep and, when he awoke, all the tribe were dead of old age.

Any hill might look insignificant, with only a few scattered trees and dull rocks, but within it might be unchartable crystal vaults, seas, floating islands, sparkling people, talking birds, a learned boar. That particular hill he never discovered again, however much he searched. Sometimes he was glad of this, remembering the trinket.

Older folk explained that in the Other World lived gods, and mortals restored from death by a golden cauldron, though there enjoying another vision, another language, which they could communicate to those on earth only at Sowing Time, Midsummer, Midwinter.

To reach the Other World was possible. The quickest way was to be blinded by an eclipse, a favour from sky gods who transported you there instantly. Otherwise you had first to cross borders – a fence, stile, ditch – then undergo some test, answer some riddle, recite a verse, difficulties planted to make the Pure Land invisible to the ignorant and malicious. No such challenges had he yet encountered, and whether the regular disappearances of both young and old meant welcome admission to the Other

15

World he was afraid to ask.

People wished to be buried on some border, neither in their homes nor out of them, so in the centre, which was magical. The Other World itself had no boundaries, was neither above nor below the earth, neither wholly part of it nor wholly separate like the sky. It had no sun, yet was lit by sunlight, brighter yet softer than earthly light, and divided by no seasons. Mortals sometimes stumbled into it, as if by chance, though priests taught that accidents never happen. Usually, such fortunates remained but briefly, then, as if from a dream, awoke alone on a cold hill or under a solitary larch, with deranged memories and thirsty for dew. A few never returned.

No prayer, training, virtue, could win favour from a god or entry to the Other World. Strangely, an outcast, smelly, drunken, violent, might suddenly be transported beyond men's sight, often for seven years, to return incoherent.

The very old muttered about a slave who had accidentally stumbled into a highland cave, ascending and descending simultaneously, as if drunk, the unkind said, then found gleaming pools and meadows where all were young, without death, sickness or tears. They removed his stained rags and, smiling, gave him thin green silks, together with his favourite dish: broiled venison, roasted apples, yellow wine. Later he yearned to come back briefly to embrace his mother. This was allowed, with warnings to keep utter secrecy. Leaving twigs to mark his track, he reached home but could not resist describing the games and enchantments he was already missing. Departing, however, he could see no twigs, he never found the cave, and perished starving, not drunk but witless, the unkind added.

Contemptuous of such tales, the Widow stood tall as a temple door, and bards croaked that when a lover desired a beloved of three colours – raven-black hair, blood-red cheeks, snow-white limbs – he need only look at her. At this she looked more contemptuous than ever.

Her son was by now begging to learn more about his father and brothers, for the wind, roaming through trees, lamented those lost lives. She reproached him for asking questions, but told him a little, though nothing of blood and conflict. His father, she said, had ridden the Chaldean East with its four rivers, succoured the poor, watched the usual magicians change mountains to honey and back again: he fed thousands with a single fish, spread the gifts of peace. His sons had virtues that, like song, uncaged the flapping spirit, and they had all died of goodness.

When she finished, the unkind kept silent. Forbidden to celebrate feuds, battles, weapons, the ageing bards could only

16

praise illustrious laws and genealogies of the swaggering sun and slender, subtle moon, and the wonders of cauldrons. Three drops from the Great Queen's cauldron gave you mastery of time, allowing you to ride with the dead, also with the unborn, and – the bards lowered their voices in fear of the Widow – a youth from the East who would overcome all the wide world. He was, they grumbled, clever as a salmon, brave as a bull, radiant as a kingfisher.

The boy also heard more of gods, usually but not always friendly: of Taranis, who makes thunder, the Nine Maidens, who drive storms across the sky, Nodens the Silver-handed, horned Cernunnus, Llyr the sky chief with his three daughters, the winds. With one, Creddylad, he fights at Midsummer before loving. He is also, at certain periods, the moon. That, the Oak Priests declared importantly, is understood only by the few, and people closed their eyes respectfully.

Some insisted that gale-haunted Llyr loved that daughter too madly, and that at Sowing Time she escaped and two chiefs struggled for her weeping body.

Gods could be human. Blood-drinking Teutates, Esus the Summer, Lug the Light. Mabon the Sun breathed life into the sky.

Brighter than these were goddesses dwelling on islands or beneath lakes, on frozen mountains or in blood-streaked groves. Some awaited you at stiles. A mare-headed goddess sent terror and tempest into dreams.

The end of each year was the Night of the Gods, when gods and the dead mingled with the earth-bound, all worlds joining in uncanny light. They left behind stories which, lit by brilliant dawns and heavy dusks, were repeated in the hall, save of course those of battles, hunts, even night rides. Nor did the Widow countenance talk of demons, often called 'Noble Lords', 'the Mothers', or of bandits, the 'Peaceful Ones'.

Stories had to be repeated exactly as they had always been, for to omit a word, misuse a rhyme, was akin to an ill-performed rite, impairing several worlds. Stories did more than provoke laughter, sorrow, spite; they could cure the sick, damage enemies, enchant and beguile. An earthquake, lately, or 'once upon a time', had been caused by a singer arrogantly replacing 'white as a swan's wing' with 'pallid as bird lime'.

Music hovered in the words behind words: in the dark torrent, the blue stream, wind's lament and summer rustle. One bard loved to sing,

> Winter snarls as the summer dies,
> Wind bullies the low sun in weak light.

The Widow's son listened, motionless with awe. He now knew of a queen who had been changed to a butterfly, though a god's son then gave her a glass hut in which he nightly restored her. Eating a nut in a badly chosen month, a chief's daughter found herself deep underground with the nastiest of the dead. Cernunnus could be stag, tree, a cry, a bowl of sunlight. All was both more and less than could be seen. On pots and jars painted men were always melting into birds, twigs, leaves; curled lines were suddenly snakes or paths through the sky.

There was also the Bear Chief, who had existed since the beginning. Such excitements he absorbed, pondered and doubtless misunderstood.

In this way he lived, contriving to speak only with those exalted men, the smith and the swineherd, and permitted but one companion, 'Badly Fed', who was dumb, perhaps from having stepped into the Other World and been forbidden to describe it. He was also black, having been born at night. Once, wishing to reach the moon, he had climbed a tree but, deciding he was little nearer, waited until he spied the moon in a pond, then dived in with shining eyes.

Meanwhile, the boy was growing, escaping, not only to Badly Fed but to other boys and occasional girls. For this, he would often be beaten, for, like most women, Mother had more eyes than were visible. He would not yet, however, swim with them, for nakedness, like rhyme, had mysteries which both tempted and dismayed.

He was beginning to feel expectant. Perhaps he was to be favoured by a god. Perhaps Teutates was hungry again.

3

People were murmuring that the Widow's son still had no name, was only Nix Naught Nothing. He was growing tall, his chin already flecked with pale gold, but remained exposed to demons, like a baby who, through namelessness, was protected only by candles burning away the noxious spirits.

A bard, wrinkled as the nut he clasped, draped in shabby feathers to assist the flight of his words – winged words, the boy told himself – mumbled that at Dagda Time, the beginning, eight powers of speech had floated from the sky, and woman stole seven. This was deemed a rebuke to the Widow. Yet her unwillingness to name her son was understandable. A name might tie him more closely to his warrior ancestors, lodging him in a world she could not control. Fearing the bloodshot past she shrank from the future, though time, the Oak Priests told her,

18

was only a snake swallowing its own tail, but, by withholding a name, she fancied she could preserve the boy even from snakes.

Naming was tricksome. If you pray to a god and name him incorrectly, you may be punished, though to refrain from prayer can be worse. To name your child after a divinely protected chief is prudent, yet the choice is sometimes made at the instant when protection is withdrawn, so that the child is blotched, maimed or unwitted.

While the demand for his naming slowly loudened, the boy was making interesting discoveries. Apparently, his hair, fingers, feet, the little spear between his legs, were linked to stars and the Other World; particularly his head, within which dwelt the spirit, the soul, itself deathless, thus rendering a head, particularly that of a notable, powerful beyond reckoning, a casket of treasures. That explained why a new bridge, gate, house needed a freshly cut head buried beneath it to ensure survival. Dead people's heads were cut off to release their souls, and to possess such a head usually assured respect from the ghost. He suspected that the chest, always tightly corded, by mother's couch, contained heads. All knew of the chief who sliced off his enemy's head and made a ball of the brains and earth. The ball, still bright with the dead man's spirit, able to extinguish fire and shatter stone, eventually killed the chief. This was not told in the hall, but all knew it, and of the Bear Chief, very near, very far, slaying twins and red-haired children.

The Bear Chief was seldom mentioned. Silence hung about him, though people knew that on special days he had to sit motionless with his feet between a girl's thighs.

Once the Widow's son saw his own spirit, a glistening bowl with sinuous lines foaming into dew-drops and feathers, drifting into the light opened by a candle fixed in a skull.

One rainy day he was wandering alone on hills, hoping for he knew not what, but imagining that something was waiting, perhaps kneeling by the path, weaving by water, lurking in tree-tops that sometimes whispered, sometimes howled. The path itself was irregular, the sun now on one side, now on the other. A bright slope suddenly gleamed through grey, sodden air. Could it be a patch of the Other World? Then it was blotted out as he turned by a heavy mound, and at once shivered, sensing himself watched.

He halted, looked about him and saw, at slingshot distance from behind hillocks almost level with him, a head. The eyes were dull, the hair strewn with mud, chin resting on tufted grass. All was still. Then, abruptly, it vanished, leaving him scared. Had it been Cernunnus, Lord of Heads? Or an Alder King who would cure ague, though he did not have it? Despite Mother's precautions he knew of Con of the Thousands and Mesgrega the Golden who were challenged by strangers to behead them, then be beheaded. A mystery, the priests explained, not everyone could understand.

He nerved himself to go forward to a path that led down to the forest. Soon he saw the head again, in a clearing, gazing from yellowy bush and dripping red tears, staring from eyes unblinking as if painted. It must be unearthly, from behind the air. Seen nearer, its eyes were rimmed with black. Turning aside, he ran, once tripping over a root, falling, recovering, then seeing the head a third time, between trees, aloft in dim, frail space. Now his blood quivered, also his legs, for he saw that it was spiked on a pole gripped by an unseen hand, perhaps one of the Forest People. He fled. Nothing further alarmed him, no bird changed to a twig, no hare quivered into flame, a butterfly remained a butterfly.

Returning, he said nothing. He had learnt to keep secrets, knowing too the dangers of curiosity. You could know too much. However, he realized more keenly that something was astir. The old men were whispering, their lined, parched faces looked worried. Possibly a Bird Man had been seen at last, or the glittering hand of god Nodens had pointed towards himself, showing that because he was ugly he soon must die. But no, they were concerned with his namelessness. Were he not named by Mother, others might name him, maliciously, drawing down evil. There had once been an unnamed boy whom, without knowing why, people began calling 'Heavy', then 'Too Heavy'. Later he was found strangled. His ghost long plagued them, accusing and cursing, until expelled by a satirical verse.

A name, the old men insisted, was more vital than an open gate. Gates themselves were controlled by names which entrants must evoke. Your own name, carved on an enemy's sword, would paralyse his arm.

One day the boy saw the grey-beards stationed in a half-circle around his mother, seated above them in dark blue folds, her hair bundled with a green ribbon. Anxious women and slaves were listening though pretending to hear nothing. A few dwarfs and hunchbacks had been brought in, for luck.

An Oak Priest in bird-shaped cap was speaking, too low for the boy to hear. This man knew the magic of writing and could dispatch soundless messages to all the worlds, a skill granted mankind by a god who once cut seven signs on a birch. When he ceased, he doffed the feathered cap, and stood back. Others began chanting the customary tributes to the Widow. Her teeth were a shower of pearls, her face the golden flush of the moon, her hair wheat bright, her wisdom the envy of the Other World, her pedigree stretched from sunrise to sunset and back. Soon, however, she interrupted, harshly, for in truth her hair was grey, her few teeth were black, only her strong voice survived from her pedigree, and this bade them disclose their great matter before they spoke further of her ancestors, those gods, magicians and, alas, warriors.

'Lady, for your son to remain without a name, to be beholden to himself alone, is a darkness and grief, a rejection of gods and forefathers, more ill-omened than cross-eyes or birth when an owl screeches. Retribution will come of it. The born and unborn beseech you to remedy it and restore the future.'

She listened, she frowned and she scolded. What! Was she accused? Were her wits a madman's frolic? Was she no man's daughter but misbegotten by wind and fog?

All, even the Oak Priest, crouched in terror, abjectly mumbling, until her railing suddenly ceased. She stood up, grew taller in her anger, then sighed, soft but startling, her hand swept through her grey tresses, which dropped like a waterfall. She was unsmiling, very stiff, ominously mild. 'It shall be as you wish, this very night. I shall bring the name. It is my pledge. Whoever has ears, let him use them.'

Namings were performed just before midnight, an auspicious borderland. So the boy was roused in the darkness and escorted naked to the last palings of the settlement. A flask of dew was produced, touched by fresh sun and tired moon, on a frontier between earth and air. It was sprinkled over his head and feet, hands and little spear. Then his forehead was anointed with pig's blood, for purging, though the bards had sung that he was faultless, was indeed purer than Mabon the Sun. Bowls were swiftly filled with milk, to appease the hideous Mothers, the Noble Lords, the Peaceful Ones and the Great Queen. As the precious liquid touched his little spear, his skin rippled, like tiny mice scuttling over him. What would he be called? Surely any name would be too large for one so ill-visaged? His ears were huge, his hair like wild heather jaundiced by too much sun.

From the dim, stirring concourse, faces were lit here and there by a husk of moon floating between thick clouds. His mother's voice tolled: 'I have bent to your wishes. My last, most beloved son has a name, which is his due. He will be called Stay-at-Home.'

Fires were lit, milk was poured to Nodens, though he might have preferred wine or barley juice. There was singing and dancing, and the boy was forgotten. Some of him was glad, enjoying the enflamed uproar, some of him was disappointed.

21

His name bound him more closely to his mother's watchfulness. To name anything both enhanced and limited it. Even gods lost some power when they let their names be known, especially their secret names. Henceforward they were confined to the exact, the possible. He was told he was now secure for ever, like a favourite hound, like a threshold. Yet he fretted. The dark trees and airy hills now seemed insufficient and paths were eager to lead him beyond them. His name slowed the pace of life, frustrated his impulses. He still climbed trees with Badly Fed, looked for the distant tower, but was discontented.

A shepherd was known to have encountered three swans which in sunlight changed to naked maidens. This troubled rather than enticed him. He wanted to see them, yet closed his eyes as if fearing blindness. When he fondled his little spear he felt nothing.

One morning, on pretence of gathering wood, he hurried away. The grass was still damp and he wondered whether dew was part of night or morning, and whether it was softer than water. He knew, moreover, that he and his shadow, orchards and birds, love and pain, feasts and hunger, were mysteriously united in the Great Queen, though this was bards' stuff, not yet to be fully revealed.

He wandered his usual paths, yet much had changed. A bird called, but as though to him alone, as if it were one of his dead brothers. Only the Oak Priests, however, understood bird talk. When he gazed into a pool, he realized that he was not malformed, indeed less ugly than he had so long believed. He was not, indeed, beautiful as the thousand butterflies that bards enjoyed praising, graceful as the silks of the Other World, nor did his hair glisten as in a song of lovers, which the bards sang, sang perhaps too often, but he was tall and straight, and his eyes were full and blue, blue as the sea, old women assured him, though confessing that they had never seen it.

His mother, thinking herself alone, had once sung, 'Seeking solitude in the pathless sea', which made her young and strange but, seeing him spying on her, listening, she was angry, and he never heard her sing again.

He moved on through stillness. Bird and insect merged in a low hum beneath broad leaves. Soon another sound intruded, scuffling, irregular, quite near. Forest People. They were seldom seen, were sometimes hunted during famine but said to be shy and harmless. They settled quarrels by having the sick, the witless and deformed imitate the disputants, mocking them into peace. He swiftly realized that the sounds were those of horses and at once held his breath. No horses survived amongst his people, but, like pigs, they were beloved in the Other World, to which they might lead the wanderer. Some held that daily a horse pulled down the sun, letting night flow over earth's rim.

He slid behind a tree. Birds squawked, then went dumb. A branch clicked. The horses' feet were heavy on the thick, heated air, through which water was running. Harsh figures must be approaching, fierce from some dolorous tower. He peered through shrubs. The animals were nearer, nearer. He could now see the glimmer of a stream. Very timidly he moved a little forward, then stood amazed.

Three strangers were watering horses, from whose necks dangled dried human heads. The men were young, fiercely bearded, tall. Long knives glittered at their waists and they wore bull-hide jerkins still fresh and hairy. One, the broadest, ruddiest, had a face slightly twisted under massed hair, red as Lot the Light in his sunset splendour. His white horse had ears dyed red, and dyed on his arm was a hawk.

Stay-at-Home knew at once that the Hawk Youth had already seen him. The others too were straightening, turning, patting their mounts before the red-haired spoke, slow and distinct, as if to a simpleton.

'Young friend. Of what people are you? Of what region?'

The others chuckled in no very friendly manner. The questioner waited, eyes a frozen brown, mouth cruel. The boy was dumb, very afraid. Questions always alarmed him, answers were difficult. The red-haired young man still stared in silence, the other chuckled again. To reply that he was named 'Stay-at-Home' when he was far from home would only confuse. He was young, but no friend. His people shared blood with the Boi folk descended from a great fish, but to utter this might sound boastful to these three, who were at least princes, perhaps from the Other World. Really, he considered himself still Nix Naught Nothing, but hesitated to make himself seem even less.

'Let us hear you speak,' another stranger said slowly. 'To remain silent is insolent, as even a slave knows.'

The boy trusted the Hawk Youth most, and, stammering slightly, trusting his spirit to send him soft words, tried to describe the hall and the huts around it. His spirit, indeed, allowed him more. Perhaps for the first time in his life he nerved himself to ask who they, others, might be, seeing them already mounting their horses, apparently satisfied that he was without importance.

The Hawk Youth deigned him a nod as his companions shifted their steeds to another path. 'We serve the Bear Chief, whose sword flashes fiercer than lightning.'

'But where is he?'

They all frowned, suspecting he was mocking them, then, at his innocent eyes, grinned. 'If you do not know,' the third said in his turn, 'you won't last long in the wide world. You should also know that his sword and spear settle all questions. With them the Bear Chief pursued the noble White Boar and the Seven Pigs to the edge of the world, then to the world beneath. With them he is lord of all under the sky, indeed he is rather more. Now, go home, and learn your lessons.'

This adventure too he kept to himself. Yet he could think of little else than the Bear Chief. Dim tales revived: raids for a magic cauldron, a child born from a tree, protection from a circle, strange love from twelve flashing stars. Of sword and spear, of course, he knew very little.

Days now seemed shorter but more vivid, part of dreams, those shreds of the Other World. Here he reached the tower always turning to the sun, and within were twelve Chestnut boys and five Beech girls, one of whom he rescued from bear talons. Tall stones trembled when he began counting them, then danced before toppling into nothingness.

At noon he might feel a brooding presence behind the light: it could be a red head, gleaming cup, the mysterious sword, about which Badly Fed might know but would have no words to describe. He was no longer a child. Mother was sadder, greyer, smaller, at times drooping into shadows, always brooding over her dead, who perhaps visited her by night, their spirits seeking the cauldron of immortality.

At last, Stay-at-Home could no longer keep the three riders to himself and, as if pressed by some imp within, he told his mother of them and their fellowship with the Bear Chief. She was much alarmed, and forgetting her own edicts against curiosity, which, she had so often said, had left him fatherless, she asked questions, not all of them understandable. Were their feet winged? Were their arms scarred? Had they sung?

His replies, however, were vague, and anxiety did not leave her face.

When he next left the hall he was scared of her rebuke, but she no longer seemed to notice and he ran out joyfully into the sunlight, making not for the woods but for the smooth green hill from which he had once seen the fleeting tower. The sky was empty but for a white cloud and brief streak of birds. Climbing, he fancied he saw, below, a fox, once perhaps blood-brother of a chief and now, in the way of things, likely to be the Chief himself. Reaching the summit, he was surprised to find a circular tarn, surely new. He sighed contentedly, cooling his face and legs, then sat watching the sparkles. In the warmth they began enlarging, becoming a golden mass so dense and bright that he closed his eyes and was at once asleep.

He awoke in terror. The golden pool had vanished, in dry dust were three great steamy dogs, underworld hounds, blacker than a goatherd's teeth or the holes between dreams save for their fangs, yellow and dripping and six eyes flecked with angry red. They crouched together, their nerves maddened by him, their growls like the earth stirring. Already he was fleeing, his mind gone; he had only blind, frantic urgency to escape the teeth at his heels, those eyes like a fatal net, the breath like a fire curling to overtake, the snarls. It was in the dream in which, breathless, rushing, you cannot move and, faster than birds, dangers pile up around you. Now a leaf hung, swollen, menacing, then a cackle like wood tearing, a swooping shadow, and still the furious tongues scorched and his spirit shrivelled. He was failing, the dogs were almost alongside, dust spewing up at him, black masses famished and snapping. A gigantic paw ripped out at him, missed, dissolved, was back again, his heart breaking its moorings. Wild pains gripped his legs. He could not breathe, his sight was fading, he was nothing in nowhere, collapsing before the huge muzzles, about to be broken, torn, until, at this last, the chase slowed, fell away, the snarls crumbled, the animals, panting, sodden, were down on the turf, frustrated, but cowed, controlled by a figure who but an instant before had been only a shadow under a leafless tree but had now stepped forward to catch the boy as he fell.

Red hair, crooked nose and mouth, a slanted, perplexing grin, fierce, barely controlled eyes, an animal youthfulness. On his bare arm was the wild hawk. All this, Stay-at-Home, sobbing with exhaustion and relief, felt rather than saw in scattered jabs within himself. The dogs slunk away and, with unexpected gentleness, he was laid on moss, sunlight falling quietly around him, the dogs themselves teased into slumber.

He lay in dreamy, absolute trust, slowly recovering breath, content with the rich crawl of warmth on his limbs, the return of bird and insect, while, still standing, his rescuer gazed down through unsteady brown eyes, his smile balanced between mockery and friendliness.

He must have slept a little, but soon, with sensations of glad inevitability, he saw the Hawk Youth kneeling over him, touching his cheek, his neck, his long fair hair, saying nothing, still smiling. Lying still, he felt the hands glide lower, his tunic and kilt peeling off like bark. Stroked, then caressed more firmly, he no longer believed himself ugly. Now he was hot, now cool, now rigid, now astir and trembling, soundlessly turned this way and that, naked, by the resolute hands until the red head lowered, his little

25

spear tingling while he slid back into nothingness. The pressing fingers were like snow, melting on touch, the lips enclosed him utterly, belly, arms, little spear, giving silver, delicious anguish, an incredible relief. Later he thought of the tremulous instant shaken between dusk and night, the surge of a ninth wave so cherished by bards, a pennant flourished, then slowly, slowly drooping within acclaim.

Afterwards they stood together on the shaded edge of the forest, the subtle boundary subject to no time, no mortal commandment, a sign from the Other World.

At last the stranger spoke. 'It is farewell and not farewell. I follow the sun to the Bear Chief. One day you may follow. They call me Gwalchmai.' He grinned so that his teeth seemed large as pegs, 'the Spring Hawk. Others call me Vine Shoot.' His laugh was harsh, his hair flickered like flames, his face twisted, in malice or scorn.

5

Fear and joy, soothing pain, loving surrender, tender crushing, did they mean he was now a blood-brother? Gwalchmai and the Bear Chief haunted him, he prodded more deeply into fireside stories, the smith's grumbling songs, the swineherd's rough jests. The Bear Chief hunted the Noble Boar and the Stag with the Golden Horn, wrestled with the sun, traversed nine worlds. He rode the sky, thrusting between stars and, protected by three apple goddesses, slew small children as winter ended like a handful of smoke.

Stay-at-Home was impatient, for, in the familiar hall, he again felt himself clumsy, ill-favoured, awed by too much sameness, too little future. He had hopes, he had despair, circling like bats, but the hopes stubbornly refused to soar. Even in high summer he was nagged by frost's tooth.

When he wished to help a blind shepherd, the man desired no help and called him a moon-begotten fish. He rescued a hound from drowning, and the hound bit him and trotted away.

Fretful, sullen, challenged by lack of existence, he accosted his mother, rudely throwing down his cap.

'My son, what is hurting you?'

'I am sick at heart because I am nothing in nowhere. My life here dwindles away like an old sparrow.'

Such words as these she had long dreaded, but her voice was calm.

'And what do you desire?'

'To depart, to seek the wide world.'

26

He spoke loudly, daringly, then faltered, and could not say that he must find the Bear Chief.

She was angry, she raged, then became disconsolate, sinking into mournfulness. She wept, and he hid amongst the sacks and pots, until, after three days, she relented, called to him, then embraced him with a lovingness he had never seen, telling him that he could go with her blessing, on one condition. To safeguard himself from the world's violence, he must wear a many-coloured coat and peaked cap, a little bell at each shoulder, the signs of a fool. These would ensure him protection, for fools are loved by the Other World, and reverenced by many mortals. His several colours, moreover, would confuse demons, appease the Mothers.

'You must listen very carefully, treasuring my words as your father should have done. You must be friendly to whomever you meet, respect advice from the aged and feeble, show respect to hermits. Cherish all that belongs to a woman if she is your true love, and respond to her cry whether she has beauty or whether she has not. Remember that though you are by no means handsome, you are of noble lineage. Ask no questions from whomever you meet, give thanks for all that is offered you with a smile, for your smile will win you friends. At all times use few words, for words are packed with treachery and, however fair-sounding, they can be bells to flatter your enemies. And again, be sparing of questions, for they can bring about dangerous answers, perilous journeys, terrible loss.'

On plea from the old men, she allowed him, though unwillingly, a spear. He had not demanded one and accepted it cautiously. It was light and smooth, not made, so she had insisted, by a smith, but of soft wood, without magic, its tip blacked by hot ash. He must swear to follow no man arrayed for battle, even the Bear Chief.

He was too happy to demur, even the fool's attire excited him, he clasped the frail spear as he might his true love, thought yearningly of Gwalchmai and could scarcely wait to be off.

The very next day, having embraced his black friend, Badly Fed, he set out into the wide world, seeking the path of the sun, though clouds were full, closed by an ill-tempered wind. The bells chimed from his shoulders, on his back were five loaves. At nightfall, fancies scudded, now high, now low. A gate became a stag, a log was a fox, then again a log, though a larger one.

After three days the trees, with the cawings and rustlings, chatter and slithers, fell away, and he emerged on to a rough track undeniably curling towards the sun. Soon, at a crossroads, he found a piebald horse, neighing as if in long-awaited greeting. He kissed it, for here indeed might be a blood-brother, and fashioned a saddle of spruce twigs. The horse would surely take him to the Bear Chief.

27

At the second crossroads he passed shrouded figures, bent heaps of rags, lamenting, which betokened an approaching death, perhaps his own. He had nothing to give them but one loaf and a smile, then he rode on. Sunlight fell freely, the horse turned aside, moving through meadows strewn with tiny flowers, gold upon white, Day's Eyes, beloved by the Great Queen in her summer mood. He did not forget to look out for a hermit to revere, but none appeared. Bridges, ditches, stiles he approached carefully, always with an invocation. Sometimes the dead were there, cowled but invisible, at posts, branches, boulders. His horse might indeed see them, animals being able to see even the Other World, though unable to describe it, such being fortune's gifts.

The third crossroads seemed empty, though the horse was uneasy, tossing his head in need to escape. This certainly meant that ghosts were lurking, perhaps the hideous Mala Lucina, a hag half alive, half dead, white face streaked with ruin, hair like crushed snakes, who preyed on human blood. However, the good horse carried him safely on at a fine trot, the bells jangling reassuringly – for demons fear bells.

Each day was polished anew by a fresh sun. Though he occasionally glimpsed fair-robed women standing on distant hills, he encountered no one and was glad of it, for Gonfan the Smith had warned him against friendly travellers. These could be followers of the goddess Badt, who ingratiated themselves with the unwary, shared provisions, offered protection, then strangled them to please the goddess.

Once, he awoke from beneath a hillock and found beside him a golden cup brimming with wine. He drank gratefully and without surprise, for he expected such gifts from the wide world and feared no trap. Briefly, he then saw everything more vividly, more exactly: brilliance of grass, loops on a butterfly's wings, spots on a sun-ray, but these soon faded and when he looked for the cup it had vanished, as though dissolved by the sun.

He rode on. Reaching a ford he halted, for, though shallow and clear, it was another boundary where men met gods, suffered ambush, were felled by unseen hands. So he did not cross but went upstream along the bank until he reached another danger, a bridge, no less. Bridges indeed were more hazardous than fords. Some were narrow as a rope, and across them the dead passed, some to the mirthful Other World, but a few to a lake of torment, a vale of blood, a vault of despair filled with headless betrayers.

The horse had stopped of its own. Yet the sun lay on the farther side of the dazzling water and he was certain that he must proceed towards it. Nevertheless, the horse refused to cross, so that at last the young rider jumped down, cajoling, pleading, even weeping a little, before being able to drag his new friend across the planks. As he did so, a strange pang crossed his heart, convincing him, wthout joy, without sorrow, that his mother was dead.

This indeed was true. Bereft of all but her names, she listened once more to praise of her ancestors, then, very quietly, died, alone on her high seat.

Her son, meanwhile, felt dull and sad, resolving again to obey her last commandments: ask no questions, avoid fighting, take the rings and shoes of his true love, could she but be found.

While he rode the high road towards true love and the Bear Chief, his mother would be moving the faster along the low road beneath the earth, to her birthplace, her spirit returning to its first dust, east of nine rivers, west of seven hills, north of three haunted wells, like a fine-spirited horse, nearing death, and seeking to return to its earliest fields.

He had dropped tears, but for himself, and his spirit soon flared, for sky and earth bubbled with promises, grass and light, breeze and leaf alike urged him forward. At any instant, when least expected, Gamalchai the Hawk would reappear, his embrace, sweet and painful, streaming as if from the Other World which could be found but never sought. He forbore to ask questions about such matters, thus saving himself fatigue and obeying his mother.

One afternoon, riding, he saw some way ahead on a bluish moor a dim shape that slowly revealed itself as a coarse, black tent. Here would be food, laughter, a soft couch. Laying aside his spear, leading the horse to grass, he ventured to the entrance and stood wide-eyed. Could this be the Other World? A girl was asleep on rich, bright coverings, hair raven black, her cheeks blood-red, her neck and shoulders snow-white, as in the best stories. There could be no doubt of it, she was his true love and there, on a silver stool before him were love's gifts: eggs, fine meats, yellow cakelets, a flask of pure water. These he had been told to accept, and at once did so, having made a sign to placate the threshold. Then, refreshed, he looked again at the inert, gently breathing girl.

Did he awaken her? Of course not. Sleepers must never be disturbed, having perhaps briefly departed from their bodies, to roam vast realms. To be woken suddenly might make a sleeper lose his way, possibly for ever, deprived of his body, so that at best he became a firefly or spider. This girl, in her loveliness, might be one of those who change to a swan each alternate year, or, like Blodenwald, to a flower, to an owl, or, like pretty Essylt, to a swallow.

29

As he stared, hearing only the contented munch of the horse and the girl's hushed breath, he saw further gifts of love. A golden ring glimmered on her finger, two blue sandals lay near the stool. Life was opening for him like an enchanted gate.

Kneeling beside her in love and trust, he began removing her ring. As he did so, his bells tinkled. She stirred, her eyes opened, large and jewelled, showing neither surprise nor alarm, probably soothed by his attire, for fools are messengers from the Other World, subject to no mortal law and possessing rare secrets, though of these they cannot speak plainly.

Suddenly smiling, seeing her ring glimmering in his hand, she reached for him and gave him a kiss. Now she awoke properly, seeing that within the fool's dress was a personable youth with gold hair, fine, simple eyes blue as Mabon's bracelet, elegant limbs. Naked, all men are identical. Her lust sharpened, then teemed, her flesh craved for him and she threw aside her coverings, eager for what might come.

Nothing did. For the first time he saw fully the secrets of a girl's body. She was beautiful but to be feared, a cold summerhouse, a forbidding field. What other youngsters, certainly Badly Fed, enjoyed readily, he shrank from knowing. No pleasure stirred him, his little spear was limp as a worm, he felt ugliness clamped on him, unmistakable, withering. Foolishly clutching her ring he looked everywhere save at her. True love, evidently, was less than bards' praise and old men's boasts.

She lay back, withdrawing, then her anger flashed. Her long black hair shook, her cheeks flushed redder. 'Are you not a man that you see me thus but can take only my ring, like a greedy jackdaw? You are witless indeed, ignorant even of the nature of rings. Dolt, simpleton, scullion, petty scavenger! Soon you will be seizing my shoes, my gloves, as if their only import is of silly ornament. Otherwise, while joy hovers and dallies, you move not even a finger. That stalk of yours must be no more than a dead corn-husk. Fool you are, fool you will remain!'

She turned from him so that he could see only her hair. He was relieved, he was sorrowful, he was mightily afraid. If this was the Other World it was a jumble of deceptions, a surface highly polished but cracked. Almost at once the tent darkened and a bearded man bestrewn with metal and blades which could only be swords stood in the entrance, his eyes the glare of a forge.

Stay-at-Home jumped up, his bells ringing as sharply as his own fear. He trembled, then, remembering his mother's teaching, that he should be friendly to all, he outspread his arms in greeting. But the dark intruder thrust him aside, and cursed the girl beneath them.

'I shall eat and drink with you no more, your bed has the stench of middens. I would slash off your wicked hands, but they will be needed to bury this menial, this absurdity, who has stolen what is mine, and wishes to lord it here in bed and out of it.'

The girl did not stir and, clanking, ashine with wrath, he swung back. 'Fool you are, and will die in your folly.' He grabbed the youth's shoulder, thrusting him outside into the noon sunlight, vowing that he would spatter grass and heather with blood, and indeed showed every sign of doing so. Instinctively, Stay-at-Home contrived to grab his weapon but it was immediately knocked to earth and splintered, his very life about to follow. He was slapped and battered, kicked and half throttled, the warrior too scornful to finish him with one stab. The young man was perforce resisting without movement, wrestling without strength, in a prolonged whirl of agonizing delirium. Always falling, he was ever on his feet, screaming but silent, gasping his spirit away while the sun shone and the good horse placidly munched. Such pain, such helplessness . . . the blows fell from some infernal hammer, ever more huge. Again he was thrown, dragged up, his throat squeezed, head savaged, guts smitten. A red daze enveloped him, he was sliding into a chasm, nauseating and endless.

Yet – was it an instant later, was it a day? – he emerged from the chasm and, behold, his mighty assailant was outstretched before the tent, groaning, mouth open, blood oozing from between his teeth, from a gash above his eyes, and from a hole in his metal tunic. Astonished, still breathing in starts, his thoughts smudged, Stay-at-Home stood irresolute, indeed helpless until, robed in pale yellow, the girl approached, stepping as though the ground was too hot, and with no eyes for the stricken warrior.

Her voice was low and hurried. 'You have rescued me from this midwinter troll. I shall go with you, following at your horse's tail, punished by my own cruel words.'

Still bewildered, he saw only her dark hair, swan neck, yellow robe, for she did not dare look up. He was about to risk touching her but the bleeding man groaned again, and his heart once more misgave him. Stammering, he told her that she must succour the fellow, perhaps from death, but that he himself sought the Bear Chief.

She wept, for the Bear Chief was enemy both of herself and her man. She was swollen with tears but at last moved to tend the wounds and drop soft words, while Stay-at-Home tended his excellent horse, who had seen all, more indeed than he had.

As he prepared to ride away, his thoughts were in better shape, soon convincing him that he had again been rescued by the red-headed Hawk of Spring. Furthermore, he had been assaulted on the tent's threshold, which might have given him uncanny protection. He at once saw that, on the scarlet earth around the prone warrior, were footprints, one set, two sets, and, ah, three sets, showing that another had indeed been with them, seen by the horse.

The girl approached him once more, with another spear, bronzed, which she placed in his hand. No longer pleading, she was very composed, ready to devote herself to the fallen man. As he listened, Stay-at-Home thought sadly that she could indeed have been his true love.

'Go now. You are indeed simple but not witless. This will not harm you. Nor will the spear. You will be loved, you will earn a new name and touch many hearts.' Her eyes saddened, shadowing her face. 'By ways of search I myself came to suffering. Fare you better. And keep my ring, to remember her whom you lost without having won.'

Her touch was soft as a mouse, he kissed her, watched her stoop, firm, without pity, over him so strangely overthrown, then rode away. Before him was perhaps the Hawk, certainly the Bear Chief, slayer of giants, hunter of boar and dragon, whose father was an all-knowing head and who possessed three birds that spoke in mortal tongues of Now, Whenever, and Because.

Side paths and open gates tempted him to stray, but he gave them no heed. He sang, the merry words drifting within him and of themselves sinking into rhyme. He was at one with the green, the hills, the birds. He had used no weapon, had gained a ring, life was a fair path of rules and rewards. His spirit was leading him, no evil eye glinted, no man changed to a wolf, no headless creature perturbed his horse, he was blessed by hawks, the distance to the Other World was slender as a hair.

Thus he travelled, under the yellow sun and the white cloud. At each well he dropped a leaf or petal honouring some nameless presence far below. By night he heard the fox's bark, the owl's scream and once, in sleep, trying to clasp a dim figure neither naked nor clothed, he slipped over a crag and awoke dripping with shock, but at dawn all was well, he was happily riding forward, past empty hills through which shone white ribs, surely those of giants who had built the world in Dagda Time.

Sometimes, above waterfalls, beneath cliffs, he saw, too far away, always too far away, a grey stone tower, though the more he gazed the swifter it receded, drooping into mist and leaf, with the allure of long mounds where dead chiefs and queens lay buried, upright in chariots, their slaves, horses, dogs around them, adorned for the Other World. Once, through spray, he glimpsed a hillock which briefly gleamed as he heard, was almost certain he heard, thin, errant music. Hastening, he then found no hillock but a pit, wherein lay a wooden cart, rotting amid bracken. Later, under the faint stars he dreamt of a mighty chariot buried in a vault which was simultaneously a mountain stronghold. He was glad to awaken, for the chariot might drive him down a nether road.

Now he met more bustling life, no hermits or wise old men, no magic rune or swineherd aglow with witty spells, but several rough hamlets, small crossroad fairs thronged with pedlars' booths, horse-sellers, dicers, tinkers, bull-tamers with daggers, story-tellers chanting and boasting – the valour of the Boi, craftiness of the Parii, Belgic cleverness. Everywhere, as a fool, he received laughter, greetings, embraces, a cupful of wine, a brooch, and to all he gave his smile, not radiant but shy and trusting.

Roads were teachers, whereon he met no murderous devotees of Badt, but water-diviners, metalworkers, carpenters, bards with song and law, all hailing him as one of their fellowship, though his hands were clumsy and his songs unskilled. But he was fair as a sun prince, a girl said, without having seen one. Men too fondled his bright hair, foretold fine fortune. His gold ring was admired, none attempted to steal it or molest him, and though he said little, he was felt to be a favourite of the gods. Respectful to the old, asking no questions, never demanding their names or revealing his own, he occasionally contrived to speak of dew, towers, gates, so that his wisdom and secrets appeared profound. Sometimes, though indifferently, he mentioned the Bear Chief, hoping to learn more without directly asking.

'The Bear Chief! Dear young sir. . . .' All knew. of the Bear Chief with familiarity somewhat alarming. He ploughed the night sky with horses larger than dragons, at his Queen's beauty the earth trembled, he was wiser than Nodens, more controlled than Llyr, his soul had the strength of ten thousand banners, the weak died at his glance. This was exciting, but he was glad not to hear again that tale of the Bear Chief slaying children, having been warned by a head that a New Year child would supplant him, a tale apt to darken the air and, some added, hush the birds. Of the Bear Chief's sister and lover, perhaps the Great Queen herself, Lady of Waters, nothing was said or could be said.

6

Had he journeyed twenty-one days? Forty? He had ceased to count. The horse remained amiable and patient, though they were ascending steeper hills, the paths flintier, dust rising from spurts of wind, within which seemed lamentations. Up there ahead were dull shapes. Trees? Homesteads? The wailing continued, now high, now low. Moors were squaring into fields where cattle stood in plumes of white steam. Rounding a terraced slope and an outcrop of stone, bones, old rags, he reached disorderly rows of hovels before which tilers, woodmen, herdsmen, women with hair like dirty snow, and urchins were moaning, beating their heads in dust, raising them to look askance at his many-hued livery. Above them, on a pole, were two heads tied together, eyeing both sides of the path. Only the children waved him greeting and a small girl ran up to take his hand, happy, until harshly called back.

The Bear Chief was dead. The sky had failed, the sun was losing strength, the air was rotten with grief. He led the horse towards the thick bulk of the hill, a honeycomb of caves, before the largest of which, crowded with pigs, hens and small asses, bedraggled mourners had gathered, supervised by men and women with spears taller and sharper than his own, which he thought best to keep lowered. Their faces too were hostile. Did they believe he had come to slay the Bear Chief? They parted from him reluctantly, suspicion shining through their tears.

He paused, uncertain whether to enter the high cave or go farther on, but at once a dwarf in a yellow jerkin trotted forward importantly, ordering a churl to care for the piebald horse, then moved to the entrance, signing for the newcomer to follow him. This he did, grasping his spear so tight that he could no longer feel it, though still mindful of trailing it in the dirt, as was seemly amongst strangers.

Armed guards did not demur at him. Within, the rough high walls, streaked with damp, were lit by rush lamps and painted with swarming beasts, hunters and sharp pegs. Mists hung, concealing corners and cavities. On a ledge barely within the light, a row of heads glimmered above hanging, blackened pots and soiled weavings ornamented with leaves, birds, snakes, stags, griffins. All smelt of dung, apples, smoke, moist hair. Further groups stood grieving, most of them surrounding a low stool on which a boy crouched in a red cloak slightly too large for him, his bare arms daubed with blues and blacks, a shabby bear-pelt across his knees. He was holding, as if unaware of it, the birch rod used against witches. His eyes, his manner, were dazed. Behind him, in long blue robe woven with green wings, half in shadows like the heads above, loomed a thin figure, probably but not certainly a man, with pointed chin, sharp nose, antlers cunningly tied to the head. Before the crouching boy, kneeling women upheld three wooden birds on long poles, occasionally lowering them, so that they appeared to whisper into his jewelled ears. On another wall was a carved human image with a bear's

34

head or mask, naked, with little spear dangling to his knees.

The intrusion of a fool aroused not frowns but scoffs, particularly from the men, grim in rounded, feathered helms, iron rings and bracelets, bronze greaves, their corslets thick with weapons. The boy on the stool remained motionless, unseeing, gross words were flung, while the dark-mooded women grinned, one laughing hoarsely, perplexing, for she had never been known either to laugh or weep. To many, her laugh showed fleshly desire, unnatural at so critical a time, and a squat, harsh-featured man with a broken nose, scarred face and mouth, chin smeared as if with greyish moss, brown sash trailing from his shoulder, seized her by the hair and struck her thrice with a cudgel. 'You welcome with sounds of pleasure this upstart nobody and will accept in exchange this penalty, the more dolorous the more deserved. There and there, so be it!'

This fellow, Kai, was lord of the dead chief's retinue and blood-brother of a King Salmon, a fish he was thus forbidden to eat. The salmon is upholder of wisdom which, in Kai, was never much seen.

The girl left them, not weeping, not sullen, but with grace, even dignity, while Kai, looking about him at the fixed, glum faces, began taunting the silent Stay-at-Home, who wished that he had more than the yellow dwarf to protect him.

'Here now, we see a Lord of the Spear, survivor of countless and accountable battles, who has come to rejoice in our sorrows and seek lordship in our weakness and sorrow. Honour him, all of you, honour him as he deserves. That is, for nothing at all. Beardless, impudent, unbloodied Peredur! Hear his silly bells!'

For Peredur, though it may contain other names, was understood to mean spear-bearer.

Before any could applaud Kai's ungraciousness, the dwarf gave a sharp cry, clacking, imperious, much at odds with his stature and wizened, inconspicuous face under a tattered hat.

'Not so. Not so. Peredur he may be, yes, you can call him that, but it is by no means a name to mock. He is also, though he may be in no way eager to boast of it, a Deliverer. Hearken to this,' the dwarf continued sternly, 'there are some of you who listen, or pretend to, who will not die until you realize the truth of it. Which of you can remember when I have been in error? Not one of you.'

His lips parted unpleasantly, the seamed face greyed, as he touched the bewildered youth already striving to think of himself as Peredur, though to add 'Deliverer' was indeed foolish.

The dwarf paused, and a short stillness was broken by a raucous, half-approving growl from all but Kai, who frowned mightily and fingered his weapons. The painted boy, seemingly the new Bear Chief (what curious folk these were), attempted to nod but could look only nervous, his head too heavy, though none were attending to him and the thin, robed, horned outline behind looked even thinner and more frozen, before fading into the gloom, remaining but a blue tinge, more akin to the wooden naked image than to the people breathing and watching in this lofty cavern within jittering flame lights. Peredur wondered whether the creature's earliest forefather had been a cloud. Most now seemed disposed towards goodwill, but while the dwarf awaited some acclamation, a black-browed, small-eyed warrior cloaked in ragged skins and loyal to Kai, lurched forward, mug in hand. 'I shall,' he announced, 'with or without the gods, deliver the Deliverer,' and, this said, emptied the mug over Peredur, who at once jerked up his spear, not to strike, but instinctively. As he did so he slipped slightly on a dead fish, and the dwarf, swift as a cat and infuriated by the slight inflicted not only on Peredur but on himself, none other, darted between the insulter and insulted and, to the amazement of all, the former collapsed, blood spurting from his belly. Indeed, he was mortally wounded, some dragging him away, the rest gazing in horror at the young Deliverer who, barely aware of the resourceful dwarf, stood petrified by the sickening gush.

Later all, even the reluctant Kai, agreed that the youth must have slain the man who had been, in truth, somewhat disliked, even by the Bear Chief; slain by an unlucky glance, as if from a bard who, as all well knew, can blind, maim or kill by pointed words or silent curse. Fools can sometimes do likewise.

Meanwhile the dwarf, who had bustled away, now grandly reappeared with the dead man's cloak and sword, awarding them to Peredur who confusedly donned them, obliterating the garb of folly and entering fully into his new name. But he remained embarrassed and, in horrid silence, he thought it best to step to that boy huddled with the Bear Chief's fur over his lap, queerly perfumed, lonely, and despite the solemnity of his stool and posture, looking very frail and unprotected.

Moving through uneasy men and women distorted by unsteady lights and irregular granite, he bowed low, looking into the boy's eyes, convinced that they were scared and pleading. At once he yearned to embrace him and promise him succour, relying on his new name and the inexplicable felling of his late bully, but did not know what best to do until he could seek counsel from the dwarf. So he merely uttered the friendliest words he could muster.

'Till I am old and failing, I shall have no delight if my lips praise not the Chief and my arm refuses to aid him.'

Words remembered from bards, and which, though the boy

seemed not to hear them, won a murmur of approval from the rest. The dwarf then escorted him out to a small cave where he could sleep, also reporting well of the piebald horse and scolding those who wished to disturb his new friend.

Peredur's arrival had interrupted the death wake which now resumed. For three days and nights, between howls and low dirges, the Bear Chief's deeds were chanted and counter-chanted by bards in groups of three, men bearing willow branches, women strips of apple bark, all in the cloaks of feather and bark, reminding Peredur that birds and words shared some origin kept secret by Oak Priests. These bards, he learned from the assiduous dwarf, usually had mortal mothers but fathers from the Other World. 'So it is,' he chattered fussily, 'so it is.' But whenever, despite his vow against curiosity, Peredur asked him about the new Bear Chief, he received no answer save a derisive smile, a fitting penalty as he told himself later, in remorse. As for the old chief's goodly deeds – the warriors recited them endlessly – well, he had cut down princes like barley, had seized a silver comb from the head of Troit, whitest and most sanguine of boars. Ah, the Bear Chief and his three stalwarts – Kai's upthrust chin implied that he had been one of them – had chased the beast for thrice seven days and nights. One of them – and here the chin tilted mightily – changed himself to a raven flying above the boar and his brood of seven. The raven summoned one boarlet to confer with the almost exhausted Chief. 'We won't speak to your Bear Chief, we are busy enough without disturbance from you.' The boar then devastated forty lands, his sons were successively slain, but at last the Bear Chief grabbed the comb and the white boar rushed into the sea, causing a wave that destroyed seven islands.

Peredur also heard of a scheming sorcerer, Klinge, always 'beyond the farthest mountains in their white caps'.

All listened intently, bunched close together in the warm, frayed air. Some stories bestowed enchantment, protection from black magic: others fostered loyalty and courage.

Throughout, holding a blunted sword, the young Chief sat deferred to by slaves, ceremoniously served, yet given only perfunctory respect or even recognition by Kai and those of the greater sort. His eyes remained glazed, as if he had chewed the valerian mushroom which at once transfers you to the Other World, though your body may remain visible to all. Beneath his daubs he was pale, sometimes turning towards Peredur, as if in anguish. Peredur would have stepped forward to embrace him, pledge his aid, but the dwarf always tugged him back, angry and warning.

Near him, squatting on dirty mats, might sometimes be a

37

former Bear Queen, dishevelled, begrimed, completely shaven, her head oiled and ashine to still her magic. The head, seldom moving, resembled a swollen hazel-nut. At intervals the bards reminded her in lustreless tones that she was guardian of the dead chief's cauldron but that her successor – where could she be? – was taller than the midsummer sun, fiercer than the spear of Queen Medb the Fierce.

Gazing at her sunken frame and haggard demeanour, Peredur felt a new sensation, pity for someone older and still more powerful than himself, though plainly less so than Queen Medb the Fierce. His new name, given in mockery, he preferred to the old. But he had best remain unobtrusive, despite the poor Chief's unspoken plea. The dwarf, Bohort, continued to safeguard him, for all feared his railing tongue and agreed that dwarfs were familiar with the Other World. Because of so much lamenting, he was Peredur's only companion save for stray animals and certain children. Peredur, tolerated but not accepted, thought kindly of him, as he did of the girl buffeted by Kai whom he did not see again, though he heard later that she had wedded. Of spirited nature, she allowed the husband her bed only for a year and a day, when she returned his gifts and left him, as custom allowed. She was always called Laughter Loving, though in truth she only laughed that once.

Unexpectedly, thrillingly, Peredur fancied he saw, within a distant cave, Gwalchmai – lean, reckless, mocking – amid the mourners, but he received no sign and the slanted face, covered with shadows, was already gone. He was sad, remembering marvellous feelings, lilt of the flesh. But perhaps the Hawk was in some underworld with the Bear Chief.

At dusk, the third after his coming, came frantic acclamations, then the thud of weapons on leather shields, wooden shields, wild stamps everywhere, torches, gaudy lights flaring. The old Bear Chief had returned, revived from underworld congress with his sister, mother and lover, the Great Queen. Beside him, under a crudely cut arch, was a young queen, her golden head like dragon-fire, though indeed it was a wig. A warrior's coat, metal and leather, covered her, she had knives, her eyes were as powerful as the Chief's. Before them, heated, was a mighty cauldron of Scythian bronze, incised with stars, spirals, flames.

While Bear Chief and Bear Queen clasped arms above the steaming cauldron, then dropped in a wooden doll, eyeless, neither male nor female, the boy on the stool was deserted by all save three Oak Priests in bull-masks, blindfolded so that they could see no ill omens. Pipes began, and nonsensical songs – 'Why does the hare run, why the bright grain?' The boy was now of unearthly pallor, his paint having dropped off. His red cloak was ripped away, leaving him naked. Once again Peredur stepped towards him and again Bohort restrained him. Out of obscurity emerged the thin, blue-garbed antlered one who, very slowly, as if drugged, pulled the unresisting lad outside by the hair. Propped against a tree, horribly inert, he must drink a cup of blood, then receive a spear in his breast.

The body was escorted to the river, where Kai had it placed on a circular wattle-raft, pelted with dung, old shoes, unseemly animal parts, then released, the blunt sword thrown in after him. Occasionally a hand from the flood had been known to receive it, but today no hand thrust up.

Peredur was weeping, ashamed that he had not dared to protest. The Bear Chief did not appear to notice him. He was broad, bandy-legged, black-eyed, neither young nor old, with small, moist, bearded face on a head too large for it, with huge hair striped like a badger's and never permitted to be shorn. It bulged behind him and, when unrolled, covered him like a cloak. His expression was resolutely unmoving, as if stitched. He wore hide sprinkled with iron rings, a strip of grey pelt wound round his right arm. Peredur remembered that whoever sacrifices another must disguise himself as a wolf.

When at last the Bear Chief greeted him, it was with suspicion, owing to Kai's talk of deliverers and spears. Then he unexpectedly grinned, soothed by the newcomer's slender face, white hands, almost girlish face. His voice sounded rusty. 'I hear you are a simpleton with a horse to be laughed at, that you jump like a scorched cat at the sight of weapons, and yet, by knavish trickery, have lost me one of my followers. We certainly need no deliverance from such as you, but you look in need of warmth, and mead, and unless you kill two more of us you can have both.'

His unpleasant laughter was repeated by all around, and having expected nothing, Peredur was not disappointed, though saddened by the gibe at the faithful animal and by the thought of the dead boy.

To celebrate the Bear Chief's rebirth, a marvellous event followed. No less than the sight of the Three Daughters of the Great Queen, Lady of Birth, Love, Death. They flew over the domain disguised as birds, inciting so much blood fever that, on a day chosen as auspicious by the antlered one, all warriors were summoned for a raid on the North King, 'Lord of a Thousand Chariots', who had wickedly, wantonly usurped a long-exhausted salt-pan, at a time that none could now remember.

The Bear Chief's voice rose above his feather-mantled bards, jurists and praise-singers, themselves men, and his satirists, most of them women.

'I vow that in my own presence a thousand chariots, a forest of spears, are as one. My glance will melt the spears and loosen the chariot wheels.'

Curses were thrown at the enemy's names, and jests about their weapons, and barbed mockery from the women completed the declaration. Like lascivious dances, satirical rhyme can thwart sorcerers, turn fingers purple, scatter the groin with poisoned warts, and worse, much worse.

'Without the Bear,' the bards intoned, 'we are nothing. Without us, he is less.' This, however, displeased him and he sent them away without gifts.

The war band soon set off under flying strips woven with ravens, wrens and the bear, above all the bear, together with brilliant twists and knots. Also a wheel, wooden, with an iron knob in the centre. The Bear Chief and Queen were both laughing, astride their nags, surrounded by companions marshalled by Kai. With them were the nine women who ranged the aftermath of battles, scavenging, stabbing, robbing. They too were armoured in leather and bronze, and one bore a wooden image, plumed, with a silver hand. Older men alone rode. Girls wore small leather kirtles, the youths were mostly naked, even their strong, ridged little spears unprotected, a few standing proud as if battle were already at hand, inflaming them. Each threw away a stone, which swiftly became a pile. All remembered, or claimed to, the Bear Chief routing the foe, any foe, forty times before sundown, twelve times after it.

Peredur watched. His spirit was not kindled, he had no hankerings for vengeance, he was separate, obedient to his mother. Yet had the red Hawk summoned him to battle, he would have followed him. Fleetingly, he did once believe he saw him near the Bear Chief, but no summons came. Again he was Stay-at-Home, though taunted into holding a heavy sword, which by mischance he dropped. 'You are', Kai exclaimed, before taking horse, 'lord of nothing at all, and have no strength to deliver even a spider. You are but a stammerer. Brave deeds avoid you, you lack power even to frown, and you do no more good here than fleas do roosters.'

Several applauded this insult, the face of the Chief was closed and expressionless, though, like all chiefs, he presumably contained mighty thoughts.

Peredur was not wholly downcast by Gwalchmai's absence or silence. Twice he had been saved, there must – in the stories there always was – be a third. They shared a sort of blood.

The antlered one was invisible. He was apparently neither wholly man nor absolutely woman, and might be in seclusion in a wolf's lair, licking his spirit clean of the boy chief's killing.

The warriors clattered into the distance, and Peredur sat in his small cave, served by Bohort who had cleared it of a number of dirty bones, some surely human, torn away the webs and wasps' nest, and rebuked the bats. He was often joined by officious hens, indifferent cats, a few old women, and, more particularly, by children. They sat quietly round him, awaiting a story. He told them of Badly Fed climbing a tree and seeing stars splitting and foaming, the dead disputing at a gate, a headless man on a stile, dancing boulders that could never be counted.

'Our Peredur,' the children said.

So he lived, through quiet, glossy days and moonstruck nights. He was pleasant to all, but wary. Hens, children, gifts from the unknown might be deceivers from terrible Badt, or from the Other World, testing his soul.

Daily his good horse came to nuzzle him and sometimes seemed about to speak. He told himself that he was learning much of the wide world. Sometimes, as he made grass rings for the children or watched Bohort prepare beans, fennel, fish morsels, he heard from high air a flute, sweeter than a blackbird. It reminded him of joy with the Hawk, until Bohort spoilt it by declaring that such music cured toothache, for the torturing worms would peer from the tooth to listen, and then could be removed by chewing bread. Peredur never had toothache and disliked hearing that he might contain worms.

Days went by, sunlit, calm. He would watch certain leathery women training boys in weapon play, adroit feints and dodges, skilful shield use. They were reminders of fierce queens of old, Aife, Scatlach, Medb, blue-faced Keridwen, and those tireless lovers, Grainne, Deirdre, Essylt. All were loved by the Great Queen, had tamed horses, founded cities, borne blossom in the Other World. He gazed long at smiths limping in their glowing forges, grim, swarthy, absorbed, forbidden women or boys while performing their craft, sometimes healing wounds though magic verses which they might whisper into the weapons they drew red from the fire. The air was murmurous with old tales, voices sounded as if from far distances, often half heard as they spoke of a wolf swallowing a god and devouring the moon. There were so many secrets that he wondered how anything was known. Yet many secrets seemed known to all. He learnt that the antlered one could utter three strange laughs and possessed a thick chest containing heads preserved in cedar oil. A creature of glooms, depths, abrupt reappearances after long absences.

The bards sang alarmingly of the Bear Chief's five hundred wives but evidently almost all were long gone. The children said that there were three Bear Queens, sisters born on the same day, all of the same name, sharing the Chief on days chosen by the Moon Goddess. Whatever the truth, she had a lover who rode to her in a cart, a foremost warrior, ninth wave hero, bearing a lance dedicated to Lug the Light God, whom the priests at Peredur's old home sometimes called Lot.

From women, Bohort, from children, Peredur learnt more about gods. They had no chiefs, they never died, but, like all the worlds, were maintained by the struggles of fire and water. Also, when the Bear Chief needed a new councillor, the antlered one would drink a potion, then sleep, and whoever appeared first in his dream must be the councillor. From him all knew that the sky contained twenty thousand criss-crossed steps, visible only to the instructed and certain of the dead. Stars were torches set on round stones, maintained by elves, as guides to the utmost reaches of the Other World.

Once he asked about Gwalchmai, but received only uneasy glances, and a warning stare from Bohort, and again he remembered that questions should not be asked.

After seven days, at the trembling bridge of dusk, Peredur saw the outline of a woman, a monstrosity, riding up the hill on a yellow mule which she whipped with scarlet thongs. Her ugliness was easier seen than imagined. Blackish face and hands, high, raw-boned, tufted cheeks swollen as if by four apples, rotting straw hair, nostrils like blood-rimmed burial-pits, sow's ears, mouth a thick muzzle, eyes mean and slitted, fangs gorse-hued, belly lumpish beneath filthy gown, legs bony, back bumpy like a sack of roots. Her jaw was long as a dagger, with small tusks curling from it, her brows hung in thin, sable tresses, her hands were satyr's claws. She could be none other than the fearful Mala Lucina.

Bohort was unconcerned, even appeared not to see her when she halted, standing before Peredur as if from a poisoned dream, eyes gleaming through slits, armpits stinking like fox earths. His spirit sank to trash. Unable to flee, imprisoned in horror, he heard her voice, startling, low and melodious, at evil odds with all else.

'I am Gundrygia the Beautiful. On you too is something fair, almost sweetness, though I find no name in you. Youth, my violet eyes, fairer than most women's, tempt me beyond my deserts and yours. To win my love you must embrace me lovingly and kiss my mouth, as all men desire. Then perhaps I may allow you what all men desire more.'

He was crusted with fear, bemused, his spirit drifted. Never had he been called fair, it was mockery, and, pierced not by golden desire but the iron dart of loathing, he inwardly shrank. So Gundrygia disdainfully flicked him with her whip, but he felt nothing. 'I now see what you are and where you are likely to go. So be it.' And she rode on where people were gathering to greet her with signs of welcome, which baffled him.

All that night Peredur was tormented. How could he be a hero of bitter love and evil conquest? Another tale returned. A youth, blithely naked, flees the Great Queen. Frantic to escape her wiles he becomes a hare, but she is already a deadly hound: he is a snake, but she is a crane: he is a fish, she is an otter. A wren is pursued by a hawk, a speck of grain then swallowed by a hen, who, as Great Queen, bow in hand, bears a child whom she places in an osier basket and consigns to the waves. Some held that the child was saved, growing to be a slayer of monsters, others that he was soon a lord of the Other World, and yet others – Peredur shivered and sweated – that he was famed as a deliverer. Such deliverers came only once in a thousand years under a glaring comet, yet who knew when a comet might not be at hand, exposing all secrets and disguises? Now he could feel the lash of the scarlet whip.

Next day the Bear Chief was back, at his horse's neck, heads clotted with dried blood dangled like crimson blossom. The bards eagerly assembled. The foremost head had been filled with sly skills, so that something of these must now lie within the Bear Chief.

Acclamations echoed through the caves. The Chief's sword had flashed lightning, a crow had hovered above the battle, the Great Queen or Bran the Blessed. Refraining from magic, the Bear Queen had been foremost in valour.

The bards proclaimed that their own praises, curses, satires had blinded thirteen enemy leaders and scalded their rivals' tongues so that their taunts fell short and their weapons wilted. It was swiftly known that human and animal blood-brothers and ancestors and Other World kindred had swarmed to help the Bear Chief. Bears had devoured eleven archers, a white boar led a charge, ravens plucked out wicked eyes, a daughter of Llyr had blown back the enemies' weapons into their faces.

All marvelled that the bards described so precisely the miraculous onslaught which they had not seen.

Each warrior swaggered in new finery, taking back a stone from the pile, which, in the end, had somehow enlarged. A mysterious trophy. That night, within a circle of tall grey boulders, under stars flashing like distant war helms, like watchfires, the tribe feasted the Bear Chief and the Bear Queen. Platters of steaming meat abounded, blood-red cups foamed with wine. At his inconspicuous place Peredur was amazed to see, in and out of the massed, raging faces, the hag Gundrygia in the place of honour between Chief and Queen. None seemed offended by that tusked, hideous presence, indeed Kai and, yes, undeniably, Gwalchmai, and many others, were belauding her loveliness as the flight of nine and ninety swallows, her eyes the jewels of Mabon, her skin clearer than the dew of the Isle of Apples. Peredur could not believe it, there she sat, a bag of vileness, told to whatever passed as her face that her hair was golden honey, that her smile healed like the Bear Chief's dread mother, lover and sister, Lady of Waters. Another stool was empty, he learnt that if a coward sat on it he would be swallowed up by the earth or be seized up into the sky by fiery hands. He felt no temptation to move from where he was seated.

None, however, had an eye for him, certainly not Gwalchmai, eating ferociously, drinking anything within reach, his head fiery in torchlight falling from the guardian stones. Everything flowed. Tensions between light and dark, stars and earth, loosened. Children and hounds wandered happily between feasters. Eloquence unfurled, words soared and swooped as flames scattered the huge shadows and whirled into unearthly hues while, inside the great cave, wine was placed before the heads on the ledge, which had earlier been caressed and placated. Each warrior, riotously applauded, recounted his deeds, the Bear Chief, slumped in high chair, golden torch glimmering, was anointed with dew, had earth dropped on his shoulders, was given a pig-shaped loaf, a brown cloak, and a cake fashioned like a boar's head. The antlered one, very blue, whom none dared name, taller than usual, appeared as if from stone and, over a fumy cauldron, performed magic. He squeezed mud and a squirrel leapt from his hands; he stared at a knife until it bent, shook a kerchief and a jewel dropped from the air. He stroked the cauldron and, visible in the steam, were vague pictures: a giant hammered a snake, naked youths rode through sky, transfixed a wand with an arrow, sang to stones, climbed transparent towers on floating islands. The mounting wine, the elixir and fumes, made all heady, waving, bright yet indistinct, while voices again rose for the Bear Chief, giving life to the outlandish beasts and fruits moulded on cup and platter and the cauldron itself.

> 'He deals doom as wolves savage sheep,
> War-lord, deadlier than his own word,
> Gives stallions to bards.'

Bear Chiefs stride unshod, drawing strength from the earth, their riches stream from the Other World, they outmatch Bran, ride faster than Llyr, beget scores of children in a single night. Peredur noticed that his own Bear Chief, eyes closed, mouth open, was showing no disposition for any of this. 'Of all who ever lived, Our Lord is alone in wisdom, prowess, generosity,' the bards intoned, repeating the last word thrice, before adding that he was braver than the Nine Hostages. The Bear Queen likewise received their fruits of understanding. She had been created from a pomegranate and seven waves, was in cordial descent from a thistle.

Kai then rose like a battle-cloud. When he lifted his shield the sky had fallen, shattering a battalion of spearmen. He had smitten off nine heads, nay, eleven, captured a spectral ram, been applauded by the god Taranis who had brandished an emblem of a circular table, slung to earth a maiden warrior with three hands and but one breast. When he subsided, exhausted, voices shouted for Gwalchmai to speak or sing, but he merely winked to himself, gave his insolent, lop-sided smile, and kept to the wine.

Peredur was drowsy, perplexed, astray. He had come seeking the Bear Chief who did not need him, nor did the Queen, nor the phantom antlered one. This world of weapons and boasts was alien, he should have heeded his mother. He wanted only Gwalchmai, intent on yellow wine and contemptuous of all else.

When he roused himself he heard the loathsome Gundrygia, a voice that, issuing from a pit of corruption, lulled all that heard it. They fell silent, there in the flamy dark under the brooding stones in warm moonshine, metal glinting on dark blue.

'Many days' journey towards the sea . . . ', she was intimate, tempting, 'on a high mountain, the Summer Princess lies imprisoned in the Place of Wonders, awaiting deliverance from the wisest of the brave.'

None save Peredur could see monstrosity, her voice was all, enveloping her, touching each of them. They must be imprisoned by her spells. Clamouring, stirred by lust for the Summer Princess, desire for the Place of Wonders, or both, the seething men wildly besought the Chief to allow them to go forth. 'What others can achieve in a year, we will perform in seven days,' Kai said, and the Bear Chief assented as if glad to be rid of them all, for with dawn tingeing the clouds, scarlet lights trembling on haze, bards had began cursing him, for ugliness, cowardice, cattle-thieving, stinginess – repeated thrice to avert envy from the Other World.

Peredur, at last using his new name with some confidence, felt he should accompany the quest for the beleaguered Princess, for had he not been greeted as Deliverer? But Kai's sooty brows were as if sewn together, his voice scoffed. 'Did you not stay behind from battle, asking not one question, uttering not one plea, as a man should, when we forsook you? Did you not slay our companion in some vile and secret way? Are you not an outcast, despised by all save a peevish half-man? You came, a fool from nowhere on a raggle-taggle beast, with toy arms and milky smile. You stay in your place, with loons and old men and leave real quests to men.'

Gundrygia remained to all eyes save Peredur's the fairest, but he could see no more than a gross, repellent pillar of flesh and verminous instinct, exhalation of swamp, midden, snake-hole. She had told others that he had treated her cruelly, contemptuously, and deserved only ridicule.

Once, when she said this, Gwalchmai was standing near, sardonic, grinning, but affecting to hear nothing. He was already armed, foremost in the expedition to the Place of Wonders.

Thus Peredur was again abandoned. The Bear Chief ignored him, Gwalchmai had not come. There must be some link between them, a pulse, the string of a harp waiting to be touched, but silence remained. He looked for the girl Laughter Loving, who had endured a blow for his sake, but she was not to be seen. He knew from Bohort's eyes, from his own spirit, that he must depart, so embraced the dwarf, sought the piebald horse and rode away alone before dawn to find the Summer Princess. He must think himself a Lord Lover, yet follower of Gwalchmai who pursued his quarry to the end of the wide world and back, could change at will to swan or wren, win further names, saunter in and out of the Other World, live for ever on the lips of bards.

He had a horse, a ring, a hard spear that he must not use. Even venomous Gundrygia had admitted that he was not ugly. Feeling his ears, he was at last certain that they had some delicacy.

7

Summer was failing. Peredur rode south, dreamily, according to the inclinations of his worthy horse. He had much to ponder: the Summer Princess, Gundrygia's fearful visage. And why had Bohort hailed him Deliverer? True, gods used the awkward, the moonstruck, children, and the malformed, lending them secrets apt to confuse the mighty.

Again, riding, he saw, or seemed to see, the distant glint of glass towers, one of which might hide the Summer Princess, beautiful as blossom above a lake. Once, at a turn of the way, he met a boy who demanded a kiss. Yes, of course. The boy then promised to do anything asked of him. Peredur plucked a yellow flower. 'Go to the Bear Chief's dwelling and seek her whom they call Laughter Loving, and give her this, for her kindness.' The boy gladly assented and Peredur nudged the horse forward. He

46

saw a river, a shining skein rippling between russet trees and grey cliffs, passed lakes, each with its nymph, the priestess, and, deep down, the cups and chariots, bodies and chariots cast in for the Great Queen. He hurried past, fearing the naked women, who fluttered through dreams, glimmering in green twilight, beckoning towards freedoms repulsive as Gundrygia. Perhaps she came from the Other World. The Other World, remember, contains no opposites: the squalid is lovely, radiant youth has memories of the aged and crabbed, shapelessness has shape, absurdity reveals truth, in dreaming is waking, in ignorance is knowledge, in death is life.

Peredur asked the piebald horse whether his love for Gwalchmai and disgust for Gundrygia were identical, but the animal forbore to answer.

He sighed, learning that if life is simple it is simultaneously difficult. A leper, cruelly cursed in flesh, is always blessed in spirit. Such is the dispensation of gods.

From horse-traders, pedlars, even urchins, he learnt more. Far down south, two eagles had been born of a harlot or wolf, they had built a city, one then slaying the other so that warm blood would give life to the city wall. This upstart city might become dangerous, people chattered, but, were the tribes to unite, they could crush it easily. Yet tribes often won battles, then quarrelled over spoils, so that the defeated recovered. Such was fate, people said. But was it?

Glancing about him, he sang to the horse's ears an ancient song:

'Shapeless bracken is turning red,
The wild goose raises its desperate head.'

And felt sad and joyous at once.

Leaves were falling, soughs and grunts abounded as boars mated in the undergrowth. The sun looked old, blood red, and he met fugitives from the north frightened by the wolf with snapping jaws that hunted the moon. They spoke of a fire shortly to devour the world, gave him a basket of loaves, praised his horse as gift from Nodens, and hurried on. He saw girls hiding from the west wind which fertilizes, was shown a boulder placed to block down a ghost, and queerly split, perhaps by a strange laugh from an antlered one. All this, but nothing of the Summer Princess.

On he went, not lonely, and afraid only when, as he had done long ago, throwing stones for sport, he killed a swan, clumsily inflicting pain. Why was he always so clumsy? Weeping, he endured utter, accusing stillness, he had spoiled a purity, then felt a light touch on his forehead, sign of forgiveness.

The Bear Chief he was forgetting but not Kai, that harsh face smeared on the furry head and packed with spite black as crows and who needed cruel trophies. Nor the Hawk, reputedly son of the sun god, who could love and guide him, yet did not.

By a nettle ditch he met an old man, surely a hermit at last, seated under an alder, most of the leaves dried or fallen. He wanted to ask his name and fortune, but questions should not be asked. The old man was friendly, spoke kind words to the piebald horse, who nuzzled him familiarly; and was glad to accept a crust from Peredur. His wrinkled face was grave. 'Soon you will be entering the Visible Strange to face one of three temptations. I can tell you only this much. You are in danger from none but yourself.'

He sighed, then closed his eyes. Shadows were thickening, he soon seemed part of the tree, and Peredur had to forbear mention of the Summer Princess, though to do so might be a fourth temptation.

Thanking the hermit he rode away and, looking back, saw only the alder bare against cold green sky as if the other had never been.

So much knowledge was filling him that he might need a second head, knowledge that would ridicule Kai, despite that brotherhood with the wise salmon. He knew that sky and air were kept alive by gnats too tiny to be seen but packed with vigour sufficient to crack the brightest star; on an island dedicated to Llyr's ungrateful daughters, all births and deaths were forbidden. Men followed secrets drifting from farthest east, behind the north wind, home of the Great Queen. He knew from his mother that secrets could not be hidden for ever. A secret could be whispered to a stone, and, after nine score years, a singer's voice might shatter the stone and the secret leap free.

Each day was yielding him a new haul of sensations that unfolded into words: Cavernous, Allure, Slogan, Battle, Dapple, Fur Slipper, Bedazzle, Egypt, Crave, Lurch, As If, Grail. The last he *envisaged* as a polished, many-sided lump which could create flame by bringing down particles of the sun.

So his soul was lustred with steep heights and watery depths which, uniting, exalted him, *as if* he were one of those before whom sun and moon bow down, though only to his patient companion could he tell this. The word *Nearly* began to recur. He was Nearly a man, Nearly beautiful, Nearly a deliverer of the Summer Princess.

Days were shortening, the sky dwindling, though not forbidding random hints of the Other World when least expected. They were

48

woven within the common day. Unusual light flickered along shores, hovered over summits and gates, and above the moon, messages from Lug. He never paused to explore further, for Other World gifts, never what they appeared, could be risky.

Nothing could be disregarded. At sundown, trees were purple, conqueror's hue. A colour might be a path, a hoof mark the presence of Cernunnus. Shrouded Mothers lurked on hills, satyrs slid through marsh wisps sent by wicked Medb. Sometimes a breeze, a tremble on water, a crow flapping across the sun, reminded him of the crafty sorcerer Klinge, of whom he knew nothing, save that he hid behind mountains, throwing enchantments at the world. At such times, he remembered Bohort's warped face nodding encouragement, and, in wonder, he at last realized that the little creature had loved him.

Cold stiffened, snow fell from a tiny sky, obliterating many certainties of the Summer Princess. He was enclosed in a pale, stagnant haze, riding into the Visible Strange, hideously alone. Yet the horse trotted on, confident, only occasionally stumbling. The greyness agitated him, and because witches cannot cross water he was glad of the many streams. Also, the water might inspire him, though it had not yet done so.

8

Midwinter days were dark, the sun unable to wrest itself from frozen waters. Trees were dulled, spiked. Peredur reached a land of grim villages and ageing, haggard people, amongst whom the dead were never mentioned, so that no past was remembered. He heard nothing of the Summer Princess or Place of Wonders, only of the Dolorous Valley, Dire Peak, Three Grievous Visitors. Neither friendly nor unfriendly, they allowed him a place at meals, very scanty, but he was disinclined to linger. Indeed, with half-knowledge of spells, he tried to detach his spirit and in it sail over hill and valley to the Place of Wonders, but half-knowledge was insufficient. In this cold, windy twilight, a Summer Princess was as unimaginable as an Isle of Birds: more probable were Kai's charred eyes and bragging tongue, Gundrygia's tusks and fangs. He must depart.

All was barren. Ravines were now empty, wattle huts abandoned or left to outcasts who, at his approach, barred their doors. Clouds could be low enough to touch. Even the horse now quivered uneasily in this weird frontier between known and unknown. Trickery was everywhere. Friendly hills changed to fog, a welcome pool was but rising mist, a bridge faltered, then dissolved entirely. Was this a penalty for twice killing a bird?

It might be so, for, after seven days, he reached a shabby pond at which, holding a fishing-pole, sat another old hermit, much resembling the first. The white brows frowned at him:

'You have raised your hand against the beloved of gods.'

Desolate, Peredur produced his last crust, offered his flask. The old man groaned, but accepted the pitiful sustenance, very slightly softened.

'Where do you go, young sir?'

'I seek the Summer Princess in the Place of Wonders.'

'Seeking is easy. Very often it is its own reward.'

'I also need shelter and rest.'

'That is sometimes too easy, and with no reward. But go down that track and ask entrance from whomever you meet, in the name of the fisherman.'

Peredur was surprised to see a crooked path leading down to a wall of mist. He thanked the old man, who had spoken as hermits might be expected to speak, and left him.

Descent was slow, the piebald horse was even more uneasy, bare branches whispered 'Danger', the mist pressed against him, deepening as if from marsh as he moved, dragging the horse. He wanted Gwalchmai, who did not come. As if at some fugitive signal, frost glimmered and he shivered in deadening chill. His teeth chattered. (Later, a crude drawing of him struggling on a sinuous path gave rise to a story of his overcoming evil disguised as a serpent.) Bushes touched him in warning, the slippery earth trembled, a briar lashed his face, then a moth, ancient, dusty, big as a starling, slowly brushed him.

The horse whinnied distress, but, as if at another signal, the mist cleared, the earth tilted, revealing, straggling a patch of swamp, seven lean cattle, very still, as if blind. A little beyond them was a mossy, rotted palisade impaling several heads, pocked and peeling like fallen apples. He pushed through and saw rounded, dilapidated walls, no Place of Wonders, no House of the Sun, but the lonely goose-grey tower he had seen so often in and out of dreams. His spirit slumped, but he could only go forward. The silence was unnatural, no bird sang, for there were no birds. Before the tower, from a solitary tree, hung a small rusted gong. He struck it, the sound was low, hollow, foreboding. He waited. Perhaps the gong was a precaution against demons. He was afraid. A wall was more than a wall, a door more than a door. He knew no password or sign. Then, as the heavy door creaked open, he remembered the hermit.

A bald, unsmiling man peered out at him. Peredur's speech was unsteady. 'I seek entrance, in the name of the fisherman.'

The man at once stood aside for him. 'The fisherman does you honour and my lord expects you in hope.'

Inside was a low-roofed circular hall, a few candle-dips glowed,

showing that the central pillar was a thick tree-trunk on which
was carved the wheel of Taranis. Painted on one wall was a faint
tree encircled by a snake and from the blackened ceiling hung a
dry bunch of corn, blackening in smoke from a desultory fire in
an iron basket. On a further wall, also discoloured by smoke and
damp, was daubed a staring, menacing boar. Fatigued, hungry,
Peredur wondered whether he had joined the dead. Slowly,
fearfully slowly, he knew that the Other World was very close,
but that he lacked the word, the charm, though which to see its
clear, full radiance. There were only these dripping walls, dimness,
the cold. The man had gone. Then he heard a groan, 'Fiercer
than fire, more biting than ice', and saw in a recess the lord
outstretched on a low, planked bedding, a pail filled with bloody
rags beside him. Could he be the god Bran, wounded in the heel
by a poisoned spear? His hair and skin were grey as ashes, he
was enfeebled by a grievous wound, unseen, though, Peredur
realized, not in the heel, but the worst that a man can suffer. By
his head was a reddish brazier, but, despite this and fur mantels,
the lord shivered and fretted, gazing at the newcomer in strange,
painful need, while, now visible on the farther side, a girl
crouched, emaciated, stricken, a dull circlet of beads round her
shorn head.

'Youth,' the lord's hoarse voice issued with agonized effort,
'you have delayed long but are indeed welcome.' His dull eyes
contrived to widen, then gleamed a little, so that Peredur imagined
a dawn but could say nothing. He was bewildered, his wits
astray, so that the cracked face dimmed, the lord gave a small
heavy wail, his eyes closing in torment.

Peredur felt shame. He was a speechless intruder wearing a
false name, disappointing all who saw him. Anxious to utter
some comfort, he could merely fumble stupidly, with no thoughts
but the question of what ailed the lord. But to ask such a question
would show only his simplicity, and he had been groomed too
long against questions.

He could say nothing, yet something was expected of him: had
he to heal the lord of his monstrous wound, or even slay him?
Blushing, yearning to help, he was powerless. Occasionally, like
a bird or wolf, he could know the thoughts of others, but here,
raw, nervous, oppressed, he knew nothing.

The lord was still, perhaps insensible, the girl rose, gaunt with
reproach, though, crossing, she gave Peredur her hand. 'Come.'
Could she really be the Summer Princess, liable, by some flake
of the Other World, to be transformed to the glistening and
sportful? Was this the House of Glass, one window displaying
only rain and mud, the other revealing flowers and birds flashing
through sunlight?

Seemingly not, more an abode of Mothers. He now glimpsed

51

fleeting, shadowy presences, heard dim sighs and complaints. He was threatened by the demonic.

She led him deeper into the tower, to a cell where a table was prepared for some joyless repast. There were stale sweetmeats, crumbling loaves, a solitary candle, several listless women and a few meagre children with baleful mouths. He seated himself beside the girl who offered him two cups, each half filled. He reached for the nearer then, sensing some warning in a child's eye, took the other. The girl's hand whitened on her own cup, and she averted her face. The twilit air was tense. He drank a thin, bitter wine, none spoke, the children soon filtered away into darkened recesses, until, startling as ambush, the place was suddenly alight, with four lofty torches escorted in by skinny youths in grey cloaks, their leader upholding a thick, many-sided jewel which glittered, winked, threw off greens and reds and blues, tumbling together under the flames, sharp particles of an Other World sun.

While he wondered, laments surrounded him and another youth appeared, quite naked, skin drooping, hair frayed and unkempt, clutching an upright spear whose tip dripped blood. A chill draught rustled the floor straws, the mournings loudened and two girls streaked with fear or illness passed before him to the naked youth bearing a green stone dish in which he saw, horrified, floating in blood, a man's head, dabs of gold on cheeks and hair, blue on the eyelids. They raised the dish to the lance, then, kneeling, placed it on the floor to catch the blood drops, then withdrew with the youth, all covering their faces. Peredur's heart quaked, for the red mouth in the dish had started to grin. He recoiled, then saw ants swarming around the lips.

A cry rang though the tower as if from all the world's torments, another drop splashed in the green dish. A network of grieving eyes trapped him, he was numbed by mute accusations, guilty pains, and strove vainly for a supplication, song, answer, convinced that these stricken faces had pleaded many times before to wanderers as ignorant and foolish as himself.

Dazed, he found himself back by the wounded lord, seeking words of comfort, struggling to ask the question, but his throat filled with knots and he uttered nothing. So awed was he by the tortured man, bleeding lance, severed head, that he believed himself confronted by the god Belenus who, at a certain moon season, died that peoples might live, live more abundantly, but whose lingering death blighted all around him.

Peredur's silence further distressed the lord. After a thin, pinched moan, he turned away, covering his head with the furs, like a famished animal who has sniffed meat but failed to trace it. The girl's face went hopeless, though she made no rebuke and led the young stranger to an upper floor. Here he lay uneasily between midnight and dawn, the turn of the world, awaiting cock-crow to expel the malignant spectres of darkness. The stillness was grim, the tower was rank as pig swill, mouldy as a crone's neck. He dropped his belt. No sound. Crossing the floor, opening a door, needed much effort, as though he were under water. Every movement was very slow, laborious, barely possible. The chill bit. Clammy mist hung at all levels and he met no one. The lord's couch was abandoned, the tower itself was smaller, narrower, about to fall. His thoughts sickened. He might be in a temple to the Great Queen, despoiler of heads, deceiving travellers, exacting vengeance for unknown crimes. Or perhaps the place was thick with plague from god-smitten Egypt.

He struggled outside into the dripping morn, finding his horse too dejected even to lift his head. No hermit was visible, the tower was receding into soft, damp obscurity. Feeling himself accursed, he rode slowly away, unaware of where he was going, aware only of the bloody lance and remembering a tale of a hero stabbing a gracious queen, then beseeching forgiveness from her ghost. But from the slashed throat no word was given.

9

Midwinter. Sky and tree had withered. Loneliness paralysed: the heart was stone, sluggish blood crusted the rib. His soul was lost, homeless. He had a ring, token of humiliation, a name awarded in mockery, a secret name already lost. He had slain gentle birds and felt no sorrow for his mother. He was but Nix Naught Nothing, defiled like a grave-robber. Yet he could not explain his failure. He had obeyed his mother, respected old men, refrained from questions, impaired no custom, and been rewarded with a world that lacked true colour and in which all numbers were unlucky. He would never forget the floating head, the racked, unspoken accusation of the wounded lord. All mocked.

In a drear, windswept hamlet, he spoke of the diseased tower, and an old woman rebuked him.

'If you saw anything, it was not meant for you.'

'Who was it meant for?'

'For none but the Deliverer.'

All was untrustworthy. The Other World had faded to mire and grime, gods were mere tissue. Gwalchmai was no more than a treacherous foundling cast off by the Mothers. His smile could melt gold but his laugh was pitiless. The light itself moves on bended paths, the Oak Priests taught. Yet, smooth as silk, blue veined, his little spear would tingle, mindful of a joyous occasion, begging release.

The horse plodded down rimed tracks, through raw, dripping woods, across sodden moors, while the Summer Princess doubtless endured rescue by Kai. They would be scowling at each other in a House of the Sun that ever turns on its own base to receive the splendour of Mapon, while a fledgling deliverer was lost under a frozen moon. South and north were but one, a morsel of nowhere.

Unprotected, virtually nameless, all beliefs scattered, he scaled snow-striped passes and helped sad folk burn logs to revive the sun. He sheltered from bladed winds unleashed by the Blue Storm Hag, Llyr's wife. He envied those capable of three strange laughs. He sucked hot bones thrown away by a girl who, having sneezed out her soul and lost it, refused all comfort he could offer. Already he was far from the wounded lord, the little procession, the green dish and floating head. Seeing a hawk chase away a wolf he felt better, fancying a sign from Gwalchmai. But the piebald horse neighed, the hawk started up, stunning itself on a tree.

A wild man, shaggy, fierce eyed but friendly, gave him a muddy drink which made him see beloved hues: raven's blackness, snow's whiteness, apple's red. He also saw, as if through thin webbing, Gundrygia, her atrocious outline merging with a girl in old tales who fell asleep for years and years, briars growing round her hut, nettles bestrewing the path, until at last a man pushed through, saw her lying alone, and treated her so that she awoke dappled by her own blood. Again he remembered the green dish, and shuddered, up here on the iced lip of the world, the wild man snoring beside him, besotted with mead, root or berry, like the famous thief who drank so much that he felt a terrible beak daily ravage his liver. He craved the powerful spirits of his father and brother. Were these more than an invention, dreamed by the mother he had deserted? 'I shall be buried in no chariot, reach no Other World, I am no Deliverer.'

From stray wanderers, he knew of cities of the dead, far, far away, surviving some angry retribution, by flood, fire, earthquake, with great staircases leading nowhere, vast buildings inhabited only by flitting ghosts, wild gardens where now kings and chiefs were brought for burial. Was it to such a city he was being led, through snow and gale, in a life that was but a hateful trick of the Great Queen? Her convulsive love pointed only towards death.

The Place of Wonders could be but the fabled realm of magic lying between lake and shore, visible to but one eye in thirty thousand.

His pack of grief was heavy, he was destined to end through a false gate, amongst vampires, to be savaged by a boar, or led to deceptions by a spiteful white hart. The Summer Princess was only a whisper. His own names had been bestowed in ill-will, thus insufficiently, so that, like the dead, he was neither in the world nor out of it. His spirit was negligible, incapable of the lustre sometimes flickering from the skin of a Gwalchmai, like the words behind words.

Very slowly, as if on rusty hinges, warmth revived, the sun, still weak, pushed aside clouds, winds lost tongue, the sky ceased to groan. Purple alders loosened into green. On the first warm day, with leaves unfurling and birds noisy, at full noon, there was a roar like that of bulls mating and, confronting him, was the Red Chief – red hair and face, arms and legs, red hat, red cloak, knee-plates and sandals. The very earth glimmered red beneath him. He held a sword in one hand and, in the other, a red cup stolen from the Bear Queen.

'Here is a girlish youth on a fanciful mount, very pretty, yet trespassing in my path like a silly claimant, a sham deliverer, on a hobby-horse, with weapons a little too manly for him, thus needing a better master. Dismount your clownish charger, my young friend, and strip, then yield me those fine trimmings of yours, doubtless taken without leave. When I have also been allowed that curious but serviceable horse, you can go your way and array yourselves in leaves and bark, or, if you care, go naked, as you must lack withal anything to dismay the weak creatures of these parts.'

Peredur was dismayed, the red, taunting apparition had him at its mercy. Sometimes a man left his own body so that it remained mindless, uncontrolled, without regard for its own furies. Such a one, ferocious, demented, he must now be facing. He still shied at using weapons, and, could he but do so, he would never worst a Red Chief. The other was advancing, slowly, gleaming, in terrible menace. Peredur, still mounted, closed his eyes and prepared for the slashing blow, the death gasp, but then, from neither behind nor before him, he heard, or seemed to hear, a chuckling voice, from none other but Gwalchmai, though, opening his eyes, he still saw nothing but the glowing, threatening mass, blood-hued and merciless.

'Let us see,' Gwalchmai, somewhere, was subtlely amused, 'let us both see this empty ox display his magnitude. I enjoy the throw of knuckle-dice, I love the stupendous wager and the play of chance. I shall hazard that the red ox will fall before the gold. Answer courteously, but move not one step back.'

So Peredur, though his attire contained no gold, drew breath, held firm, and in pleasant fashion smiled across at the Red Chief.

'I would gladly give you riches, in friendship, but I have none, and I do not care to strip myself for a friend unproven. But I give you good will and, in return, ask for that red cup in your hand, so that I can indeed fulfil my part as Deliverer, and restore it to the Bear Queen.'

The Red Chief would hear no more urchin insolence, he swept his sword through the sunlight, aiming straight, then, down a slight incline, rushed at Peredur, so recklessly, and so enraging his senses, that he ignored a thick black root protruding before him. He tripped, whirled to earth, broke his neck, moaned, then lay still.

Peredur stood amazed, while churls flocked from byres behind the trees, bowing to him, presenting fruits, milk, wine, coloured shawls, rejoicing, for their master's cruelty had changed loyalty to hate. A one-eyed fellow smote off the dead man's head with the red sword, and had soon tied it to the piebald horse's neck. Gwalchmai had already vanished, and the one-eyed now spoke.

'All know of the wounded lord, but only the poor and humble can speak of him. He had vowed his powerful body to the Great Queen, who rewarded him with wide empery. But the wicked, spell-mongering Klinge, though far away, ah, young sir, always so far away, was jealous and sent who else but a beautiful temptress and he lay with her and enjoyed her as any man would, and in anger the Great Queen cursed manhood, his great tool lost magic and he lies bleeding and corrupt, awaiting succour, but who knows from where it will come? It will not', the man said sadly, 'come from such as I. But you, sir, look a likely youth, and may know what best to do, and what we can do in help we shall do. In token, we must give you the red cup which you so wisely sought from the beast who is dead.'

Peredur thought awhile, letting his senses calm. Then he beckoned to two others. To one he said, 'Take this red head to the wounded lord, with all speed, and in hopes that it will relieve his sufferings.' And to the other, 'Take this red cup to the Bear Queen. Tell her that Peredur sends greetings and returns her own. And forget not a friendly word to her whom they call Laughter Loving, and to Bohort the dwarf. Of a lord named Kai, beware.'

They hastened to obey so mighty a warrior whose looks belied his prowess. The rest then escorted him to the Red Chief's daughter, who was tied to a post amongst tall pots daubed with red dragons. He hastened to cut her thongs, she kissed his smooth face, praised his sapphire eyes, feasted him well, sent rich oats to his horse, then offered many gifts: magic dice to forestall death and sickness, a luminous glass cube she called a grail, to attract the sun, a whalebone casket. Also, indeed, she offered to tell the story of a dolphin and nine marvels so precious that they could neither be named nor described.

Peredur, however, shook his head. 'I can accept nothing, and must hasten away. I am pledged to the Summer Princess in the Place of Wonders, and, gracious as you are, you are certainly not her, though of course you may be finer than any princess and probably are.'

Three times she pleaded for his love, nine times she kissed him, but without avail.

At last she smiled sadly. 'You seek more than you understand. My love should have contented you, but I see that it will not. Go, therefore, but know that the Summer Princess is sought by all men and many women, but is loved by none. That horse of yours will lead you to the mountain over there, still so faint above the forests, and beneath it you will find a lake. Hidden within bushes is a boat. Row out, and in the centre of the lake you will find the Place of Wonders.'

Parting, she gave him twelve kisses, which he endured with good grace, patted the horse, and set out for the mountain.

The piebald horse gallantly jogged towards the mountain, sniffing as though he recognized familiar sights. Soon, before them shone the lake and, indeed, behind bushes glossy with new flower, was a trim boat and, before long, leaving the horse to a friendly ploughman, he was landing at the Place of Wonders, seven high towers circled by wide courtyards, all in white, gleaming stone, shining like glass in the fresh sunlight.

He passed through an arch into a court in which were five dark green yews clipped into roundness. In the second court was a silvery fishpond, and, in the third, two statues, small but live, squatting over a chequer-board playing a game of stratagem, black against red. He fancied a chuckling voice was urging him to place a wager, and, remembering his contest with the Red Chief, he chose the black. However, the black lost, the players, no higher than his knee, departed, somewhat stiffly, one having taken from him his bet in forfeit. At this, inexplicably overcome by rage, he seized the board, rushed out and tossed it into the lake. Immediately he was ashamed, also astonished, for never before had he felt anger, a sensation splitting, scalding, shaking him beyond himself.

Worse was to come. As he hesitated by the lake, thin trumpets sounded, throwing silver on golden air, a drum beat, hounds growled in grey and white scurry, gates swung open for the Summer Princess, and, behold, she was Gundrygia.

There was no doubt about it. None, of the utmost good will, could mistake that atrocious hag: the peg-like teeth, massed hair

57

poised to uncoil and strike, the sow's ears, the vicious little tusks. A carrion self. No bard, even at his most florid, could find words for her stench, or, if he did, he would stand petrified. Her voice, as she halted before the trembling youth, was unchanged. Still that uncanny softness with music within it, though her lower lip shone horribly and her eyes were poisoned.

'You have already besmirched my name with insult and now do so again and now you inflict more injury upon me. That chequer-board you have so petulantly drowned is one that I cherished. Luck is embedded in it and henceforward I shall suffer further misfortune.'

What greater misfortune could she suffer than her own monstrosity? But he could ask nothing, only reply: 'I shall recover the board, my head upon it.'

'Your head will indeed be upon it, should you fail me. So listen. It is more important for me to recover my treasure than to scourge and hack you, as you deserve. To succeed is difficult, but, if you obey me, it is possible.'

'I shall obey whatever you lay on me, very willingly.' Should she demand a kiss, this would perhaps not be possible, but, her hideous visage losing some streak of menace, she continued, her voice very low but distinct: 'You must slay the stag with the golden collar and single horn sharper than the sharpest, who ravages my woods, drinks dry my ponds, impales my people. You must dare the woods with a single hound, who will sniff out the stag and drive it towards you. Then you must use your wits, which seem but few, your judgement, which hitherto is lacking, and your luck, which, by all reports, is prodigious. When you return, if you do, you must obey one further command. Now go.'

A hound was brought, together with a strong bow and sharp knife, at which Peredur inwardly shuddered, but perforce he must swear to do her will. Soon he had escaped her noxious breath, and the Place of Wonders was behind him. On the farther shore, the hound appeared to know where best to go and, having greeted his horse, Peredur followed on foot, despondently, doubting whether he could fan up the anger or resolution needed to injure a living being.

Once within the trees, the hound darted off, leaving Peredur to wander at will. All was still, the very leaves hung as if painted, the birds silenced. The dangerous stag must be close, and indeed, very soon, when the sun was at its highest, at the entrance of a glade a gleam flickered on the brown air, and there came a great stag with a golden collar, lowering his horns while the hound snapped behind it.

Peredur stood dismayed, the beast, angered, red flecking his eyes, began advancing, a thick, scraping noise in his throat, the horn as deadly as any Great Queen. Peredur fled, not knowing where, and was swiftly out of the wood and racing towards the lake, beyond which the seven towers rose white and aching into the rich sky. The fierce, steamy breath was upon him, the hoofs thundered, he was almost down, amongst the reeds, but, at the sight of water, the murderous stag slackened pace, and, in the space of a stone's throw, he had drunk the waters dry and, quite near, the chequer-board lay red and black on the mud, drying in the heat.

Peredur had not cared to move, for the stag was between him and the emptied lake. Refreshed, the stag remounted the bank and was at once rejoined by the snarling, snapping hound. The stag glared about him, unable to transfix his agile assailant, then saw Peredur but three spears' length away, and moved forward, encouraged by the hound, to renew the chase. Peredur dodged behind one bush, then another, with fingers almost numb fumbling for an arrow. The horn was again tilting, an eye was fiery, stamping hoofs whirled up dust. Almost at the last, as the menace loomed over him, he fitted an arrow, shot wildly, missed, then again, vainly. He had but one arrow left, was enveloped in the monster's breath, he aimed, badly, but as he discharged the arrow, the hound leapt on to the stag, making him veer abruptly and receive the missile in his heart, so that he thudded to earth, golden collar awry, horn cracked.

As Peredur recovered his senses, the hound panting contentedly beside him, the air brightened and he saw, standing nearby, a girl in long green and crimson robe, more beautiful than a praise-singer's rapture of Grainne and Essylt, and certainly fairer than any Bear Queen. Tall and slender, she had Other World shimmer. As you will have guessed, her hair was raven black, her skin snow white, her cheeks apple red, but her grass-green eyes glowed in anger.

'Whoever you are, slave or master, you have slain my dearest companion, my most cherished ornament, making my life desolate.'

Her voice sounded half-familiar, a lost echo, but, transfixed by her smarting eyes and white, flushed skin, he could remember nothing. Here was the real Summer Princess. He could only stammer: 'I was entreated, commanded to do so by her of the Place of Wonders over there, to whom my word is given. But tell me how to win your forgiveness and I shall do all that is in my power, and indeed shall strive to do more. Tell me who you are and what is your sacred name.'

'What I am named I cannot tell to such as you, thief and killer, and as for her to whom you are pledged, she does not stand with the loveliest in the world. She is my enemy. You despoil and harrow me further by your talk of her.'

'She does not stand with the loveliest and she is my enemy also. Yet I am bound to serve her. To break pledge to the living or the dead is to wound the spirit, sully the name, pluck an unlucky number. I must restore her that board you see there, with which I foolishly meddled, to save her from some worse misfortune. When I have done that, I shall follow your wishes, and gladly.'

The language of bards. Nor was he mistaken in using it. Slowly, reluctantly, her rage abated, the green eyes settled in harmony with her other beauties, and burnished their radiance. 'Do what you must do. The mountain here is lofty, but I know of one higher, and within it dwells danger that is nevertheless your salvation, should you wish to appease me. Follow that same hound for seven days and, at the foot of that mountain you will come upon a grove wherein is a stone hut of long ago. Call out a challenge, keep your wits handy, and wait.'

At this she withdrew into the forest and, calling the now friendly hound, Peredur reassured the inquiring horse, then stepped across the warm, still dry mud, recovering the board, and sought Gundrygia in the Place of Wonders. There, amid the pure whiteness of court and tower, she was waiting, a snakepit presence, her scowl as malevolent as her body. Yet her voice was mild as she took her prized board and gave him thanks. He told her of a nameless girl whom he had wronged, though of her beauty he said nothing.

The haired, venomous face crinkled, the tusked, fearsome mouth opened over the terrible fangs. 'Is she fairer than I?'

'I cannot gainsay it.'

'Did you embrace her?'

'No.'

'Did you wish to?'

'Assuredly.'

One flat eye winked, the other shook as if from spotted fever. 'You can serve her this once, but on one condition.' The grin chilled him all over.

'You must tell it me.'

'On condition that you embrace no woman, no man, until you next see me. Also you must leave me that ring I see on your hand and bring me back the reddest stone in all the world, and then obey one further command, which I shall not yet reveal.'

Disconsolate, he could only smile, bow his head, pull off the lost girl's ring and drop it into the greedy, bloodshot claw. Soon he was riding away, the hound loping before him. Though wondering about the unknown enemy ahead, he felt little unease, here in soft sunlight and wide, flowery meadows, though sometimes wishing he had gathered a verse from the Bear Chief's satirists, which could maim or crush a foe. Only once he felt dismay, fearing that perhaps his opponent would be none other than his beloved friend the Hawk.

After seven days, all was as foretold. A vast mountain breaking the sky, a dark clump of trees, the outline of a stone hut.

Night was near and he resolved to delay the challenge until morning and, with his two friends, lay down to sleep. In dreams he did what he had been bidden, crying his challenge before the hut. A fierce man glided out, black as Badly Fed, a ruby blazing beneath his tumbled hair, but, seeing Peredur, he turned away, weeping piteously, bemoaning his ill-chance. 'You are protected by a vaunted name, stronger than three thousand knives. I, who have earned more, receive nothing.'

Thrice he repeated this, the ruby fiery, his spirit groaning, and who could dispute that the stone was redder and deeper than any in the wide world?

The sun was high, Peredur awoke, the hound licking his hand, the piebald horse astir, and, by him on the moss, was a ruby, reddest in all the world.

Nothing more. The hound was already making towards home, the horse too was turning. Thankfully Peredur took the ruby and seven days passed without adventure save that, at a crossroads, he found a black man resembling the one in the dream, though smiling and friendly. He wore no ruby, though a lighter patch gleamed on his sable brow beneath the tumbled hair. He offered to share his wine and loaf, laughing softly as if over a shared secret. Peredur too laughed, gladly assented, and they spoke of other things, the rejoicings at Sowing Time, the tribulations of Llyr, the loves of Essylt, until, with handclasps, they rose to depart.

Nearing the towers by the lake which was again full and sparkling, he saw the beautiful maiden awaiting him. Ah, the Summer Princess. She said nothing, her face, clear and fine, was neither scornful nor welcoming, but, silently, she stretched out her snow-white hand and touched his sleeve.

'Peredur, I can now forgive you for slaying my only true friend, and, in return, you can kiss my cheek.'

'That I cannot do, for I have made a promise to her across the lake. And indeed, your forgiveness is my reward.'

The green eyes flared, the dark lashes quivered. 'Am I always to be second in your foolish pledges? Am I so inferior to her? No man has treated me so. Is it her you desire?'

Peredur lowered his head, very desolate. 'It is not, and you know it, but I must submit not to her command but to my own

61

promise. To break a promise risks too much and injures whatever name we possess, however small.'

'Then look at me again.'

At once he saw Gundrygia standing where the maiden had been, more swollen and disgusting than ever, fouler than the vilest sore, gripping her scarlet whip, the sunlight itself besmirched. Lumpish, scaly, under a dirty cloak, her flesh was astir with the leprous; her small eyes under tufted growths and hideous warts were grubs, and they seethed and shone evilly at the sight of his ruby. Only her voice was human.

'Name me.'

But he was too nervous to speak. To utter the name of such a monster might be to smite him with its own curse. Yet he had sworn to fulfil one last command. He attempted to do so, but the word stuck; he whispered, he stammered, and failed utterly. Angered, she slashed his face and the pain cut sharper than a knife from the three thousand. 'Peredur, you are a fool, were a fool from the start. You heeded your mother's words without question. At the Bear Chief's dwelling I greeted you by no name because you deserved no name. You shrank even from your hidden name, if indeed you risked claiming one. Fate was blind in allowing you to be called lord of any spear, for you lack both strength of arm and purpose. To the wounded lord, your fine delicacy forbade you to ask the most simple question, though to seek answers out of love and pity is to render the most wicked spell to nothing. Either you are shamefully timid, or too witless to be regarded, a fool bathing in his own folly. Any mortal who seeks good for his fellows would from very prudence have asked the wounded lord's title and lineage, then, from compassion, his ailment, and afterwards, from need for knowledge, from brute curiosity which keeps the wide world moving, the meaning of the severed head and the bleeding spear. A question, simple as an egg, can free us from the dark and baneful, it can splinter Fate, divulge Fate, defy dead custom. To fear answers is to fear understanding and the future, to despise your soul and whoever tells you otherwise seeks but to ensnare you for ever, and force you to turn your back on life. All questions are simple, answers occasionally less so, nothing is unanswerable nor should it be.'

There was sorrow in her voice, at odds with the crawling hair, tusked visage, scabrous body. Peredur was sunk in shame and despair, his spirit a bird dead after a few hops and chirps. He knew, moreover, even as he placed the blood-red stone into her grasp, that he had not escaped her last command and that she too would not forget it.

Dry throated, he trembled as that crawling, inescapable head, damning as the Mala Lucina, lifted, intent upon him. 'You have sworn to do my will and are forsworn by denying me my name. Now I shall try you once again. You must embrace me and give me true love.'

She was waiting. Flight was impossible. Trying to close his eyes he still saw her ghastly stare. Were he blind, he would yet remain trapped in an unearthly hue. He must reach for his soul, and obey. As his arms encircled her, they felt her quiver as if she were dropping a cloak and, awaking from stupor he saw, resting on his breast, no Mala Lucina but the green-eyed girl, slender as a sapling, more lustrous than Essylt, and who had cherished the stag with the golden collar.

She took his hand and led him to her bower up above the world, and at once they were together on a blue, shimmering bed. He gave her a score of kisses, she returned them lovingly, but then drew apart, her eyes both teasing and sad, and he knew that he was failing her as profoundly as he had the wounded lord. Her mantel was still knotted at her throat, sleeves still hid her slim shoulders and arms. She fondled his bright hair, then shook her head. 'You have more to learn, more to dare, and for me to instruct you would not serve you best, it would not serve me. In order to return, you must leave me, before I can fulfil your love, for love me you can and surely will. Your journeys have not yet reached your real name. By false vision and unreal fears you saw me only as a diseased hag, and would not attempt to try my spirit. Now you have overcome much of your ignorance, but must still venture forward.'

She was stroking his cheek, allowing him more kisses, though returning none. He felt rejected, not by her, but by himself, and her hand strove to soothe his tears. Her words were soft.

'You need fear no more. You are no broken blade. You have been deceived by the visible. The least seen can be the most powerful. The tiny berry can poison the conqueror, a city still unknown can rise up and astonish the world. A sigh has as many shapes and signs as a grail. Colours within colour. There are those who stand outside the light, yet observe keenly. Listen now, you will see me again but not when you expect to, and though you must never forget me you must not seek me. We are like arrows heading for the mark, but arrows not shot by ourselves. And I believe this. To two alone can I give my love. One, whose name you know but whom you will never meet, makes my heart leap and my blood quiver, but we can never entwine, no more than a larch can entwine the moon. He is very kingly, has gifts of all the worlds, but lives in order to do wonders, then destroy them. He is malign, he is in everlasting misery, and his pain is a howl from the underworld. I am in his power, but am also out of it. You will understand, you will understand, for you are my other love, so that you must not fear the name written within you, Deliverer, which the wise Bohort could read, and first uttered, to the scorn of Kai, who in all his life has delivered only scullion's jokes and cruel ways of battle. My Peredur, you are not what our bards call a son of the morning, beautiful as radiant dew, but you have that for which no bard has yet crafted the word, and which will outlive beauty. Do not grieve. Too much beauty tries me as much as too much grossness, but you delight me. Your dear eyes will revoke many promises, your voice will move stones, build cities, dislodge hills, so that the jealous will yearn to rend you blind with twigs of sharpened mistletoe.'

He listened, not wholly believing, yet trusting, for she was a bright stream, a birch silver in western winds, a Summer Princess tender but strong.

'My Peredur, we can reject gods so fiercely that they will favour us immoderately. We must often beware the soft, kneel to the cruel. In a tree can lurk a man, in a man can hover a girl, and tree and girl can teach without words. When you enter cities, you will know the lure of decay. I have outgrown pity, but this is my misfortune, I may recover it when you know my body which you have yet to learn to love. Yet all this you have always known, without daring to believe it.'

Her hand was in his as they lay on the bed together, and as if through the sun he heard her say:

'You must return to the suffering lord, and in this too you will serve me. I myself am imperfect and need aid – and am confessing more than you are ready for. Klinge, whom simple purity rejects, tempted me with promises not wholly false, never entirely true, and in my wretchedness forced me to deceive his enemy whom you know as the wounded lord who has lost his magic weapon. Stricken by my treacherous beauty, sorrowful for his lost powers, powers you have yet to find, he has lain enfeebled, tortured by dark lore and mocking desire and spreading ruin, murrain, famine. Some vision of Eastern blood and cruelty, dispatched by the Great Queen from a wicked past, haunts him, as he groans for the Deliverer who, wishing only to console him, will heal him. Had you asked your simple question, he could have named aloud him who had conspired against him and corrupted my feeling. The spell would have withered. Though you saw the emblems of his torments, by keeping silence, you concealed your compassion. Thus, though your soul is guiltless, you yourself must atone, and recover your name.'

Now she too was weeping. 'Klinge placed a curse on me too. I cannot fully love another until I most fully hate him, and I find that this I cannot do.' She was desolate yet strangely calm, taking his fingers as though counting them. 'Lasting hate is rarer than enduring love. You may journey your life through, and discover neither.'

Very reluctantly, yet resolutely, she rose, standing over him, tall as a lance. 'You must leave me this very day, before, fatal to both of us, I try and keep you with me, like the lover in stories, pretending not to see the bright sail, the banner, or hear the trumpet.' Her spirit clouded. 'Yes, you must go back to the wounded lord, on that good mount of yours, the most faithful of all, though Bohort, and Laughter Loving, who will laugh no more, must not be forgotten. You will discover that the shortest way may not be the swiftest, and indeed, though you are awaited in the East, you must therefore take the path to the West.'

She was already fading. Her voice came from a distance as he still lay motionless. 'Remember my words but strive to add those of your own, for love of me, love of yourself and love of what is greater and lesser than either of us. Now go. We shall not die before our time.'

10

Summer, summer, rebirth of spirit, polishing of names, large splendour of stars, murmur of leaf and bee, the drift of swallows, flashing motions half seen from the Other World, glances building bridges between lovers. The head buried in the field sprouted with golden harvest. New words dropped through Peredur but he was too exuberant to clutch many. Like the horizon, like hills above midsummer dusk, which was, yet was not.

He was convinced that with Gundrygia he had escaped the glare of the Great Queen, indeed was winning her smile. Or, he trembled excitedly, could Gundrygia herself be the Great Queen? A lady of orchards, birds, glass heights, groves and sometimes blood. But beyond all, he thought of love. Separated for years, lovers can yet unite: pretending to be statues, motionless, waiting, they can unfreeze, released in common joy.

Tireless as a cloud, the hound led them through easy passes, friendly steadings, sunlit meadows. Meeting a lithe, spirited youth, alas not red-headed, who had quelled a storm by diving naked into a lake and bedding the water-nymph, he felt neither envy nor fear, but fellowship. Later, tribesmen were burying a woman who had been unusually fat, then mysteriously shrivelled. Peredur was no longer backward with questions. Voices were quick to respond. The more she ate, the gaunter she became. She consulted an Oak Priest who advised gifts to the moon; she juggled meals to fit lucky days and unlucky numbers; she ate five mushrooms at twilight, but all unavailingly. She was thin as a stake, and people only laughed when she gasped that she was to bear a child. Soon she died, and there dribbled from her an adder. The priest announced that, as he had suspected, she must have swallowed a deadly egg, which fruited a young serpent that consumed all she swallowed.

Peredur also heard more chatter of that new city over the mountains rising from a brother's blood and protected by twelve books handed from the Other World.

Once, he saw women, fierce-browed, grouped before a rocky henge coated with mist, though elsewhere the sunlight was a strong yellow. One of them, blood at her fingernails, clutched a head. But they seemed not to see him and, of themselves, the hound and horse quickened their step, as if avoiding a shaft to the underworld. He heard afterwards that in this region had lived a famed head-hunter who had pursued his love through seven worlds and, thrice nine seasons before, in false triumph, he reached her, only to realize that he was clasping an apple tree.

After twenty-one days the hound unexpectedly left the path and they were soon on a wide road, joining a procession of Boi folk, master head-collectors, on pilgrimage to a camelot, the House of Light. 'Come with us, you of the bright hair, and you will be a forerunner.' Not understanding, he nevertheless accepted a bag of simples and, when he chewed one, the sunlight flickered, hills and grass swayed, and almost at once he was with them in the temple of Lot, holding not simples but white pebbles.

The temple, in a wooded vale, was concealed from all but an eye in the sky, and known to be the middle of the earth, an exact boundary between seen and unseen. It had seven walls circling round each other in an unmoving spiral. All had a different colour, the highest being green. Above them was a blue dome with painted golden stars, through which a bronze sun and moon imperceptibly moved. Columns within the first circle were hung with masks of horses and men, decorated with the familiar curls of fancy and transformation: trees becoming girls, leaves midway to birds, feathers flowing into twigs, lovers drowning in their own tears, cauldrons dropping magic liquids. As a star over the sea, glittered the Great Queen, with the warning that loss is gain. Drawn perhaps in blood on the second circle were two axes, dedicated to the sky, and a flower to the earth goddess. Voices intoned in an unknown tongue from somewhere impossible to discover.

Peredur's first day was a fast, in honour of a newly cut head, lovingly nursed by white-robed priests until escorted in a casket of gold and petals to a darkened oracular shrine, whence it could utter wisdom amongst those disposed to listen. At dusk, having

66

eaten hazel-nuts, all partook of a warm, lustral bath beneath a
bronze, three-horned bull. Purifying evil thoughts and ignorant
dispositions, the water also cured ague fevers and sore elbows.
Then they reassembled under a hanging, violet, transparent veil,
behind which stood a shaven priest, a circlet of ivy fringing his
pallid head. All responded, as taught, to his half-sung questions.
   'Who are you?'
   'A name.'
   'Where are you?'
   'In the underworld.'
   'What is the underworld?'
   'A bundle of limits.'
   'Where are you going?'
   'Out of the underworld.'
   At the kiss between dusk and night they entered the Court of
the Rowan, and, in moonlight, drank pale-green juice, heavily
spiced, bubbling from a stone basin and poured from a skull
crusted with scallop shells. Peredur was soon drowsy, awash in
dreams. He mounted invisible steps into pale-blue ether. From
above his sleeping body he saw the three-horned bull dismember
a beautiful youth, the limbs collected by three wailing Mothers.
An eyeless head chanted unknown words. Herdsmen's staves
pierced a goddess whose blood unfroze snow, which very slowly
became giants, uncannily white, their faces tortured as they
erected a dark-blue curtain, already changing to a sky, behind
which light trembled through a multitude of holes. Lying inert
with many companions he was simultaneously trudging over
rocks, lost in mazes, convulsed by winds.
   On the second day the pilgrims gathered under yellow walls
on which a silver hand glimmered through scented fumes, a
shower of petals fell wavering from the dome and, suffused by
the fumes, emerged as birds which at once vanished, though
there were no windows. The haze cleared, bird-men were grouped
on a dais, waving censers heavily aromatic and lulling. Now,
hung with small bells, clappers on fingers, with speckled wings
and hairy cloak, a bearded shaman dizzily capered to wild
drumming and piping through a hail of flowers, cloak whirling
about him in a ring as he emitted cries that came from all sides,
cries animal, mortal, divine, infernal. He gesticulated and, from
the air, spread a fire-rimmed table at which sat eleven masked
figures, one stool empty. He gesticulated again, the scene emptied,
replaced by the world tree which, one hand on his mouth, the
other over his ear, he smoothly ascended, up, up. The music
stilled. Now he was outspread as if knotted to the trunk, before
shaking himself free and, with a low, thrilling call, pushed
through leaves to the top. He lifted both hands, the tree shrivelled,

had gone utterly, leaving him hovering aloft until he gradually sank, to be hidden by a mass of dancers who, to the shrill ecstatic pipes, mimed the tale of a divine child born to Nodens, worshipped by sages clad as hersdmen as he lay in an osier basket amid green stalks, green leaves, tiny lights flitting like elves, flashing from many-sided cups, mirrors, dishes, which Peredur from his trance called grails. With a sudden cry the shaman stepped from a wall cradling a metal vase. Peredur by now was seeing and hearing little, though afterwards recalling a monstrous flame, then bird-song, and, through purple, a lake being wrapped into a cauldron and on transparent wings flown to a crystal grotto.

He wakened alone in a cell of six silvery walls moulded with green knots and mulberry cups. Beside him was a flask of dark liquid. It tasted both apple sweet and charcoal bitter, bringing sensations of lying in darkness, at once asleep and awake, ghosts drooping around him amid the shine of cauldrons. He pushed at a gate, it remained fixed. He desisted, it opened of its own, revealing a vast, blue, airy cup tilting to drench the earth with dew.

On the third morning each received a new name, and Peredur was now Perceval. When asked its meaning he could only shake his head, though others were quick to answer. Champion of the Bowl, Life Deliverer, Traverser of the Lonesome Vale, Piercer of the Vale of the Mystery of Nodens. Doubtless all were mistaken. Leaving the temple he found himself dumb for seven days, but trusted Lot for protection.

He had been welcomed back not only by his horse but by a white hart whose eyes resembled those of the now vanished hound. He rode confidently through a wood, meeting nothing perilous and, seeing a shadowy form crouching by water, he felt no unease, convinced that before acquiring his new name he had been seeing the world as if through tissue.

Abruptly, as though it had pushed up through dim, damp earth, the grey tower was before him. Again he saw mists, dark rasping stubble, seven lean cows, the palisade with its rotting heads, and, faintly luminous in shrouded air over the gateway, the head of the Red Chief.

Unhesitatingly he rattled the door. The same man opened it, but this time smiling, begging him enter. Yet, within, remained the chill, the wretched lady, the suffering Chief writhing beneath his skins, sweet herbs strewn about him against the horrors of his wound. Here was no Belenus or Bran, but a man mortal as himself. Peredur hurried over, knelt, and in his eagerness forgot to ask title, lineage, or anything save: 'Dear lord, what ails you?'

The lord lay back, very quiet, agony ebbing from his face, his limbs at rest. By simple compassion, a spell was broken. Slowly, picking up words as if they had long rusted, he smiled comfortably, and told his tale of beauty and jealousy, immoderate desires, retribution and pain, the constant attempt to escape it by ritual and imprecation. With the telling of the tale, the pain was ebbing.

Rising, Peredur saw before him the lady, her worn face restored, glistening like clover as she passed him a cup decorated with tiny leaves, points of light, circles. Draining it, searching about him, he finally saw from shadows the spear, tipped with blood. Dipping the blood on to a rag from the besmirched pail he smeared it over the lord's oozing wound. At once the dim vaults and damp, cracked walls were brilliant, resounding with joyous song, and from without came the fresh sough of waters, happy lowing, the whirr of birds. Perceval too was elated, at table with the lord, eating from a platter of fish, glad of the world awaiting him.

Three

The Japanese entertain a wise concept, very different from the
Christian concept of redemption. Like our idea of martyrdom, it
has application to both theology and aesthetics and through them
shapes the moral view of the universe. Their word is *Utsuroi*,
and it means, at face value, the point of change. It locates beauty
at the moment when it is altered. It implies an acceptance of flux
and of transformation, for it means that it is not the beauty of
the cherry blossom that gives the highest pleasure, but the
knowledge of its evanescence. The fugitive emptiness between
one palpable state and another; the shadow's leaping lack of
substance; the ephemeral dappling of light under trees; variations
that are undone on the instant – all these answer to the idea of
Utsuroi. It depends on an understanding that time is not linear,
not one event after another in a chain, but an overlapping
sequence of the same shapes, as in a shaken kaleidoscope.

Marina Warner

Gods – we project them in bold provisional sketches,
and destiny crossly rejects them into the past.
Immortals, nevertheless: our spirit questionly stretches
and hearkens out the one that will hear it at last.

Rilke

1

I, impoverished son of a petty Swedish knight though in descent
from King Eric Ploughpenny, was seeking my fortune farther
south. I had nevertheless, because of some verbal fluency, received
a commission from the King of Swedes, Wends and Goths to
deliver loving greetings and refusal of a loan to his Beloved
Brother, Co-Dweller in Christ, Exalted, Lofty, Peerless and
Sanguine Duke, Titular Chamberlain to the Emperor Most Holy,
Most Roman. Also Commander of the Golden Fleece, Designate
of the Virgin, Renowned in Heaven, Watch Guard of the Holy
spirit, and born under Jupiter, as a ruler should be.
   I had been promised private audience, but the Duke then

dreamed of three funerals, so that eventually I had to present my missive before most of the court on the Feast of St Martin of Tours, preceded by a solitary trumpeter which, I was assured, was a considered insult, the Duke already knowing all of my gilded and embossed parchment. In my dispatch, I of course emphasized that my own monarch's renown, echoing throughout Christendom, had forced His Grace to allow me seven trumpeters, five heralds extraordinary and three bishops on bended knees intoning the royal name. Such are the ways of courts.

Observant on travels, I became familiar with the niceties of diplomacy, the feints, the elaborate compliments wrapped around exquisite rebuffs, smiling evasions, sly nuances. I learnt much from the tale of wily Pope Alexander II who, to successive pleas from envoys of the English king during his quarrel with his tantrumy archbishop, invariably replied, 'We are glad that the King is so good. May God make him even better!' Confidences exchanged without intimacy suited my temperament, rather than battle, tournament, dice. I enjoyed the occasional woman or page but sought no grand licence. Reasoned debates at an opulent table, saunters in June arbours, solitary rides through glossy landscapes contented me. My books and music rolls, my measure of gossip, outbid invitations to join a crusade, loot Baghdad or Trebizond, climb glass mountains, assist a madman to harrow Hell, risk myself to avenge an imaginary hero.

Like a playing-card, the court was more than it seemed. From the cat-faced Venetian envoy, I learnt how to praise with a smile, without a smile, or, blatantly, unobtrusively, not praise at all; how to read the Duke's squally countenance (he was nicknamed 'the Florid'), the transient values of particular saints, rumours of artisan unrest or the French king's humour. When a cat tactlessly changed sex and the Black Brothers demanded to arraign it, the Venetian soothed the Duke with information that the animal came from Morocco, where such behaviour was commonplace.

Hitherto I have told Perceval's tale in traditional manner, careful to include tedious brothers dying in futile combat incited by a father himself not very substantial, though, like the Merlin, like indeed our Blessed Saviour, replenishing the world's glamour. I have negotiated with degrees of truth, for Perceval's own witness was never impeccable and, at crucial events, was stammering and contradictory. I have had to fill gaps from suspect testimony, grope towards the essence. Absolute truth is unlikely, often uninviting. A learned monk has written of history that some parts are satanic delusions, others are poetics, some truthful, some merely appease folly.

72

I too have witnessed the curious and ambiguous. Proudly, Sieger von Ekstad wagered a single ducat that he could slay fifty horses in an hour, and won. A Mantuan ambassador alleged his descent from a Cretan mountain, which indeed bore the same name.

Another famous name was construed as a need to fulfil a prophecy, which burdened Armente di Aventura in proclaiming that, as the thirteenth of his line, he would be hailed in Paradise itself as Dragon, after he had slain such a monster. He was anxious to acquire so illustrious a title, but found difficulties. Though scholars, troubadours, mendicants, pedlars, tinkers, gypsies, often professed having seen a dragon, their directions were confusing, so that Armente's life, though vivid, was taxing, occasionally ludicrous, and, on his thirtieth birthday he carelessly hurried over a cliff towards a clumsy shape on a far distant horizon. Thereafter, his family always walked stiffly, hands to sides, to avoid rudely injuring his ghost.

A name still roots us, imprisons us in the definite, limits or expands possibility. I would not, like Marguerite du Vercellière, name my daughter Earth-shaker, or imitate Wide Acre Martelli, who christened a son Odysseus, Greater than God. Names must be endured until by chance, will, or Fate we win others. Whether Fate exists is certainly the largest question I have yet encountered.

On Perceval's arrival at the Duchy, from some vague East which, whenever he spoke of it, seemed always outspread under an azure sky dazed with too many gods, he at once enjoyed distinction because of his name, ambiguous yet as if out of romances, usually interpreted, however obscurely, as 'He of the Cup'. I had met him earlier, at an alpine pass, and was immediately charmed by his slim frame, skin clear as dew, agile, debonair eyes, violet under hair richly golden in the heat. I spoke, not of my adventures, negligible, not of my loves, trivial, but of random encounters in castle, university, lawcourt. He smiled courteously, nodded at set intervals, but obviously heard little.

Perceval seldom fully described or explained and, if striving to do so, resembled an excited but stuttering child. His memories filtered through words seldom less than clumsy. I must sometimes ascribe to him words of a later writer, that no sooner do we express something than we devalue it.

He did mention some tribe where cripples, particularly amongst children, were deemed exceptionally wise, and used as magistrates. 'A one-legged boy', his face looked distressed under the litter of fair hair, 'was hated by other children. They were jealous. He was pelted, almost killed. I led him away. They were all silent. Perhaps', he struggled for coherence, 'they were ashamed.' But I wondered whether they really were.

When he heard that a man and his donkey had been burnt at Dijon for sodomy, his eyes and shoulders were stricken.

He found difficulty in speaking of Gawain, mysterious Spring Hawk, incest's child, who slew a lord for stretching out his hand in greeting. Gawain was said to have wounded a king, raped his daughter, and been driven away, laughing and swearing, in a filthy wagon, showered with dung, offal, worn-out shoes.

'I lack love,' Perceval mumbled. 'Poets sing of its changing happiness to desert, loneliness to Paradise. I am denied happiness, I find no Paradise.'

He did not appear too disconsolate, indeed his smile was playful, as though loss was a courtly Other World pastime.

The question-and-answer traffic of his youth still perplexed him, and of these too he would speak as if measuring some barely discernible obstacle. They sounded ill-remembered scraps of ritual kept secret even from the twelve disciples and of course proscribed by our ever watchful and fatherly Church. At the back of the mind hovered the condemned Templars and Cathars with their furtive adoration of idolatrous heads, magic cups, less than omnipotent God; their ambiguous loves which forestalled new births on an earth they held evil.

'Yes, yes. . . .' But Perceval seldom listened. In my company he could be wholly unaware of me, avoided my eye, looking only at the spaces around me. If he did seek love, I had not met anyone likely to win from him a love that I would have found satisfactory.

2

Flamboyant or subtle, from Arras, Bruges, Tournai, hanging at all levels within towering apartments, the tapestries entwined with the court itself, so that in later afternoon, by wavering sconces, elongated and waxen figures unfroze, seeming to join procession and dance, prayer and conference while live counterparts suddenly stilled in dramatic posture as bells rang from a campanile, a horn sounded, caps doffing, bows prolonged at a majestic entry, ceremonial presentation, orotund announcement. Amid fanfares, aloft, in sumptuous golds and crimsons, blues and greens, angel and noble hunted beneath gigantic oaks, above bent, swart peasants, though woods agleam with stags, wild men, leopards, then across landscapes strewn with giant hares and lilies, past windmills, over bridges, down roads on which exotic Asiatics led elephants against mighty Alexander. Ahead rose pale turrets half concealed by exquisitely detailed foliage, trim points and lines like spray, and from which slender hands dropped marigolds to knights, like mounted castles, plumed, slitted, jousting in roseate courtyards. Hercules, the Duke's forefather, was everywhere; naked by a fountain, in lion's skin, in chainmail, or, as Seventh Champion, in the Golden Fleece. He bestrode all worlds: guildhall, port and Olympus, meadow and lighthouse, rival of the Emperor, rival of the sun, Hercules, lover of the moon, world saviour, slayer of plague, sky runner, feasting the Hours and Months, bearing infant Dionysus over a yellow, tumbling flood. Years back, he had returned to Italy, calling himself Rienzi.

The Palace was a warren, not ramshackle but confusing, each hall, gallery, vestibule, chapel with its own unmistakable lights and shadows. The Duke's private chapel, rimmed with gold and turquoise, dedicated to Holy Poverty, held the Venetian goblet from which St Louis drank his last, a pieta of enamel, diamond, onyx, a bust of Nero, foliated, and with emerald eyes. Covering a profane, indeed Bacchic mosaic were golden vestments woven in Paradise and once worn by St John the Divine. Mercury was carved on St Mark's amethyst ring, a vial contained the Saviour's blood, a tiny crystal box splinters of the True Cross and Ulysses' mast. Hidden was a blackened toe of a Holy Innocent. Much of this was coveted by the French ruler, often called the Spider King and despised by the Duke as a clerk in breeches too large for him. Never had the Spider King ventured on crusade and entered Jerusalem through arches of rose, myrtle, Muslim heads; he had inspired no epic or geste, a hundred thousand infidels had yet to surrender to him. He had overthrown no Knight of Calatraver, had dislodged no pope, found no Templar treasure, had never flown through air to rescue Andromeda, had not even slept with Helen's ghost. True, the Duke himself, *objectively speaking* – a phrase recently disinterred and now fashionable – had deigned to accomplish none of these, but was always about to and was perhaps unconvinced he had not yet done so. An assiduous reader, he knew so many tales that he fancied himself as within all of them. 'Achilles and I . . . ,' he might begin. Above an arch had been embedded a human head, to give it life, though the Archbishop, theologically adept if but recently baptized, insisted that, in reason, the chapel enlivened the head. I noticed that a painted lintel stone was misplaced, so that Jesus blessing the children was placed amongst the Deadly Sins.

The Duke had been dangerously pensive when I risked telling him of antique Roman emperors building themselves arches of a height that made them as if for giants. Here, magnificence and gloom were adroitly balanced. I knew of low rooms where braziers smoked and Black Brothers examined suspects, while beyond, under lofty ceilings, dancers twirled and bowed, mummers mimed comedies, singers lulled over flutes and lovers loved. The latest alchemist, from Marseilles, had already caused famine in eggs, many thousands consumed in an experiment which he swore would bring benefits inestimable, the least of which was eternal youth, though I had to report that he himself was old.

Each in his cell, physicians dispensed essence of fennel to improve sight. One informed me that the fashion for washing was thinning the skins of the rich, so that their susceptibilities were more vulnerable to satire and malice. The most distinguished physician, Étienne de Frésnay, wrote a treatise concerning plague remedies. Aptly, plague occurred, and he was pelted and his house destroyed, for having caused it. At court he was Lord of Functions though none was sure what these were, nor, despite three separate salaries, was he. His brother-in-law had the distinction of being beheaded at Trier on the evidence of a ghost.

In almost every courtyard, sumpter panniers were stuffed with richly dyed brocades, opulent samite, dazzling green Syrian damask, Muscovite furs. Weekly I described the munificence of Brabant, Ghent, the bustle of Antwerp and Amsterdam, the bobbing looms of Flanders, the brisk mercantilism of Bruges and Ypres. Daily I saw consignments of oranges from Castile, wagonloads of Rhenish wine, English wool, Venetian books, Alexandrian spices; Levantine mystics, shield designers from Maastrich, armourers from Bologna and Toledo. Hucksters, scenting a provincial novice, offered me goat's milk brewed with rue to save me from leprosy, teeth of male vipers against bile. I declined an elixir compounded to avert the end of the world. A Jew from Montpellier knew the secret of confecting dragon's blood paste to ensure invisibility. Eager to worst the Spider King, the Duke besought him a barrel, but lugubriously the great man told him that his last jar was in the Sorbonne, much valued, and that seven years were necessary to prepare it, under a rare conjunction of planets. The Duke was mollified only when a Court of Chivalry assured him that invisibility lacked honour.

Everywhere, I repeated though cautiously, my missives being preyed upon by spies, was contrast. The court rose high above loom, ship, bank. A trained reader would realize that it could rise too high.

The household mingled formality with accident, Fate was tempered by caprice. Much of the Duke's father, the Old Duke, still lingered, in portraits, as a shade in the Spring Pavilion, in tales of his practical jokes. One of his bridges jerked the newcomer into a pool, artificial winds opened ladies' skirts, certain books drenched the reader with soot. In the Sanctuary of Jason, with its door so low that even the Duke must stoop, so that his visits were few, a false step induced thunder and lightning and improper water from Medea's statue.

Daily I sauntered past noblemen and prelates stalking forward with processions of clerks, notaries, chaplains, heralds, archers, squires, concubines, sometimes wives; also apothecaries, surgeon-barbers, pastry-cooks, hawkers, minstrels, conjurors, Jews, choristers, physicians, jesters; also Liége illuminators jostling for commissions, magi with prescriptions against the hairy star, or flaunting maps of Hell – Hell, sited between a Sicilian volcano beyond reach of the sea, and bordered by fires which roasted the unbaptized urchins.

I felt the Palace was indeed the centre of the world, open to all save devotees of the Spider King, and even they could be charmed or bribed. A glance could reveal the sculptor Ghiberti who had devised a sugar cathedral, an Augsburg master printer with a book of praises of the Duke from all universities save Paris, a brother of the busy Earl of Warwick, usually staring as if obsessed at a tapestry of a Spartan hero betrayed to executioners by a kiss from a false friend. Strutting Genoese chattered with lumbering Bavarians, quarrelsome Orléanists, Englishmen stiff in opinions and demeanour, dandified Neapolitans, many too obviously Saracenic, skilled with the fork, which the Black Brothers condemned as heathen, sacrilegious, but not heretical.

For my King I was careful to list each petitioner, inventor, confessor, pardoner. Slyness, or courageous effrontery, was needed to hint that the Duke, boon Companion of God, ever required pardon. I avoided Boanerges, Son of Thunder, a youngish, soiled pretender to some fief near Tunis, at present stolen by infidels. He gave an elaborate supper, forgot to pay, then disappeared; was understood to have challenged an Arabian philosopher to magic him into a fish swimming in wine. This, if true, lacked foresight.

Throughout day and night, bells rang, not only for the hours but, at irregular intervals, to warn off devils. Devils fear bells, save in Russia, where winged imps dwell on church-tops and are at their most mischievous during the pealing. The oldest corners of the Palace, the Aachen crypt and the Strasburg Arch were smudged by decay, or, some held, by Christ's favourite bird. This was never identified. It might, I learnt from the smiling Venetian, be that goose which, filled with the Holy Ghost, helped lead the First Crusade, and was doubtless a descendant of those worthy geese chosen by gods on a famous occasion to save Rome from Perceval's people. These ancient quarters were kept strewn with daisies, St Margaret's favourite, though all knew that it had also been beloved by the infamous and proscribed Great Queen, now vengeful from the suppression of her sacrificial fumes.

The Palace gardens were Christendom's glory, envied by Pope and Emperor, traduced by the Spider King, surrounding the Palace in luxuriant oblongs and circles, furiously tinted rectangles and squares. Myrtle and cypress recalled resurrection and hope. I would pace with expression of importance the Knot Garden, intricately patterned by knee-high hedges looped and tangled, enclosing tinted rocks and pebbles, diamond-shaped levels of thyme and rosemary. An arch of Hadrian medallioned with tritons and centaurs separated the Garden of Aeneas with its pronged evergreen and spiky bushes and dwarf pines, from the Garden of Dido, where roses and plaintive marguerites glowed in light mellowed by old walls or under a weeping statue. Beyond was the Garden of Wildness, thick with bristle and briar, nettle and grass, through which Pan leered, carved dwarfs and Medusas silently muttering that life could end suddenly as the flash of the swan in an adjoining lake. The garden's exact centre was a circle of moss, luminous at dusk, guarded by boulders topped with unicorns' horns. Lawns of thyme, lavender, dark-green turf ranged to all boundaries, set between tall, curved hedges with stone seats, useful for love and intrigue. Above a dark pool glimmered a stone heron known periodically to fly away, though always returning on the edge of sunrise. Everywhere, in basin and pool, cascading, or still as paint, were water and naked forms, white, silvery, pale green. By delicate mechanical arts, Neptune would break surface with chariot and horse, his trident jetting spray at observers. By tricks of light the bright mosaic bubbled liquid-like on a blue wall, appearing to merge with a real stream foaming beneath, falling to a pool from which two white-marbled nymphs and one black enticed shaggy satyrs. Herbs, if plucked under correct stars, cured all ailments. Symbols were worn like opinions. Roses showed the five wounds of Christ, the transience of love. Vineyards recalled the Bacchic sap, the Saviour's love, lilies were dreams of purity, orange blossom reiterated to unwilling ears the delights of virginity.

I was careful to gain audience with the Archbishop, who enjoyed the resounding appendage of Protonotary General, Seneschal and Particular of Ghent, a city he avoided for its hubbub, impiety and intimacy with the English. From him I learnt no more than that the world is not supported on four celestial columns but by the Will of God. More interesting was the ex-Comptroller of Requests, pustulous, moist-eyed, shambling, whose fiscal beliefs had encouraged him to promote coinage designed swiftly to disintegrate, thus having to be spent rapidly, thereby stimulating commerce. Though his reign was brief, it had several imposing sequels. The Duke, though somewhat impoverished by his counsel, valued his company, while unable to abide his successor, regarded as the foremost banker of the age. Often at the Duke's elbow was the Sieur de la Rivière who spent seventy thousand crowns in five days at the behest of certain Savoyards who gave in return a lock of Christ's hair, three slices of St James stolen from the Spider King and a possible cause of war, a sty from St Matthew's lower lip, a parchment in Latin on which scholars made adverse comment written by none other than the Holy Ghost, and a box, seemingly empty but guaranteed to contain the heart of St Pulchrindia, visible only to the perfect, relatively few, and kept from the gaze of the Duke. The Sieur, very thin in all but his mouth, was gracious to me, as he had been to Henry V of England, whom, perhaps unnecessarily, he had instructed on the winning of battles. The monarch, however, was ungrateful, as monarchs usually are.

The court abounded with skills. An Andalusian grandee, until ejected for malapert seductions, enriched himself by inventing a language he professed had been known only to Solomon, Alexander, Hercules and Agamemnon, which he made available only to a wealthy clique. To confuse Death, Maître de Quatre Chiens, so ancient that he claimed acquaintance with Priam and had been painted by St Luke, seamed as M. Fouquet, the Duke's rhinoceros, would totter through galleries in archaic robes or crouch naked, walnut-stained, in a forge, feigning a limp. He told me that male Jews had periodic issues of blood, like women, curable only by blood from a sacrificed Christian.

The Duke disliked poetry; it had, he declared, feeling but no meaning, and he preferred chronicles, but retained a Noble Poet, known as Monseigneur, who, at certain ceremonies, stood in high, gilded buskins, out-topping the Duke himself, in imitation of the Emperor's Noble Poet, who paraded on stilts and enjoyed posing as the Merlin, obligatory seer of ancient chiefs. Though speaking familiarly of such versifiers as Walahfrid the Squinter and Theophilus the Hungry, Monseigneur refrained from quoting them, and the extravagance of his own conceits suggested some internal barrenness. He who owns much, craves more, he would say, smiling, for he was very rich. He himself accepted literally the wisdom of Peter Lombard, that to love one's wife is more sinful than loving another's, though his wife was glad to agree. Intelligent, spirited, with hankerings for those more comely than Monsigneur, she was apt to quote St Jerome, that whoever loves his wife to excess is actually an adulterer.

The Duke believed in marriage vows and, unlike his father, was awed by Holy Writ, and, when disobeying it, was angry, usually with others. Casual amours he now disliked and indeed, though his father had assiduously hunted women, his heir had earned clerical rebuke for a chastity unseemly in a prince. Later he married an English princess, at present absent on pilgrimage.

His Grace was apt to juggle with confessors, according to the state of his conscience: his favourite, a Milanese, taught that only the pure should procreate, but that these would not wish to. This perturbed the pious Duke, for he had sired a daughter, thus incurring the disadvantages of impurity and lack of a male heir. This daughter was now married to the Emperor.

All this was very different from life in my own wooden villages and desolate winters, manic springs, flimsy enchantments and early deaths. (I brood, not for long, over the distinction, if any, between 'early deaths' and 'short lives'.)

Birds dyed blue and yellow, released at the Easter Fast, the most lordly of Palace banquets, were hailed; then abandoned to fly wildly about the halls, until, braining themselves against stone or reaching the gardens they were pecked to death by others outraged by colours displayed by those in no way superior to them.

Visiting notables were welcomed with trumpets, feasts, jousts, and the plaudits otherwise reserved for master chefs. I supped with the amiable nobleman obsessed with art and chivalric pageants, styling himself King of Hungary, Jerusalem and Naples, with the habit of painting on glass and addressing ladies in verse. An English embassy brought twenty-one caskets of gold, followed by a resplendent youth, the Wonder of Cyprus, who arrived with no baggage or attendants. His manner was authoritative but his talk lacked authority.

I was privileged to salute the Greatest Doctor of Palermo, a Jewish master, ant-waisted, in golden raiment and with black slaves. His nose had been pulled out farther than he might have wished, tilted slightly upward as if encouraging something grosser farther down; Monseigneur once hung his cap upon it. He was renowned for having sold three bottles to the Queen of Naples, one containing a glance from Venus, the second the smile of a Holy Innocent, the third, later purchased by the Pope, the breath of Jesus. I was invited to attend his cures, none of them actually novel in technique or result. To heal a Moravian's impotence he took a wax model of the youth's little spear, then lit it to purge the demon. The member, however, dwindled to almost nothing. Less controversially, he prescribed live spiders to be swallowed against rheums. Informing the Duke – whom he addressed as Your Altitude, which sounded irreverent – that he, the Duke, had the honour of being thirty-ninth in descent from Noah, he expected instant riches and, his expectations unfulfilled, departed in dudgeon.

The Other World was not overlooked. Prayers pattered on all sides, especially between Christmas and Lent, the Lengthening

Time. Prayers to St Apolline, who soothed toothache, to St Uncumber, who disposed of spouses, to the Virgin of the Broom Plant, Virgin of the Palm Leaf, Virgin of Dew and Protectress of Hunters. The Grand Prior of St Gervase-en-Guyau mentioned that, throughout her life, the Virgin spoke only four times, though he was contradicted by the Archbishop's mignon, a talkative Gascon, stating that the occasions could not have been less than forty. The Prior had but one leg; as a youth, he had had the other lopped, on assurance from a mountebank – splendid word – that a missing limb increases virility. Unwisely, on the selfsame day, he devoured pink fish without knowing it, and never wholly recovered, for his patron, St Finian, was grandson of a salmon, thus resembling the uncouth Kai. I myself learnt more from chatter than from prayers. Chatter in arbours – to the scandal of Christendom, the Abbess of Neuchâtel had overnight grown a beard after prayers to St Uncumber, then written nine plays: chatter in turrets – in Aragon a moneylender had been gibbeted for belching on a royal occasion. The Basques lacked a word for God, and were indisposed to invent one; William de Hainault abducted a duck girl, who bore a daughter, perfect save for a duck's head and neck. Infuriated, he had the infant hanged, then, repenting, prayed so vehemently that she recovered, but henceforward could not speak but only quack.

Foremost, I had to observe the Duke. He was always courteous, but Perceval's arrival prevented me from becoming an intimate. My dispatches must have read erratically, for the Duke was inconsistent. He drank infrequently, but, when he did so, was immoderate, so that in a single bout he might abjure a treaty, cancel a mortgage, insult a legate. He had, perhaps, some residue of animal ancestry, or, as sometimes happened, two souls, ever conflicting. This irregularity was, more conventionally, attributed to a maladroit combination of Saturn and Mercury though, more probably, due to his mother, who, pregnant, had lain in an apartment hung with violently contrasting hues, reading tales of valorous bravado. His Grace, wrote a chronicler, was a choleric man of overmuch fire and air. He composed music, noisy but inharmonious, treasured his father's books, misquoting them at important ceremonies.

Professionally, I had now to watch more closely, for a crisis impended. This had long been predicted by astrologers, but planets, though laboriously charted, often confound the prophets.

3

There had lately arrived Cundré, Princess of the Holy Roman Empire, after months of intimacy with Duke Sigismund of Austria.

The Empire had shaken with the transports of ecstasy, fury, accusation, hectic reconcilation he had exercised in his famous castles; Sigismundsfried, Sigismundsfreud, Sigismundslust, Sigismundsburg, Sigismundskrön and Sigismundseek. Cundré was a May child and all knew that in northern regions such offspring are the healthiest and most sanguine. The Duke liked to claim these attributes for himself though, born as he was in January, this was but nominally true. Monseigneur had composed verses honouring those May children, slaughtered by Arthur, the Bear Chief.

Like Perceval, Cundré was much travelled, though the more communicative of the two. She soon entertained us with tales of a dark-skinned, Southern race who, forbidden to name the dead, prided themselves on their thoroughly misleading history, boasting descent from the moon and protection from a hero disguised under the epithet 'Dirty Pot'. Their ruler was a severed head. Cundré spoke Latin, Hebrew, Arabic, Persian, French, German, was versed in rhetoric, geometry, astronomy, music, poetry. From the start, however, she was distrusted by the court, feared by the populace and denounced by the clergy. She had fits of laughter, unexpected and wild, and never explained. Under certain moons she was reputed to become a giantess. The same source, at best indistinct, held that she had been glimpsed as a mermaid in the Babenberg river, then hunting bare and alone on moonlit Bohemian uplands. These may have been vulgar images of her rapid changes of mood. More serious were whispers, at first stealthy, that she was a spy from the eastern warlock Clinchschur, a castrated sodomite who had dispatched her to entrap the Duke for his own secret purposes.

Her arrival elicited much reciting of Bavarian love poetry, to the mortification of Monseigneur, who was late in composing his own. Voices trilled throughout the Palace, chanting:

'Cunning prospers but briefly against noble love.
Dry timber snaps and crackles in the thicket
To accuse the prowler.
The watchman awakes,
Many a fight is roused in park, on heath.'

At this time noble ladies were more languorous than formerly. Leaving their husbands to assist the Duke's matters, they and their elegant, formal lovers would recline under trees or ardent tapestries, studying the richness of peony and lily, the intricacy of rose, also complaining of wounds from the sharp moon and bemoaning, with sighs and intermittent giggles, the fate of wronged and loving Dido, and Branwen Fair Breasts who suffered the Third Dolorous Blow. They wept over romances. To be loved for oneself alone, could it really have occurred, would it ever happen? This Cundré, in spirit and appearance, harked back to other days, to Isabel de Montfort-Tosny leading the charge, the Empress Maud slinging swords at Stephen de Blois, to Joan, ever victorious until losing powers when her magic sword broke on a whore's backside.

These new times suited the men, who disliked hearing of valorous women from ages even more antique than that of Maud and Stephen. Names resounded like gongs, like the clash of whales: Sichelgaita of Salerno, Alberada of Boundabergo; Queen Grundiperga repulsing a seducer by spitting; Hrotswitha of Gandersheim, whose plays outraged many but gratified herself; Brunhild the Visigoth, who murdered eleven kings, blood-vaunted as Camilla of whom Virgil wrote that her mighty axe smashed through armour and bones, spattering her foe's visage with his still-warm brains. Poets remembered, or affected to remember, Atalanta, Hippolyta, Judith. Court ladies turned up their noses at Tacitus' note that the Britons made no distinction between sexes when distributing army commands; and, in seemly fashion, they admired Charles the Bald who knew how to yoke women. His incessant prayers for children kept his wife abed, bearing him eleven.

The Duke himself would speak, though disapprovingly, of the many treatises written by Christina de Pizan.

Into his world there now came this Princess Cundré, preceded by scents from Asia, the courtyard of Paradise. Such scents were outriders of beauty at its haughtiest as, at the Palace gates, she accepted a yellow iris but complained that it was not purple.

I myself saw her disdainfully fondle the unsatisfactory iris. Her crimson, steepled head-dress was coiled so high that it probably invited jealousy from Heaven, her extravagant feathers offended the pious, the whiteness of her exposed breasts disgraced modesty, and because of the length of her *poulaines* she was accused of aping men's sexuality, though men themselves appeared not displeased.

Cundré entered the Palace on the Feast of St Arculf of Gaul, of him who had found the imprint of Jesus' knees at Gethsemane. That morning had almost witnessed catastrophe. Hastening to honour the saint, the Duke had stumbled, an upset in ceremonial that might have jarred his planets. The day was, furthermore, Saturday, honoured by the Pomegranate, the importance of which could scarcely be exaggerated yet the significance of which was imperfectly clear. We were relieved only when that learned physician of the Duke, a Saturnine, explained that insensibly the Duke had stumbled by intention.

A tournament was swiftly arranged to honour the Princess, at which her effigy presided under a gold and scarlet canopy, mantled in green, sign of new love and scandalizing the multitude. The Duke, visored and anonymous, jousted to much applause and Cundré's replica was greeted by his own alabaster statue, arrayed as Lancelot, last knight of the world, plumed blue for fidelity to the fairest of all. The crowd's tongues jangled, for the absent Duchess was well loved, but the Duke, despising crowds, never noticed their moods. Also, fearing nothing, he enjoyed challenging taunting, overthrowing adversaries. Only against ribaldry was he helpless.

This tournament, a minor affair, that of the Vase Unparalleled, was won by an English knight from the Honour of Richmond, though, because he used a new mechanical device which, at the instant of sticking, enabled his spear both to emit flame and a bell-like sound, a Court of Chivalry was at once instituted to debate its propriety which, twenty years later, it was still doing.

Cundré could exhibit more than trim courtesy. In rages she spat even farther than the Cardinal Legate and though, in pleasure, she spoke more nicely than many, she could also relapse into lewdness, blasphemy and mirth that might have stilled Attila and pleased Nero. Often calm, even meditative, she was as energetic as the Duke. She was soon unpopular, from her habit of writing on a tablet her witty objections during sacred discourses preached before the sovereign. These she then presented to him. We held our breath at the audacity but the Duke, feigning comprehension, laughed noisily, to the chagrin of the Archbishop, who later abused her for trying to rival the Blessed Virgin. The wording of this comparison was injudicious. He added that she was known to relish crimson roses, suffused with the disgraceful blood of Venus.

The people overnight hated the strange Princess. In brothel and alley, loft, tavern, mill, indeed within the Palace, they murmured that she was the banished Juno. Impudent nonsense, a visiting cardinal retorted, at best she was Hecate. I myself wrote to my King that she might possess some of the lubricious qualities of Ishtar, Whore of Babylon, Isis, perhaps Cybele, whom Perceval in instants of anxiety still called Great Queen. Anxiety was justified by reports that the Great Queen was male in the forenoon, female in the afternoon. Of her nocturnal status I could only guess, though I heard from the Venetian that some years ago she had been adopted in Rome as defence against Lord Hannibal. The Virgin, my informant gave his crafty smile, had filched her loving compassion while shedding her cruelties.

Rumours blossomed around Cundré. She gave her lovers pelican blood to increase their ardour – certainly it would not have increased mine. Unicorns notoriously avoided her, but whom did they not? They were known, to put it decorously, to sleep with their horn in a virgin's lap, so that perhaps no virgins existed or, indeed, that virginity was disreputable. Judgements lacked charity. Cundré's Slovak opals, certainly stolen, harboured plague; her wit, inscribed in those unpleasant tablets, was born in gutter and stew.

I first met her, a few days before Perceval's coming, at a feast honouring Messer Pietro d'Angeli, whose masterpiece, *Hero and Leander*, had depicted Leander not swimming, but climbing a tree, this enterprise being easier to paint. She was courteous, but the slim, green-blue, somewhat teasing eyes, under hair black and tumbled in a network of jewels, gazed round rather than at me, probably affronted by my hard face chipped by northern winds. I could easily envisage her shimmering in the baleful glow of M. Clinschur, who wove spells behind oriental mountains which presumably he had created from a butterfly's wing, a demon's glance, a secret thought of Satan's. I could report little more of Clinschur. His nose was reputed curved like a dwarf's scimitar, his black magic developed in recompense for castration by a furious husband. He was known to have given life to a naked girl woven into a carpet, presenting her to Julius Caesar, who called her Cleopatra.

Cundré at once enraptured the Duke, hitherto so faithful to the Duchess. Her tongue, other tongues wagged, could maim a man at nine paces and her left buttock sported a cross and circle, sign of tiresome Venus-Astarte. This detail I had to accept on trust. She had laughed at the suffering Christ. The Duke, however, now wrote to her daily, sometimes hourly, on Modena parchment sprayed with attar of violets.

They were constantly together. Motets and canzone honouring the Duchess were transferred to her, poets laboured on epics of famous loves: Lancelot and the Bear Queen, Lord Diamaid and Lady Grainne, the Sun Lady, Sir Tristan and his paramour. The Duke commanded leagues of verse from Monseigneur, who, delighted, declaimed cheapjack lyrics on demand – infrequent – imagining himself Ovid, indeed better. The ladies, though disinclined to hear much of the Princess, would demand his song of Tristan, wounded, where else but in the genitals by the poisoned blade of the Moholt of Ireland while slaying him in deliverance of Cornish children sent in yearly tribute to the Irish king. The royal daughter, Essylt, cured him by sucking away the poison, which, the ladies agreed, would have damaged her feelings not one whit.

The Duke did not hear, or ignored, rumours ever more scurrilous, breeding like field-mice. From countess to scullion, none held the intruder a real princess. My dispatches could reveal only that she had come from Prester John's empire, where mountains are golden and rivers wash up diamonds; that she was penniless, wanton, had fled the Isle of Nine Women, a Thracian whorehouse. She had, all agreed, been hired by the Spider King to extract the Duke's secret purposes. But no, insisted the blue-toothed Master of Aachen, jealous of Messer Pietro who had hastened to paint her as the Virgin, in opulent blue, gazing, somewhat professionally, at a naked archangel. Undoubtedly, if not Juno, she was love-child of Venus who now resided within the Horselberg, where she summoned the unwary to seven years tingling lustfulness under weird lights, evil images, indecent mirrors and song. I knew of vain attempts to induce Cundré to supper on a small, fashionable islet, for witches being unable to cross water, she would be shamed. In addition, she had once concealed the sun in a cave, causing twenty-one famines. She was Lilith, the Devil's lover.

Altogether, Cundré was a reminder, perhaps unduly emphatic, of Blessed Paul's stress on woman being created for man; also of Bernard of Clairvaux's reminder that her face is a burning wind, her voice the hissing of serpents. Noblemen, however, less rigorous, gave Cundré sighs, protestations of devotion, unseemly confidences. Southern love tales, with their desperate couples and absent husbands, were dangling before the Duke's court new patterns of ecstatic lament: brilliant towers soaring above the blackest abyss. And despite Cundré's wiles and stratagems, there was expectation of something further, the holding of breath before the approach of a saviour, though few yearned to be saved and all had the protection of a singular duke.

4

Thus, throughout the Duchy the Princess Cundré was being cursed as abominations of mysterious Clinschur, more potent because of uncertain existence; as daughter of sinful Troy and noxious Asia, so far removed from the stern Roman virtue of our all-providing Duke. Probably, the apparition of Perceval prevented more active protests.

He came amongst us unknown, from nowhere very discernible, treated in outlying provinces as a licensed and somehow exotic child of peoples once ferocious and unbridled and, in defeat, awarded a glamour and innocence never wholly trustworthy.

The Easter carols had been danced, spring grasses now rippled in Western breezes, sunlight tutored urchin leaves, birds exchanged comments, the air was blue and silken, torn by no storm, ruffled by no cloud, poets and painters strutted as though nature were obeying them. Interesting discussions sparkled. Did women acquire souls at birth, or three days later? The Archbishop offended the Princess by querying whether women possessed them at any time, thus being at one with Jews, Muslims and all animals save the Duke's favourite hound, Bayard, and horse, Brutus. The Duke agreed to this last, roundly affirming that, as titular Archbishop of Arras he would excommunicate all who denied it. 'Very true,' the Archbishop said, careful thereafter to please the Princess.

The sense of expectation increased, though vaguely, even stealthily. Only years afterwards did chroniclers affirm that the season had abounded with obvious portents, a child, hitherto dumb, exclaiming, 'He will come', a boulder splitting to reveal a well-worn rhino foot, a gypsy born with two heads.

The death of the Visconte de la Roche was at first thought to resolve the curious awaiting. He had drunk horse dung in Sicilian wine, to soothe his coughs. This it did, but the fumes suffocated him. Earlier, he imagined he had saved his soul rather ingeniously. Commanded by the Gospel to sell all and give to the poor, he sold his estates, rendering himself destitute, then gave the purchase money, eleven barrels of gold, to himself.

His passing, nevertheless, did not dislodge the apprehension hanging over court and street. Speculating on the possible political significance of the Princess's hold on the Duke, I was carefully watching the busy, throbbing turmoil outside the Palace, the gaudy colours, market imprecations surly or raucous, the escapades of felons, tinkers, scholars, the stolid, secretive concerns of merchants and guild-masters. Wandering alone, I would sit listening in tavern gardens.   'My grandma saw nine moons up there in the sky. They gave her no comfort. And they say it means . . . this new matter of the Duke's . . . they say . . . '

'Hush. . . .Trouble may come, but don't hasten it.'

'Trouble has already come. He'll give her a little Jack-in-the-cellar.'

'By no means little. The Duke's . . . I've heard. . . .'

Experience had taught me that the populace has beliefs far older than duchy and empire, held throughout Christendom and beyond. The tiresome proverb, 'Rain at Christmas is midsummer's joy', was repeated unquestioned through centuries of error. I knew of a priest almost killed for refusal to walk on water, a girl admired for her ability to crumble sunlight, a friar wealthy from teaching the secrets of flying. Perhaps people possess two brains, one for everyday use, the other seldom used, often never. Sometimes I suspected that Perceval possessed neither.

A few months before he reached here, people had been scared

by drunken centaurs at the Feast of All Souls, when the dead mingle with the living, candles in hollow cobs reminding us that such lanterns had replaced skulls. For them, Virgil was no poet but a magician who had built Naples from eggs and surrounded it with glass. From a statue of him standing on a book, they imagined he read through his feet. The old duke was remembered not for his political adroitness but for once removing his cap to a smith and freezing a forest. Minor terror swept the weavers' quarter when a rose bloomed in February and, throughout the capital, cocks crowed at midnight.

The Bear Chief was remembered. Poets and minstrels from York to Brittany, Wales to Anjou and Tuscany, were recalling him, inexactly. A funeral statue of the English king had borne Arthur's arms, three golden crowns on flat blue. His forefather, Henry II, had, at accession, received goodwill from Avalon. In shabbier places, Arthur was known to have pursued Troit, the magic boar, through three worlds: he had stolen the Cauldron of Inspiration from the murkiest depths of Hell, had conquered Rome, vanquished the Burgundians, freed Britain from Teutons. His three wives had identical names, and worshipped the heads of the giants and monsters he slew. That the Duke possessed a town named Avalon increased his own lustre. One tale the court ladies particularly enjoyed. Arthur, Gawain, Lancelot found a castle in which a squire sensed horror. Lancelot, investigating, counted three hundred oozing corpses. Fastidious, adept at love and courtesy, he rejoined his noble companions at the fireside, and all three laughed noisily throughout the night.

Children, Perceval believed, had some of Arthur's magic, despite Augustine's opinion that children's innocence is more in physical weakness than purity of heart. The lords of the Isle of Ruegen had been enriched by the discovery of minerals by children tempted into seven years sojourn in the underworld. The present lord was reputed, by merely thinking of a gold cup, to make it appear.

Popular fantasies were mercurial, sometimes dangerous. Influenced by the English, the Duke's towns were unruly. Executions, particularly of the rich, provoked savage ribaldry. Attending trials, I recognized wit more nimble than in Sweden. Condemned to die, one fellow appealed to some biblical text which, he admitted, was long ago lost, but which justified theft.

'If the holy text is lost, how do you know of it?'

'It was I who discovered it. Then some rogue stole it.'

'But how did you discover it?'

'From a vision.'

'But you cannot read.'

'Our Lady read it to me.'

'Then let us hear you quote it.'

'Messers and great folk, to reveal secrets of the Other World is forbidden, and in asking me you are risking not your souls but mine.'

He then pleaded, rather reproachfully, that, if he had committed the felony, he would have done so at the Feast of St Engelforth, when all was permitted save war and sodomy. The assessor declared that the calendar contained no such saint. 'That', the accused retorted, 'can make no difference.' His manner convinced several, though others were outraged by his lewd chuckles when reminded that Joan the Maid had assaulted Paris on no less than the Virgin's birthday.

Notwithstanding his repartee, he was condemned: the mob gave him an ovation, a wealthy clothier promised support for his children, he drank seven jugs of wine, then, the rope already prepared, a reprieve arrived from the Duke who, amused, had consulted his conscience and, citing a precedent antique, perhaps mythical, had confirmed the sentence but ordered the felon to return to the gallows a century later. Afterwards, he was again caught stealing, but refused to go to his death unless accompanied by a drummer to whom, by an archaic, long-disused law, he was actually entitled. The long-suffering Duke, if slightly less amused, applied his original sentence, and we heard no more.

In the Cordwainer's Street a wise man gave a boy's toy to a pregnant wife to ensure a son. She bore a girl. The toy was examined by an apothecary, a monk and a notary, who merely quarrelled. Then a pedlar intervened. Pocketing a fee, he removed the toy, explaining that he had discovered a minute fault which he would soon remedy, and, next year, a son appeared.

I have mentioned calendars. Humble folk cherished, often secretly, the older cycle of festivals overlapping with the Church's: Sun Birth, Lug's Day, Witches' Night, Day of Boundaries, sometimes with surreptitious offerings of flowers on some ancient stone or broken image, a coin dropped into a well, hazel-nuts laid on a rounded hill. More rarely, a child was bricked into a new wall, a body found curiously stabbed near a commonplace cauldron.

Such folk distrusted clocks, insisting that years were inventions of priests. Priests might declare that only three dates really mattered – the Creation, the Incarnation, the miraculous departure of Huns – too vague to be disturbing, but common folk knew more: that Monday was mysteriously linked to willows, and women, Wednesday to almonds and hammers, Friday to quince, apple, and a queen who should be nameless but sometimes was not.

Emperors and popes came and went, alliances collapsed and

regrouped, but the year continued, holding peaks and abysses. At All Souls, glaring fires repulsed sorcerors, doors were left open to the dead, and many, not myself, saw the Wild Hunt and Hell wains trundling away souls. On Pancake Tuesday, little cakes were devoured for St Fornax, Roman Lady of Ovens, the disapproving Archbishop told me. Chiefly, I fancied, people believed in Fate, though unable to define it. This, the Archbishop said, was blasphemy, yet not wholly untrue. I suspected that Lug, the light, remembered at Lammas, attracted the deepest loyalties. Wavering only at Christmas, light was entangled with numbers, which only priests claimed to explain, though they refused to do so.

By decree of Duke and Commune, an enormous clock unexpectedly appeared, built by night into the Guildhall Tower of St Joseph towering above the central market. Unease was instantaneous, veering towards panic, the morning swiftly toppling over into a fishmongers' petition, a weavers' protest, a deputation, soon dispersed, from armourers' apprentices. I recognized here the primitive terror of numbers, census, of the precise, together with conventional dislike of change. Since Eden, sunrise and sunset had bounded the day, monastery bells tolling the hours, not always accurately, but pleasantly, and, furthermore, routing demons. People desired nothing more. At Dijon they tossed a scholar into a cesspool for proudly announcing his calculation that Paradise was exactly 9,382 leagues from Earth. He was rescued only on confession that his calculus came from Byzantium, and all knew that Greeks were liars. That Byzantium had fallen to the Turks was further proof of their sins. In much pain is much retribution. Paradise, as everyone knew, was an enchanted isle floating off India, where Alexander had paraded with more glory than profit, ending in a magical underwater boat, where he still is.

Huge crowds, still dissatisfied, now thronged the square before the Archbishop's palace, known unofficially as Bribery Farm. Eyes were agog, necks craned to the immense, inescapable clock. Angry exclamations tossed above the huge buzz, fists shook, spit leapt, the hubbub fierce as in England and Italy where voices clang like hammers.

'Eek . . . the nasty thing!'

'Get it smashed . . . it's another plot . . . '

'Burn the rich. . . .'

All clocks were suspect, but this staring, moonish apparition was worse, for its golden hands pointed not only to the hours, familiar, if scarcely loved by these fairground Annies, bathhouse Megs, water-cart Harrys, yellow-sacked bakers' daughters from stews, the scholars from Ireland and Brittany, and the retrograde

'Followers of Lucifer' adding their mischief . . . but, consternation, towards minutes, those small unpleasant additions to the day's burden, alien to most here present, and inducing sensations of being scrutinized.

'They're robbing us . . . taking away our liberties. Scoundrels.'

The poor man's day was being chipped away, the old, leisurely journeyman hour given formal divisions. It was inhuman, perhaps diabolical, a crushing accumulation of extra time which all overseers would note, sharpening their eye for lateness, doubling penalties. Minutes! Each had a number, probably a name, which authority would keep secret.

'Life's getting worse, no doubt of it. . . . First it was whips, now it's scorpions. Stars are freezing white.'

'We must look to our rights, eh!'

Yes, labour periods would be stricter, discipline straiter in field and yard, workshop and warehouse. Every chink of the day would be listed. The crowds, swaying in browns and yellows, were already seeking leaders, who were indeed fast appearing. On ornate plinths, trestle-tables, fretted roofs of stall and booth, from window and step, agitators were bawling and gesticulating. Dialects and phrases might differ but their purport was identical. Lords, master-guildsmen, the portly, unassailable merchants and bankers, had but one end, to increase work-loads without paying for them by nailing the day with these sharp and deadly minutes. Nay, with worse, for, brothers, hold your tongues while you consider further. Authority, not content with its minutes, was chopping them into *seconds*, impish with malice, yet rigid and undeviating as their horrid cousins, numbers. Only the Saviour's lacerating wounds could rival this enormity.

Outcries briefly, momentarily subsided as lances poked up at the Arch of the Celestial Entry, sunlight flashed on horse armour, breastplate, plumed casque and, reluctantly dividing, pulled by fearful suction, the mass recognized the Seigneur Superintendent of Walls. He was popular for having unsuccessfully pleaded for the remission of a fish tax, also because of his children. He had wanted only five, but some busybody told him Pythagoras' assertion that odd numbers, being masculine, were troublesome. He thus insisted on a sixth and, at the birth, held rejoicings so energetic that none noticed the mother had died. This caused much mirth and made him a favourite.

He was no favourite that day. As he rode forward, mantled in fur despite the heat, gold coins glittering on his helm, the air parting grandly before him, the clock showing five minutes to noon, fists clenched, dung was hurled with distressing accuracy, curses shouted, people began closing in on him and his retinue so that, with what dignity he could muster, very little, he was compelled to retire, backwards, wiping his face.

Jubilation. 'We need ladders, brothers . . . we need fire and stones. And axes. Don't forget axes. Hammers, too. We need all these things!'

'Take the lead, friend. . . . Smash the accursed thing!'

'If God knew his business. . . .'

I was above them on an exquisitely moulded balcony with the Venetian, who murmured that the offending clock must brace itself for the stake. 'Since our Black Brethren believe in timelessness, they should be willing, even eager, to lend a few hammers.'

We then perceived that a further diversion had quelled the seething uproar. Threats subsided, caps were fumbled, then removed, a woman's cry deepened a sudden, awed stillness and once more the ungainly multitude parted, presenting an avenue for a slim, bareheaded figure, fair hair like a halo, clad like a swineherd in a Morality: coarse brown jerkin, rough gaiters, tattered cloak drooping with some elegance, turquoise bracelet on one arm, presumably to induce some virtue or other. I saw, very clearly, Perceval.

The population watched, breathless, transfixed, as neither fast nor slow, but sauntering, he moved on, face upturned to the clock up there blocking the sun, forecasting noon. Halting, he gazed up a little longer, before giving a tiny shrug and, smiling slightly, contemplated the thousands, friendly but not ingratiating.

A long, trembling hush was revoked by an incoherent shout which immediately released the furies and bafflements. Clamour swept the wide square, climbed turrets and pinnacles, gables and balustrades, monuments, belfries, vaulted roofs. The Venetian retained his small, appreciative patronage of interesting events, but I feared for Perceval, alone in the turbulence and mystery of crowds. But again, as if a baton had dropped from some jewelled, controlled hand, the wild hoots and threats shrivelled, for Perceval was singing.

His voice was not unusually loud but very clear, reaching me without effort, caressing the open-mouthed multitude, tender though not sickly, the tune antique sounding, angular, insistent, never quite fixed, gliding around a half-melody fractured into small, inconclusive divergences which almost but not quite repeated themselves, neither wholly returning to the source nor poised towards a completion. Something seemed for ever withheld, like, I thought afterwards, the singer himself. The words were in a tongue unknown even to the polylingual sophisticate at my side.

Perceval sang; first a few, then all, knelt in the mud and dust, heads bowed, receiving the solitary voice, its quavers and resonances, pleasing yet unearthly, as though from some long-faded brightness: that of a god stepping from a tree, a chief pulling a sword from a rock or flashing a grail to ignite a pyre. The infamous clock leering over us all was forgotten.

'They should be comforted,' Perceval told us later. 'All people seek music.'

I myself considered that very few did so, though many endured it.

The song broke off unexpectedly, as though he had carelessly forgotten its ending. Then he held up one hand. The turquoise gleamed, his smile beckoned; in long rounded shuffle the massed kneelers hoisted themselves up. He spoke, a divine youth with promise of the great holiday.

'His Grace the Duke loves you more than he does time itself. He requests, he begs, your favours for his new ornament, he implores one favour more. That each of you accepts from his bounty fifty florins.'

A gasp, a silence, then a vast roar surged through the painted, opulent city: 'Long live our gracious Duke. May our Duke and his Duchess live for ever.'

Back in the Palace we joined a solemn procession to salute not the Duke himself but his new suit of armour from Toledo. While acclamations swelled from without, to the clamour of trumpet and timbrels, we doffed and bowed to this burly, glinting counterfeit, fixed, legs astride, black, embossed with gold, on a stage draped with crimson velvets under a purple canopy, the casque mounted with the inevitable Hercules stabbing the Hydra, a mass of silver and scarlet heads hating each other as much as the hero. The cuirass was blazoned with Venus and Mars trapped naked in the net of the divine smith. I fancied that the armour would be too small for the Duke, though it had cost him five villages and a municipal charter. He often proclaimed his intention of leading a crusade and enjoyed being hailed as Crossback, and on the shield glowed the ruddy cross, emblem of holy wars. I imagined him galloping wildly into the sunrise and as if in afterthought capturing Jerusalem.

Meanwhile, the populace was escorting Perceval to the Palace, plaudits showering, sashes waving, pots and pans clashing, bells starting.

'The Deliverer ... the Deliverer. ...'

From what had he delivered them? From the whims of great ones, from forfeiture of laboriously earned time, from the year itself? Exhilaration replaced thought, they cheered a new hero, a new spring.

We did not linger with the resplendent armour, for its owner,

93

mighty before the Lord and now a sullen Lord of Welcome, hearing the uproar, had summoned a levee in the Blue Throne-room. Trepidation followed, a later chronicler mentioning that the painted angels in the Duchess's chapel lost colour. The Duke himself had been ill-tempered for some days, because a Castilian deputation had presented him with a Cordovan boot, silk lined, superbly crafted, at once soft and tough, but what, he demanded, can a boot do without its brother? Was he, with all his sins, a cripple?

The Duke enjoyed referring to these many sins, his manner inferring that they were superior to the virtues of the rest of us.

I now saw him enthroned, backed by a tapestry of Hercules declaiming before his twelve archers. Beside him the Count of Malmédes held a sheathed sword denoting the promise of justice. This nobleman had been born under an icon, to make him holy, though the icon was of squat St Paul, and Malmédes was not holy but ugly.

Current was a belief that the Blue Throne induced in its occupant sensations either of pain or intimations of marvels. The former appeared in ascendant, for the Duke looked what could be tactfully called sombre. With him on the dais, adorned with flouncing lions and suspicious leopards, were squires flaunting silver pennants sewn with green unicorns while, under the marble steps, heads level with the Duke's sandals twinkling with diamond dust, were stationed, like statues chastened by an east wind, the lords of Flanders, Artois, Mons, Hainault, also the Lord of Functions, doing nothing in particular. Several others were entitled to join them but six was the number of the Holy Ghost, God himself was content with but seven spirits before His throne, and for more to stand before the Duke might be blasphemous, though he had once suggested that they might provide conditions for a miracle. Miracles still occurred, often inappositely. A French peer had prayed for an exciting event – and behold, the Hundred Years' War. A Dutch merchant shouted that his wife was worse than Eve, and she gave birth to a toad.

I could distinguish the ex-Comptroller, then Monseigneur, in his high buskins, one gold foot on a mauve stool and dangling a feather: nervy, quick-eyed, awaiting the chance for a witty remark. In his carved, elaborate stall the Archbishop peered through weak eyes, having, rude folk gibed, been half blinded by his halo. Near him, winking at the Sieur de la Rivière, thumb in mouth, lurked the Sponge, ducal jester, who absorbed all he saw and heard, then squeezed out sallies, conceits, repartee. In spangled cap, lop-sided face awash with professional mirth, he had deftly slashed off the pocket of the Governor of Héballt.

At the rear had gathered several hooded Black Brothers, dark rebukes amongst the glitter. Fitfully influential, they did not flourish here as freely as they wished. Conventionally pious, the Duke would declare that he himself was guardian of his people's thoughts. 'They share my beliefs, and if they don't, I give them a shaking.'

The Black Brothers pursed lips, but did not yet care to dispute it.

Galleries were jammed with ladies, jewelled, brocaded, with hats exquisitely tapered, but the Princess Cundré was not amongst them. The Duchess's supporters were numerous, and did not wholly credit her reputed pilgrimage. They were, moreover, stuffed with her relations' gold: sound Yorkist currency.

Shortish, but thickset and powerful, swarthy beneath the tasseled cap worn slightly askew, the Duke was leaning forward in formalized impatience. His brown eyes, usually very clear, often sportive, sometimes suspicious or vindictive, angel's eyes, the court archivist wrote, more than once, were now twitching angrily, aflame with the tidal passion that periodically chastened the Duchy, alarmed Pope and Emperor, entertained the Spider King. His squarish face, now slightly moist, was mottled, confirming that renowned floridity: his hands trembled, so that the white and orange pages did likewise, while the capital too shook, resounding with his exultant subjects. On the gilded tripod beside him twinkled a crystal chalice topped with a scarlet casing, to preserve his wine from the breath of inferiors.

A prince, it has been said, is he whose blood is visible, strung blue beneath the skin. At this instant the Duke's blood, glowing and fierce, displayed all signs of its lineage from Hercules Tyrannos, its gleam reinforced by his scarlet and emerald surcoat emblazoned by the Star of the Holy Ghost, bestowed by the Pope for victory over the Turks, a subtle hint that his beloved son should bestir himself and actually fight them. Two upright lines, very straight, deepened on the Duke's cheeks, joining his thin, straight mouth in an uncompromising triangle.

We waited, scarcely breathing, all save the Duke, for such a man does not wait, but merely allows time to drift past him. None dared show any recognition of the tramp and stir now at the gates, and the thunderous shouts.

'Deliverer. . . . Deliverer. . . . He has come!'

With some daring, Count Malmédes, ascended the steps and whispered to the Duke. He was another whom God was happy to contemplate. While he continued his almost soundless confabulation, I recalled his marriage to a lady rich, kindly but of marked disfigurements. He had heard, though from Monseigneur, that these could be cured by a whole-hearted embrace, ugliness often being a disguise for exceptional beauty.

95

His embraces, however, must have been inadequate. Sensitive about baldness, he died some years later strangled by an immoderate growth of hair induced by some alchemist's lotion, a gift from fabled Clinschur.

'Deliverer. . . .'

The gates were opening, the guards repelling most of the crowd with pikes. Clerks at their rounded tables bordering us grasped quills, ready to pounce on history, stabilize it, correct it, embalm it for ever. They would erase the unthinkable, the disgusting insult of some intruder from Mongolian barbarism, Moroccan squalor, Levantine nastiness, or of one of the slum messiahs who at intervals cause trouble and are hustled out of the inconveniences of life.

When, accompanied only by a page with a lighted taper, Perceval, in soiled travelling clothes, his gaiters loose, evoked giggles from the lords and ladies, prelates and officials, led by the Sponge, the Archbishop permitted himself a silent sneer. Perceval, though, showed no nervousness, no very discernible respect, more an amiable curiosity as he strolled gracefully through the sparkling ranks, the giggles dwindling, until he reached the Duke's feet, somewhat pronounced in their wide, ornate sandals. Here he waited, still curious and agreeable, folding his hands together as if clasping a rose.

The atmosphere clouded, tinged with intimations of thunder. The Duke remained leaning forward, glowering, his restless eyes stiffening in affront. 'By St Joachim. . . .' But Perceval's answering smile was guileless, friendly, even affectionate, making him very youthful, the glistening head and blue, airy eyes those of a scholar awaiting comment from a trusted mentor.

The Duke's expression, nevertheless, as the Venetian murmured, promised three weeks' wet weather. His voice did not improve on it.

'Have you come as a usurper, malefactor or common defrauder? They inform me that you now stand between us and our people, holding up your hand like a prophet!'

'It was, Your Grace, very little.'

Self-deprecatory, slightly stammering, words struggling against a tide, the swineherd from old tales, Perceval was respectful but by no means pleading, indeed radiating an assumption that the Duke's rank entitled him to no more superiority than that which is courteously granted an older man. 'Almost nothing,' he added, his hand as though smoothing wool.

Ladies were fascinated, but the Duke's anger leapt high as a steeple, terrified pages recoiled, the Archbishop smirked at his own knees. 'You open my treasury to all the world, and more, you rob me of a year's revenue from Alsace, and joke to my face that it's almost nothing.'

Hovering on the fringes, the Sponge swiftly looked up, scenting an upstart rival, while the Duke's patchy face glowered; he breathed menacingly, like a minotaur. Perceval, unperturbed, smiled like a child graciously accepting a gift of inferior quality. 'No, Your Grace, yet I had better, after all, call it very little. But I show sorrow, for offences, even when imaginary, remain offences.'

The ladies gave swooning smiles, their lords frowned perplexedly, but the youth's modest demeanour did not disarm the Duke, now red as a hedgehog's guts, and braced to shout, when the Sponge, striped mauve and white, bells in his peaked cap, flourishing a white wand, intervened. Ever ready to stretch his licence, he quipped in epicene drawl, 'Here I perceive a lover. A lover of beans.'

The men growled a ragged assent, beans denoting madness, but, aloft, though a few ladies tittered, most looked grave, unhappy for the handsome but vulnerable stranger.

Abruptly, the Duke rose to give summary judgement. Fiery eyed, broad, he was formidable, and I myself shuddered for the hapless victim. The whole court went rigid, even the Sponge's daubed face stilled, and Monseigneur, who had edged behind a pillar, doubtless envisaged the opening line of a tragedy. But then, before the Duke could open his majestic mouth, Malmédes, almost dropping his sword, sneezed, the Sponge called out insouciant benediction, the Archbishop, in reflex, crossed himself, and Perceval, glancing round, gave a small sympathetic smile. The tension lightened, then, after a silence, threatened to resume, the Venetian's almond, experienced eyes turned on me with an expression of warning, as though he expected me to utter some foul rhyme, or stroll towards the Duke on my hands.

His Very Exalted Highness the Duke commanded the attention of all Christendom by his flair for the unexpected. As though stepping down from a Trojan tapestry, he slowly, probably gratified by the anxiety, then fear, which greeted each step, descended, halting before Perceval, the young David. His bearing, his finery, his face now youngish and frank, gave him an illusion of overwhelming height. We all drew a sharp breath as, without warning, he grasped Perceval's arm, his face cooled, and the celebrated voice, so often sounding like enraged waters, was mild.

'It is undeniable that in appearing to rebuke a stranger and guest, I was within reach of tarnishing my honour.'

Immediately a consort of strings, drums and pipes began a sonorous march, the florins of Alsace were forgotten, and a curious thrill sped through these illustrious folk, finding many targets. Another favourite. A change of policy, the entire Duchy astir. What would Princess Cundré think, if indeed, while serving truffles and love-potions to the Duke, she ever had time to think?

This Duke, with one of these endearing gestures that erased resentment at his many faults, won extravagant popularity, not by removing that offending, almost criminal clock, but by stopping its hands at noon, the moment of Perceval's arrival, where they remain to this day, or so I am told.

5

Perceval greeted me with a rather nervous embrace, and addressed me by a wrong name. Once more I reflected that, though not quite beautiful, he was haunting like his own song, a gleam from the unnamed, hint of the unseen. In new attire, he was neither modish nor foppish but carelessly debonair. On special occasions, which were numerous, he was apparelled from the Duke's own wardrobe: white doublet, silk girdle of brilliant scarlet, green and black tunic, white mantel fringed with ermine and secured by a triangular amethyst. He was hailed as Knight of the Swan, also as Knight of the Grail, more risky, for the Grail, whether or not it existed, and despite various disputes about its shape and function, was anathema to the Pope and proscribed by the Black Brothers. Duke, Princess, councillors delighted in him, ladies surrounded him like flowers, drawn by his azure eyes, easy charm, and thoughts of his wondrous little spear, surely so long, so ivory. Actually, this last was no more remarkable than my own and, on evidence, less ambitious, though more finely tapered, its pink mitre faintly but enticingly visible through a foreskin almost transparent, tempting many fingers towards plucking, not least, perhaps, his own. That soubriquet, Knight of the Spear, was mere wishful thinking, like most of the ballads of the day. Ladies noticed, with appetite, that he bore no willow wand, token of rejected love. Even the Archbishop allowed that, though his errors might well be grievous, they seemed but few. God, Monseigneur admitted, was in pleasant mood when he planted a soul in Perceval. Holding a reception for him, Monseigneur, emulating his imperial rival, honoured us by briefly appearing on stilts, though with scant poise, in an apartment unsuited for them. Perceval himself, I thought, might be more of a poet than Monseigneur, collecting secret names from worlds visible to the rest of us yet usually unobserved.

Never seeking me, Perceval suffered my company without complaint, perhaps glad of my lack of flattery, which made him call me M. Dry Bone, later applied to an unpleasant sickness. I

98

imagined him a figure of simplicity, but not simple-minded. His occasional stammer implied modesty, but modesty seldom quite convinces me. To deny one's vanity can be a way of admitting it.

Outwardly he was friendly to all, to flaxen page, yellow-maned countess, black envoy from Morocco, a beggar at the gates. He was gentle, smiling, though at times the expression in his eyes was distant, even absent. But with indulgence-vendors, grinning friars, blatant intriguers, and Black Brothers, his smile vanished, his countenance ceased to glisten. With them his stammer returned. Indifferent to possible danger, he would incline one hand, polite enough but in absolute dismissal.

When not summoned by the Duke or occupied with predatory Cundré, he would allow me to show him the intricacies of the Palace and give certain warnings, for which he thanked me, though with no evidence that he had listened. From his delight in the gardens, I suspected he preferred trees to friends and councillors. As M. Dry Bone I would never be his lover, but was accepted as dependable, a contrast to the opaque and fleeting: the suggestive dusks, cruel rejections, enthralling quarrels, tiny lyrical pastimes, the tragic midnights and tormented dawns. I was a temperate region where he could dally at ease, leave without elaboration, reappear without explanation. I may have been a curiosity from the world of cabals and a method of which he professed, perhaps with some truth, to know nothing. I could envisage him in tempest, shipwreck, plague, very little concerned: a stare without a face. He would hear my own activities as he might music, not complex, but too distant to be properly heard.

At his arrival, more children appeared in the Palace, richly clad, from where I know not. From the start they followed him in small, excitable groups, joined by grubby street arabs who dodged guards and insulted officials with graceless impunity, jeering at the others' bright trappings until stilled by Perceval's reproachful glance. Then all would join together, beggar and princeling, seated around him as, all stammer gone, he found copious words to fill his stories, make them laugh, weep, then wonder, rapt at the resources of the wide world. He would regard them as he did flowers, as if concerned less with their colours than with their brevity, their vulnerability.

I too might listen, and later, question him. Had he really stolen a girl's ring, escaped the Red Chief? Had he passed through Isles of Birds, Apples, Women? His smiles were wistful. 'They are not reached by water.'

He himself enjoyed stories about children, his own credulity was remarkable. I once tried on him an episode at Santa Domingo de la Caljada, in which a pilgrim boy had to mount the gallows for theft of two chickens, but, too late, the chickens, roasted perfectly, stood up and sang his innocence. Perceval was grave and unblinking. 'They too were innocent.'

Between his two favourites, the Duke strode his domain, like Hercules casting gigantic shadows. Perceval he saw daily, though the young man never besought an audience. The Duke allowed him so close that his state robe touched his feet, a privilege I did not covet and which displeased the Privy Chamberlain of the Cape.

Perceval's ambiguous 'Lordship of the Cup' aroused a few salacious sniggers, but without real animosity.

Cundré was a different matter. The Duke was in a period of jovial calm, as though, I reported in cipher, his fervour for her, fraught with the perils of an extra sin to his tally, was balanced by Perceval's courteous passivity. He had, however, little small talk, was always on the throne, issuing pronouncements to benefit eternity. His love whispers might have toppled Mount Atlas.

What was Cundré thinking? We shall see. Meanwhile, throughout the Duchy was fear of her becoming a giantess. She was the reverse of the beloved, unseen Duchess. All knew, it was undeniable, that, laughing like a screech-owl, she rode nightly on a horse pallid as moonlight, pursuing fearful lovers, and that whoever lay with her 'was lost to this world for seven long years'. Grosser tongues spoke of her pleasuring herself with a goat. 'You are simpletons,' said a groom disdainfully. 'She rides no horse but a white boar, she pleasures herself with a pestle made of finest gold.' He was envious. The Archbishop merely considered that she had tried to trap not only the Duke but God Himself, by casting spells learnt from Clinschur on each letter of His most secret name.

To Perceval, without offence to the Duke, she displayed immediate affection, and there was tavern talk of a usurping Trinity, in which the last was first. The song with which he had stilled the clock riot mantled him with Orphic glamour, so that he was popularly revered as grandson of Orpheus, even Orpheus himself, a status somewhat parlous because of underworld associations, dispelled only by a scholar from Utrecht, who patiently reminded us that Orpheus merely depicted pagan jealousy of the future Christ. Perceval, he continued, losing interest, was probably related to the wise and loyal Joseph of Arimathaea, whose eyes wept wine.

Already rumours were about, breeding like spring hares, that Perceval had healed a child smitten by lightning, also a lord wounded by vile Longinus' spear that had once torn the Saviour; or, voices lowered, castrated by *her*. *Her* now had multiple meanings.

Hearing such absurdities, Perceval smiled, fondled his sleeve, and said nothing. I like to believe he winked at the children. 'They say that you are Son of the Sun. Surely you can be no more than the nephew!'

He smiled again, but did not reply, and we soon heard that his father had died fighting almost alone against Pompey, Lord of Nineveh, and his ten thousand knights and now, worshipped as a djinn, was splendidly embalmed in Baghdad. Perceval himself, by his sweet smile, had disarmed Mi Porter, a rich merchant's lion. Throughout Byzantium he had been hailed as more radiant than Hylos, Absalom, David, Ganymede, and Vergulaht of Ascalon. He had rescued Sir Tristran from the jealous Cornish King, succoured Sir Persides chained to a rock, outwitted Kai, and when banished Lancelot, son of Lac, wandered mad and lonely, found him on the joyous Isle and jousted with him for two hours.

I remarked that his inimitable military reputation would now avert war with the Spider King. He shook his head, as if reminded of something else. The pile of stories rose higher. He and Lancelot had routed Mordred's three hundred. He had accompanied Erec when he won Schoydelahurt from Mabonagrin, son of Poydiconjunz, who had raped fair Imane de Beaufontane. The tongue grew tangled and sore on such names. I chuckled at these exploits, and at my friend surviving the ardours of the Terrible Valley, Lonesome Peak, Place of Wonders.

Even the Duke was overlooked in this saga. On the Mount of Mourning, brave Perceval had slain a black serpent whose tail held a stone which, if grasped in one hand, filled the other with gold. A girl had yielded him the Nudosi, pebble of invisibility, which perturbed some ladies and enlivened others as they imagined him watching unseen while their lords ploughed them naked in bed. Listen . . . listen. Our Perceval had been feasted seven days by the Empress of Cristinobyl the Great, at which the Cartographer General shook his head, had reached the Paradise of Birds, that isle where Lucifer's fallen angels changed to Irish swallows, singing for ever on the World Tree in a dewy garden. He had visited the Grail, described as Persian temple, had once been loved by the Seven Cobblers of Britain, been trained by nine witches whom he later slew, sending their heads to the Soldan. By faith in the Saviour he had removed a mountain. At this, the Sponge jested, with sour credibility, that, lacking prethought he had thereby crushed a city. His unofficial status as saint was enhanced by dubious reports that his undergarments contained lice.

'All this', I used my Dry Bone manner, 'is unusual but not unbelievable. St Michael, after all, is sometimes a cloud and we

101

have Monseigneur's word that there exist swan knights, royal wrens, thirteen species of dragon.'

'I am neither wren nor dragon, and have never envied Michael.'

I enjoyed questioning him, without always accepting his answers.

'That old tale of the Bear Chief always wearing green because seven was his Fate number and green its sign. . . . But did he?'

His smile was faint, his eyes careless. 'Not so. I remember his brown cloak. Never very clean.'

'People say that you and Gawain accompanied Arthur to Hell. Gawain the Hawk.'

The smile flickered. 'I never did so. But if a man knows the approaches to Hell, that man is Gawain.'

A brooding pain grazed his face, forcing me to make no further demands. Casually I mentioned his reputation for chastity, admired rather than envied, to which he gave only an enigmatic shrug, though his eyes were suddenly boyish and merry. I wanted to know more of the Grail, that dark mystery disavowed by the Church, reviled by the Black Brothers, despite some chatter about its holding Christ's blood, being used at the Last Supper, and much else. What was this tale of a Persian temple? Had he really seen a magic cup glimmering in a whirl of dust?

He looked weary, passing a hand over his eyes. 'I remember very little. But grails. . . .'

He stopped, looked uncomfortable, as if caught fibbing. I refrained from asking about Arthur forcing the Castle of the Turning Door, which secluded the Grail, but being forbidden to see it, losing all save seven companions.

I was restrained by his habit of smiling confidingly but speaking as if to himself. Evidently, of the Grail and Gawain he already felt he had said too much, yet he spoke more, in his rambling, unsatisfactory way, as though from a book he could barely read.

'The sky was very blue, hard blue. Clouds slid across it like white sails. Sometimes I saw, or I dreamed . . . hollow mounds, and, inside, chariot-wheels, drinking-horns, pale gold cups, dimness . . . sometimes a yellow crocus shone through. Mists became castles, which dissolved at my approach. Things always do. I could be scared in forests. Stillness . . . a charred smell, like that of boar. So much seemed awaiting me on the verge, like a tree, a stone, colour, await the singer, the painter. Wise people patiently expect deliverers. They don't always come.'

His face, girlish smooth, flushed; he was clumsy within his grace, his recollections too crowded, refusing explanation. His voice drifted away. 'In England, you know, a boy and girl emerged from beneath the earth, attracted by bells. They were green, from a land of green dusk. The boy was weak and soon

102

died.'

'Did the Princess Cundré see such sights?'

I had already realized that they were by no means strangers to each other, might indeed have arranged, even conspired, to reunite at the Duke's famed and generous court. I also knew that I would receive no direct reply, indeed, he gave no direct reply, merely resuming slow memories of bright hill and plant, bird and butterfly, of dew, neither rain nor mist, falling when the light is not night, not morning. He seemed to be unrolling an old manuscript, sharing secrets small yet powerful, diffidently, against some inner ordinance.

'There was an Irish poet who described his songs as making difficulty out of clearness. He was kept seven years in a dark hut, to perfect his craft. . . .'

He himself read little. I would observe him with silken ladies in turret or arbour handling a book but intent not on the words but the margins lined with flowers and beasts, scrolls and foliage, elaborate fancies of English and Flemish masters.

He hesitated, his stammer returned. 'There is always . . . I can't quite see . . . opposites meeting, door leading to door . . . things floating. Fishers of men. . . .'

I quoted Boethius. 'This discord in the heart of things, this endless war of truth with truth.'

He nodded, ruffling his hair, perhaps relieved of the burden of pursuing Boethius.

Several times thereafter he spoke of a hawk in days of trouble. This I understood. His random flashes of emotion had charm, but I was less open-eyed at this than were the ladies, the Duke, and, probably, the Princess.

'I seem always in search of castles.' Momentarily his full lips pouted, his eyes were petulant. 'Their high view over a world free of boundaries. A view into. . . .' He stopped, helpless, then smiled apologies. 'I had heard of a land named Thule, always ahead, perhaps forbidden.'

'By whom?'

He ignored me, speaking more to himself: 'I was in a castle, far south, talking to a troubadour. Upstairs, a lady was suffering. The lord was away fighting, he was always fighting. He once killed a man for refusing to proclaim aloud that his mistress was fairest in all the world. The troubadour spoke very beautifully of chess, starlight on roses, a purple glove. But blood was dripping down the steps from the lady's room. I pointed to it, but he was wrathful at interruption. But . . . ' – Perceval's blue stare was one of astonishment – 'he smiled, he laughed, then said that the sight would give him a new stanza.'

Throughout I sensed that the fuller his descriptions, the less

103

they revealed, like those of a mystery initiate which in some fashion he was, or thought he was.

If his wanderings had enlarged his curiosity, it was very different from my own. He lacked interest in the properties of light and water, salts and minerals. My talk of Roger Bacon, Albertus Magnus, he dismissed with a glance at a passing girl. Hell he believed in as a sort of milestone, and Heaven as fluctuating within his own head. This, I suggested, should not be said to the Black Brothers. He accepted life without displaying much concern for it, and appeared convinced that harm would come to him only from himself.

Like others I responded, not to his looks and manner which so captivated the Duke, but to his vagueness which yet seemed purposeful: his perplexing allusions, his elusiveness which had something of the exotic, his simplicity. He really believed that birds are the dead, able to fly into the Other World, that they perpetually strive to communicate with the living.

Might I learn more by lying naked with him? He would probably have consented from courtesy, not desire, but I desisted. In our subsequent adventures we had, often enough, to share bed or pallet. Only once did I make a suggestive movement, which he repulsed so gently as to imply anxiety to spare me disappointment or fatigue.

'Strangeness . . . ' – he made it sound commonplace – 'ripples between floor and wall, along edges of fields. Lures.' His face creased, deepened, as it did at mention of Gawain. He spoke of past events as if all were of equal import: an invitation to adultery, song of a grasshopper, abandoned rose, prospect of a crusade. The events themselves had a quality pertaining to him alone. In Umbria stood a boulder, usually taciturn, but, when sprayed with water, it emitted thunder, on which villagers prospered by charging travellers for the miracle. Perceval arrived there during a drought, when thunder was useless. He offered a special prayer, and told them a story, not very pious, of St Jovian, which made them laugh so much that tears came, reminding the clouds to drop rain, which they soon did, copiously.

'Once I came to a place where three roads met. An old beggar cast down three arrows and advised me to select one and follow its direction. It led me to the Duke. And to you,' he added in generous afterthought.

He mentioned heads more than saints, and I learnt that the head of St Andrew, deposited in Rome by the learned Pope, Pius II, was curing sick penitents.

London was long defended by the head of Bran until Arthur dug it up, wishing to defend the town by his own deeds alone. Friar Bacon – Perceval showed a disposition to giggle – consulted a brazen, oracular head of his own making. More recently, the Knight of Giac, before being drowned by his wife's lover, besought decapitation, having sold his head to the Devil in down payment for privileges thereafter. At this, Perceval for once almost laughed outright, then looked so contrite that I did so too.

6

I was not neglecting my duties. I had to assess the intrigues, numerous as monks in Bologna; also the political webs covering all Christendom, the Duke, Emperor, Spider King weaving in the centre, the Turks hovering on the edges, the Spider King pausing only to negotiate for the sale of the finger with which Thomas probed the Saviour's wounds.

The Duke was currently the most powerful, ruling from Friesland to Arles, his lands united more by coinage than by language and tradition. He was industrious, his smile stirred hearts, his promises were splendid, though behind them he was secretive. He seldom delegated responsibilities and his rare attempts to do so were usually ill-judged.

At accession, having dutifully planted a cypress at his father's mausoleum as a token of rebirth, not expected to be immediately fulfilled, the Duke, austere of purpose, denounced all wars and combats, aggrieving the promoters of tournaments and backers of knightly champions. Later, however, nudged by rebellious French vassals, which included himself, he was inveigled into armed conspiracy against the King, a conspiracy known as the Good Fortune of All. In this, he accidentally won a battle, which he conventionally ascribed to God, but remained intoxicated with victory. Lacking measure, still youthful, he became dedicated to charge, breakthrough, the uttermost, preferring defeat to indecision, his easy ways hardening into a see-saw of storm and calm. The Good Fortune of All dissolved in jealous rancour, but the Duke was reputed to dream of making himself a king, successor to Charlemagne, Alexander, Agamemnon – the names themselves sounded like the collisions of lions. Humbly addressed as Crossback, he would regularly agree to storm Jerusalem.

Exciting government, remarked the grey, stealthy Spider King, is usually bad government.

The Duchy's frontiers, lengthy, irregular, were largely defended by their rulers' fame, by the spectacular and resounding, and the gifts of the marriage bed. The West gaped at the Lille banquet for the old Duke, at which Olivier de la March, in woman's dress, lamented falsetto the fall of Constantinople, seated on an elephant led by a giant; a boy in silver tissue warbled on a stag, musicians

105

played M. Dufay's motets from within a giant pastry.

Such pageantry disguised the absence of river, mountain, even broad highway to protect the provinces, particularly from the tough, merciless Swiss. The prosperous north could rely on mercenary archers and freebooters and thirteen new Augsburg cannons engraved with dolphins and myrmidons. These were still unused, though one had recently exploded, killing a donkey and three children, whom the Duke irritably demanded be canonized, a favour not yet granted. Some held more effective, preserved in an opalesque reliquary, the foreskin, no less, of St James the Less, purchased by the Duke's grandfather at a cost of eleven feasts, fourteen hogsheads of Tuscan wine and three dowries of second-rank princesses. Whatever its military potential, the relic had assuredly procured several rich harvests, a flock of sacred cranes out of season, and a rebuff to the Spider King.

The transaction reminds me that in Cologne Perceval saw Moses' rod for sale. An Aragonese grandee paid a hundred thousand marks for it, then discovered a gross deception, for the rod was Aaron's.

I had to include in my dispatches matter more routine. A Provençal poet, scornful of the details of a world merely visible, proudly unaware of Cundré's arrival, entered the Court accompanied by a cat on a samite cushion, to read aloud his new verses which, I suspected, he had, with changes of dedication, previously recited throughout Christendom.

The Duke, Cundré beside him, politely stroked the cat, awarded too much gold, overcame his misgivings of poetry, composing himself to listen, agreeably enough until he realized, not least from the Princess's grimace, that he was being offered reams of elaborate praise of the Duchess's virtues, physical, moral and ancestral. Moreover, he was being rebuked for not roaming the world and at ford, bridge, crossroads, declaring her beauty equal to the Virgin's, her soul infinitely blue, her wifely decorum envied in Paradise. A reference followed to the Duke, redeemed from utter worthlessness by his sovereign lady. Praise for him was only that he was lauded by mice, encomium too subtle for its recipient, whose glare would have withered butterflies. A rhymed concession that a prince's spittle cured lepers failed to appease the Duke's lowering frown, for he could not abide these unfortunates, forbade them his dominions, ordered them to be burnt when captured though, as he always hastened away in zeal to escape them, this was never actually done.

At last, though by now Cundré was quietly laughing, the Duke jumped up, violently gesticulating for us to depart, the poet injudiciously imagining that he had enflamed the great man into frantic desire for the Duchess. This he united, rather unconvincingly, with praise of chastity, Christ's lily of the world gleaming on the boundary of Paradise.

He received customary rewards (the Duke scoffed at pettiness, by which he generally meant the Spider King): a black palfrey, which he sold, a room in the Palace, which he did not want, a golden buckle, which he mislaid. He inferred, however, from the Duke's demeanour, that our poetic sensibility was limited by our barbarity and hastened to Tours.

I had to watch incessant movement abroad. East Prussian Teutonic knights were imposing Germanic religious and racial codes on Balts and Slavs by the sword. They possessed a round Table of Honour at which the twelve foremost brothers promulgated savage decisions, though weakened by defeat at Tannenberg by Poles and Lithuanians. They remained pledged to save Slavonic lands from Slavs. I rejoiced that they were not pledged to save me.

The old Duke had been devoted to ceremony and custom, though with acute awareness of grosser realities beneath. 'This Monarch', a Milanese ambassador asserted, 'is a profound observer with concealed intentions, and unaccustomed to give without thought of receiving.' Neither duke was one of those who court milkmaids and dispense justice under some immemorial oak.

The son likewise respected tradition, on which his sway so much depended, though he could make staggering gifts without prospect of return. Pride was a necessity both for his complex inheritance and for himself. His Cap was often held aloft on a golden lance to avoid the common breath. Regularly, his standards were unfurled, to bless his realm. Revering Alexander, Hannibal, Caesar, he spoke of them as old and admiring friends. His apartments displayed mosaics of His Grandiloquence Sir Amadis of Gaul, William the Marshal, el Cid, the Black Prince. In ancient courtesy he once sat on horseback in wind and rain discussing with the Emperor how they should enter Trier, the former wishing them to ride fraternally side by side, the Duke arguing that he himself must ride behind. This he did, but his magnificence made the Emperor appear a menial outrider.

I was alert for his hankerings towards kingship, his envy of others' titles, particularly the remote and luxuriant. Exchart of Ravenna, Baruc of Baghdad, Lord of the Golden Horde, Catholicus of Hromgla, Turkoyt of Itolse, Shadow of God. From a great Bavarian poet he would extract earth-shaking names: Kings Papiris of Trogodjente, Milon of Nomadjentsin, Translapins of Rivigitas, Zyrolan of Semblidoc, Amincas of Sotofeititon, Lysander of Ipopotiycon, Jetakrane of Gampfassach, Kyllicrates of Centrium, Thoarsis of Orasegentesin, forbidden to marry, for his radiance would consume the beloved; Serabol of Rozoharz, Amaspartins

107

of Schipelpjonte, who saw a nightingale in the moon. Such names did not trip off the tongue too smoothly.

The Duke was delighted when I informed him that ancient rulers had been awarded divine honours and enjoyed being addressed as Saviour, God Incarnate, Visible God. Rather wistfully, the Archbishop showing uneasiness, he demanded whether such titles still appertained. He was overjoyed when an embassy arrived from the Lord of the Conquest, Navigation and Commerce of Ethiopia, Arabia Felix, Persia and India, outraged when this was revealed as merely a King of Portugal; was enraged, then mollified by an offering of sweet apricots, delicate as a page's cheek, brought by the Bey of Algiers' choicest eunuch, Frobenius. This personage, very gross, had acquired some fame for discovering the Garden of Eden and bringing back various herbs. Eden, he squeaked to me, was surprisingly small, beyond Babylon, towards China, a land surrounded by a porcelain wall whose brilliance repulsed marauders, and where Frobenius had bought poison of the upas tree which, he said, was imaginary, though its fruits were not. The Bey apparently retained a very old man who had met Jesus and seen him restore a bull to life at the request of St Sylvester.

This Frobenius was crafty. He was offered a delicate choice of Lenten gifts: a bag of gold, or a bag of the Duke's droppings. To accept the former might be sinful, it would certainly be vulgar, which was worse; to reject the latter would affront the Duke. Frobenius decided that to prefer precious gold to inferior was wise, and grabbed the metal; then, for one cheap brass plate, purchased the dung, explaining, after three bows, that in securing the ethereal and sublime, he would not contaminate it by offering mere lucre: the illimitable could have no market value. He then compared the Duke's generosity to that of the Spider King, imagining this to be a compliment. Furious, the Duke dispatched him to the ruler of Ferrara, with whom he had quarrelled.

Because of the Duchess's absence and Cundré's installation, some were watching the Duke with misgivings. The ducal pair shared much good sense and courtesy, perhaps concealing some grievance or guilt from lack of a male heir. Long ago the University of Leyden had presented her, while pregnant, with a dagger, to ensure a son, but, perversely, she bore the daughter. People grumbled that the University should of course have given it to her on the marriage day. God's will, the Duke grumbled, but said that the heir remained his daughter, the Empress, which endangered the realm.

Now the Duke's angers, frets, affections were more impetuous, he was drinking excessively and was too often closeted with lascivious Cundré. The outcome vied with the Turks and the evil fashion for Ovid, in whose pages Jupiter mentions that Fate has decreed the destruction of the universe by fire.

Perceval was welcomed as a rival to Cundré, a restraint upon the Duke.

I had met few less endowed with quotidian virtues than the Duke, though in ways scarcely despicable. His humours were ill-balanced: he was shallow, his thoughts so close to the surface that they leapt out headlong, betraying State secrets as often as minor rudeness. Now he was withdrawn, now fierce as a Breton fisherwoman. Choleric in face and temper, he warmed himself with constant expectations, hated asking advice and, still more, resented accepting it. Sparing him my own advice, I thought him rather endearing.

Increasingly he was ambitious to knit more closely his lands scattered in France, the Empire, the Low Countries and Switzerland, though the last were ungraciously disputed. By bribery and promises, however, the Spider King was taming his rebel lords, scheming to isolate the Duke. There was continuous revoking of pledges, forswearing of brotherhoods, breaking of alliances. Formerly, to crack an oath would have injured the universe but today, with oaths violated weekly, the universe was unperturbed, dispensing the regular round of harvest and birth, Plague and Turk.

The Duke, consulting no one, had recently annexed Alsace, gratifying the commercial classes for its markets and ores, though they were displeased by the subsequent taxes. Here, as in Sweden, all but a few monks desired a better life, but grudged contributing to its cost. Thus had Rome fallen.

The Spider King murmured offensive witticisms but sent no protest. He was wily, unscrupulous, and far-seeing as a merchant, which the Duke particularly despised. He often smiled, in a quiet, unfinished way, thus resembling Perceval, but, also like him, never laughed, might not have known how to. I should like to have seen the two of them together. Unobtrusively he was fostering Swiss anxieties of the Duke, who borrowed money from beefy Londoners, keen Lombards – loans between allies, he termed it, though it was being noticed that he referred to repayments as 'honesty without honour', which, I was forced to report, was not reassuring.

I remained undecided about the future. There were tendencies with predictable outcome, perhaps indeed dissolution in universal fire, as forecast by M. Jupiter, but my dealings were with people, and these can behave unexpectedly, sometimes rejecting their own hopes of plenty. At Crémiaux the Jews departed because of the Hebrew tax which they deemed extortionate, thus removing the town's prosperity. Left ruined, the populace nevertheless rioted when the Spider King encouraged the Jews to return, by modifying the tax. A proverb should have emerged from this, but proverbs seldom assert the important.

One proverb runs, 'Who knows a tall man who is wise, a small man who is humble, a redhead who is faithful?' Proverbs attempt to control the future, are very boring, and seldom convincing. In this story, at least, there is a faithful redhead.

Court and Council contained several factions. The Chancellor, seldom visible, close associate of the Old Duke, trusted though disliked by the son, was opposed by two upstarts and their following, 'the Starlings', so named in mockery of earlier dissidents, 'the Crows', mostly executed in the previous reign. Both represented manufacturing and commercial guilds and communes, together with Jewish purveyors of drugs, optical glass, and, by rumour, alchemical treatises. The Guardian of the Unicorn's Footprint, a valuable sinecure, was traditionally a Jew, none knew why. The present incumbent, jovial and witty, had a deformed shoulder because, during his mother's labour, his father had declaimed an inappropriate verse and, by mischance, devoured not a dove's breast but a fox's shoulder.

To the still largely smothered discontent led by the Starlings, an unstable quantity was, inevitably, the Duke, now wilfully bemused by the Princess and indeed by Perceval. Often now, courting their admiration, fingering that Papal Star, the Duke spoke of leading Christian armies against Islam, outshining the Spanish crusade against Moors. This project dismayed Starlings, Jews and most bishops, who feared the expense, though pleasing the common folk, who believed, on inadequate evidence, that Turkish flesh was tastier than spiced peacock. Rather too often the Duke wore the crusader's cross, to which he was entitled only by the looser conventions of wishful thinking. He had lately appointed a Commander of the Right Wing, who then tactlessly died, his marble tomb provoking rumours that Mahomet had transformed him to stone. Alternatively, that God had made adverse comment on the Duke's delay in starting for the East.

Despite the instant unpopularity of the Princess, I saw that the populace still trusted him. God's Chosen, voices bawled gratefully, reassured by his intimacy with their beloved Perceval. Moreover, the Duke's grandfather had been captured by Turks and had, in fact, much enjoyed his sojourn with them, but the Duke owed it to his Name to redeem the dishonour. Loyalty sprang like a falcon released.

There was an additional matter which I hesitated to include in my dispatches. Considerable pothouse discussion was stirred by

110

the Conversation of Gamalean, an anonymous tract surreptitiously read out in loft, slum market, under bridges, read silently in quarters more opulent. This predicted an Emperor who would crush French, Hungarians, Jews, Slavs, confiscate Church lands, slay clergy, usurers, lawyers, then reign for a thousand years of universal prosperity. Other tracts followed. Some held that he would emerge from the Black Forest, others that he was growing up in Bohemia, born under a sacred head. All agreed that 'Scribes and Pharisees' were doomed, virtuous informers would replace the rich with the pristine freshness of Goths, Lombards, Vandals purging old and sinful Rome.

The latest belief was that the Emperor Gamalean was already amongst us, who else but the Duke, himself undeniably hinting of preparations for mighty events.

7

In describing Perceval and the Princess, I have to infer much from his halting disclosures, her quips, usually cryptic, and from courtiers' untrustworthy opinions. My own intuitions, accurate enough in diplomacy, were otherwise liable to error. Thus I imagine him wandering the lofty, shadowy Gallery of Illustrious Knights, dominated by a tapestry of huge Alexander scattering dwarfs and down which tall suits of armour stood ranked, spectral shapes from dream, monstrous hybrids, beaked and plated, tusked and feathered, swollen, distorted by the dull light, gauntlets now vast, now submerged in shadow, helms growing fangs, shields hanging as if to break the world. He would not be scared, but concerned, occasionally astonished, asking himself unusual questions. Where did the hollow sky turn solid, did the earth have sharp corners? Were dreams sent, produced, or did they merely occur?

Together we watched a puppet-master excite derisive mirth in presenting the Spider King dancing in Hell, tweaked by imps, though jocularity dwindled when a Scots captain revealed that the fellow possessed a puppet of the Duke with grotesque carrot nose and top-heavy limbs, used for performances in Paris. The Duke, hearing of this, uttered an oath that threatened delicate bowels, then forgot it. The usual ceremonies continued. A procession was delayed because an archdeacon saw a hare, or thought he did. An Irish poet arrived, dirty, grinning, mendacious, intoning,

> 'Through faith in the Threeness
> Love of the Oneness
> Of the Creator of Creation.'

111

This at first gratified the Duke, who imagined that the jingle was in praise of himself, but, learning better, withdrew his favour. Monseigneur at once reminded the newcomer that the Blessed Rodbert had condemned the Irish as deceivers and stragglers, and advised him to depart to Mantua, where, he added, the ageing Ovid still dwelt. The poet gratefully hurried away.

Perceval was welcomed in all quarters. His purity was already famous; at his approach, Plague stayed her touch. Meditating on a parterre, he rescued a sick bird, taking it to his apartments, though later he opened the door to oblige a hungry dog, which at once devoured the sufferer. Perceval, a man-at-arms told me admiringly, was distracted between compassion for the bird and gratification at appeasing the dog. At my own response, Perceval showed the nearest he could show of umbrage.

Perceval was also acclaimed for securing repentance from a murderer by presenting him with a tame sparrow, inducing the rogue to show tenderness, thus winning pardon from the ever-magnanimous Duke. Less happily, Perceval's respect for cats and love of mice entailed messy outcomes.

Ladies who sought his love were disappointed. Dalliance, he felt, gave little save recollections of sadness, and we understood that, while respectful to the Duke, his affections, such as they were, were pledged to Cundré. She, I suspected, received less from him than she craved, but more from the Duke than she wanted. Perceval, quick to embrace, kissed only reluctantly. He wept more easily than he smiled, she discharged that repellent mirth, loud, but lacking the quicksilver of youth. Tears she must have scorned. I myself have always regretted not having known her better.

Beneath these grandiose matters, two damsels – a period word I try unsuccessfully to avoid – pleaded that Perceval should settle their quarrel. They had gone to an April pool to see, in its depths, the face of their future husband. Unfortunately, they both saw that of Perceval himself. They rushed for his judgement, he told them to become nuns, they squealed ecstatically and did so, thus solving his own problem, though, not, perhaps, theirs.

I believe that his presence at court replaced the fashionable *debonair* with *charm*. This I cannot define, but can describe, in that to the ugly and disgraced he was as winning as to the beautiful.

I must again emphasize that he descended from peoples, vanquished but not ruined, peoples of boar, torque, spiral, gaining peculiar status by eloquence, curious skills, angles of impertinence. His simple spontaneity dazzled, perhaps I should write dazed, though it may just have held something of a not quite sober chess-player. Also, many love their victims, without

112

realizing that, deeply, they fear, even hate them. In his way he was as palpable an enchanter as unseen Clinschur. His deft use of the fork inspired a verse from Monseigneur. A shaft of light, it hovered over a white flake of capon, a dark-brown morsel of venison, circled above fruit in bright, exquisite dance before spiking the prize, which then drifted to his lips so effortlessly that it seemed to alight there of its own, while he listened and smiled to the lovelorn, the sly, the preposterous, his eyes trusting all.

His trust, of course, could be misplaced. Humanity, we are told, is sinful; we do not need to be told it is grasping, spiteful and jealous. In shrill descant, other voices began, not yet prominent but fateful. His art of the fork was no Christian practice. He was secretly a pagan, half-brother to a blackamoor begotten on the infamous Belacane of Zazamanc by his errant sire while serving the Baruc of Baghdad, Preserver of the Gates of Paradise, Wielder, notably in bed, of a miraculous lamp. Perceval was enveloped by stories in fabric invisible but gleaming as the Hesperides. His birth had been an illicit concoction from water, earth, numbers, supernatural head, artificial beast. He had entrusted his soul to a whore, he consorted on mountains with Syrian hashish fraternities. Were he to laugh, he would emit roses.

Already it was part of history that he had cured the Roman Emperor Justin of a suppurating wound which poisoned fish-ponds, and been rewarded with seven purses, which he gave to the poor, who then grumbled that they were owed twenty-one. He had striven to rescue Paolo and Francesca from the underworld, had tamed Prester John's phoenix and, chasing a hallowed pig into a glass tower, had grasped an enchanted bowl or mirror, been struck dumb, been freed by a mystical question.

All this chroniclers assiduously recorded, pausing only to invent a poetic ending, plug a lacuna with glamorous detail, as, at times, I must do, though reluctantly. History easily induces loss of faith in mankind, though rereading may restore it. I had scant faith in an account of angelic Perceval, in despair at failure, reviling God, then travelling a thousand leagues on a dolphin.

Thus he walked within an aura burnished by the half heard, overheard, misheard, while, as the Venetian perceived, caressed by the Duke, applauded by the mighty, being followed by cooler eyes, who mistrusted his simplicity as they had that of Blessed Francis. Perceval would pluck flowers, somewhat apologetically, not for their medicinal properties, virtues, astrological links, but because he enjoyed their shapes and colours. For him, the curve of a river was not Ulysses' bow, the light of a dove no reminder of the Holy Ghost, the movement of light across a statue was not a symbol of the soul in transit. Like a child he happily saw them, happily forgot them. Like music, like beauty, he obeyed his own laws. I think he did believe that bridges would by night vanish from the world, but often reappear at dawn, though not always as he had last seen them. I had seen him in early morning smiling in wonder or relief, look uneasy at dusk, expectant at midnight and, at noon, he sometimes sighed for Gawain.

Music engrossed him. Never fingering harp, dulcimer or lute, he would listen rapt, eyes closed. Song was a gleaming muscle, glittering nerve, indifferent though he might be to a lyric addressed to him, beginning 'Thy dear and maiden eyes'.

The Duke had awarded him his most serene Order, nine windmills, a river-mouth, and gifts ever more lavish, while he contrived to nod pleasantly at the ruler's unexacting, oft-repeated jests, never flattered him, and deferred to him no more than to anyone else.

After a love bout or quarrel with the Princess, the Duke would summon him to listen, condole, soothe, before passing him on to do likewise to her, who never needed it. Significantly, as his popularity mounted, the vilification of Cundré redoubled, and a weaver was publicly flogged for asserting that by smearing Arabian gum on her thighs she flew without wings to Lapland and back under the moon. But, but. . . . Perceval's intimacy with Duke and Princess was angering the Starlings, who had failed to bribe him. Indeed, politics he found so alien that he believed, or affected to believe, that Cato and Cicero still lived with the Emperor Frederick II, himself long dead. His hours alone with Cundré provoked frowns from the staid, though these were few.

The faces of the Black Brothers still remained as blank and ungiving as their ᵣ.bes, though their eyes missed nothing.

Embarking to Isles of Love, the Princess was always a bowsprit ahead of the Duke, with a smile sweet as a lily and as cool, yet within it mischief lurked, seasoned though good-natured. When, after a half-imagined rebuff, the Duke resolved to be curt and aloof at their next occasion, she wrote that she was indisposed. He swore to reply to no more letters, but no more letters came, and he was soon scribbling strenuous apologies for what he could not remember.

Acclaims for the Duchess he did not deign to notice, though the Pope himself was expressing grief, less for the Duchess than in fear of the Princess accepting some tiresome anti-Pope howling in Brunswick. The Pope himself, I afterwards knew, very imperfectly. Attractive in conversation, he would arrange events small but memorable: a feast amongst precarious Roman ruins, which once brained a cardinal, an expedition to an Etruscan bullring . . . so as to mention them in his writings, embalming

114

himself in history.

The Duke felt no need to embalm himself anywhere. His emotions surged to the peaks, toppled to the depths, neither condition registering him as a nonentity. Happiness, he might have believed, resides in discontent.

On a whim, he ostentatiously dispatched to the Duchess a superb cloak of ermine, which he described as worth the ransom of Arthur. It was also, the Venetian murmured, an emblem of chastity.

To return to Cundré. I never felt she was greatly interested in herself, nor that her self was a compact, rounded identity, but rather an amorphous spread of moods, more complex than the Duke's, obvious only in her effect upon others, of whom, unlike Perceval, she was so shrewdly aware. He appeared insensible of influencing any but himself. I could never envisage Cundré alone, meditating, engrossed with a story, a carving, teasing out a prayer. Like her new protector, she hungered for movement, diversity, clash of intensities. Perceval was always alone, particularly amid revels, receptions, watching jousts and hunts.

She had compulsive needs: for vengeance inflicted without pain, for rapture grasped without expectation. She wrung satisfaction from despair, mordant information from triumph. Statecraft amused her like children's romps, at the Other World she gave a worldly-wise shrug, though she once wondered whether God experiences sexual spasms while watching human lovers. She could have discussed little with the Duke, who talked incessantly but said little, seldom straying far from high-flying but conventional love metaphors, turning aside only to reiterate the necessity of enlarging the Duchy. I imagined him lying with her in desperate and agonized silence, awaiting renewal, not of his Duchy but of himself.

Elsewhere, for our Duke, light and shade were usually identical.

His subjects now had the uncanny belief that Cundré was stepchild of some tricky planet, probably Mercury.

'I tell you, sir, though she glistens like Diana's bum, she bears no children. What am I saying? She bears too much. Bees, handfuls of blighted grain, horrid cats tailed like Jews and Englishmen. Ugh!'

An insolent master miller presented her, as if in tribute, with a sieve, its golden mesh heaped with diamonds and ebony, arousing spiteful grins, for sieves betokened virginity. Some added that, if held to the sunlight, the wires outlined a boar's pizzle. Not so, it would be the Duke's, a Flemish purist objected. Though he had never seen it, he declared that a model of it hung on the di Florio statue of St Luke in Brussels. As for Cundré, she kept the diamonds and ebony but returned the sieve, as more necessary to its donor.

Monks were insisting that she had been sent by God to test the Duke's continence, a test he had failed. Some pitied her, for beauty is damned, a bequest of Lucifer, Babylon, indeed Sodom.

Perceval was often seen with Cundré, or with the Duke, or strolling between them in the Gardens of Aeneas and Dido, calm between squalls, the Princess carrying her elegant scarlet knout. Spies flitted between tree and hedge, their reports enflaming the popular agitation. She was a fount of sorrow, ban on salvation, curse on marriage, soul beyond cure. She would drag the Duke to perdition, then Perceval, the land itself. Begetter of strife, revoker of honour! The Duke, ah, the Duke! Rugged Perseus bewitched by gilded Andromeda.

Pothouse Aristotles, libellous maltsters, asserted that, nightly, she grew tusks. Nonsense but not rubbish, for, in truth, in some of his blood Perceval had secreted a fear of her. Aspirer to ideal love, he must cherish such fear. Outwardly frail, his independence was stubborn. In a society that sought champions, his mild smile dispersed them. At the song of Master Hugo Brunec.

And now I see that with its very fulfilment
That love a-dying which once gave sweet wounds! . . .

Flowery ladies fluttered and sighed, with dramatic eye-rollings, but Perceval looked gravely acquiescent. He submitted to trials, but those of his own choosing. Neither pleading nor arrogant, he probably gave the Duke scarcely more than an occasional though affectionate thought.

Beside a lake, within which its toy pinnacles and domes quivered like elfin celebrations, stood a Saracenic pavilion where the Duke might hold his Council, to the inconvenience of all. Water, Monseigneur pronounced with condescension, encouraged wisdom and strict lines of architecture.

The Duke, with unprecedented graciousness, had presented Cundré and Perceval with its keys, confident that here they would do not more than swap praises of himself.

I well remember arches and marmoreal pillars, the tapestry of a heron flying towards a castle above mounted hunters, a lady brocaded in green and gold turning a mirror to a snowy, enchanted unicorn. The last of the three rooms, the Bower of Flora, had a canopied bed scrolled with angels and eagles flying indifferent to Hell, sulphuric yet enticing. Lust, scowling naked on a goat, was routed by Chastity, resolutely astride an amiable Pegasus, watched lasciviously by Priapus at full stretch. In a

116

sandalwood chest lay the copper-gilt chalice once touched by Juno travelling to visit Oceanus and Tethys. Stained glass windows depicted glaring Elijah, a wild man in skins, tramping a glen with knobbed and unseemly club. In an oblong recess appeared to hover an alabaster Virgin and Child, from Sicily, though the Child was female.

Perceval and Cundré were a sparkling pair, the dark and the fair, with their slender limbs, small expressive hands, he with pellucid eyes and imprecise smile, she with proud stare, finely moulded breasts. I envisage them pacing the little rooms, goblets flashing between them across a jewelled table, Cundré in samite robe, pearled head-dress lofty above her pale forehead. A trace of the far off, the Scythian touched her lustrous, rather narrow, irregular eyes and ripe lips, her heavy jewels, small, dangling crystal beads, powerful rings. In daylight she looked soft and tempting, but by moon or candle hardened into the barbaric and inexorable, which may have belied her true character, though not totally.

Only once did I join them in the pavilion. With her he was more fluent than with me, whom he seemed not to notice. 'Nevertheless, a most beautiful word is . . . evening.' His face went startled, his voice stumbled as if at an unexpected discovery. '*Evening. Night* I can never trust.'

'You say such things.' Those slanted eyes accosted us, pupils sad within their green radiance enlarged perhaps by nightshade juice. 'Our roads are different. But whatever I ask you, with all your *evenings* and *nights*, you never reply.'

They smiled, as if at some secret joke. 'Your questions make me search my memories, but so many are dreamlike. Naming what we don't know yet think of continually. I see a cup of green stone . . . or is it a dish? A lord spoilt for love. . . . Meanings change like sea lights.'

Her mouth blossomed, her voice was throaty and foreign. She mocked him, glancing over to reassure me. 'Do not I contain all that you need name? Am I not the cup of delights? I am called so, too often! You have to look back even with your hand in mine. You are blind to the woes of the world which make our poets swoon. Are you not certain that you may not be the lord spoilt for love, unable to forget that fates, furies, Nemesis are always goddesses?'

Clearly they were continuing a dialogue long familiar, for ever inconclusive. She teased not only him but herself, demanding words still formless. They were Other World folk, bright, evanescent, scarcely touching the earth. At the Last Judgement, he would droop into sleep, while her powerful repentance would deceive even the dark angel.

117

He was thoughtful. 'Did Jesus prefer love to knowledge?'

She stepped apart, refilled my goblet, gazed at the woven heron. 'He was very young. His love often faltered.' Silence dimmed them like a cloud. She fingered a violet cushion strewn with golden bees. 'I was ward not of Jesus but Clinschur. With him I learnt both.' Her laugh was scornful. 'I realized, rather late, that his strength was only magic, meagre, even pitiful. Twelve times he failed at my golden passage, which others found easy enough. His twelve labours! Our great magicians finally accomplish so little. A Merlin spied on his enchantress from a tree, she passed nine times before him, and left him trapped for ever. Clinschur, why, he tried to turn water to wine, and . . .' – her trilling laughter matched her eyes – 'produced only vinegar. When he crossed the Bosphorus on foot, he sank half-way and had to be poled out by fishermaids, yet . . .', she sighed contentedly, 'he taught me to love water, swimming, stroking the river from a boat as we glided towards the stars . . . and wine.'

'Bathing in dew?'

'Yes, that too.' She affected gratitude, not to Clinschur but to Perceval, head bowed and intent. 'I closed my eyes against the sun . . . I saw, I still see, tips of butterflies, crimson skeins, green specks, sheets of colour no rainbow has ever swallowed. But true colours, true blood, came not from Clinschur but from another. He was cruel and savage. Clinschur would have transformed him to a toad, or tried to . . . but I awoke from centuries of sleep.'

The three of us stood at a casement. The blue lake was briefly cobbled by the breeze. He appeared to overcome a choke, then spoke easily.

'I never belittled magic. Somewhere I heard of a girl who, twice a month, left home for three days, on pledge from her man to ask no question. But his mother, jealous, taunted him for weakness until at last he followed her into the woods. Concealed, he saw her reach a pool, remove her girdle and throw it into damp grass. At once she became a snake, glittering, beautiful, vanishing into the earth. He said nothing on her return, but when her next time was due, before they rose, he stole the girdle. She made excuses not to depart, he said nothing, she fell ill. He demanded where she always went. Bitterly she accused him of breaking his pledge. Their quarrel was violent, he threw the girdle into the fire, it hissed and crackled, she writhed in agony, then fell, flattened herself on the rushes, and died.'

His wide eyes turned first to me, then to her. Her cheek briefly lay against his. She murmured, 'You still know so little about us.'

We watched the shining lake, sunlight wrapped over a bridge, birds swooping. She continued, 'Poets sing of kisses and

118

fondlings, much of it absurd, some of it true enough. I have dreamt of the strongest, wisest, most beautiful, but such are but the tragic romance of distance. Hollow valiants. Dregs of time. Loveliest but not loving.' Her head was averted, her voice toneless, even gaunt, stricken by the weaknesses of power. Was she thinking of the Duke, about whom her wit could be caustic?

Perceval said slowly, as if testing his powers, 'Gawain said of a Spanish knight, killed at Acre, that, pressing from darkness, he unfolded towards night. His wife said that.'

'Dead husbands.' She was restless, trailing to an arch. 'Our desires for those we can never meet. Hérault and his maiden. She warned him they would be sundered if he struck her three times without excuse.' Her smile was sardonic. 'He was at first careful to make his blows defensible to lawyers, but later grew careless, and soon lost her, giving out that she had become a seal. But so many, even the Duke, feel for women, only like slaves thanking their master for a thrashing. Their Holy Virgin flatters them and stills their consciences. Their Eves and Helens bear the blame for the thoughtless heroes, even for the clumsy gods.'

'The Duke. . . .'

He was unable to say more. In tall head-dress, she was the taller; commanding, prophetic. 'He thinks he loves me, he deals out no blows, but such love will harm him. He demands huge rewards, terrible penalties. He can be morose as a debtor, he can laugh us all out of the window.'

Perceval brooded. Their intimacy was unfailing yet inconclusive. The pavilion fitted them: ornate, exotic, haunting, but scarcely a home. She appraised him, friendly, not critical, her hoarse laugh forgone. 'You pass for simple but you have your own knowledge, as I have mine. You too can unfold to the light. We both read our riddles, survive our ordeals.'

He took her hand, though only his eyes caressed it. 'I saw three drops of blood on snow, and at once saw you. But . . .', he foundered, lost her hand, 'I remember it all at strange times, often unwanted . . . a bridge reaching softly into death, mists in the bright sun . . . fishers, gods, thriving on our disappointments. . . .'

He was picking words like a child at play, intent on fashioning what the elders would never see. She smiled, cleaving to their difference. Together they were stranded in the Duke's fiery gaze, but dukes could be as insubstantial as this pleasure-house.

In another silence, a silence not dead but waiting, the Duke himself joined us from feeding his carp. He soon sensed her anger at his intrusion, but addressed us all with finely balanced courtesy, inviting the three of us to supper with the Chancellor.

I was sensible enough to decline, but, at his suggestion, remained here with the wine after their departure. The sun was

119

lower, bud and petal, leaf and branch flared against deep, rich sky. Children's voices unexpectedly swarmed over the gardens, spreading networks of joy over grass and water, reaching the three figures pausing on the Palace terrace.

Seeing them so gently at one, I again wondered whether Perceval's wavering dislike of outright carnality might be a device to prolong its early attractions, a barely conscious realization that in much pain is much pleasure, that waning can be worse than eclipse. To Lancelot and Hercules he preferred Narcissus – the less he heard of Gawain, the sharper he saw him.

The Duke gave whatever he laid hands on, Cundré gave nothing. A gift from Perceval would make one of those occasions that sound better than they really are, like reading the airy verses of William of Aquitaine by primrose light.

8

'The soul, dear and respected Lord, is smooth as an egg, yet rough as the Ardennes. It is round, yet shapeless as sea. In my *Daphne Pursued*, I show it compounded by the flash of a kingfisher, the fall of a wave, the echo of a Breton lament, the instant of love, the spirit of Arthur. It is the dazzle behind a cloud, the recognition of unity between the usual and the strange.'

'Monseigneur wings his words and sends them beyond Heaven itself. Very elegant, but are they very true? I have heard on most excellent authority that the soul is an egg itself, with three further eggs inside it.'

'Neither of my noble and blessed friends can be wholly correct, or only nominally so. More specifically, it cannot be gainsaid that the soul is a dew-pool, now wet, now dry, from which life emerges, to which life sinks.'

Heads tilted, hands raised, the glittering councillors paced slowly away, to comfits, sugared oranges, ginger heaped on silver trays, held by yellow, motionless pages, leaving me to withdraw from behind a pillar. Their brittle talk was yet a reminder that the aura of powerful souls is said, not by me, to affect the weight, texture and even transparency of the air. This might explain the moods unsettling the Court. The unquenchable Duke, behaving like a warship under squalls, was now grandly contrite for having slapped out a girl's tooth in a dispute about cherries, his groans as usual making the hearers feel vaguely guilty. There was also a dispute with the Pope about the recent elevation of Grand Prior Maximilien des Roches to an important see, Maximilien being aged nine and sharing a bed with the sodomite Seneschal of Five Bridges.

The year mellowed under broad sky, huge butter-coloured sun. As if from a missal, our world was scrolled with black and blue birds, larkspur, bees, rabbits. A small embassy paid respect to Bayard the Swift, magic horse, given to Charlemagne by sons of Ayman and whose whinny could still be heard at midsummer. Down dry roads a deputation arrived from Mainz bearing the Duke a casket containing a jet ring which would paralyse demons. This was on the festival of St Duncanus, beatified for leaving his footprint on the sea. The ring was wrapped in parchment enscribed with verses to the Duchess and an outraged clerk muttered that the Duke had passed it to Cundré who, a demon herself, destroyed it.

A quack spoke of a barnacle tree in Thrace which bore not leaves but geese. The Chancellor, overhearing, grumbled that it might hatch chickens, butterflies, but geese never, the man was a superstitious liar, to be seated with such menials as tutors, chaplains and the better sort of friar, if such existed. Then a miracle, second class, occurred in the cathedral. An image of Michael bowed its head during an anthem extolling peace. Some, surely exaggerating, added that it had also sneezed. Interpretations differed, and the Duke, ever preparing for a crusade, was angered at the archangel's tactlessness in seeming to discourage it.

He himself had fever, due less to Cundré than to prolonged hiccups at the Sponge's strange, lewd imitation of the Spider King. Procuring, at some expense, an Egyptian elixir from a donkey's liver, he worsened, and his jealous physicians declared that the compound cured only blindness. The Duke's rage was so strenuous that it jostled him out of bed and he at once recovered. Years later, I wrote that the Duke always pushed to the limit all save his intellect. His spirit coursed the world but his judgement remained whimpering at the fireside. He galloped reinless into himself. Once, at Council he began weeping uncontrollably.

'Gracious Lord, who has offended?'

Through tears, he glared with wild astonishment. 'Hector died. He was killed disgracefully. There can be no forgiveness!'

A monk, his face grey, bare as a crow's, plucked my sleeve. 'Have you heard. . . . It's all over the city. . . .' Apparently, on a planet, Pluto, known only to astrologers though not yet discovered, mechanical contrivances forecast death, calculated the movements of Plague, and fashioned mirrors that reproduced not only figures but voices, and sometimes the thoughts behind them.

All this was the usual stuff of courts. Mingling with it were more cryptic allusions to Gamalean and his universal empire, perhaps a compliment to the Duke, perhaps not. Also, at Ghent, Bruges, Liége, discontent was loudening amongst weavers, always, as prices rose, seeking a scapegoat. Malcontents agreed that the Duke was too distracted by his lusts to hear their grievances, but that Cundré was to blame. She was the hail that destroys, her peacock feathers were a bequest from Medusa, her intemperate desires endangered the exquisite celestial harmonies, themselves affected by mortal misbehaviour in proportion to status. Thus Antony and Cleopatra bruised a constellation, a petty thief might slightly dislodge only a star. The perversions of Emperor Domitian gave birth to a comet.

Cundré never stepped outside the Palace, which heightened the libels upon her. Those beliefs that by night she changed to snake, vixen, she-wolf, made few envy the Duke and his naked ardour. To avoid pregnancy she was said to roll on the floor, smeared with honey, then mixing it with dust, sweat, flour, and making tartlets which prevented frenzy quickening the womb.

The Venetian's face went as near as it ever would to a vulgar grin.

Fear of unrest forged a pact between Starlings and Black Brothers. These hearkened to the stricture of St Bernard. Intellect, scholarship were endangering faith and godliness. To accept God's immaculate mystery, await, then obey divine inspiration interpreted by holy Church, was needful for salvation. A Dominican who unexpectedly squatted in a street, refusing to move or explain, was deemed exceptionally pious. The Duke, grumbling to Perceval that he was exceptionally fraudulent, had to agree to provide a trumpeter whose calls pealed whenever the virtuous one gobbled or swigged from lavish offerings, whenever his bowels emptied or his prayers croaked.

Ostensibly Perceval and Cundré were unassailable, protected by the Duke and, it was said, by Cundré's occult wiles learnt from Clinschur. Yet I was alert to the dangers to which no favourites are immune. Perceval at present was the less vulnerable. His presence made talk kindlier, less lascivious. Even the Sponge's malicious wit dealt lightly with him, joking only that, in sport, casting a javelin at a tree, he had pierced a knight, who had lamented his death by a weapon so vulgar. Perceval thereafter vowed to touch no weapon more. Certainly, though avoiding jousts, he was accepted as manly enough, and I heard no criticism even from stalwart champions. His modest yet firm bearing silenced would-be rivals. He was, people repeated, on insecure evidence, born under Virgo, propitious for a soul sensitive and inquiring.

I was wary rather than anxious as I saw him, blithe and innocuous with Duke and the hated Princess, part of a romance remembered most vividly by those who never knew it. Romance is a trick of time. An effigy borne upright on a funeral chariot becomes a future hero; the dead within hillocks merge into dancers in enchanted castles stirred by fairy blood. A chronicler assured me that Perceval had been seen at Joppa in a cathedral carved from the bones of a dragon slain by Perseus, St George, or both. Supposedly, too shy to make a simple demand, he was denied a beautiful Angevin princess, nonsense enhanced by his halting speech and mysterious allusions. He was sometimes called Lord of the Red Tower.

Some stories, however apocryphal, held some gist of truth. He caressed a child, this aroused jealousy, the girl was stoned by her friends. He was begged to succour a village impoverished by drought. Given a forked rod he stood in an arid gullet, the fork twitched like a frog, water suddenly gushed and Perceval departed to comfort a sick woodcutter, and forgot to return. The gush became a flood, wrecking the church and village, sparing only the monastery, which had disapproved of his coming. There are indeed regions where a 'Perceval Miracle' survives like 'Pyrrhic Victory'. Similarly 'pointing the finger of Scorn' seems derived from a description of Perceval pointing at a clothier who always compelled his wife to walk three paces behind him.

My wariness increased, conscious of Fortune's Wheel, an image hateful to the Duke. Yet plaudits for my friend gilded the summer and gratified the Duke as testimony to his own perception. When clouds sailed low, peasants declared that Perceval must be approaching, the atmosphere itself craning to see him. Reputed, erroneously, to lack body hair, he seemed thus akin to angels. But from a tavern I heard voices:

'Jesus, did you know it? If not, listen well, for I do know it . . . Jesus was deformed, to save his blessed fellows from lust and deception. The young man in our Duke's bed is beautiful. . . .'

The imputations were a gift to the Black Brothers.

Those who had never seen either, proclaimed his likeness to an image of St Francis carved at Brabant, though I myself failed to perceive it, possibly from its absence of nose. This, too, would aggrieve the industrious and public-spirited Black Brothers to whom simple virtue, unselective generosity, indifference to hierarchy were as much a nuisance as our Saviour Himself would have been, restrained as His respect was towards clerics, notaries, the rich and the law.

Once, by the lake, Perceval was listening to the Duke praising Cundré. A bird alighted on his shoulder, Perceval murmured some politeness, and a report was soon speeding through the city that he had charmed it into chirping to the Duke some vision of the Other World. His resemblance to the Mild Saint was complete.

More questionable still were accounts of his raid into Hell with

123

Arthur and Kai, his acceptance of strange gifts that risked the soul. Particularly indictable was that rapidly growing conviction of his embracing the Grail, mystery beyond life, at the exact centre of the world, thus securing unique powers. This last, so beloved by common folk, outraged even the most frivolous prelate and benevolent friar. The Grail, they pronounced, was best avoided, whatever its connection with Christ's supper, Christ's blood: it might also be a profane oracle guarded by a demon with swollen, corrupt genitals, annually blessed by a goddess with a name proscribed against Plague and earthquake. As for the magic, ever-flowing horn or cauldron, some shadow of the Grail itself, it was wrecker of maidenheads, vessel of perversity, exciting women below the girdle and making them seek powers grievous to God.

Poets quarrelled about the Grail. Some held it a green stone used to control nature and reason by combining physical opposites and, by discharging illicit energies, transmuting dross to gold, thus enabling adepts to enter Heaven without having earned it.

'Righteous folk, know ye not this? The stone was once bound to the head of Lucifer, brightest of God's beloved. At his fall it dropped to earth and, until it is found, he must wander, tempting the unhappy and weak. Should ye chance upon it, fear for your souls, avoid the lie that it will save ye from death. Blessed Aquinas has taught us that the true Grail is the soul of Mary, neither stone nor chalice, and visible to none.'

From such associations, Perceval could be judged no true Christian but akin to Clinschur's rival, Merlin the Christ-hater, able to become cat or bird, but seldom observed doing so, for such persons prefer agony at the stake to indulging in such rude display of talent.

Servants and spies were informing me that the public boxes hanging on churches and guildhalls for popular petitions were being crammed with complaints not only against Cundré but, now beginning, against Perceval, as a deceiving infidel or Greek, said to have once descended to the underworld. In truth, he never mentioned God, or Christ as God, but merely as initiate, explorer, scholar. This was unwise, for all scholars were disciples of Lucifer, particularly the Irish.

With agitations noisier, sometimes brutal, the Black Brothers at last moved, ordaining that, without exception, all Grail stories were trash of scullions, fantasies from wicked cults, which alleged that, if you stared at the Grail for two centuries, nothing would change save your hair: that every Good Friday a dove flies from Paradise to leave a white wafer on the Grail. Whoever saw the bird should shoot but not eat it; the wafer, of course, was poisoned.

124

Perceval remarked, rather too casually, that the Grail was too bright actually to exist.

At court, most believed, without much interest, that the Grail was a crucible wherein chemicals perverted the coinage, and that those hoary old bleeding spears were not of revenge, hatred, or medical properties, but the rays, lascivious but healing, of the god Lug, in which girls fondled themselves or each other, naked. This, however misleading, heightened Perceval's attraction for ladies and did him no harm with their lords, always ready to encourage their concerns elsewhere. As for the Duke, he exclaimed irritably that he cared not whether the Grail were stone, jewel, dish, mirror, cup or good red herring: the only receptacle – he used another word – worth possessing belonged to the loveliest of all women.

Chap-books appeared claiming that the famed chastity of Grail seekers disguised their addiction to sodomy.

I overheard Perceval talking to children, more fluently, more expressively, than he could ever do with me. They listened agog. Somewhere, *out there*, an arrow's length above the earth, was a dim, grey town where only ghosts dwelt. All knew of it – I did not – many had seen it in childhood and would see it again. When I mentioned this to him his eyes, blue and childlike, looked puzzled, as if I had made an abstruse jest. 'I don't read Aquinas,' he eventually said, in that tiresome manner of answering a question that had not been asked.

That week I learnt that in disreputable bath-houses, stews and underground chapels, dead Arthur was depicted in bearskins, with vast priapic cone or swollen club astride a goat, apples at his neck. Priests and Black Brothers announced that he had stolen an altar, used it to outwit a dragon, then feasted from it, very drunk. Very sensible, I agreed with the Venetian. Arthur had slaughtered babies, even his own son. His Table Round, so pleasing to high-born ladies and benevolent knights, was but a vile temptation from Lug.

These condemnations were waves, rising against the gleaming Palace but always falling back, while within, the ornate ceremonial continued undeterred, led by the besotted Duke and his paramour, who had herself induced a fashion for the Saracenic, Chancellor, ex-Comptroller, Sieur de la Rivière, Malmédes, even the Archbishop, though in capacity of Protonotary-General and Particular of Ghent, dressed in turbans, trailing green silken sleeves, attending the Duke and Cundré and Perceval with wines of flashing, Eastern vintage, which they drank on a vast, circular damascene carpet outspread in a meadow, all feigning unawareness of the quiet rain.

The sun lashed fiercer as summer wheeled to a fiery peak and, as if rhyming, the factions and rumours coalesced into unpredictable opposition to the favourites, to a whispered war policy, to the lordly disdain for markets which guaranteed the ducal House. Dark memories were stirring, with complex ramifications not wholly understood to this day.

Years back, a French king, beautiful, secretive, ruthless, and needing money, colluding with a weak pope, had destroyed the Knights Templar, top-heavy with wealth. One accusation was that they were Guardians of the Grail, lovers of idolatrous light in which they adored a magic head, embalmed and polished with carbuncles in its sockets, that of a dead Grand Master, initiate of Eastern mysteries. Allegedly they had been linked with Provençal Cathars, self-styled seekers of light. Doubtless they had muddled the teaching of St James, that all gifts good and perfect derive from the Father of Light, because, to the horror of the Church, they insisted the world was the Devil's handiwork, profanation of divine light, stinking breath of the Great Queen.

Another French king, another pope, had wrecked the Cathars, but Christendom soon realized that crusade and stake eradicate old tales no more than cannons, printing press and edict destroy elves, devils, Mothers, Clinschur.

The Grail, then, was daily more solidly linked with fearful notions surviving in outlandish regions and remote castles, in which the Devil shared power with an imperfect God, notions reaching back to the Bear Chief and Dagda Time. The Fall was no garden orgy but periodic failure of imagination, to be redeemed by will: salvation lay in no Other World but in enlightenment. Hell was wilful rejection of such knowledge. Even Jesus had admitted that this world was unreal, but an act of faith could transform it.

The Duke's city buzzed with Grail chatter. The Cathars had addressed the Virgin, or Great Queen, as Grail of the World. I myself entertained a supper-party with a tale of Emperor Constans, deposed and exiled, pursued by the ghost of his father whom he had forced into the Church, before making him drink from 'a grail of poisoned blood'. I was uneasy when Monseigneur, with delicate smile and perhaps indelicate purpose, spoke of Perceval, 'our beloved friend', curing a knight by displaying the head of a red chief whom he had overthrown beneath a red tower. I attempted to transfer the escapade to wild Gawain, but no one was listening.

Crisis was impending. Wherever Perceval appeared, crisis generally did impend, without his knowing it. Common people were learning that man needed no Black Brothers, no archdeacons, and, a few might add, no Duke, though dukes were at least manifest protection against Turks. Women shuddered with unchaste terror at ideal Saracenic love exuded by Grail tales, in which maidens bearing fruits heaped on snow with cups of immortal elixir glided through Syian gardens naked or in accursed green.

Such tales evoked seven formal university debates, in which the Grail was dismissed as one of the baubles by which men live.

Few, however, listened, for the wisdom was exchanged in Latin and a majestic peroration was given in Greek, which none but the speaker understood, or appeared to understand, and, though commended by the Duke, who knew neither, it was no help to Cundré or Perceval, or, at distant remove, to the Duke himself. Verses were circulated, praising wronged, hapless 'Dido', the Duchess, whose sufferings, perhaps death, threatened the English alliance and cloth treaties. As for Cundré, she was none other than the Cathar witch Esclamonde of Foix, child of stale juices, whose spells enabled her to survive fire and dismemberment. Worse, much worse, the Princess was an artificial body manufactured by Jews to drag the Duke to inferno.

On walls and pavements was daubed the hooded crow, popular image of Cundré, on which people spat and pissed. Other representations showed her with stabbed loins, pus-swollen breasts, porker's feet, snake-hair, tusks, and a bottle containing Plague. A chronicler asserted that her wily thighs poisoned all the world, she was vile Salome, she had – lower your voice – jeered at sweet Jesus as he bore his cross.

'I hear', the Duke smiled heartily, 'many tongues and little sense. Let babble run its course.'

While it did so, the Princess continued to exercise her witticisms, incise her tablets. The movements of her lips, the light in her eye, were ironic, critical and contemptuous, a reminder that for such as her even the renowned Duchy was not the world's centre.

As for Perceval, whatever was plotted and invented in furtive places, the spectacular court cherished him as true Grail Knight, simple and lustred. A painting, much applauded, showed him riding through a golden, autumnal haze spreading between roseate hills. It still hangs in an Artois mansion and has performed an attested miracle.

Nevertheless, Fortune's Wheel was relentless and I watched it uneasily. Incessant applause does not finally ingratiate. Even in the Palace I now detected germs of dissent, notably in an account of Perceval's 'infidel brother, Badly Fed, and may he long remain so'. I believe the epithet 'airs and graces' was first applied to Perceval.

The Starlings and their allies were rife with beliefs in a conspiracy of 'Templars', employed by the Spider King to disrupt the Duchy at whatever cost and with Cundré as go-between. Inevitably, the treasonable insignia included a head, sealed in silver, rescued from a sacked Templar stronghold, said to be that of Arthur.

Summer passed, with tourneys, festivals, theatricals. With autumn, Starlings and malcontents, followed by ducal spies, gathered in the Chapel of the Master Coopers and, grandly obeisant, presented the Duke's representative with a silver rose, fashioned by Jan van Clessons. They knew that their ruler, always impulsive, ever suspicious, would be riled. Indeed, pocketing the rose, he swore that it was certainly condign, probably malfeasant, its sexual reference was discourteous, that it was not gold was insulting, and from his favourite window he could hear a ribald song, nasty as an ulcer, acclaiming its petals as his five most despicable sins.

10

I was necessarily debarred from what follows, various versions of which were swiftly known, the most convincing being that of the Venetian, whose resources were more ample than mine.

Winter was stark, river and canal froze, fields were snow-smitten. Even Palace gaieties dimmed, though, to preserve harmony, processions were slower, more punctilious, ceremonial exchanges more elaborate; banquets too were prolonged, repelling mutters of famine and disorder, sennets and drums smothering dangerous coughs and groans.

To awaken the sun, crack the ice, and also, I suspect, from childish love of noise, the Duke one noon ordered all his cannon to be discharged simultaneously. A resounding explosion, a roaring masquerade of Jovian thunder rocked the city, precipitated births, set animals howling, but winter remained unperturbed. As the Venetian put it, as an example of experimental science it scarcely passed muster. He himself then suffered an ailment curable only by eating apples and black beans soaked in a prostitute's girdle. All were readily available.

Perceval too was unwell, attended without remission by the Duke's most intimate physician with regular bursts of entry from the rash monarch himself. He would have fared better at my own lodgings, fresher and quieter than the Palace with its clocks, bells and erratic intrusions. The Princess, shrinking not from danger and insults, which she enjoyed, but from chills, secluded herself from all save the Duke, who regained floridity as he railed against the disloyal weather, impertinent Spider King, busybody Swiss and refactory weavers. He could never understand why food was at is costliest when it was most needed.

Outside, under spectral trees, misty belfries and ramparts, the sky low and thick, in short days of sick light and barred doors, much was shrouded and menacing in the vast, looming stillness, the season of famished dogs, dead children, the wolf at the gate. Like markets, fairs and certain low-lying taverns, the mills beyond the city walls, secure from authority, often sheltered the illicit and factional. Here people from many diverse quarters exchanged news, sold teeth of the hanged as cure-alls, complained of taxes, prices, favourites, until, at a signal, tiny but unmistakable, they withdrew to some inner room or cellar.

One such mill, two leagues down-river from the gate of Hughes the Mellifluous was frequented by Starlings. Here, on a late February afternoon, the slap of mill-wheels harsh on the raw air, the sails honking in wind from iced marshes, a suspicion of rooks under the eaves, some thirty figures in dark cloaks and baldrics, unobtrusive collars and hose, high hats with low brims, gathered in a vaulted granary. Among them, several bulky women had scrupulously obeyed the strictures of Clement of Alexandria against female bathing. Several groupings were arguing, united against the Palace but less unanimous in policy towards Spider King and the Swiss, their forms swollen by the dingy lamplight. Amongst them, ignored but welcome, sat a portly eunuch, quietly watchful by a low brazier, its reddish glow streaking faces and shadows. Faint peaty odours mingled with those of damp garments and flesh staled by winter. The talk was being directed against 'Aeneas'. A leader, his voice monotonous as a lawyer's, intoned accusations, to which supporters added baleful chorus.

'Vile seducer and seduced, he nears sight of land, the unknown shores. God sees all but stays His hand, forcing His creature to punish himself.'

'Yea, ensnared by wiles, he grasps the land where rules the Babylonian sorceress, plunging into her dank thicket, lying deep in the bestenched ditch. She too, friends, will be cast out by those who must strangle shameless Aeneas in his pride and pomp.'

'She is worse even than Carthage. She is debased Calypso and monstrous Circe. Her titles are shit-shot, she forces rings on to her lovers, even children, that deform them, even *him*, into the bestial. She will burn on scalding nails.'

'She deserves more. Hearken. An hour spent naked with that crow, prey for her talons and worse, is forty hours in the time good enough for the rest of us. Aeneas, abandoned by God, is two thousand years old in iniquity. Grail-scrubber!'

'I have heard . . . missives from Utrecht, messengers from Basle . . . that troops are preparing for the spring, the Devil willing, to meet on the frontiers. We must thrust down our hands to find gold.'

Lamplight wavered, the brazier shone more luridly. A burly, pocked leather-master intervened, stuffed with self-assurance. One could imagine him saying 'How's business?' to Duke, to Archbishop.

'We are massing against more than intemperate lust for a rank woman and impious, parasitical wanderer. Lust can be forgiven, desertion of a lawful wife is wicked but not always dangerous. No, brothers . . .', his smile condescended to the relationship, 'the sin here is pride, self-lust, ruinous not only to Aeneas but to us and our livelihoods. The pride that destroyed Alexander and Roland, the pride of Ulysses and Nero, of Jesus Himself. Pride, mark of Satan. . . .' He was making it sound a treasure forbidden but delectable. 'We must pledge ourselves to purge this our land, create a true garden scraped clean of wallowings in jewelled sties.'

He receded into dimness, was replaced by a friar, a Black Brother, face and hands fish-pale against the robe reddened and phosphorescent from the burning coals. All held breath, save the impassive eunuch who seemed to stare deep into himself, for this cleric was a known agent of Guildhall magnates vehemently supporting the Starlings' opposition to the Duke's demand for subsidies towards his promised crusade. He was more, he was gaunt incarnation of winter gnawing into bright and heedless summer. His authority tolled with iron-clad resolution.

'He who has captivated Aeneas imperils the soul, debars grace, imprisons his victims in cells without bars or locks but which no light can penetrate. But God the Avenger is translucent and when in its outer darkness a thought stirs, it can never escape the skin with swiftness enough to evade God's eye. Unless it submits to guidance and chastening, God will have none of it.'

The crowded listeners stirred uneasily. Hunched, with heads dissolved in steam and gloom, they waited as the Black Brother took from his robe three dolls, two male, one female, held them aloft, then dropped them on to the embers which at once sizzled in small blue fires. Handed a small, knotted bag, he burnt that too, many hearing, or seeming to hear, a tiny hiss or fluttering, imprisoned scream. A flame darted up with startling brilliance, greenish, then pearl white and hard. Departing soon after, after

130

much handclasping and whispered pledges, each had to pass another fire into which to thrust a glove, brooch, scarf, kerchief, even, despite the piercing frost, a shoe.

Though I saw none of it, I sensed a sinister power creeping upwards to where Cundré lay in her warm bedizened bed, Perceval reached for cool wine, and the Duke held Christendom in his great hands.

11

A Professor of Statecraft from Deventer, journeying to the Confabulation of Grantz, announced that Perceval's natal chart was more propitious even than that of Jesus, and rendered Mahomet's nastier than Pan's. 'May Pan suffocate in the stink of his armpits,' he said casually, adding that Perceval's blood was cleaner than Jewish blood, itself notoriously darker than Christian, soiled by transgressions. In return he offered to sell Perceval, now recovered, a vase of stuff taken from a dead dragon and useful to forecast an eclipse. Perceval courteously paid for the gift, which he then refused, uninterested in eclipses and the Professor's talk of lunar orbits.

Winter was slowly loosening grip, more quickly after citizens thronged to the Field of Mercy, generally used for hangings, where children never played but sometimes danced, fearfully. There they saw in uproarious relief the battle between young summer, green and gold, festooned with daisies and blue ribbons, and snarling ancient winter which in shabby furs, holly and rime, was riotously overthrown. Lovers were back, whispering magic at a stile, on a bridge, leaning together over a wall.

I then heard that, for all his magnificent protection, Perceval was to be examined by the Black Brothers in a Preliminary, for being a secret Templar, and having built a room where no shadow could exist, and where the Duke was worshipped as 'Apis'. That Perceval could have built anything was laughable, save that the Black Brothers seldom looked to any but unearthly truth. He would also be arraigned for possessing a Scythian bowl used by the lethal assassins of Alamut, was indeed a Widow's Son, for this was Cathar code-name for an initiate. Had stated that Christ the True Vine was none other than swilling, infamous Dionysus, boasting with charlatan miracles that whoever drank of his cup would be one with God. Worse, he consorted in bed with Gawain, Apollo's wicked mignon. Perceval, moreover, was devotee of the underground cult of Mary the Cauldron, horrid counterfeit of the Blessed Virgin Rose of the World. His concern for animals now prompted the legend that he worshipped a calf. His very name

131

signified that he had lifted the veil of Isis.

I told myself that the Duke was now far more powerful and, besotted as he was, would protect Cundré from the mob, Perceval from the Black Brothers by the force of his name. 'Just so,' Perceval said, in his smiling, irritating way, in which he would confide in obvious enemies or suggest impossible plans. As for Cundré, she was back amongst resplendent suppers and garden picnics. Not exactly good, she was certainly not evil. Rich, she extracted nothing from groaning serfs and tormented miners, only from spendthrift lords. Contemptuous of the world, she aspired neither to save nor destroy it, dwelling in her beauty like a maiden within an ice tower or on an enchanted isle.

A Preliminary, though short of a formal Inquiry, was still dangerous. On condemnation, the accused would be expelled from Mother Church and handed to the lay magistrates. Black Brothers' toils could suffocate the most innocent. The last, M. St Léger, a delightful, if frivolous companion, liked by all, had been charged with impersonating the imaginary god, Bran, and was branded on both cheeks for simultaneously lying and posturing.

I was professionally interested to find that here, as in Spain and Naples, the Black Brothers were resented only by rulers and the great. Nor were they widely feared: indeed, their secret tribunals and occasional burnings were deemed safeguards against the noxious unseen. Had not St Paul himself mentioned the weakness of God? 'Their words are as slippery as an eel's tail,' a vintner told me, but in admiration.

The Princess sent me a rare summons. I hastened to the south wing and was greeted by obsequious, stealthy, Eastern faces. Her steward, a Nubian in violet sash, raised his white wand and, as I seated myself on a wide, cushioned divan, yellow wine was brought, much spiced and thick with raisins. Cundré remained unseen. On the Duke's orders, her wines were passed through a golden mangle, against poison. The arched rooms, with curtains and no doors, had tall, painted stoves, very warm, and I felt my wits softening in this and with the wine, the drifting scents, the sweetness of burning apple wood. Through haze glimmered tapestries, intricate carpets, the curtains, Arabian vases and plates, the cushions of cloth of gold called saranthasme and woven with silver turtle-doves. At irregular intervals a light bell sounded, muffled by the thick atmosphere. No crucifix or psalter was visible, no hound or gliding, indifferent cat, but, by the windows tall and angular, birds slept in heavy, jewelled cages. All was enticing yet untrustworthy, like April opening to marvels promised but often tardy. Near me I saw, painted on Florentine boards, languid shepherds, their nakedness as if honey-spun, exchanging gentle handplay. Farther away, solid amid the flimsy

132

and wavering, were small, lustred chests, elaborately corded, reminders of Cundré's reputed avarice and cupidity.

I drank more, aware of being watched. Half glimpsed through an arch and a casement hung a crimson valance, a line of blossom, an arc of blue sky, while a concave mirror reflected from somewhere beyond a green, sumptuous bed, black and red mask, a Moorish doll, eyes closed as if in dream, a peacock feather. Eventually a slight swish roused me and, framed in an arch, was the Princess, bareheaded, in mauve silks criss-crossed with scarlet, breasts massed with sapphires, the black, cloudy hair strewn with fiery stones. Her stomacher was bordered with pearly, moon emblems secreting her own lunar qualities of change, power, invulnerability. Momentarily she contemplated me, without evident pleasure. Already drowsy, I thought of Perceval, his first sight of her, bemused in callow fears: foul glare, porcine skin, venomous coiffure, teeth like tent-pegs in a mouth bluish as if dreadfully bruised. She approached, neither friendly nor hostile, though a tiny shadow touched her brow and her voice was caustic, fitting the high-boned, capable face and strong hair.

'You have come here, though perhaps too late.' She flinched as if against cold, despite the airless heat, then smiled, though without perceptible feeling, seated herself beside me, and took my goblet, drank from it, before a turbaned blackamoor slave entered and soundlessly placed crystal flasks, a jug and long-stemmed cups on a low yellow table between us, and withdrew as if on a warm draught. Her scents descended on me, crushed from bardic islands. She gazed before her, her slender form tensed, her customary good sense, wit, experience apparently forgone, needing help, though even now to be accepted with more irony than gratitude. With her appetite and reticence, her legend, her undemonstrative purposes, she was far from the cowled, the clerkish, the conspiratorial, even though in her world of courts and journeys, her smiles, silences and embraces must be too often mere tactics.

My own words strained against the dense air and her own brooding expectancy. 'You listen to washerwomen and flounder-mongers, mendicants and mad preachers?'

She reflected before nodding. The shadow deepened on that snow forehead above grave, green-blue eyes. 'Yes, who could not? There is danger, yet there is always danger. Influences, schemes. I have feared a few enemies, though not your washer-women. And not for myself. Such as I do not get hanged or burnt, though occasionally we get poisoned. . . .'

I knew that she was speaking not only of herself but of Perceval. She paused, rather than hesitated, examining the floor, black polished wood flecked with ivory, matted with herbs, dried

133

violets, early primroses already wilting at the edges. She touched my hand as she might the cushion beside her. 'He trusts you, in his way. But whom does he not?' Her voice was lulling, affectionate, but indisposed to linger in favourite recollections. 'When he was received by His Highness, he begged him never to ask who he was, so that he could remain.' Her laugh, though subdued, was real. 'You and I know who he is, though we may not agree, and words are imperfect. You and I, he and the Duke . . . we can all love, but our notions of love, our beliefs, are so different. Our Perceval turns aside from lovers at play as he does from the hunting falcon.'

Before us hung a vague, tapestried conceit of buds, huge and swollen, in purple winds, crimson leaves unfolding within a sky inflamed as if by furious angels. Somehow, it forced me to think of Clinschur.

'Princess, I recognize love and have occasionally felt it. I cannot credit belief in it.'

She too sounded reminiscent. 'It cannot be taught, even by me, though I might come the nearest. Certainly not by him, who can teach nothing and would not wish to. You are too sensible, too quick to notice. A true man of your calling. As for the Duke. . . .'

Her sigh revealed little. Irony? Compassion? Disdain? The bell sounded, went silent, deepening a sudden stillness between us.

I was curious. 'In earlier times, days of gods and Titans . . . so much fear and blood, brother killing brother . . . was there love? Was Beauty really beautiful? I think of love and beauty long submerged by awe, horror, servility, struggling towards difficult, even agonizing birth. But here I am no scholar.' I wanted to add, like any courtier, that her own beauty was luminous as our northern lights, as Assyrian brocades, that those eyes, alien, now bold, now withdrawn, must have seen so much unimaginable by Duke and court, but I desisted from doing so. She had had her fill of the high-flown.

Cundré looked away, but I could see her face change from snow to thin pallor, her hands tremble within the jewels. I knew at once that she would not reply, that I had agitated her. She had known bloodshed, the repellent, perhaps she needed them, sensations beyond the permissible, as she did ripples of delight, exquisities of colour, subtleties of touch which reached towards those of Perceval but for ever failed to unite.

The silks rustled, their opulence, perfumed and jewelled, were helpless against sadness, the taint in all of us save the Duke, who might suffer the worst by lacking it.

Alone with her, I realized yet again that she excited in my loins no commotion. I preferred bodies slighter, slyer, more lively and fleeting. In Cundré's presence I felt diminished, more of a novice than I really was. And she too looked beyond me, for the more gleaming and perhaps the more frail.

As though I had not spoken, or spoken only of Monseigneur or the Sponge, her next words seemed tranquil, reflecting on some absurdity of court gossip, to which I barely listened. Her accent, never wholly definable, was slightly hoarse, pressing now light, now heavy on words, with unexpected effects: a serious rejoinder might hint at the comic, a perfunctory statement appear solemn. Occasionally she said yes when she meant no, favourite's privilege which, even in the Palace, encouraged stockyard ribaldry about her reputed and numerous children which assuredly did not exist.

Abruptly, at odds with her usual flow and grace, she moved over to reverse a small, gold-rimmed Tusculan hourglass almost hidden behind the stone water-jug. The gardens outside were silent, the Palace itself could have been overcome by sleep.

'He is befriended by fortunate planets. We are told. . . .' Her mouth drooped caustically at one edge. 'They bridle the universe, their whims counter its momentum. Whatever they illuminate, they mark its destiny. Our Perceval is controlled by neither sorrow nor greed. His goodness, if goodness it be, alone can harm him. This Grail, whatever it may be, is perhaps no more than his own radiance that wins him false friends as much as peace of soul and a name for questing. But an imaginary Grail can still alarm. At Thebes I heard of priests inventing a god, and one noon, to their horror, the god spoke.'

She waited but I was silent, almost numbed. She nodded, as if hearing me agree. 'He survives ordeals known to most of us, without entirely facing them, wears garlands not always merited, regards life itself as an accident that affects all but himself. You may show yourself at council and conference. I too have counselled some few lords, we may both perish forgotten, but his fame will reach to the ends of the world, his smile overcome kingdoms and empty a caliph's treasury though his understanding, even his awareness, reach no farther than his own pretty nose. Without laughter, without jests, yet he may be the wiliest joker of us all.'

A small, rueful petulance underlay her laugh, making her human and accessible, no tinkermaid Isis or half-pay Venus, but a concubine of proven excellence. Trying to imagine her tumbling and twining with the Duke, both naked as glass, I found it easy, also reassuring. Suddenly I sensed flames within her, straining for release.

She was now sipping wine, musing, that accented voice with its queer distortions needing special attentiveness. 'They may drive us both away, leaving you with your documents and busy

135

concerns.' Her intonation rendered me ignoble. 'We are beyond their railleries and offal. We may also be beyond the Duke's guardian hand. Not such as we can look to the guards and holy Church. The Duke can summon the world to rescue us, but break himself in the doing. We can only soar.'

She became more intimate, not tender but friendly, her humour delicately self-mocking. Yet her mood could change in a trice. The glitter not in, but on, her narrow eyes, melted, and I was astonished to see tears, though her voice was cool and steady. 'The Duke . . . he has torrents of words but no ears. He is a lord of feelings, a world in trouble. He pulls us towards him, like a chanson from a green dell. But these plants of his. . . .' Her shrug was not weak but decisive, then she murmured with a gentleness that made me suspect I too had tears in store, 'Like Clinschur.'

Her hands, white and sparkling, were restless, thriving on pain and on the lush, oppressive atmosphere. She seemed unaware that much of what she was saying she had already told us.

'He mutilated himself, in anger at living with the second best, knowing that his tricks and skills would never land him amongst the great. Hector despised him, Alexander turned his back. He can deal out death but inspire no life. He is always outside, gutted by others' greatness, and seeking payment from such as me. He likes to believe he has chained me, that my kiss rots whoever receives it.' She lowered her head. 'It may be true, I flee from him, but distance is no escape, no remedy. I feel his need, like a succubus.' She was distinct, a little defiant, not confessing, not pleading, speaking as she might dictate to a scribe. 'Perceval will never need me, the Duke for all his alarums needs only himself, and not always that. Those like you need only information.'

Her laugh was mirthless, birdlike. In her strength and anguish she could be a real princess, sustaining the siege while her husband battered far-away Turks or chased Andalusian milk-maids. 'They seek perfection, the impossible. So my poor Clinschur takes refuge in magic, my Perceval in his being himself alone, my Duke in rage and power. Power, medicine for failure.'

She told me what must long have been obvious enough, even to Perceval, so liable to mistake symbols for reality yet abiding in little else but symbols . . . that his wounded lord was beset only by anxieties and guilt, infections from her own beauty as foreseen by the morose and vindictive: that the rigmarole of spear and vessel was made obsolete by the smile of a Perceval. But I doubted whether this could finally doom a Clinschur.

The delirious hues of curtain and tapestry, lapsing during her talk, recovered, making a routine of fantasy. Gulping the wine,

I was within luxuriant orchards and foliage, hearing bells from an exarchate's summer-house, the radiance scarcely hurt by an executioner aloft on a scarlet and black podium in many-coloured jester's stockings and tunic, velvet gloves and staring, unblinkered owl-mask. As rich light hardened I strove to listen, with diplomat's ears.

'The Duke will win nothing by force, yet it is force that drives him, the despair and hope of mortals, like a paradox, breaker of bounds.' Again her speech, so singularly pronounced, veered abruptly between the solemn, the teasing, the tragic, the wry. 'He is limited only by his opposite, yet what, yet who, can it be? To discover that, he may destroy us all, and establish his name for ever, and,' her smile rippled happily away, 'precisely one day.' She said carelessly, 'There goes the golden charioteer with his eyes on the sun. The people are justified in their fears, but seek victims from those who have done them no injury and could never do so.'

12

Amid smoothly enunciated patter and dazzling rituals, the crisis was very near, though so few cared to notice it. Amongst the plumed and sashed, pearled and ringed, smiles were fixed as if carved. The Duke remained a political virtuoso, tortuous and shrewd, but scaring the Council, liable to wreck all by caprice, too much talk, over-magnanimity or rancour. And never a skinflint, he tossed too many coins to multitudes he never had time to observe.

Much derives from misunderstandings. I would smile at enthusiastic pilgrims tramping to the relics of St James at Compostela, unaware that the blessed feet had never touched Spain. A scribe had miswritten 'Hispanium' while intending 'Hieruslem'. I chuckled with the Venetian at the broken heads, broken wits, inflicted by the granite likeness of Señor Matthew the Wise, because of a belief that the more violently the head touches the statue, the more enduring the wisdom received.

Tavern wiseacres continued to mouth their doubtful premises.

'Friend, it's known that the cunts of Jewesses are sharp, knife-sharp. That's why their men lose their lives. Sliced off! They pretend otherwise, of course. Putting the blame on God.'

'The holy name be blessed. God's, of course.'

'Can God fast? If so, it explains the birth of Satan, who lost his soul.'

'The soul, now . . . it's shaped like a radish.'

'Nonsense . . . it's like a bean.'

Such as they were belabouring Palace gates with cries for the Duchess to return and chase away the strumpet Princess with a consecrated broom. Their charges could fill a book and indeed are in danger of doing so. She was lily of Hell, womb of horror, cauldron of impurities, scion of Clinschur, a witch from Thessaly, fearful fisher of men who exhausted the Duke and with him the realm. Suppliant nobles carried toads' feet in her presence, precaution against evil. She had declared the Holy Christ female. Her laughter would split purity itself, she revolved behind the Duke like a pernicious comet, she was a barrel of malpractice, an Astarte in bed and out of it.

Could worse be imagined? Certainly. A radical preacher did so daily. Cundré, he raged, had boasted that the vaunted Grail, goal of the righteous, was concealed in her loins, desired by many, entered by too many, a legacy from that hideous, blue-faced Great Mother, who, from her jagged crag, still evaded God's commands and spat out murrain and plague.

I must add that several scoundrels, lop-sided in reeking outhouses, sniggered that God Himself lusted after Cundré, and that Jesus was their bitter fruit. Too drunk to notice Black Brothers, like Stygian spectres, they dribbled accusations that Jesus had been bored too easily, deserting the world too early, his promises empty or sardonic.

Without reference to Duke or magistrates, they were swiftly bound, then led away, never to reappear.

The urban mood, nervy, apprehensive, was quickened by the insidious, thrilling spring, the green flush on trees, blue and white hyacinths, the night sky flashing the Archer's insignia. Yet it assuaged little, God seemed to have dropped a bleary wink. People half remembered the gross behaviour of notables, aped so strenuously by Apis, the apish Duke. Such goings-on, such wholehoggery! Lord Jupiter straddling a swan, Pasiphae defying all limits with a bull, rampant as a Jew's profits! In scallywag legend, Arthur and Gawain so coupled with their sisters that God had blanched as if at the skull of a matricide.

The Archbishop was stricken with forebodings, after seeing a cart reserved for the condemned. Meanwhile children, scuttling behind their elders, swapped Perceval's stories, jostled to sit near him, pluck his sleeve, treasure his footsteps, the poorer, verminous from dogs, clutching bits of glass which, they cried, had fallen from the sky, itself bounded by a circle of crystals. The cleverer, shrewd sons of Mercury, were lectured by a friar, about God's creation consisting of forty glass globes? Why? an impertinent girl demanded. The friar answered shortly that Aristotle had said so. More fool he! the child yelled in a sort of triumph, before spitting on the Duke's ebony floor. On being told that the gibbet

138

would claim its own, the children retorted that Perceval would protect them and tie a millstone to his soiled neck.

Only the Grail bored them, suggesting a banquet to which they were uninvited or a heap of dirty relics.

I was feeling that while current imprecations made Cundré too diabolic, they were also making Perceval over-immaculate. Dependent on one man's passion, her position was shaky, but popularity itself is undependable, a brilliant porcelain khan in an urchin's hand.

He was waving aside my misgivings with courteous disinterest. I wondered whether, despite his curious allure, I greatly liked him. His unfinished sentences, evasive replies, made me impatient, his talk was mostly teasing hints. I often felt for him as I might for a sunlight morning, a radiance fleeting but unreliable. Outwardly neither boy nor mature man, he had purpose which he could not share. His disposition was angelic in being unnatural, needing neither the exquisite pleasure nor refined pain that sustained Cundré, nor the rough agitations craved by the Duke. Sometimes I yearned to wring a cry from that delicately smiling mouth, force tears from the untroubled eyes, wrest some appalling confidence from his monotonous amiability, those intimations of self-seeking secrets perhaps known only to Gawain.

I had heard only one unpleasant utterance from him. A pretty squire was continually interrupting rather unusual questions about music, love, the Turks, addressed to an ugly, broken-nosed doctor of renowned intellect who would usually pause before answering, so that the tiresome squire, with the bad manners that too often accompany good looks, hastened to answer them himself, very ineptly. Finally, Perceval, who had been waiting with unexpected concern for the doctor's replies, murmured, from beside me, 'Young and pleasing sir, I wish you were dead.'

The next day he was. Climbing a tower into a lady's room, the youth stepped on a rotted stone, was pitched head-first on to a courtyard and perished. Thereafter, the parents held regular feasts in his honour, to which Perceval was of course invited, though on claims surely less than authentic.

Small green linen strips were being found on ledges and doorsteps. What did they mean? A threat from Islam, the eldritch grin of imps? Possibly a connection with 7, for the Duke was approaching his forty-ninth birthday, which, the Archbishop assured us, could be very inauspicious or most propitious. Several lords had remarked that they or their wives had been dreaming of green fields, forecast of death.

Perceval merely said that spring had come, as if wondering at his own serene perceptiveness. Then a countess known as 'Ditches', because of her deep pocks, found a dead bird in her hand. Better a bird than a rat, Perceval comforted her, but the bird was a starling, with political import of which he professed ignorance, and he no doubt felt unhappy for having insulted rats. From the Sanctuary of Jason, six visored figures emerged, only one of them living, a chronicler wrote severely.

Perhaps more aware of crisis than he affected, the Duke ordered what he called a Diversion to greet an unimportant Dutch bishop, whom, in the event, he omitted to invite. The bishop's women, the Venetian smiled faintly, always conceived, though as he himself thought children offensive he cursed them for doing so. Actually, the occasion was a tribute to Perceval, who must have assisted in some of it.

The Diversion, known to history as the Masque of Redemption, like so many others, may have implied more than it revealed. Policy could be conveyed through degrees of salutation – embrace, kiss, shrug or some ornate display. This last could also appease the Other World or repel vermin, as the image of Our Lady of Ghent, fearfully, grotesquely carved, famously saved that city from Plague, together of course with the prayers of the Proto-notary-General and Particular. Spectacle could also be designed to rebuff popular opinion.

We gathered in the Hall of the Holy Ghost, ashine with tapestries of elongated riders slanting towards hounds and stags on a lion-hued plain lined with distant towers. Before us seven circular carpets, each with a different planetary colour, lay like islands before the dais, the spaces between strewn with cloves, nutmeg, aromatic terebinth, dried juniper which, endlessly crushed by dogs and servants, were ever more pungent. Between two pillars behind us, on both of which the Old Duke's initial was carved within a chaplet of ivy and rose, hung a green quilt fiery with gems chosen for powers of healing, consoling, inspiring. Troubled, his eyes swollen as if from belladonna, the Duke sat apart in a small pavilion of gold-threaded brocade, its dark cords slanting to jewelled pegs. Even in garish hues and against his sparkling collar, he was unwontedly pale. On the stool at his feet, Malmédes was also strained, inattentive to the extravagant shimmer.

We swiftly realized that Perceval was absent, and I surmised some political action. The streets that morning had been even more turbulent than usual, warning me of something unusual. The Duke's loneliness was reinforced by another absence, that of the Princess who now seldom appeared in so large a concourse, though she might be watching from some peephole in a tapestry, so that the eye of a Juno, Alexander, Florizel might be more alive than it seemed. The dais was constructed like a giant scallop shell, its grooves alternately purple and crimson, the ochred foreground having on one side a closed, silver door.

We quietened at a sign from Monseigneur, upright near the Duke and cloaked in sumptuous feathers to enable his precious words to fly throughout the world. From shadows trumpets ˙pealed, then all were still, gazing at the silver door. Strings were plucked, a viol dropped thin, high sounds, a sackbut croaked, a few silvery calls spread from a small gong. Lamentations rose from a hidden choir, a youth crossed the darkened stage bearing a spear tipped with red, eliciting nods from men, smiles from ladies, unseemly, though without easing the Duke's dejection. The youth was replaced by two girls, virginally white, one bangled and red masked, the other with neat, demure mouth and eyes under soft gold hair, each with a burning taper. They danced about each other until four countesses in scarlet gowns clasped by pearled girdles brought in ivory pedestals and a round table which they gracefully set up, before making room for eight duchesses in pale blues and greens, coroneted with myrtle and bluebell, and displaying gold for wisdom, emerald for faith, ruby for charity, cornelian and jasper for I know not what. Four held flaring torches, the others an ovalled shield planted with glass knives and a giant diamond cut like the sun in splendour. This they stood on the table; illusions of light at once transformed the stone to a chalice, grass green with two round, weeping eyes, then to a horn, a gleaming disc, a latticed casket, a square of pale, glistening samite, finally a single ray before which all knelt, trembling. Fragrancy at once tinged the Hall, as though spice chests had opened. Out of the air gold cups hovered about the shield, seeming to foam, suffused with rainbow splinters sharp as fish spines, before the cups dissolved into a foliage of hyacinth and may. A velvet veil dropped over it, slow music began, and, as if miraculously suspended on all sides of the glittering ray, hung six glass vials in which balsam was lit by small pointed flames. Further light revealed a Moroccan in knightly surcoat, one eye covered with a golden patch, high buskins making him a giant. His hands flashed with beryl and sard, he was about to speak or sing, but, very slowly, awesomely, the silver door was at last opening, the lights dwindled, only the ray remaining steadfast, and, to a low carillon, four squires bore forward a litter supporting a dying king, his black coverlet woven with bears, ravens, wrens. The Moroccan, huge and dim, lost his pride, made humble obeisance and stood mute as the king lay prone, striving to make an imploring gesture at the ray, his hand palsied, his features ravaged. A single bell tolled, a queen attired in what was termed, probably erroneously, taffeta of Ninevah, knelt by the litter, first throwing away a ring, then uplifting a sceptre chased with emerald and shaped as a serpent-encircled tree of

141

life. Again a trumpet, grave, warning; all prostrated themselves, the veil fell away, revealing emptiness where the shield had lain, and on the drawn shoulders were seen white and gold wings. As lights strengthened, the ray shone with intolerable intensity, forcing eyes to close. Recovering, I saw the black knight reaching for the spear mysteriously floating above him: grasping it, he let three drops of blood anoint the suffering king, who at once revived. The round table was aglow, not with the shield but with roasts, sweetmeats, wines. Squires with yellow gloves and white towels served the king, now seating himself to dainty music of harp and lute. All hailed a fisherman in brown, simple garb, who from a single fish filled each plate.

The ray dwindled away, but a multitude of changing lights created Other World strangeness, both numbing and thrilling, the masque ending in a way about which few would agree, so dazzling were the effects, so crowded and fleeting the patterns, so abstruse the allusions, a veritable Feast of Perceval. Many confessed they had seen marvels neither wholly in nor out of the huge, glistening shell: a tree bright with birds, a glass hill, an empty throne around which tall flowers wavered, shook, became maidens singing thanks for deliverance. Though I myself did not see it, Monseigneur described the black knight overcoming a skeleton within tissue of flame and mist spun by a mirror. He explained that this, in compliment to the Duke, displayed wounded pride cured by unsullied humility, an interpretation difficult to accept and, the Venetian murmured, in very questionable taste.

I had seen, or thought I saw, the spear gleaming upright on a night sky and holding, drained parchment white, then gradually blackening, dissolving into the night, a head. At this my nerves iced, my forehead was sticky with sweat which briefly blinded me, all was as if glass had rippled, for the head was surely Perceval's. Waking, I could see the dais had emptied, but none could applaud until the Duke consented to do so. This, however, he did not, but remained fixed in disconsolate trance, magnificent but blank.

There had been no head on a lance, the Venetian assured me, merely a fire-ball perched on a rickety pole, but illusions can nevertheless intimate some clumsy truth. The masque had been, as I suspected, part of a grimmer process, the Duke's attempt to pre-empt a blow delivered at even more than his beloved Perceval, by an authority potentially outbidding his own. Some months back, he had granted Perceval twenty-one servants, grossly unnecessary. I with real work required only three. After some time Perceval, unconcerned, noted several missing. Then more, as if at some surreptitious abduction. He said nothing, might perhaps have felt relieved of their tiresome attentions, but finally only four remained, all young, with fear behind their affectionate eyes. At their plea, he embraced them and promised to speak to the Duke. Before he could do so, on the day before the Diversion, a Thursday, Day of Jupiter and the Eagle, half submerged in the Feast of the Annunciation, he had, in his usual trusting manner, been strolling the streets unattended save by an inevitable cluster of children, helpful to beggars, friendly to the old, when, outside a chapel ostensibly abandoned, he was halted by three priests, one of whom touched his breast with an osier rod, used to divine criminals and a signal of formal arrest. The children fled, cursing rudely and dodging attempts at capture.

Very soon he learnt that he was in danger of being pronounced Infamous, or even Contumacious, or, worse, Indifferent, to be spewed from the mouth of the righteous. 'Mercy is Justice,' the spokesman told him, 'the loving father punishes his own child, else he has no love.' If guilty, he would lose all hope of becoming bishop, provost or abbot, none of which he desired, or might become excommunicate, which he would scarcely notice. On his brow the priest's thumb made the sign of the cross, and the harsh voice ordered him to forswear delusion for ever.

Perceval awarded them his amiable smile as if glad of new acquaintances and was escorted peacefully away to the Tower of Righteousness, the Black Brothers' bastion, where he was promised a Preliminary, dark counterpart of the masque. Searched, though not stripped, he was found to carry only a purse containing a bay-leaf. This, though, was by no means blameless, being one of sixty ingredients requisite for transforming a child under seven into a goat. His intimacy with children had of course been noticed. The leaf was at once sentenced to be hammered, then burnt, by a Brother in white gloves.

Perceval was locked up for two days – three would have excited comparison with the Saviour. Treated respectfully, he was then taken to the adjoining Sanctum of the Innocents, mantled in black crape, escorted by Black Brothers, in pairs, holding green crucifixes and accompanied by the red-robed Prior of the Disciples of St Peter. Had he fled he would have been condemned, for innocence does not flee. That he did not flee, might also damage him, implying both arrogance and trust, not in spiritual authority but merely in the Duke, itself blasphemy, the Duke in God's eyes being less than a speck.

I knew that in such proceedings, witnesses, allowed to appear for the accusers alone, were nameless, the accusation itself often being ambiguous. Anonymity was held a most loving precaution against curses uttered by the accused. Death itself was the greatest of mercies, freeing the sinner from further sin and claims to damnation.

The Sanctum, raftered like a barn, was dominated by a towering black canopy upheld by funereal shafts and topped by a crimson S, for Salvation. All windows were shrouded against sunlight, street cries, cart noises, the effect underworldly. The Holy Ghost was present, guised as the number 6 carved into a wall. A crescent of thirteen Brothers, robed, hooded, faced the accused. On their left, representing the Duke, a steward in dark tabard with cord of gold facings, granted no stool, was forced to stand throughout and allowed no speech. His head, Perceval remembered, seemed to sit on the neck rather than derive from it. No onlookers were permitted. God Himself, like all authority, thrives on the shadowy and mysterious. On a table, stained greenish by antiquity, stood a wooden effigy masquerading as the Virgin, the rigid, angular face, slitted eyes, faint line of mouth showing no pity. It wore a short tunic which left one breast bare, and hunting boots. Wired to her head was a worn bow-shaped ornament; one hand held an apple, the other a rudder. Perceval acknowledged it as if recognizing an old friend.

The atmosphere dulled, menacing, sententious, receding still farther from the busy, raucous city. Painted ears and carmined lips, dangling chains and spiralled bracelets were unimaginable here. Honour had no station, was indeed reviled, like all notions of chivalry, as contrary both to divine and papal supremacy. When Jesus praised, rather seldom, or castigated, too frequently, He was far from considerations of Honour.

The Preliminary began with a question, delivered pleasantly, even off-handedly, as to whether Perceval ever went to confession. He replied in like manner that but for this engagement he would probably be at confession that very moment.

A thick tome was produced, from which came a recitation from the red-robed Prior, his face strained as if from prolonged chewing of gristle.

'Among God's miracles some are articles of faith like that of the Virgin birth, which the Lord wished to remain incomprehensible so that faith in them be more worthy.'

A Brother then addressed Perceval, placidly stationed between two monks in thin, dark gown and within reach of the obscurity quietly surging up wall and pillar, within which, under small circles of candle-flame, heads, quills, parchments glimmered, and, another parody of the masque, the cowled shoulders resembled swollen bats' wings.

'You are besought to reverence this most eminent Chapter, licensed before God by our most holy Father, superior to all princely tribunals of this transitory world. Allow yourself, dearest son, to remember the words of the beloved Pope Boniface, eighth

144

of that sanctified name, that without obedience to the Roman Pontiff, none can escape perdition.'

This was uttered without threat or admonition, in a manner indeed avuncular, though the beloved Pope was remembered as boastful and greedy, whom the French king had literally scared out of his life. I could imagine Perceval listening to this trained expertise with the appreciation he more often gave to a lyric, a lady's story or dog, not exactly eager but never bored or dismissive. Several times he must have nodded in an expectant gratitude disconcertingly sincere, though it would not have ingratiated him with the ecclesiastics. He was like a guest smiling over an invitation which he felt in all modesty was not wholly deserved.

Another Brother continued, with deference like that of his predecessor, 'You must fear nothing, for the incorrupt soul is incapable of fear. It is more probable than reason itself that should you have erred, others, possibly of magnitude even loftier than your own, are more blameworthy than you. Remember, our dear Lord, yours and mine, was no respecter of crowns, and Herod remains Herod. Therefore, do not dissimulate, treat us as you would your living Father, do not fear to confess all or doubt our love and infinite forgiveness. Perhaps in your novicehood you are liable to infantile deception by evil in high places, by the allures of towers, apt to bow the knee before demeanours resplendent but void, unwilling, in your undoubted goodness, to dissect princely opinions. Therefore, our hands will merge in imploring devotion, our eyes swim with compassion reinforced by zeal; for you to win grace and lasting forgiveness you should not wilfully blind yourself like the most of mankind. You should willingly, generously confess all, divulge your abetters, for, in the Lord's service, all pledges are revoked, all oaths are cracked, loyalty can be sinful, we might even say malapert, the condition of a potter, not forgetting a swineherd. A promise forsworn, we assure you in humility and respect, can ensure salvation.'

I doubt whether Perceval, in his novicehood, had learnt sufficient to understand that grace and lasting forgiveness, uttered in this shrouded, atrocious place, entailed the privilege of being strangled before the flames reached him. Exquisite consideration, sapphired language, sympathy profuse, indeed overflowing, almost concealed his arraignment for handling a Templar cloak. He told me later that he felt he was being gently but inexorably edged into a quicksand. Before further indictments a white-haired cleric, benevolent Good Shepherd, graciously acknowledged the teachings of Augustine, that mercy to those in error would prove merciless to those endangered by error. As if prompted, an assessor, hitherto unnoticed in a tall, shadowy pulpit, holding a candle, in a voice finely modulated, decorated by a small, admiring smile, recited the great words of Christ Himself: 'I am the vine, and you the branches. He who dwells in me, as I dwell in him, bears much fruit; for without me you are helpless. He who does not dwell in me is cast away like a withered branch. Withered branches are piled, thrown on the fire, burnt.'

Eyes perforce followed the candle as he slowly descended back into gloom. Another voice resumed, monotonous like a chapel bell, reading from a scroll long as a butcher's arm. Perceval must accept with loving consent the possibility that he had, doubtless in tyro thoughtlessness, created a depraved copper woman through a diabolical cauldron bequeathed by the Jewish warlock, Simon. He had foolishly transformed a flower to a girl, from lust; he was unhappily of the lineage of heathen Small Folk and of Water Spirits who had sired the crazed, mare-inspired Plantagenets, whom God had cursed. He might have carried into the Duchy a casket of infidel delights vulgarly termed the Grail; at Hainault he had stepped through a mirror without breaking its surface. That he had imprinted his likeness on a napkin while drying his face was ceremoniously expunged, but not the lesser charge that he had blasphemously called St Francis 'father' and that the radiance of his countenance, goodly as David's, was deception, concealing heathen defilements. If any such matters were true, a mild voice interjected, the young man might well be tending towards the incorrigible. It was even said that he strove to accomplish miracles and was criminally circumcised.

Perceval, who had been listening throughout with agreeable mien, occasionally tempered by a small wondering pucker, scandalized them by offering, with all respect, to disprove this last, but was quietly reproached for irresponsible levity. Paul, in his wisdom, let all remember, had distinguished between visible circumcision and the circumcision of the heart.

Perceval bowed, as he might to fellow guests in the Palace. It was true, he murmured, that to disprove circumcision of the heart was hard of accomplishment. He opened one hand, respectfully regretful, then closed it.

Quiet accusations continued. He had trusted no Holy Church but only women, one of whom could not be named in consecrated air. He had been careless, trafficking with infidels, worshipping three drops of blood on snow, had unwittingly corrupted little ones, to Jesus the least forgivable of sins. In this the speaker was earnest, anxious for Perceval to realize his manner of folly; the Saviour might have been correct, though final agreement, nay, concurrence, was not yet established. Jesus, he explained with refined patience, though Perceval had shown no dissent, no discernible sign of anything, had not foreseen the Sacred

146

Hierarchy when pronouncing on sin. God could not err, Jesus conceivably could.

Speaking more rapidly, another mentioned that the exact relation of Son to Father was a mystery not here to be discussed, certainly not debated, even should the most cherished limb of the Church wish to do so.

Perceval pleasantly disclaimed such desire, and faces creased with satisfaction. Would he now agree, then formally confirm, that earthly sufferings should be a welcome access to God's love? At this he at last stirred himself to observe, with requisite deference, that suffering should be avoided, especially that of others. The faces lost satisfaction, and he was informed, with a severity doubtless reluctant, that the good disciple loves his judge, and loves him more dearly even if, by mischance, or God's secret purposes, he was condemned, not justly but wrongly, for this would ensure him more glory than the judge, who would now be in greater need of love.

Befitting a duke's companion, Perceval neither demurred nor pleaded. I can clearly see him, like a lady's description of an angel, daintily brushing aside a smattering of gold from a cloud, then giving that amorphous smile. He did volunteer, during some pause, 'I trust all men's goodness. Ill favoured though I be, unworthy of you all, least of the children of light, I may yet be accepted with my brothers and sister.'

This caused offence, even consternation, for apparently, though not lacking logic, reason, grammar, the words contained an error, a heresy, and a scandalous allusion. Though he willingly agreed that a man of flesh could be far from being a child of God, his manner was considered pert, his seeming guilelessness was but guile at its most subtle, akin to that of the crafty Merlin.

Clerks wrote, shrouded dignitaries shuffled in and out of yellow light and, at last, sounds penetrated from outside, like distant sea-fret. On slanting rafters, shadows squatted, united, drifted apart.

'You are one of those who wilfully loosen the thoughts of the simple, the wilful, the ignorant, whose wanderings and idle talk prepare paths for Antichrist.'

I have always believed that this was the first occasion at which *idle talk* was uttered.

Heavy with sighs, melodious with regrets, the Preliminary was veering towards Formal Examination with, at the end, the hook, pincers, fire, but, forcing outraged heads to turn, a disturbance, a raggle-taggle babble intervened, advancing with the inevitability of an avalanche. Most Brothers were rising as outside guards were overcome, doors smashed, and a crowd rushed down passages waving axes, chisels, hammers, spades, screeching

147

demented profanities and clamouring for Perceval. Most were
children, ragged scourings of gutter and hovel, convinced that
Perceval was already on the cross and that his poor heart needed
them. Children, vicious, elemental, inspired, always disregarded
and maltreated, but capable of a crusade of killings, of unutterable
loyalties, led now by a lame but ecstatic scrap of flesh, wild-eyed,
ardent as Lancelot and flourishing a stolen image of St Pelaga,
who loved youth.

Parchments, candles, books were scattered, tables overturned,
ecclesiastics chased, pelted, mauled, the Hall itself at once shabby
and absurd in the rush of sunlight. Perceval, very calm, was
hoisted aloft, his hands outstretched as if for birds, hailed as
sweet deliverer and born into streets aswarm with cheering
multitudes, the ragamuffin journeymen, artisans, jobless. Within
the tumult the full-throated anthem to Perceval was also acclaim
for the Duke, whose subjects, faithful as unicorns, were restoring
him his own. In universal merriment, the children's moment,
grievances were forsworn, the wicked princess forgotten, death,
fever, the gaping belly had no place. History, of a sort, was on
the rampage, galaxies of legend exploding. Bells pounded, tugged,
people said afterwards, by no hands, songs mounted, feet
tramped, pots and pans clattered as they might one day for
Gamalean, Emperor of Last Days, judge of sinners, or, rather, of
particular sinners.

'To the Palace . . . Perceval and our Duke . . . live for ever.'

13

Not everyone remembers that the expression 'unworthy of holding
a candle to him' was certainly first heard when Perceval was
welcomed back to the Palace by the Duke and his entourage,
upholding candles which, on his entry, all but the ruler
extinguished in homage.

Perceval's stars were of unique strength, Heaven's kisses would
free him from time's scars, the Saviour would rejoice to hear his
name and was very probably doing so, the Black Brothers' threat
to the Palace was confounded. A herald pompously announced
that *Perceval* meant Knight of the Centre, without revealing a
meaning. The people, coarse and cheerful, at once dubbed him
'through the middle'. The ladies applauded a story, not wholly
credible, of his evening robe decorated with swifts that vanished
at midnight and, at his call, returned at dawn.

The Duke too was in the ascendant. Clearly, the Diversion had
in some esoteric manner undermined all opposition. Such was
the aura of the invincible and thrice orthodox Duke.

Dirty children now put on insolent airs and were apt to slip through guards and into the Palace as if by right, seeking their hero, demanding his tales of red knights, witches loathsome but exciting, enchanted castles and magic cauldrons, and of reckless Gawain, slayer of the indescribable, whose exploits rendered them speechless with terrified delight.

Himself lacking children, the Duke noticed none of anyone else's. Had one perched on his knee he would either have been unaware of it, or have dumped it in a hound's basket.

Imagination was unfurling, matching the Duke's most flamboyant standards. With Perceval amongst us, Plague herself was shamed, nobles bemoaned their rapacity and advocates their greed. Those who, sufficiently fee'd, would trace seven divergencies from reason and five errors of grammar in the Sermon on the Mount.

In the south, a Jewish plot to murder all Christians was mercifully frustrated. The Jews had planned to use magic requiring a consecrated host and a Christian child's heart. The first was easy, but the heart, bought from a Christian household, was proved, on the Jews' arrest, to be a pig's. The enterprise was detected because stories of Perceval so affected the conscience of a pious Jew – people said that for a Jew to possess a conscience was a miracle – that he betrayed his fellows. They were all hanged, he himself being pardoned and suffering only life imprisonment.

So, with inquiring demeanour and modest gait, Perceval moved through his own stories. I heard that he had refused, and refused *advisedly*, another new term, thought magical, Clinschur's gift, conveyed from Cyprus by gypsies, of a ring signifying perpetual chastity. This he had placed on the finger of the Virgin of Dijon who, a lewd horse-dealer promptly gibed, after consideration, handed it back.

During the giddyhead rejoicings another effigy, that of the old Duke, was reputedly very drunk, and that of his son was actually smashed, on rumour that it contained his soul, for which he would give munificent rewards to recover. He had not yet done so.

Leaves flashed green throughout the land, sunlight drew silver from water. The Council discussed sending troops against the Bishop of Pouillé, a ruffian who denied honour to the Trinity and taxes to the Duke. His herald delivered an expostulation but forgot to address the Duke as Crossback. Like all messengers he was liable to be awarded superb gifts or barely human inflictions. The Duke ordered this one to be flayed but, as so often, did not bother to have it enforced, and the Bailiff winked, letting him free.

Perceval was attending Council, seated on the Duke's right in his capacity of Knight of the Centre. When prevailed upon for advice on the graceless Bishop, he responded, with admirable diffidence, that, to avoid bloodshed, the troops should be exchanged for a magisterial Missive of Rebuke, with unanswerable wording. All assented, save the Duke, who was drowsy, and the ex-Chancellor who muttered, out of his master's earshot, that the utterances of butterflies were too flimsy. His own status, however, had weakened. Lately he had caused mirth by commissioning a painting of the Crucifixion, with himself shown as a penitent beneath the cross, larger and more tormented than the naked figure drooping above. The Duke awoke, consented to dispatch the Missive, thanked the ex-Chancellor for his advice, adding, 'He that loseth his life shall save it', not explaining but pleased with the remark, which he appeared to consider derived from his own wit.

The Missive of nineteen much debated words was completed within three weeks and, commanded by the Vidam of Angiers, the deputation set out: five heralds, forty trumpeters, seven learned doctors clutching, rather uneasily, lilies twined with tresses of virgins. By, let us say, mischance, the Missive in its silken purse, with long, glistening seals, was eventually delivered not to the Bishop of Pouillé but to the saintly Bishop of Saint Paulle Maritime who, on reading it, wept three days, a rose tree withering in sympathy. In the subsequent uproar, apprentices ransacked the Genoese quarter, several perished, and the gemmed reliquary of Thomas of Sens was stolen.

At this, the ex-Chancellor nodded complacently but the disaster was kept from the Duke, who then rode in majestic procession to the Cathedral to celebrate his peaceful solution. Very soon, however, his thoughts were deflected by the inopportune presentation of a picture of himself assaulting the walls of Jerusalem, themselves small, even abject. The Archbishop, airing his new mistress as he might sheets, was alarmed, for this puny Jerusalem might remind the Duke of his projected crusade, very disruptive, very expensive, likely to injure all save the Turks. The Duke said little, but his fervid glances at the painting suggested his discovery of a secret name: Ravager, World Eagle, Tenth Champion.

More acceptable to the Archbishop, proclaimed through an alarum of massed sennets and tuckets, was the miraculous discovery by monks of St Philip of Flanbers of the arm of St George. Hitherto, arms of the great saint had been held, by some further miracle, by Cambrai, by Toulouse, by Villers-St-Leu, by the Abbey of Auchin, and most profitable of all, by Cologne, where an arm fell upon an altar from Heaven itself. The latest

150

was left-handed, disappointing those familiar with the sword piercing the inglorious dragon and wielded by the right. However, the Grand Almoner of St Gervase-en-Guyau, descendant of George himself, dispersed all anxieties. 'Who in my family does not know that the blessed saint was left-handed? It is well known that painters are misguided, wilful, and very often blind.'

14

Summer, nevertheless, was not as joyous as we had anticipated, and, though blue and elegant, and despite the Black Brothers remaining subdued, there lingered disconsolate trappings no less effective by being felt rather than seen. The Council ordained a census, always unpopular. In town and village able-bodied men fled from the commissioners, and Malmédes had, uneasily, to inform the Duke that he ruled a population almost all female and which owned no property.

From his son-in-law the Emperor, the Duke received a gold-filigreed casket which, when opened, disclosed an old shoe. Some said that this betokened a most signal compliment, comparing the recipient to the suffering and meek so commended by Christ, even to Christ himself. Others held it an insult certainly grievous and perhaps maleficent. The Princess believed it a crude hint that the Emperor was short of funds, and Perceval a little wistfully thought that in summer none needed even one shoe. The Duke, undecided, then fretful, summoned a conference, which like most conferences used many words to resolve little, and, quickly tired, he dismissed it and threw away the shoe. Experience teaches that despite clocks with their hours, minutes, indeed seconds, time is variable and deceptive, often speeding when it appears slow, limping when it seems headlong. Minutes too are different from moments, which alone, so to speak, are momentous. The moment of battle, of love, of signing a warrant or greeting a spectre . . . each has different measurement, rules, grammar. Certain eras are apparently calm when actually catastrophic. Outward and prolonged tribulation may denote swift rebirth. This is groundling stuff but relevant to what was to occur.

July reflected the passions of the Caesarean Duke, as his mood soared, only to collapse. Now we ached with pageantry, now were smothered by outbursts of abuse, grief, threats, now relieved, but by no more than the supercilious. All depended on a single personage, which not everyone identified with God.

I observed that armour had thickened, was more fanciful, more gorgeous than any since the shield of Achilles. The Duke's new gorget was of steel swollen with carbuncle and opal, his casque sported a live linnet in a golden cage topped by a giant emerald Mars holding a silver pennant. Tourneys were more dazzling, rewards, passage money and hirings of champions produced the word *millionaire*, banners were more flaunting, music more deafening. Yet beneath lurked, or seemed to lurk the unnamed anxiety which, at certain hours, eclipsed thoughts of the Duke, his godless paramour and the favourite rescued from Hell. Could this be, I wondered, but part of the disturbances excited by the search for pepper and silver, the new, exotic names from Cathay to the Azores, and by gunpowder? Courtiers affected to swoon before motet and madrigal, hunted, fornicated, usually more from politeness than ardour, sniggered at the Spider King, at the Emperor and his ragged shoe, at a passing Earl of Warwick, but Constantinople had been battered into surrender after a thousand years of glory by hundreds of Muslim guns, their fiery tongues remaking the age, so that the resounding codes of Garter, Golden Fleece, Silver Tassel, might resemble a galleon, resplendent, beflagged, vast, but with guns fixed too high above water, drifting towards barely glimpsed reefs while the officers danced and the crew were forbidden to speak.

Glory could be shredded to tatters. Already, at Coutrai, mounted knights with pedigrees older than Hadrian, armed as if by clever Vulcan or Gonfan, had been toppled into a ditch and hacked to bits by Flemish artisans, who displayed, to common ridicule, four thousand captured spurs. At Crécy, at Agincourt, lords prestigious as Jupiter perished by the wagon-load, Swiss peasants and burghers had routed the lordly Habsburgs. I could see nobles selling lands and rights for love charms, talismans, ladies' favours, for defences the most superb imaginable but pierced by crude bombards; howling, clutching at stars, baubles and ribbons; rites necessitating phrases resonant but incomprehensible, of long habit but suspect origin.

None of this could I communicate to the Duke, always too impatient for any but his intimates, and indeed, in his gusty presence, I believed quite easily that the Duchess de la Meunon was descended from the flash of Turnus' sword; that, to put it decorously, Pan had a hand in the birth of the first Baron of Vevira; that the de Fulke grandam traced her line to a she-devil so ugly that she shrivelled mirrors. Nor, despite his feeling for boundaries, phenomena on the verge, could I much interest Perceval. He nodded eagerly enough, began a sentence, hesitated, then subsided, though I believed that his thoughts continued long after I had left him.

I was forced to use my ciphers to report that despite his almighty grandeur the Duke, closeted with the Princess whom I now scarcely saw, was leaving scullions, cooks, valets, grooms, even

152

master chefs and stewards unpaid, his castles were mortgaged thrice over, and, looking close, I saw that many extravagant hangings, escritoires, chairs, canopies were soiled, threadbare, torn. Such conditions helped ruin Grand Chamberlain Marceau. Desperate for his wages, he sought the latest astrologer, who assured him that he would shortly attract a fortune. Having had to sell his horses, he hastened to the Palace on foot, slipped on dung and broke his neck. His body was sold to Montpellier surgeons for a considerable sum.

The Duke, ignoring the unseen Chancellor, was towering too high above his dominions, the wealthiest in Christendom but needing far-sighted direction of trade, industry, surplus. Lords and ladies continued lolling over marchpane and nectarine, playing forfeits, listening to the scented word and meandering chord, but pleas, complaints, silken threats were blocked by clerks, undisciplined and disgruntled and remained unread, to stifle, fester, corrode, despite warnings from the young and intelligent Advocate Significant, now sent on a lengthy mission to Prague of no significance whatsoever. The Duke had a flair for selecting clever councillors whom he then neglected to use properly. For much of that summer, when not fostering military preparedness and examining travellers' tales of the East, or entertaining Cundré and Perceval, he was absorbed with a Neapolitan trumpet guaranteed to revive the dead, if accompanied by Jesus' whip, said to be in custody of none else but the Spider King.

Of the Duchess little was heard save that she was living patiently, recovering from an unspecified ailment, sustaining the Duchy with her devotions, rejoicing daily at marvellous letters from her lord.

With some gratification the Duke announced in Council that on far horizons the Turk was bulging, frontiers were cracking, all Hungary was in flames.

'Doubtless our Lord has his faults,' a councillor would begin, very doubtfully, 'but . . .', then cease, leaving us to ponder whom he meant. Nevertheless, omens were unmistakable. Despite summer, several alders disappeared outside Liége, at Mons a willow commended by the Old Duke was blasted. At Ypres a knight, valiantly plumed, vowed to build a ladder into Heaven and indeed made a useful start. Inevitably, however, God noticed, allowing him to ascend far above the earth until finally his hands stiffened, his legs and nerves went paralysed, his servants fled and, perched aloft, dumb and motionless, he died of starvation.

For some, the strain of courts, the intrigues, captious moods, strange princesses and elusive lords of centre became too tortuous, so that they yearned for the direct challenge of battle: not for the naked, outspread mistress with luxuriant flesh and moist, enthralling depths, no misty yearnings for crowns and magic fruits, but for the austere, sparse, far Eastern marshes and wind-frozen Scythian plains where the sky begins, curling upwards towards a peak above Bethlehem, or, as the Pope insisted, Rome. A few retreated into prayer, as instructed by Brother Johannes of Mainz, who taught that prayer concentrated energies so sharply that it convulsed the soul, unfroze statues, cracked stones, induced treats from a banker. These did not occur, but the Sponge cackled impudently that when the Duke had suddenly embarked upon a prayer a table started to click.

Sniffing martial opportunities, well-vintaged warriors tramped the Palace mouthing names, vast names of ages beyond Bohemund of Antioch, Godfrey of Bouillon, William the Marshal, Knights of Calatrava and of Thoma, impeccably stored in romance. Nightly over heavy wines they regaled the Duke with heroes who loomed like primeval boulders, the sounds uncouth and ponderous that His Highness so treasured: Brandeliden of Punturtieis, Affinamas of Clutiers, Rivalin of Lohneis, Tampenteire of Brobarz, Ither of Gaheviez, Jurans of Blemunzin, Marantiez of Privegarz, Mirabel of Avendroyn, Bogedalam of Minnetalle, Karfodyas of Tripparum, Tirede of Elixodjan, Alamis of Satarchzonte, Passionjus of Thiler, Astor of Panfalis. . . . Such names might make a Cundré shrug and a Perceval giggle but they smote the heart of a duke, belaboured his senses like Herculean gongs, heralded a return to high chivalry. Moreover, a lion was said to be at hand. A lion? Yes. Alone? None knew, or cared to say. On a mission? Who could answer? Then, on the Provost's ceiling appeared the faint outline of a lion, all was explained, to much rejoicing.

Aping earlier forms, the Sieur de la Hall wrote a bundle of poems, with imagery not built to last, entreating his lady to grant him her favourite satin to display when he rode to slaughter ten thousand Turks. In more modern style, she replied crossly that he should remain at home, leave Turks to themselves, and pay a rapacious Limoges apothecary for her latest consignment of perfumed napery.

Less significant events occurred, recorded with respect and a quiet smile by the Venetian. There being no example of the Devil's signature, the chief guildsmen of Brabant offered fifty thousand crowns for a specimen, but, while offerings were many, none had yet been proved, though most people were aware that the Fiend had signed testaments with Master Trunk of Antwerp, Herr Sabbelinus of Wittenberg, and of course with Cundré, last of Saturn's four wives. A friar pleaded that her buttocks be whipped to the bone, for loss of blood reduces witches' powers.

'You know, friend, that her twat spreads vermin?'

154

'Yes, yes, who doesn't? But the Duke . . .'

'Poor man, his wits are all in one direction.'

Murrain ravaged sheep, cured only by a Gospel dipped in holy water and applied to their necks by a friar. People applauded, offending him, for he demanded more than applause. Swarthy Egyptians, voices like dry biscuits cracking, held a horse fair near the university rector's vineyards, thrilling children with shiny ear-rings and coloured turbans; denizens from Perceval's tales, their sharp eyes, wild zithers, whirling dances to tambourines, their grinning flatteries not wholly concealing the malice within. Children knew from Perceval that this tribe suffered under God's curse for having opened no doors when the Holy Family fled from Herod.

Then, worst of all, the Sponge died, secretly murdered by a cake of crushed glass, he who had jested that men perished when they saw the mirror of the world. Eminent physicians gave him blood of three hanged felons to drink, but he died nevertheless, leaving the great men explaining that the felons must have been condemned unjustly.

The Duke's wrath at the Sponge's death was vehement. He ripped off his clothes and thrashed them. He wept, summoned Cundré and Perceval, wept again, called, at frightful expense, for musicians from Savoy, then refused to hear them. He upbraided sympathetic delegates from Lorraine, taunted the Spider King, threatened the Swiss. Sometimes, with a few menials, without even the two beloveds, he retired to some peasant's hut deep in the forest, sitting through the night listening to stag and fox, to dull murmurs and strange rustles, very intent, as though at prayer.

On the Duke's return, all the rooks deserted the Palace gardens. The Duke, who normally cared nothing for rooks, was so enraged that a rash erupted on his weapon hand. Recovering, he held a mass, interrupting it to declare that henceforward anyone uncivil to a rook would be fined.

At last, during a thunderstorm, he calmed. He embraced the Princess mightily, swore love eternal, granted her two castles, only one of which he actually owned, kissed Perceval and promised him two more. Monseigneur composed verses to Hercules Triumphant and, surging through the Palace, the Duke shouted that he would hold a midsummer feast, none caring to inform him that, during his ravings, midsummer had already arrived and indeed had dared to depart. Before the feast he reluctantly summoned a Council, after a quarrel with the Archbishop about concupiscence, itself of political moment directed at the Princess, forced by the Starlings on the prelate who in general held the matter only a venial sin which he himself

155

enjoyed, as the Venetian put it, to the hilt. The Duke, swearing on God's body to give him no further audience, refused him an invitation to the feast. Predictably, he soon regretted his intemperate decision but could see no way, in honour, to evade it. The Council then assembled, the Archbishop perforce missing, under a tapestry of Love astride a rhinoceros overcoming Jealousy reining a pig. They had to decide, the Duke presiding, whether to forswear an oath in an honourable cause would constitute dishonour. Unable to agree, while the ruler stamped and muttered, the lords turned to Perceval, who hitherto had maintained his customary though concerned silence. After a longish pause he ventured that dishonour would indeed be involved, but suggested that the Archbishop should nevertheless be invited, in his capacity of Commander of Parlance, and refused permission actually to address the Duke. 'Thus,' Perceval concluded modestly, 'by keeping mute and in layman's garb, he will be in no danger of offending His Grace, who will thus neither have invited the Archbishop nor given him audience.' This was gratefully accepted, not least by the Duke.

That afternoon of the midsummer feast, the sun, reburnished, on special behaviour, wheeled through limitless blue. Bells swung, scaring all devils within range, flowers were exhalations of Paradise, loyal crowds swarmed to acclaim the ducal procession as it paced, measuredly, all heads high, banners stiff in a warm breeze, protected by God Himself, towards the Chapter House of the Golden Fleece.

The music-struck Duke, Orpheus reborn, a strenuous though tuneless singer in black, floppy cap, white and gold surcoat and the belt once owned by the Bear Chief and now thick with crystal images of knights, strode with Perceval, preceded by four score boys in blue and yellow singing the anthem 'Gloriosa'. Noble heads surrounded him, followed by ladies on palfreys and jennets shod in alternate gold and silver, their steepled hats radiant. Great lords led their entourages, their emblems arousing cheers or groans. Acclamations for the Duke and Perceval must have reached the very throne of God. Monseigneur was present in his guise of the Merlin, foretelling lasting victory, in poor verse:

'Nay, no Duke but a further thing,
Behold, the King!'

The Chapter House portals were entwined with roses and vine leaves. Butlers, stewards, chamberlains waited with precious ewers in which floated petals, to be presented for hand-washing, then, in blessing, emptied over common folk pressing for alms.

The long boards sparkled with inventions and subtleties, for

156

which the Chief Chef received a much-coveted pension, which was never paid, and a hound was cheered for leaping on to a table to claim a roseate dish of triangular, tinted cakes. Around me, reaching into a distance, were miniature castles of ice and custard, jellied monsters and cannon, polished heaps of black currants and damsons, candied oranges fashioned into elves and mermaids in Other World glow, castellations of quince and gingerbread, almond paste fluffed with cream spread over mallard, mackerel sprinkled with raisins, olives and anchovies, chicory tartlets, swan roasted with shirret, crystallized violets fixed in cowslip sauce, loaves cut into dolls, trees, elephants, a tower of red and white sugar besieged by sugar plums, peppered quails baked in cinnamon, radished herring, boar haunches frosted with salt pearls, geese stuffed with apple-filled hares, thrushes stewed with larks' tongues and vine leaves in Norman cider, heron pies swelling into turbaned centaurs, flying gods, golden rams. The usual trimmings of the Duke's bounty.

Torch flame made dramatic distortions and foreshortenings as if in a Night of Gods, so that from a towering, rounded column a tiny knight plied a gigantic sword, a stag with golden bells overtopped a moated city. Fire and shade evoked plumage from faces, evanescent eagles from gestures, a minotaur glared, winked, dissolved into dull gold. Such atmosphere, filmy, raucous, intoxicated, livened the hangings as Mars, belt awry, eyes aflame, bestrode an Isle of Women, Ulysses fondled an Augsburg gun as he might a lover, the old Duke galloped in a hunt led by a blue-winged archangel, pursuing the white deer, while, beneath, peasants loosed a ferret at an indifferent rabbit and, between trees, camels surveyed us, laden with monkeys.

Revellers were awash with clary and mulberry, Rhenish and Angevin, trumpets continually blaring. Lords and ladies intermingled, vying with spectacular raiments. Aloft, far off, very noble and impassive, mantled in blue and scarlet, diamonds on collar and sleeves, the Duke sat beneath the Cap of State on its shining lance which the potency of colour, drifting fumes and smoke sometimes made into an ornate head, upheld to draw the world to it. Afterwards, rather too late, Monseigneur claimed to have observed a certain cunning around the Duke's mouth.

The feast had begun with an alarm, for the Archbishop, daringly as Commander of the Parlance, was at once upstanding and, 'by right, custom, loyalty', delivering the grace, but interpolating it with jovial allusions to valiant David and stalwart Jonathan, which I assumed were designed to regain favour for him by praising both Perceval and the Duke's rumoured war policy. The Duke affected to hear nothing, likewise ignoring the tumultuous loyalty shouted for him, then for the Duchess, accompanied by

157

some curses for her supplanter.

The Archbishop was swiftly forgotten. I set myself to the offerings before me, and a wizened, ingratiating Portuguese leant towards me, confiding the familiar tale of an Irish magician who, for a wager, transformed himself into a jug of ale. 'But alas, a donkey's hoof broke the jug and a dog drank the ale.' He pouted, looked mournful, then suddenly cackled.

Entertainments flowed past, as we swallowed and gulped, gorged, waited to recover. Dwarfs jumped from pastry-puff hillocks, painted eggs between their lips from which, at some tinkle, birds emerged, fleeing between pillars, dashing themselves against ceilings, falling senseless into bowls, rushes, dogs' mouths. A black and yellow clown flourished a goblet, its stem breaking when he began a high-pitched song. Whistles greeted a walking pig, fennel in each ear, wearing a shabby hat circled with metal saints, grunting to a drum, plainly representing the Spider King, though even this, I saw, did not stir the motionless Duke, who ate and drank nothing, despite the dishes continuously lifted to him. A fellow flung up powder, which sprayed him like a tent, into which he vanished, then emerged as a spangled, otherwise naked girl. A monkey strolled on stilts, casually accepting nuts, drunken squires threw their half-swallowed food at a crone with three ears. A spark enlarged into a hen. It laid an egg, which was promptly grabbed by a painted urchin. The commonplaces of magic. A silver candlestick shrilled a loyal verse, a juggler flung up bottles but caught plates, a spaniel was transmuted into a boar which, by some sleight, ate the spaniel.

The Portuguese grasped my hand as if wanting to steal it. 'I think of a bubble which wavers, then dissolves, yet remains part of the whole which gains and loses nothing.'

The Mantuan envoy nodded importantly, 'Finely expressed. Well said, indeed!' Then tittered rudely.

Brilliant jars exhibited the foetus of a griffin, the pickled head of a Saracen, shrunken loins, allegedly Cleopatra's, and the hand of a Vicar Choral which had both touched St Francis and led to his expulsion for thieving. Continually refilled by ogling cup--bearers, we exchanged the oft-heard stories that rhymed with the opulent dishes. Ulrich von Lichtenstein smashing three hundred and seven spears in a month, riding through the Empire attired as Venus to honour his own fair love, forcing the defeated to bow before him, calling her name to the four reaches of the world. . . .

I have always believed that, but for the Archbishop's intrusion, the Duke would have remained satisfied with the plaudits and good cheer. As it was, while outside, fireworks whirred and flared, bright breath of Jupiter wildly greeted, within, clarions unexpectedly trilled and, acclaimed as Crossback, the Duke stood up, thundercloud against the luxuriant hues, though his collar shot fires, and his golden sleeves reached to the floor. Flushed, indeed florid, stirring his own brilliance, he dominated us, his coarse, excitable voice whipping fear from some, devotion from others, wonder from all but one, for I could now see Perceval, staring not at the Duke but at nothing, as though the soul had left his body to roam where it listed.

The Duke began: 'Fate bideth her time. . . .' He glared down, challenging dispute, his words ominous, at odds with the wines, heated skins, the hectic games, dances, loves ahead. The Venetian was for once serious. We were controlled by an unpredictable father, lashing judge, an uncertain god thrusting off hallowed restraints. I had never heard the Duke sustain speech at any length, and was startled to see scribes, at some concealed signal, hastily dragging in stools, little tables, then sat, quills raised to inspire the future, their scratches running beneath verbal bombards, now fast, now slow, accompanied by a hand gesturing in swift arcs, rings flashing angry authority, capricious, sometimes infantile, and aimed at the stars.

'Since the Fall, most of you, deaf from sin, hear God's music more rarely than you see the phoenix. Your own noise drowns it. I hold sway over chaos, the disarray of reason. Some madman from Cusa yells out that life has no centre. Absurd. Mankind, however stupid and rebellious, is the centre in God's image, ordained rulers are the axles of existence.'

The scribes hurried, the ladies went wide-eyed, the lords expectant. The Venetian's seasoned eyes examined the speaker as they might a map of disputed terrain, the Archbishop looked as if the Duke's rudimentary theology trespassed upon his own estate, the ex-Chancellor's broad features were squared into anxious grimace, Monseigneur clearly wished himself elsewhere, de la Rivière, disconsolate, scrutinized his hands as if to see that they remained present. None dared fidget, fingers unnaturally rigid were arrested on knife, cup, woman's shoulder, and Perceval refrained from deft use of the fork.

Was the Duke, I wondered, really addressing Perceval alone, pleading for admiration, even recognition, from that young, ineffable face that neither accepted nor rejected love? The Knight of the Centre! Each had his quest, never quite identified, though the Duke was scattering words like the silver pieces, themselves borrowed, which he had earlier thrown at crowds screaming for him to lower his eyes. He stood on high, four-square, embattled, victorious over who knew what, the great voice slung into the infinite, veins glowing, muddied blue on nose and cheek.

'My Name, my Honour, aspire to what the noble Augustine

called the deep but dazzling darkness of God.'

His face twitched. I feared he would topple, crash face down into the sugared conceits, creamy pâtés, dragging his glory after him, to pour away under aghast eyes, all plots sliced off in a prolonged and terrible hush. But a dyke crumbled at once, releasing a new surge.

'The blessed Saviour taught loyalty. He probably taught nothing else,' the Duke pronounced, ignoring the Archbishop's offended gaze. 'The worst beings ever known, worse even than Brutus and Cassius, were once angels.' The packed, streaky faces were startled, but the Duke swept on. 'The angels who, when Lucifer in evil vanity sought to overthrow God, joined the armies of neither, but loafed, watching, eager to collect the gains of their wagers on those they were too craven to join.'

The citation was new to me and perhaps to the Duke, for he added, 'I can give the very lines of Scripture', though he did not do so. Instead, while we strove to translate the words behind his sentences, he kept us waiting. Not tall, but made overpowering by the occasion, he reached for a massive cup of wine, already dipped by unicorn's horn against poisons secretly passed in galleries, marketed in closets, packeted in dim recesses. More conversationally, though like a slightly affronted schoolmaster, he at last resumed: 'A land at war is a withered branch, profane and licentious as Barbary. I speak from the great poet of the chasms of Bavaria. Practise humility. In distress a great man must vanquish his pride. A bitter contest.' He seemed to grin reminiscently. 'But if you relieve the distress of such a man, God's blessing will seek you out. A fallen gentleman is in worse condition than the ragged ones who beg at windows.'

A queer, splenetic despair touched his glamour as he faced us, amid the banners, falling sunlight, the bewildered awe of feudatory and subject. His eye gleamed, as did his voice, keeping pace with his finery, until, again astonishing us, he said, very gently, caressing, probably to Perceval and secluded Cundré, and with a sadness that hurt: 'I'm not an Achilles destined to perish before the thing gets done. I can offer an empire of spirit, a world-blown vineyard, and speak to you from the knight of knights, who felled the tyrant of Gath.'

He spoke so slowly, menacingly, the jewelled hand weighting the words, lights flowering his head like a nimbus, that around me several ladies hastily veiled themselves. The words seemed to descend from lofty eminence.

> 'Gods you may become
> You are all sons of the highest,
> Yet you shall die like men

160

And fall like one of the princes.'

By this forbidding prospect, which sent couriers speeding to Aachen and Rome, Paris and Vienna, Prague, Naples, Madrid, London, the world knew that the Duke would strike at his enemies and grab himself a crown.

His departure left a paralysis, cessation of nerve, restored when a drunken squire rose and emptied a dish over the nearest head. Swiftly decorum lapsed, servants and masters mingled in common horseplay, throwing loaves, smashing glass, tearing clothes and tapestries. Many ladies were screaming, some were laughing and gratified. Dodging a loaf I hastened for quiet confabulation with the Venetian.

15

Bright heels of Reaper's Month, September, flitted over roof and hill. The Spider King sent the Duke a ring cut with Syrian lettering, for which the recipient returned extravagant thanks. The gift had, they discovered, belonged to Judas Iscariot! To accept it would be blasphemy, rejection might provoke war, to destroy it could entail earthquake. The Duke remained unexpectedly calm, perhaps reserving plans behind a cheerful, if patronizing smile. Malmédes, to test the ring's size, placed it on his own finger and forgot to remove it, and the matter cooled. Less ambiguous, however, was a second gift from the Louvre, a bedizened head of St Gengault of Frisia. Its workmanship delighted the Duke, who swore heartily that the Spider King might yet win salvation. However, some tactless busybody then disclosed that Gengault was patron of cuckolds. The Duke's oaths changed direction and he abruptly left the capital, sailing for some days down-river with Cundré and Perceval, having promised respectful citizens and awed peasants the richest of harvests. On his return, surfeited with pleasure but, as ever, swaying between humours, he announced that he had been insulted, not as we supposed, by France, but by the Swiss burghers, and so grievously that, although he as a good Christian could forgive, his Honour could not. A war council was summoned, postponed for a day because not only did a hen crow but it crowed at night, doubly against nature. This, the current astrologer – astrologers' periods of favour were short – announced with some state, could have but one of two meanings. He added that an awkward planetary conjunction prevented him from disclosing either.

When the Council finally met, the Duke, in excellent spirit, declared that, at the very least, the Swiss must be punished to the very edge of extermination, as forsworn Amalekites, false sons of Anak. War, of course, was unnecessary, they did not deserve it. They were, he continued, brimming with good cheer, maggoty souled offspring of mountain madness and valley cupidity, deserving mere chastisement which he would himself inflict on what he was very pleased to call a Golden Occasion.

His demand for instant advice precipitated tense reluctance to begin, none liking to mention the forebodings of Starlings and guilds, the threat to trade, the imposition of military levies. Monseigneur was particularly uneasy, partly because his notions of combat, condemned as frivolous, actually acknowledged his distaste for it, partly because a Milanese soothsayer had predicted that he would die beneath the morning star. He had rewarded the fellow well, ordered his bedroom windows to be kept curtained, then discovered that a morning star was, in local patois, a spiked mace.

At last questions began, very timidly, none wishing to disperse the Duke's urchin enthusiasm. Even a simple chastisement, particularly a Golden Occasion, needs arrangements. Had His Grace deigned to notice the calendar? Harvest was not yet fully cut, recruitment might thus be difficult. The Treasury was empty, despite His Grace's renowned economy. The Spider King had troops on the frontier, the Swiss contemptibly were very rich and had a fine store of mountains, ill-designed, of course, but staunchly protective. The English – ah, the English – had the Duke, with his piety, learning and sagacity, an exact knowledge of maps?

Hearing this, I had a distressing vision of the Golden Occasion wandering over starving countrysides, drifting through blizzard, staggering down endless, dream-like roads towards nowhere. The Starlings, I knew, were regathering, the populace was prepared to be sullen, the Duke muttered impatiently, told everyone his secret date of departure, then turned to Perceval for better company which, in his pleasant way, he at once provided, suggesting that a carnival be permitted. This would dishearten opposition, gratify the good, attract the eyes of saints and, once again, amaze Christendom.

The Duke was delighted, though Monseigneur murmured that, despite the Sponge's demise, His Grace's fool was by no means dead.

Undisguised military preparations had already begun. Court-yards were sickly with cauldrons boiling long mandrakes in wine, which numb all pain; and saffron, the oil of which cures dysentery and the flux. Hammers clanged, all smiths were forbidden women until their task was over, none remembering why. Arsenal and armoury were astir, trumpets blew continuously for the messages from sworn allies and fiefs, usually unsatisfactory.

I was again summoned by the Princess, unseen for weeks, and was astonished to find preparations for departure. The inner apartment was almost bare. On one ledge, flowers seemed dimly lit from within, suggesting that a ghost had lately passed, not wholly unimaginable, for one of those seated amongst us at the Midsummer Feast was now thought to have been supernatural. Nor did Cundré seem wholly herself. In air bright but thin, pushed through lancets, her greeting was listless, her beauty saddened, grazed by the raging times, marred by these walls which, stripped, were too high with deep whorls of damp, the windows gaunt, the floors dirty, her very scents routed. Yet nothing in her tall figure was irresolute. In blue, simple gown, without jewels or paint, very pale, black hair uncovered, she looked younger, softer. She led me to a room empty but for an uncushioned couch, curtly stopping my courtesies, her taut eyes motioning me to sit beside her.

I had much to ask. Seated so close, I wondered, as I had often done before, whether with her I could ever rise to physical love. Probably not. A model of unvanquished beauty could be less enticing than a laughing slut. Despising the tricks and insolence of so many court ladies she solicited from me, and perhaps from Perceval, not delirious passion but neat and considered liking. She saw my glance at the dismembered surroundings. 'Yes.' Her sigh had humour. 'My time has come. I have seen no mad comet, I am haunted by nothing more than my own good sense. But my day here has gone, and his own also.'

Startled, I inferred reference to Perceval and immediately felt a protectiveness towards him that he would need more than she. However, she was gravely shaking her head, the green eyes stirred in their depths, the dark brows almost at one. Pulling silks around her, she looked hollow, her spirit haggard, drained, not by fear but by knowledge. 'No. Not him. But the Duke.'

In profile she was harder, contemplating a space between us. Her voice with its erratic accents and untraceable origins was neither wholly regretful nor wholly compassionate, but a low mingling of both. 'My beloved, for he has been that.' She looked at me again, recognizing me not as friend but as a confidant who could be trusted. 'I have learnt that those we love we very seldom need. He has granted me raptures, marvels, that we enjoyed without truly sharing. Now, amid the shouts and trumpets, he has already forgotten me.' Her smile halted, mused, recovered with curious gaiety. 'So I go. When perhaps he does need me, he will remember me as his one true love, order masses for my soul, dark elegies . . . but, in a year from today, a rumour of my return would stop his heart like a thunderbolt, then freeze that

163

undying love of his.'

Whatever my face showed must have moved her, for she kissed me, though faintly, immediately withdrawing into the latest gossip, that Sieur de Mesney had lost his voice from speaking too often of death. But soon she was grave again.

'He will never come back. He will ride on and on, and the domes and minarets he sees will always dissolve before him. He finishes little, accomplishes nothing. He grinds his meat to pieces so small that his belly remains empty, even famished.'

'And Perceval?'

She pondered awhile, then briefly glinted, though her famous, milk-white hands, usually aquiver, like moths, still languished. 'To be worshipped is no gift from Paradise, which indeed it slights. The Duke has never awarded him a serious thought, despite his favours and demands and savage affections. He sees him as I do a flower, and you, my friend, see a book in a language you don't understand but which would make a most useful gift. His own longings are immodest, but Perceval's . . .' she considered, 'he does not abase himself to power, he does not seek power, yet he exercises it without fluttering more than an eyelash, and that very seldom.' Her sudden smile had no malice, but mischievous pleasure in both men: 'And I myself, without needing it, have more power than any duke. His strength lies only at the end of the rainbow, Perceval knows it, and is willing to accompany him, without knowing the direction or how to explain why.' Her eyes accosted me fully, for the first time, genuinely inquiring, green under black, tarns on a chilled moor. 'Does he speak to you of a land of Thule?'

'He has done so. It is perhaps no land.'

'It is no land, but it is my enemy. More, it is the Duke's enemy, dangerous not to me but to him. The Duke has the nature of a poet, without the talent. Yet he has more talent than our Perceval.'

She ceased. I wondered whether she was unable or unwilling to continue. She was looking away, again part of the desolate surroundings, and, when she did resume, her tone was flat, barely concerned. 'He, Perceval, has some yearning, a poignancy, which such as you can discern more clearly than I can, a willingness to discover a truth, if truth there be. I have not, nor does my Duke. Do you know. . . .' Again her eyes widened with exquisite and simultaneous astonishment, doubt, delight, changing so swiftly to scepticism tinged with dismay. 'I enjoy not truth, of which I know nothing, merely the world with its masks, and occasional face. The rough and outcast, the smooth and the wicked, even the treacherous. I enjoy the laughter.' And her own laughter shook like a pennant against her pallor. 'Colour . . . snow blown by the wind, pretty facings gone in a trice, in

164

a *minute*, which poor folk so fear. Columbines in a dark place. As for me . . . the adventuress from sinful Asia! I am not wicked, I am not evil. . . .' She drifted away, with a smiling glance that seemed apologetic. 'Wickedness is rapid, spontaneous like the Duke. But evil . . . is it not very slow, like rot in the Palace, gradually uncoiling, spreading, staining. Evil is deeply pondered . . . Hell-smitten trinkets in hands very acute . . . schemes of the blind? No, I am not that, nor Clinschur's plaything, poisoned harlot, destroyer of Christian households! Arraigned before God, for infecting several men, not a few women.' She continued to sound witty, with mock-lewdness. 'I cannot talk of "Honour", "Names", the "Golden Fleece", shed tears on impulse, step over mountains. I believe myself incapable of the extraordinary. But the Duke . . . he has no time to learn this new word, honesty. There's power in that too. Honesty! A denial of illusions of Honour, needing no spear. A burgher's word, a grocer's bond, yet fatal to his House.'

I think that at this our thoughts went towards Perceval, who claimed no House, swore no pledges, was neither honest nor dishonest, who came in order to withdraw, having unwittingly changed the light. He could flow with love, never be shaken by lust, Cundré the reverse: both were probably unknowable.

She had, perhaps after all from Clinschur, an ability to know the unspoken. She was friendly but troubled. 'There is always somewhere else. He is good. He understands . . . much.'

Her intonation was perplexing. Wistful? Envious? Mannered? Sardonic? Rancour was not with her. She was very beautiful.

Weariness slouched between us, her sexuality faded to vaporous sheen, and though we spoke further, nothing was said.

16

Escorted by Scottish guards, Cundré left in a closed litter, following a declaration that she would return at Epiphany. The populace threw mud at her windows, crying that all would now be well, for the Duchess would be back and Swiss gypsies receive their deserts. What these were, few knew, lacking knowledge of Swiss, some believing them a pack of white dogs. As for the Princess, she had defiled the dutiful and pious Duke, yet was also culpable for abandoning him on the eve of his new adventure. She tore out men's hearts, then left for spoilations elsewhere; should be hanged for treason before burning for sorcery.

Master Gregorie, astrologist and botanist, continually discussing 'the Universal' as if it were his private estate, foretold that she would reach her destination, which he could not disclose, and

165

that the swallows would soon be leaving. Cheers magnified. She was pest, diseased whore letting the moon out of her backside. She had flown through the sky in a chariot pulled by dragons and drowned an old man in a cauldron which she had sworn would restore his youth.

Rejoicings ceased when a white rose-bush beneath the Duke's orrery overnight turned red, a bad omen but which might, as all prayed, pertain only to the Princess. The Archbishop, however, was uncertain, and the astrologers took a holiday.

Even Perceval was uncertain where she had gone. We both wondered whether in the bitter attractions of fear and pity, or in her singular turn of wit, she had journeyed to distant Clinschur, to his flowers of delight and peril, his suffering, and intoxications. I saw Clinschur as at once her hateful father, damaged lover, malicious child. She was his judge and victim, never quite escaping him, and never, Perceval for once volunteered, never quite wanting to.

Perceval, somewhat melancholy, blue eyes distrait, said, 'Yet she will never stray far, though she will not come back.' He could say little of the Duke's feelings save that he spoke boldly yet perhaps defiantly of the importance of Epiphany. Had there been a quarrel? He did not know. Choleric as ever, the Duke was enthralled by prospects of victory, the breakthrough, a royal crown, empire. The Pope had given or sold him a feather from St Michael's wing, though possibly mistakenly, I judged it that of an ostrich.

In the Palace all knew that the holy ardour of the Duke would humiliate his enemies, though a monkish proposal that he should walk on his knees to Mullery-sur-Ayré to pray to Our Lady of Victories, was discouraged. The striking of St Martin's bell to promulgate Perceval's brainchild, November Carnival, was delayed by a dispute between two foremost champions about who should first greet the Duke after victory. One, the Burgrave of Beavain, black visaged, his tunic blocked with yellow and green, with stars and new moon on his shield, claimed pre-eminence through descent from Charlemagne. By no means, the Landgrave of Detmold, scarred and doughty, responded, his descent was through a source worse than carnal. His own family was sired by a Byzantine emperor, though his name he could not pronounce and was unable to write. They appealed to the Duke, who embraced them simultaneously and declared that he would greet himself.

Eventually Carnival began. I watched from a turret. All houses had open doors, with coloured finery, and lanterns already glowing through damp air already fading. Here was the hour of lazar-house prophets, the zany *jongleur*, one-eyed huntsman,

166

the nimble-witted charlatan doctor, mountebank priest, dancing imp, on a deceptive bridge between real and false, seen and unseen. Lofty arches streaming with leaves and ribbons loomed through swathes of mist, beneath which, horses dully shining with Murano glass, trundled wagons and wheeled platforms, on which mummers and singers, tumblers and jesters enacted the joys and threats of existence. A sea pageant displayed monsters, shelled, green, dripping, periodically belching stars, weeds, smoke, from scaly throats and thickly painted mouths fretted with honed, massive teeth. On high poles were the familiar emblems; cheers rose for the dolphin, residue of famous Apollo; an ingeniously fashioned strip of cardboard became a mirror, tool of lubricious Venus. A velvet panther was acclaimed as the Saviour, though some might remember that other redeemer, Dionysus, cruel and mysterious. Phaeton steered his glistening chariot up a creaking rainbow manipulated by flowery Isis, hooted at for resembling the witch Cundré. Torches waved for a monstrous staring giantess on a wooden horse, bloodstained heads dangling from her neck, Hecate, unspeakable Great Queen of Hell. There stalked that predicted lion, with tail longer than its body, derided as emblem of Venice, as a threat to the Duke, but cheered by all children for being, very simply, a lion. Farmyard cries swirled as a boy, swart as a miner, climbed a victory arch, lost grip, fell, to lie crookedly inert, oozing, already, my neighbour chuckled, an angel in Paradise. A choir passed on in a cart with scarlet wheels obscenely reviling the knavish Spider King, Clinschur's nephew, then a tumbril achoke with decorated pigs, which was greeted with scurrilous prayers. St Joachim lurched by alongside Presbyter John, Ethiopian priest-king. The Merlin, in green cloak and tall black hat, was pelted from roof and balcony. A huge artificial hare misled pregnant girls, scared of harelips appearing on their babies. Youths of the Band of Joy in spangled hose scuttled between the tableaux, tossing powders to explode amongst the crowds, mocking the great, yelling imprecations. Near silence descended, towers, balustrades, steeples seemed dimmer, heavier, when prancing as if stung, brandishing scythes, black streamers, flowing behind them, there emerged from now cadaverous gloom the skeletons of the Dance of Death, naked skulls grinning atrociously.

Enthroned on the Cathedral terrace, receiving idolatrous love and acclamations, the Duke was encased in Mars-red Soissons steel. An image of irrefutable authority, a rock impervious to wild tides. No Spider King dared sneer, Black Brothers crouched low, Starlings hid. Augustus, Saviour of Past and Future, envy of Archangels, a tremor on whose face would paralyse Pope and Emperor. Above him, beacon in November mists, his helmet

167

blazed with the Ruby of Flanders, the war-god's eye, marvel of Christendom. 'Our Duke,' the people bawled, and the Swiss were already trampled. On the steps beneath him, under resplendent banners – the Dragon of Foix, Tusk of Marvoil, Golden Apple of Polignac, Bear's head of Arthur – was stationed a thin, sable apparation, hooded, arms folded, motionless, whose significance was nowhere mentioned but which all knew.

17

We drifted into Sagittarius, Arthur's month, propitious, the Duke said more than once. The sky, however, had turned spiteful, bitter winds sounded in the hills, early frost smudged the roads. Several hundred tents filled wagons strapped to roan, jennet and foot-slogging criminals. Metalled grooms scuttled around the horses, the Duke's Guard assembled, three hundred and seventy noblemen, esquires, archers, men-at-arms, far outnumbered by cooks, barbers, dentists, musicians, chroniclers, jesters, hounds-men. Six thousand cavalry had splendour of badge and crest vying with that of culverin, bombard, serpentine and springard, weapons of dishonour, the veterans grumpled. Weaponry was stacked amongst massed gold and silver plate, rolled tapestries, largess for cowed populations. Mercenaries, Scots, Welsh, Tuscan, were still roaring in taverns, chasing women and boys. The convoy of baggage mules, litters, wagons, barrows, pack-horses, would extend three leagues. Horns resounded as if from deep waters, seal moans from the uncharted and unchartable.

I could not but observe, as the army pushed through the cold towards the Old Duke's Gate – the least convenient, but homage from his faithful son – that all was creaking, muddled, agonizingly slow, the despondent horses overladen with metal and flesh, their steam rising as if from surly braziers. From a market cross a blind man raged at soldiers, with heads bowed against the dark wind: 'The day of the Lord will come as a thief in the night: then the heavens shall vanish with a roar and the elements melt with a fervent heat, the earth also and all its works be consumed.' I imagined a stronghold overpowering yet waxen, outspread under a fierce sun: the castled galleon, loaded with guns, yet rudderless.

When Perceval visited me I was astonished to see him, revoking his earlier vow, in light, delicately fashioned armour, holding a shield, very clumsily, so that it hung like a painting from a crooked nail. The sword was cumbersome on his slight frame and he confessed that, though his helm was the Duke's gift, he found he could not close its visor. As though parodying the Red

Knight who had earned him fame, his plume was blood red; also his gauntlet, cuirass, greaves. 'They will all know me.' His smile was abashed, and I too had to smile. We must both have recalled tales of a fiery youth belabouring monsters, felling champions, shattering half an army with magic spear. I did mention the legend of his sword which, if broken, was always restored by a magic well. He sins who disbelieves it, a poet had sung.

His nod was softly appreciative. 'That was scarcely true, though neither a wilful lie. Or so I suppose. And now, at last, a real battle.' He was sombre, a little older, one of those princes who so often encounter three coffins in a dark wood. 'It is coming. It has always been coming.' He touched his sword-hilt, by no means boastful but as if to reassure not himself but the weapon. I knew that, always horrified by blood, he never displayed fear, perhaps, unlike myself, never felt it.

Later, an absurd legend was gathered by poets that, whenever he threw a spear, it always returned to his hand. As a symbol of fortune it was apt enough, though I doubt if any spear left his hand or that he ever held one correctly. Another tale was somewhat more credible, that he knew the art of curing himself, like the wounded hart consuming wild dittany.

From the window he looked down at martial disarray. When he spoke, he was self-mocking, not abject but avoiding all pride. 'I can never resemble red-haired, scornful Ulysses, hateful and hating!'

'Resemble only yourself, not any Ulysses worn out by too many singers. No. But in your loyalty, to the Duke. . . .'

For an instant his features crinkled, as if he were striving to remember a duke. He moved from the window like a young, troubled sleep-walker before shaking his bright head free of thoughts.

'I too get a hunger . . . temptations. Difficulties, doors to be opened, bridges and thresholds to be crossed. It is not given me to discover purposes I can utter. . . .' He looked at me, anxious to remember my name. 'They make me hear old matters. The ladies and so on . . . the children. Listen.' Now gazing at me intently, so that the clatter below dwindled, he recited, questioning, not quite convinced, lines inappropriate to warriors:

'I form the light and create darkness.
I make peace and create evil.'

He resumed his usual Other Worldly tranquillity, but without explanation of the curious verse. 'Suppose, just suppose. . . .' Then ceased, leaving me to suppose, in which I failed, sceptical of lords likely to make peace, though evil was generally evident

169

on all sides. He flushed, was indistinct. 'Finding the centre . . . but it is always empty.' Head lowered, he stood very still, then said, seemingly mistaking me for a circle of rapt children. 'Sugar and spice and all things nice.' With his customary taste for the inadequate or nonsensical.

In his self-preoccupation, the chastisement ahead gave him no misgivings. My own government had forbidden me to accompany the Duke in a campaign it judged wasteful and unnecessary.

He said little more, allowed me to embrace him, gave a half-smile, a little regretful, a little resigned, and as always concluding something else, then departed. Again the city was rowdy. While horses slipped and plunged on frosted roads, very soon the Duke and his nobles, isolated from wind and cold by shut helms, salets, heavy cloaks, were riding up a gilded ramp hung with dry columbine. His own battle harness was speckled with violet and gold, jewels adrift on his purple coating beneath which glimmered ringed steel. His horse trappings, black glossy satin, were streaked with gold and topaz, as were his jambs, from which protruded immense scarlet spurs, curled like horns.

Thus had the Dukes always departed, to struggle on behalf of their people. Beside him trotted a riderless Castilian mare, representing the Duchess. He bore an ivory mace. When he bared his head to acknowledge prolonged ovations, his face was seen dyed martial red. As in some cherished *geste*, his knights flaunted ladies' sleeves, kerchiefs, bracelets, more treasured, they proclaimed, than Caucasian gold, Regensburg taffeta, riches of Cathay. The ladies themselves, forgetting to shiver, packed windows, balustrades, parapets, and were waving, crying Godspeed, though some, indeed too many, covered their faces. Muffs and wraps doubtless concealed histories of youth and sport, surely with accounts of Roosebecque in which knights piled up raw, stinking mounds of Flemish rebels, encouraged by seeing flames in the heavens. Thousands more were suffocated, having packed too closely against the pitiless riders.

My Swedish forbears, before battle, would chew a red and white fungus, entrancing themselves with Other World giddiness, indifferent to pain, reckless in assault. The Duke, Hercules carrying the world on his eyebrows, would have disclaimed such means, intoxicated by tempests induced by his will. Now he was up, up the ramp, at the very top, with all magnificence, seeming to vanish into the sky. Protected by no dittany or rune, he would wear his coronet in the conflict, however paltry, for no true knight attacks a head anointed and crowned, though, I remembered uneasily, no Swiss was a true knight.

Soon all Christendom heard of struggle, somewhere, anywhere, on the edge of the world, beginning with seven lords of the

Golden Fleece challenging in finely tempered language seven foes to single combat. This was declined, the seven champions received only taunting laughter, mud slung at their feathers and pennants, insulting whistles. Snow fell. Christmas was passed in the field, the Duke offering a banquet in which dazzling plate was more plentiful than the provender. Skirmishes followed hasty, inconclusive sieges, minor rebuffs, but from the camp Pope and Emperor received bulletins from the Duke that, on the morrow of victory, he would declare himself King.

Winter deepened, lakes froze. Unexpectedly the Duke had to abandon five hundred guns under snow and hail. Infuriated he hanged scores of captives, amongst whom, we understood, were deserters. A pall hung over city and plain, mountain and hamlet. His vanguard was repulsed in a narrow pass, the main army forced back by mere scavengers and outcasts. Defiant, he stamped his foot for a new army, greater than Alexander's: he sent haughty tax demands, promising in return the most sensational of coronations. Towns protested, villages trembled, his Florentine and English fled by night. He regathered, advanced again, himself ahead of all, mace aloft, in whirling flourish, into the dank breath of Hector. Weeks later he was dug from the ice, face smashed into pulp, body known only by certain missing upper teeth and a birthmark on the thigh. The Spider King, after so long, was seen to smile.

Perceval? I knew, without being told, as if from the flick of a scribe's quill, that he was safe, riding aimlessly in his usual unaffected repose amid blood, crashing bodies, barbarian uproar, until plucked from disaster by some unknown figure on a horse with red ears. Did he, I wondered, have a hawk dyed on his brutal arms? Probably. His presence was easy to surmise, for lovers of youth have powers prophetic and, people say, supernatural.

Four

... this smile in which man divinely recognized the fellow man, the fellow soul – the essence of human compatibility, the birthplace of human language: the smile.

Herman Broch

All sciences save this merely use arguments to prove conclusions, like those which purely speculate, or possess conclusions universal and imperfect. Experimental science alone can perfectly discover what Nature can effect, what Art can effect, what Magic can effect. It alone teaches how to test the lunacies of magicians, just as logic tests argument.

Roger Bacon

At all courts there exist remarkable individuals who, without talent, without distinguished family, and without friends in high places, achieve intimacy with the great, and finally, none knows how, become a power in the land.

Duc de Saint-Simon

1

Here at Kremitz, in the Manor of Love, all days succeeded each other quietly but without monotony. Sometimes, like a waterfall, pigeons dropped from trees, for scraps. Wheels were always turning, smoke rising, voices joining in friendly exchanges.

Most but not all couples were married: several young men shared hut and pallet without rebuke or scandal. Children played timeless games – Nick Nock, Pope's Posts, Fly-away George, absorbed and unreflective. We accepted the wisdom of Boehme: that labour and study must progress through joy, life's masterpiece.

Couples obtained a divorce very simply, confessing sadness before the whole community. Many Moravian Brothers were here, having renounced swearing, soldiering, town life. Ours was one of many settlements concealed in woods, in a fold of the hills. Dreams were haunted by no Great Captain, Saint, Martyr, or Grail floating in Other Worldly sunlight. The Gospels themselves were respected as remarkable, but, flawed and incomplete, four books among many, some of which were better.

Urban Europe was spinning with notions of mathematical harmonies, geometrical certainties, regular cosmic metres affecting constellations and particles alike. They concerned Kremitz no more than whether the earth was a divine agency, illustrious metaphor, incoherent accident. Planets might still sing, but meanwhile there was work to do.

Outside, crouching from half-starved mercenaries, shivering from ague, fleeing Plague, fighting for bread during siege, people yet bulged with suggestive nonsense or lay felled by terrors that accompanied the approaching death of the century. A trumpet had already sounded from the sky, in which peasants saw men and animals fighting. Blood had fallen over Ghent. Few at Kremitz cared about any century, or the new telescopes in Padua, in the city, and my own natal chart disclosed that, owing to chronic ill-temper from Saturn, I had been fifteen years dead.

The Parable of the Vineyard dominated the Manor of Love: work well without reckoning the fee. Many had hearkened to the shepherd, Hans Bohm, reviler of priestcraft, who had reinforced his flying words with drum-beats. Princes of Church and State should possess no more than did their inferiors, allowing sufficiency for all. At Kremitz we shared goods, rights, duties. Cooks and woodmen had equal voice with scholars and elders. Children, avoiding middens because of devils, wandered from hut to hut, welcome in all. The simple minded were respected. Meals were communal. Gardeners gardened, cooks cooked, students studied, even the idle were not gainsaid rights of idleness. Jesus, a working man, had not condemned play, nor had Francis.

The Kingdom of Heaven is within you – but *you*, Deacon Matthias taught, meant a community. 'No man hath seen God at any time. If we love one another, God dwells in us and His love is perfected in us.'

Hope abounded. Though apparently in chaos, the world was always struggling towards order. Lives seemingly worthless might yet be withstanding an Attila, a Klingsor; a coward be fulfilling an ancient ordinance that none shall save his life by shedding another's blood. Outside, Europe was shrinking. Angered by defeat at Lepanto, encouraged by astrological omens, the Turks were massing, though the Emperor left them to the Privy Council to do what it would. Very little. Muslim hordes had grasped much of Hungary, were belabouring the frontiers of Styria,

174

Moravia, Silesia. Perhaps some unfortunates now regretted the Duke, though, yes, exciting government can be as dangerous as inert government. Simultaneously, the search for silver and pepper entailed cravings for vastness and distance. Horizons stimulated like poppy-juice. Galileo had discovered Jupiter's moons, though our own moon continued unperturbed.

Bohemia, where the Boi had once hung temples with severed heads and raged against upstart Rome, was savaged by battles and Hungarian typhus. Preachers were announcing the Last Days; that Jesus and Peter had been overthrown by John and the Holy Spirit, with God exacting fearsome penalties. Or that the Devil was now lord of the world, or that Antichrist reigned, or perhaps Emperor Gamalean, and, with the century about to end, God was preparing another dispensation, replacing that which had begun when He expelled the gods of Rome.

I myself regarded preachers, zealots and most philosophers as conceited madmen, and was happy not to see five wounds in the sky; the bite of the pox was more dangerous than Antichrist. A current belief, that if a man labours for good he may be damned for pride in thinking that this ensures salvation, was nonsensical. Omens – cross-eyed children, owls, quacks from hens – were frauds: mirrors were but mirrors, not devices to trap the soul, wheels were wheels, holly merely holly. Dr Luther was a hysterical clown, bawling that he was the ripe shard, the world a gaping anus. His monstrous downpour of words made me laugh, made me shudder. Determined to escape the bloody convulsions through which zealots yearned to destroy Europe, then win salvation by restoring it, I welcomed the words of Ammianus Marcellinus, that no beasts are such enemies of mankind as are most Christians in their deadly mutual hatred. This evil century, despite the new science, had failed to transform God from He to *it*: love, generosity, reason.

A man digging, a sight once simple and reassuring, now had sinister suggestiveness. Behind stupendous walls, hooks, pincers, pulleys were at work on bodies. Great captains, dispossessed lords and knights crazed from lack of sugar, stormed through ever-dwindling pastures, hopelessly pursuing imaginary game and women. Children dreamed of Sultan Selim, surrounded by a hundred dwarfs with large heads, tiny legs, their midget swords yet able to slice off a hand swift as a bird's wink.

Prices soared; the eye, wrote a chronicler, ached at them. The Pope abolished the Turks by a formal bull, but apparently with incorrect phrasing. Everywhere the pox ate like acid into flesh, undermined bones, besieged lip and nostril. Crapulous bandits, no longer seeking forage but a riotous death, were firing haystacks, dancing around those concealed within.

175

Kremitz had no single founder. Fleeing from turmoil, families united for protection and discovered that from handclasps, communal labour, quiet speech, distress could be confounded. Refugees came from pillaged castles, monasteries, towns. Former monks arrived with Jews, peasants, bankrupt knights, threadbare pedlars, radical weavers, military deserters loyal to the Emperor's predecessor who had scandalized the respectable by declaring that he was neither Papalist nor Lutheran but Christian. Carpenters, tailors, smiths gathered here: fence and hut and bed were strong, clothes simple but firm. Prayer was mostly private. For some it was strenuous exercise, not petition but purposeful concentration, for others a mouthful of air. One should not, Jan of Zwickhau had written, pray for external gifts, but extract treasure from within. A few confessed their sins to each other, though I did not. There was no regular leadership, save for the benign influence of such as Deacon Matthias. Particular individuals solved particular problems, then retired. Children were listened to. In Jesus' words, the children of this world are wiser than the children of light, an adage controversial and enigmatic. A boy grumbled that life was worth only a peck of beans, then grinned, confessing that he loved beans. None took vows binding himself to Kremitz, to Moravian tenets. All could depart at will, though none had done so. We enjoyed some protection from a nearby castle whose lord, jocular and easy, sometimes visited, eating his share, working, rather perfunctorily, at hedge or ditch, passing us news, commending our comradeship before retiring to his serfs and armed bullies.

St Paul, worthy enough in his way, not mine, held that those led by God's spirit are all God's sons, abandoning their gross nature. In the Manor of Love, it sounded plausible. Diplomatically, assuring my station, I quoted as best I could Jesus' text, that God is spirit, and received approving smiles. My beliefs about God I did not utter, but mentioned Jesus' further maxim that whatever failed to affect the soul was inessential. More smiles. I did, however, wonder whether Jesus, with talk of damnation, had really done more good than harm.

Despondency, it is said, is a cruel neighbour, and cheerfulness pervaded. Songs for digging, kneading, baking, sowing, all at odds with the hell outside, swept by Luther's pernicious thunder. 'If women grow exhausted or even die through pregnancies, that does no harm. Let them have children until they die, for that is the reason for their existence.'

Love as policy I had hitherto mistrusted. Jesus, apt to offer it as a placebo, was nevertheless a figure of impatience, intolerance. In my childhood those who loved their children most loudly also thrashed them most viciously. A farmer hanged his favourite

176

daughter to save her from sin. At Kremitz people seemed better than Jesus, threatening no one. Patience, tolerance, were unfailing. 'Perchance, Brother, I may be mistaken' was the least amiable rejoinder I had yet heard. When a newcomer, gaunt, still yellow-eyed from tertian fever, stole a loaf, he was embraced, then given three more. Perplexed, he ate well, settled happily and was soon carving clumsy tops for children, who played with them in order to please him.

I wondered nevertheless how long we could shelter from the tempests sweeping the Empire, or perhaps more significant, repel danger from within. Life, however well ordered, can secrete aggression, the boredoms of perfection, a desire to be hanged. Trying to overcome doubts, I listened to texts, songs, memories. Memories of a forest inhabited by phantoms, of fire-worshipping Balts over-ready to change into wolves, a tree-king who periodically killed himself. Not material for Galileo, for Kepler. Nevertheless, the speakers were peculiarly blessed. Plague ignored us, violence stayed its hand, goodness deflected the monstrous. One stalwart, a Leyden merchant, had fled Catholic persecution for 'incest', having married a nun. He spoke of the Emperor playing a form of chess, always against 'a lucky one', any courtier out of favour. Imperial victory was believed propitious for the Empire, though conditions suggested that he was no adept at his own game.

Machiavelli had asserted that rulers of great achievement, who despise sincerity and know how to confuse the cunning, finally outmatch those who govern their activity by honour. He may have remembered the Duke. *Honour* had dropped from the international word hoard, the Great Captains knew it not, nor did the Pope. In Sweden, St Bridget had compared the Duke to Lucifer for his envy, to Judas for his cruelty, and, committed only to evil, murderer of souls, more abominable than Jews.

In its moral balance, quiet Kremitz could be the world's centre, an Other World where little was forbidden, much was avoided. One Brother, solidly hewn, white bearded, would read aloud from Paul, always astonished, always delighted: 'I knew a Christian who, fourteen years back, whether in the body or out of it, God knows, was snatched up as far as the third heaven. And I know that this same man, whether in the body or out of it, I know not, God knows, was snatched up into Paradise, and heard words so secret that I may not repeat them.'

I thought of Perceval with his strangely lit towers, gleams of adventure, unfinished stairways.

Deacon Matthias, patriarchal hurdle-maker, all beard and eyebrow, one of those called by Erasmus the poop and prow of simple virtue, felt all this was confirming Christ's promise that through faith we pass from death to life, that whoever loses his life shall save it. He disbelieved in vulgar immortality. Salvation was access to light; illumination; shedding of spiritual blankness. He that hath eyes to see, let him see. Christ, in many Kremitz beliefs, was a higher awareness waiting within us, perhaps not the highest, accessible but difficult, with many coevals, Orpheus and the like. The Cross was the tortured moment of decision to abandon desires comfortable but commonplace, Ascension, resurrection. Meister Eckhart, I was informed, would stake his life on the fact that, by will, humanity could pierce a wall of steel.

I was less readily persuaded by Anna, nervous orphan of about twenty, with some allure despite plain dress, kerchiefed head, clogs. Out of tentative smiles she half whispered some Greek's nonsense about the soul returning to the body four centuries after death. For her I had mild lust, unlikely to be reciprocated.

The work allotted me was to keep friendly with the castle lord, assess newcomers, oversee the school where parent and child often studied together. I arranged a small library of salvaged manuscripts and printed books. We had hopes of building a press, two master printers being amongst us.

The day's work over, we regathered from fishpond and bakehouse, mill and school, for bread, soup, occasional bacon and the wine I had procured from the castle. At meals, old wisdom was pondered, then debated in friendly humour. Life was simple as a bucket. The songs – peasant and tavern ballads. Reformer's hymns, robust Free City anthems, calmed the bruised mind, the bereaved and luckless. Messer Leonardo had called music the shaping of the invisible.

In this peaceful summer even I could feel that even if no God existed, many had something of the Divine. A star glimmered in each head, the young and the old. Without sententious pledges, brotherhood bounded us: surrounded by perils, we felt freed, as though nearing that third Heaven. Conscience guided. 'There are those in the darkened inn of the world who need no candles, but are guided by the inner light of their own goodness.' None agonized for the lunatic and impassioned. Life was sustained not by dogma but by questions. Curiosity, as Perceval had discovered, was a virtue. That lens and mathematics at Tübingen and in the City showed Earth no longer the hub of the universe dismayed few, certainly not me. The questions concerned·me less than the questioners: their natures and pasts, their secrets. They did not, however, obsess me. I was unlikely to be confused with him whom the Milanese philosopher said was the supreme martyr because he felt the most deeply.

The future seemed embalmed in this sturdy haven, but did the man beside me surreptitiously envy, did the woman smiling at the loom cherish a grudge, did thoughful Anna crave a body alongside her in the bed? What is hidden beneath the wave can be more powerful than the wave itself.

A question more immediate was that of violence. Early Anabaptists had rejected it wholly, *Resist not Evil*, and met their assailants naked, in the spirit of love. The outcome was distressing, and later they had filled Europe with battle-cries. Kremitz opinion agreed that spiritual resistance alone was permitted the upright man. Not myself upright, I was uneasy.

As often as was seemly, I retired to my library and perused the ironies of Marcellinus. From him I learnt that dreams were unknown around Mount Athos. Occasionally I tried to interest Anna, surely lustrous under the skirt, but she only stared at me in shy bewilderment. By restraining my desire I maintained it, in chivalrous fashion, which did not best suit me.

At Kremitz, girls were neither seduced nor won, but came to men naturally, like the silent embrace of sunlight and rose. They did not come to me, and in the wake of my lost lady I scarcely minded.

Sometimes, summer hush lay over the camp and we all sat contentedly gazing at poppies amid our ripening corn, at butterflies gleaming above mint and sunflower. The wise doubtless meditated, I merely thought of life as I had known it.

It might be demanded, not very insistently, why I, no obvious choice for a Manor of Love, had chosen to seek it. The Duke's death had deprived me of my mission. The Duchy was lost, swallowed by the Spider King. A few spoke of him as still living, wandering the world, in search of a crown, living with hermits, but survivors of the battle declared that he had left half his face in the ice, the rest having been gnawed by wolves. 'May the earth rest lightly upon him,' Perceval said, long afterwards. Myself, I agreed with Heraclitus that the dead are no more than dung.

I had considered resuming royal service, but was distracted by an incautious love for a married lady while sojourning with the Lord of Maastrich, hospitable enough, during whose afternoon sleep no living being was permitted on the road, no bells could be rung, no word uttered. Dogs were muzzled and birds reproached. My lady was always greeting me fondly in an arbour, but only to complain of the husband she had no real desire to flee. So much of life is a search for grievance. I imagined her, soft, listless, thinking of me as merely a figure of dream, as though colour could devise the object it tinted. She herself was scared of colour, distrusted even the light. I brooded too long over her fine but uncertain gaze, high breasts, downy fathomless loins, until, uninhibited by my host's ban on afternoon noise, Swiss and Slovaks assaulted Maastrich, I rode away, leaving her to the husband, my diplomatic skills assisting me through warring factions. Watching tiny governments rise and fall, I nodded at Machiavelli's further dictum, that whoever organizes a state presupposes that all men are mad. Bearing the irritations of lost love, I recovered more swiftly than I had intended.

Here at Kremitz I found crisis. A notorious mercenary, Crazy Ritter, expelled by his troopers for enormities outrageous even to them, was skulking in the countryside. None was safe. Once I had convinced the community that I was no killer, I received smiles and embraces, and was invited to join the debate about Crazy Ritter. Should he be welcomed as a fellow sufferer, or excluded as an unrepentant sinner? Did sin entail evil, or did sin not exist, being merely a faultiness in mortal arrangements? I disliked the prospect of Crazy Ritter, and disliked still more Deacon Matthias's argument that, in retaliating against criminals, one becomes criminal oneself. The old man informed me, very mildly, that I should treat Crazy Ritter with gentleness, while denying him my inner allegiance. Just so.

2

Occasional reports of Perceval reached me through gossip, rumour, miasmal libel. On the lost field, frantic for rescuing hands, he had thrown his sword into a pond. Indigent, he was seeking a stray princess. On the Rhine, imprisoned as a changeling deceiver, he had vanished, the windowless cell remaining locked from within. With a forbidden song he had incited a lascivious and convulsive dance mania amongst children, leaving three dead. Some simpleton had lent him money, trusting him for repayment when they met in the Other World. From himself, I heard nothing. Grateful for company, he never regretted its absence and, complete in himself as a cherry-tree, would not always have noticed it.

Kundry was more ascertainable. Fat Henry of England had demanded her portrait which his Cardinal, Butcher Boy Blue, slyly altered, so that the royal interest evaporated. In sulphurous wrath, running a black tongue into the universe, Luther damned her. Allegedly, she had died in Sodom on the Tiber, and was worshipped in Lithuania as an earth goddess.

In the library, I found a description of a Kundry:

180

Sister to King Arthur, she was very merry and sportive; a most pleasing singer; though dark in her face, very finely built, not too fat, not too thin, with hands of utmost delicacy, perfect shoulders, skin softer than silk; tall and straight in carriage; altogether the warmest and most sensual lady. Merlin had taught her astronomy and she learnt so excellently that she became a fine scholar. She spoke gently, with delightful intimacy, and was more amiable and desirable than all other women alive, when in a quiet mood, but in wrath very hard to appease.

I should probably see both again. Experience suggested that little derives from rootless chance: luck, coincidences, are superficial, traceable to niceties of existence larger than they seem. Fate comes not from planets but from ancient rules, some obvious, some riddles and dreams, abstruse tests, to be obeyed or flouted. Princesses in castles or on summits, monsters and crones, peril and devils, trolls, enemies at the ford or waiting in a maze, are messages from the blood. Discrepancies are illusion, for all are within a web pulled across the earth, unseen but powerful as atoms and mind.

Perceval's arrival at Kremitz was thus less remarkable than some versions suppose. Likewise his very survival from conflict and downfall. There are always those favoured by a trick of charm, of smile, of insolent wit, who effortlessly receive all, usually without deserving it. They are protected. Perceval's flair for bad judgement rewarded him well. I was near the gate when he appeared. Though he had journeyed far, he was still clean and graceful, despite a slight diminution of lustre in that bright mass of hair, blue eyes less pretty. The boyish face had deepened, losing bloom, though the indolent cordiality was gracious as ever. He greeted me without surprise, rather, indeed apologetically, as though a trifle unpunctual. His embrace was more polite than heartfelt, though at once gaining me admiration hitherto withheld. He happily surrendered to the common stock his spare cloak and sandals, his well-filled wallet, preserved none knew how. Glad to be rid of them, no Crazy Ritter, he was immediately at home, children summoning him to play quintain and Knock-me-down Peter. He built them a bridge, and, though it speedily collapsed, they were more grateful to him than to Tall Kasper who repaired it. To the aged and feeble he was as concerned as the best of us. His stories were no longer of glass towers, Isles of Birds, chatty animals, but of lovers sundered or crumbling to dust, complex promises, magicians doubting their spells, a headstrong lord galloping to death, of souls lost, sold, stolen by Great Captains.

181

Anna listened as intently as the childlren. Also Deacon Matthias, glad of the narrator, then quoting with affectionate nods that text about God selecting foolish things to confound the wise, and the weak to overcome the mighty. Perceval from the start induced a shift of atmosphere in which I detected from sighs, random words, confessions, our friends' recollections of homes long lost, childhoods vanished but still glistening, marvellous promises. A coloured, unbreaking flux: the dead in their mounds transformed to sleeping princesses, radiant princes in vast halls; boulders gaining blood and flesh from the dead buried beneath them: ghosts and demons routed their own names.

I believed, without being certain, that Perceval too concealed pains and fears he would never reveal: failure with others, the helpless tortured, the black quiver in a garden hitherto beautiful and safe.

'They say we're in prison . . . life, love, forced to drop away, as birds shed feathers. I've never quite believed it, though I've known prisoners . . . sometimes they become gaolers.' He was serious but not solemn, smiles gliding across him. 'I never feel my father's spirit when they invite me to sit on a charger and win a trophy. . . .' His flush was tender, he spoke slowly, against the stammer: 'There is far to go, to feel, to . . . yet in anger, I feel disgraced.'

Anger was unthinkable in those trusting features, that inquiring air of expecting some momentous decision which from me he never received. His eyes drooped, he made uncomfortable efforts to continue, to confide, but managed only what sounded an unnecessary epilogue to what he had already meticulously and vividly described.

'Often there were hedges of mist. Or I was alone under the bright, empty sky. Mud everywhere. Then a lump stirred, it was like watching a head, the hair moving, filled with lice. An English king died like that.' He frowned, evidently his words could not match his recollections, his incoherence distressed him. The mud, the sky, the English king were mere sketches of what he could not reveal. 'Laughter.' He tried again, a student striving to convince his master: 'A girl did me kindness with a single laugh. A sooty fellow limps over to punish her. There are always castles, never near, so seldom reached. On crags, above chasms, on the rim of a plain. Almost all are surrounded by dense briars or guarded by monsters. One . . . by lepers. Those I could help. Bells ring out, very suddenly and harshly. Whenever I manage to cut through the briars, soothe the beast, I find all steps broken, doors rusted or barred. Or I place my foot on the first step and a shudder strikes through me. . . . Always, on the very edge of things, where regions meet.' Groping, he had to cease, his face

182

broken by frustration, before he said ruefully, 'That's all. Overcoming and unravelling ordeals ... no more than that. I want more.'

'The land of Thule?'

He did not hear. 'There was a cave, though none other appeared to see it. There are always gaps ... not voids but entrances. But ...' – the clear eyes searched for a password – 'I was always too late. Almost everything had become dreams. A traveller, Gurnemanz, told me that dreams fulfil themselves. In my own ... an angry woman pursues me. Many arms, many faces. I become a panther, wren, grain of wheat, yet it's very real. Only when I awake is everything so receding, so ghostly.'

I felt him now choosing words not for their solidity but for their colours, part of his love of butterflies, kingfishers, bubbles, and indeed toys and games. Honest, he was also untrustworthy, not treacherous but often mistaken or purblind. Essentially, he remained in cap and bells, each chime a reminder that at Cologne he had murmured a childish rhyme understood to foretell earthquake and, after departing, had been denounced when a steeple fell on a precentor's clerk. Did he ever feel responsible for his own achievements, the good, the ill?

Despite halting tongue he possessed a sleepwalker's confidence, or the silent defiance of a child unable to feel himself liked or attractive, yet aware of secrets of an Other World. He had always delighted in the unfinished, half-glimpsed, the random eye glittering within leaves. Though unconcerned with history, he inhabited the past.

'When I saw the Duke's palace ... roofs, pinnacles, turrets like grapes ... I felt I had reached home, returned to myself. All else seemed long ago, forgotten. At last all doors were open, thresholds were unguarded. Some marvel was awaiting me, something from out of the mists, now shining. Summer had come. Stones rolling away. And I was thinking of Her ... I had dreamed of her as daughter of waves, lady of foam. I had seen her swimming the tides, riding the wind, opening arms to me at crossways. I had seen the white stag in the woods and couldn't rest until I saw it again.' His eagerness lapsed, his voice flattened. 'They hunt, they cure, and they go away.'

Could he mean himself? I was puzzled, until I remembered Gawain. Never having heard him speak for so long, so confidingly, I did not dare interrupt.

'There is a tent by a river ...' – he spoke more to himself than to me, struggling for complete vision – 'a feast is prepared, a loving voice calls, but none is within. Or a hand waves from a white hill. I climb, climb, but reach only a strange laugh in the air. A betrayal, or, yes, an accusation. A dark sun. A man who

183

has killed a bird. . . .'

Virginal in loves and hopes, he would never envy the moral swagger with which Bear Chiefs and Kais had stormed against legions, yet which destroyed their efforts to hold the West.

He recognized me again, we were brothers in an unlikely place. 'When I could not see her beauty, when I failed the wounded lord, I lost all desires, beliefs, loyalties. Time was slow. I was limp as an underground prisoner. Like a stepchild at the mercy of all, I was nothing, under steep, black sky, slanting down at me. Like judgement, but I could not feel. My nose and my horse led me where they willed. Through desolation. The lonely valley. But she returned . . .'

'There is always return . . .'

'Yes. People, gods . . . perhaps they never really depart. It's our eyes and hearts that fail. . . . And with her, and with the Duke, time passed swiftly, all was dancing. I was happy. And the Duke. . . .'

Downcast again, he could not continue, looking around as if for rescue from the trees, the school, even the hen-coop. He choked, brushed his eyes, forced himself on. 'He will not return. He was one of those poor kindly folk who looked to me . . . it is not my right but my penance . . . for a sort of cure. I still wonder what I could have done, why I appeared chosen. The world's harsh voices, making wars. . . .'

He achieved unnatural lucidity, addressing me from my own world of missions and missives, cabals and sections. 'We hear from Dr Luther . . . and from many . . . that God may cherish evil ones, and can reject those who nourish the oppressed. Jesus spoke fair words . . . Orpheus' love . . . but has become a judge. Perhaps he always was. Stern as Rome. The light gets poisoned. . . .'

I myself would from the start have quarrelled incessantly with Jesus, Orpheus would never have transformed me to a silvery fountain or enraptured statue. Attempting humour, I told him that, at the new university of Ingelstadt, Doctor Christophe Rasperger was teaching two hundred ways of interpreting *Hoc est Corpus Meus*. Hocus-pocus!

He did not smile. 'The sad, the ignorant, the cruel. So much talk of sin. . . . I feel no sin, only some burden, and the need to go farther, to reach out. Like a swimmer, like a pilgrim. Looking for new names when all seems nothing. Looking for her, also. I reach a tower, she has just departed. A frontier, she was there a week before. A dying town, they have driven her away with stones. One of the marvellous friends we so seldom see, but know are there.'

I asked something, but again he was distant, listening only to the stir and patter of Kremitz. Sunlight streamed through leaves, he had the suffused radiance I had seen when he stood with the Duke and Princess before the people, that young spirit which was yet denied the abandon of youth, the merry bawdiness, casual capers, the delicious fruits of lust. Too often he stood with hands folded, apologizing for having been born.

'The voices. . . .' He mused as if afflicted with all the hard, disputing factions of Europe. 'They say the Turks are coming, that the Turks do not exist, that we are all Turks. That the Pope is a devil and the English queen a witch. But the Emperor. . . .'

Each word flickered with interior meanings. The Emperor could be fabled Gamalean, or the High Gentleman in the faraway City, or some imaginary visitation. 'The Emperor . . . he might yet . . . he could still. . . .' Again he rubbed his eyes. 'He upholds what must be remedied. The winding paths lead to him, but there are no short cuts. Once I believed they were trodden by the dead, seeking their lost homes. But we must go down them, not craftily but patiently, knowing that darkness can help the light, open secrets, like dog-day heat opening the world.'

Glad of my silence, he was speaking as reasonably as he could ever have done. 'In the uncharted I scented freedoms, as if intended for me alone. . . . Not from pride, but from obligations taught me at the start. I was not always very wrong. An Other World existed, though it could melt at a touch. If described, if sought as a merchant seeks goods, it vanished as if hurt.'

In the contented hum of afternoon, he again lost sight of me, leaving me to wonder how artless, how credulous he really was. He at once responded with the clear, the tangible, which nevertheless resolved nothing.

'Martin Luther told us of a tall hill in Saxony, with a lake on the top of it. Throw a stone in, and gales sweep over the land from the demons imprisoned below.' Evidently he believed this but was now listening to cheerful sounds beyond, mostly from children, while feeling he owed it to me to continue. 'An old fisherman believed that mortals were once animals. Flitting through dreams, starting up under the sun, they revive our wild fears and joys. Horns and tails, wings and siren voices. Temptations to rejoin the pack. The Isle of Birds. . . .'

I imagined Perceval and Kundry, two elements coldly glittering, revolving about each other, never quite touching, bound not by passion but by unspoken spirals of wit in an unending masque.

Kundry would utter that sudden, discordant laugh. Perceval's laughter was unimaginable, perhaps eerie. Without ideas he was helpless before feelings, towards song and tale. Kundry, I thought, had ideas but no great interest in them, they were the casual sparks on an opal. The Grail, which he had seldom mentioned,

185

was conceivably a simple hope, a device to cherish lost existences, purged of the animal, moulded to a shape inviolate in perfection. Then, as if in more than chance, from behind huts, children began singing:

'The World, the world, and the sky far up
was made, was made, was poured from a cup.'

They renewed my reflections about Jesus. Though possessing considerable goodwill, I disparaged motives, not only my own. Jesus might have relished children, as dedicated to himself alone. I knew nothing of his concern for any particular child, though I was aware of a legend of him as a child miraculously drowning three others for taunting his bastardy.

'The world, the world, the sky far up . . .'

The song was nearer, but in the intensity between us my unspoken thoughts were again caught. Perceval, like children, had a flair for perceiving the imperceptible. 'I did once punish. Not, of course, with these hands. . . .' He was shocked by accusations I had not made. 'But there was Brother Irus. It distresses me to say it . . .' – he did not look distressed but insouciant, almost gay – 'he was stupid, he was sour, he said terrible things. That babies who died would still be punished. They would turn on globes of fire, burning away their sins. I was . . . angry. I told him that he would come to ill. I thought he might at once run at me, to strike, and then fall on the ice.'
'I expect he did.' I remembered the talkative youth falling so readily off the Duke's palace. 'No, no. But he dreamed that Jesus flogged him, Jesus himself, so fiercely that he awoke screaming with pain, and covered with blood.'
He smiled, if not in pleasure, at least in wonder, at life's versatility. I wanted to hear more but at last the children were upon him, surrounding him, pushing me away. His light eyes were grateful. They clamoured, 'A story. Tell a story. Tell anything you like.'

3

I enjoyed teaching children, though my method was not that of a Perceval, deprecating his own authority, and assuming that pupils know more than masters. I was also wary of them. Children are as treacherous as any Judas, as cruel as Brother Irus. I was mindful of Savonarola's Florentine Inquisitions manned, if that

186

is the word, entirely by children, waving red crosses as they denounced their teachers, friends, parents, and hurling into the flames whatever paintings and adornments they could grab, screeching against beauty and vanity. Nevertheless, work over, I enjoyed as much as any in the Manor of Love sitting in summer dusk listening to Perceval, whose quiet figure faded with the light, his voice continuing, making its own light.

'Then the Queen fell ill. She whispered to the King, "My malady will kill me, and you will find another wife. But if you choose too hastily you will harm our precious son. So take no wife to comfort you until two blossoms wave in the western wind, from my grave." The King, who loved her, shed tears, promised to do as she wished, and she died. For a while he tended her grave so well that not even a nettle grew there, but at last he became too busy, and began to neglect it, though, when the west wind blew, a faithful courtier would inspect it. You will not be surprised to learn that a day came when he heard that two white-beaded nettles were swaying in the wind. But he had quarrelled with his son, he was enchanted with a tall girl, and the words meant nothing to him, nothing at all.'

This was how I enjoy remembering him, holding old and young rapt and motionless, his words soft as a stream, his manner tender. Yet I had known, almost from the first, that his arrival had doomed peaceful Kremitz. Also, and for once I felt guilt that I did not fully lament this. I had found a refuge, it was provident, harmonious yet, for me, somewhat less than a prison, rather more than a hospital. Each day was oppressive in its inevitable order, its balance, like a zealous pastor. I thought, Worse is better, knowing how irritably I would resent it when it came.

Thus I was swiftly alert for signs of disintegration unseen by others, certainly by Perceval. Of such signs, Crazy Ritter was one, though not the foremost, for though the nobleman behind walls urged watchfulness, danger now threatened more from within our loving community than from without. True, this tiny refuge seemed like the Garden, free of the past in which wisdom corrupts, love turns terrible. Here were kindly, aged faces, competent hands, the darting feet of children loved and loving: friendly instruction, embraces, the simplicity of bread, fruit, water, of summer. Yet men like the Deacon should know that Paradise is not built in a season, the past lurks like a wild cat, driven spitting into an alley but, famished, ready to pounce. Peaceful Florence once confiscated a temple to Mars, dedicated it to the Baptist, thenceforward suffered war and siege from Huns. Then a fisherman discovered Mars' statue in the river, thrown there by indignant monks. Disillusioned, the citizens placed it, garlanded, and with barely remembered rites, on some hunk of marble, and the Huns vanished in dust, the past back in business.

An eminent Stuttgart philosopher was proclaiming that the past is a circle, history a sequence of variably sized triangles. It may be so: no great matter if it is not.

Sunlit Perceval, cornflower eyes happy, seemed fresh from an illuminated missal. He would have been at ease with the Adamites who, believing they had restored the Garden, lived naked. Accepted without question, he was loved, could give no offence: to all he gave the serious attention spontaneously bestowed on trees, flowers, a duke, a leper, an emerald-green lizard, a lame and mouldy dog. And so real to him, to the Other World. His rare disclosures suggested that it was vaguely populated, wholly ungoverned, probably ungovernable.

All this placed him and his surroundings peculiarly at risk. No lavish, unfeeling Bacchus ruthless in his plunge into life, into others, he nevertheless imposed an expectancy, a heightened awareness akin to intoxication, hitherto induced here by some resonant chant, moment of communion, domestic celebration. Sometimes eyes had to close against an intensity increasingly sharp. People deferred to him as if in atonement for misdemeanours hitherto unrealized. Matthias was calling him his son, our feudal protector begged for visits and informed me that they transfigured his worthless life, women wove him garments, mostly unsuitable. Anna bought him fruit, children carved twigs for him, which he accepted dreamily, grateful indeed but to no one in particular, accepting them not as his due but as manifestations of general and trustworthy kindness.

Unlike myself, ensconced with my books and in my schoolroom, he hastened to assist in all tasks, however menial, as absorbed in digging latrines as in proposing a game. His very inefficiency sanctified the failings of others, giving rise to much mirth and happy forbearance. A grizzled woodman, often impatient with the ill-performed, dodged Perceval's clumsy attempt on a tree stump, wiped off the splinters, merely remarking that the Lord Himself, though a carpenter, was not known to have been a talented one. Requested to treat a sick child, Perceval made suggestions from which collapse was averted only by hurried appeal to the castle surgeon, a box of lemons and, presumably, by fervent prayer. That surgeon, a former Zwinglian preacher, charged only those patients he failed to cure, to compensate himself for disgrace. Success, he asserted, rewarded itself. Much admiring, Perceval volunteered to be his assistant or pupil, from which, for once getting my way, I managed to dissuade him.

Real history seemed, for those folk, sober, but rendered childish, to have started with Perceval, one of those who, in a twinkling, change water to wine, walk on waves without preliminary training, tame bears at a glance and understand birds' speech. An old woman almost blind, hitherto dumb, unexpectedly declared that, on his coming, two stars had chased each other across the night. Actually, they had not, but soon almost everyone remembered them.

He had no message, he was only himself, or what passed for himself, the wanderer whose head was filled with resourceful dwarfs, red-haired rescuers, maimed princes and unreliable convictions. An old man revered his information that if a blind man and a sighted woman were of equal weight, the woman was heavier. When I talked to him of Messer Leonardo, his admiration, I felt, was given largely because the great man left so much unfinished. He praised some poet who spent his life perfecting a single verse, showing it to no one and, in death, destroying it. To Perceval, the fraudulent were blessed.

Anna's eyes, so indifferent to myself, shone with utter faith and love. Piqued, I imagined them, doubtless erroneously, reclining in long grass and lilacs behind the forge, murmuring high thoughts while he absently fondled her, lulled by those wistful Southern lyrics composed by those to whom love was perfection of spirit, or a dirge sung to one pledged elsewhere. Legendary improbables who had lain naked, a sword between them, may have set for Perceval a test he took pleasure in resisting. Convinced of his search for love, he surely loved most arduously when alone.

Whoever lacks contradiction may be saint or scoundrel. Perceval seemed all of a piece, and I liked him less because of it. I tended to enjoy scandalous swaggerers, witty liars, grandly arrayed and respected buffoons, more interesting by unexpected behaviour. Friars, with their polished greed and immoderate requests made excellent company, lords of misrule and mischief believing in the Devil as the sum of carnal frustrations. Cautious and diplomatic, I was perhaps necessarily attracted by rogues, whom I did not much like, and was often inconsiderate to those to whom I felt closest. Constant, even monotonous, in his affections, his behaviour, his indifference to reason, Perceval was as undiscriminating as this summer light, welcoming all in his path. Admirable, of course, but liable to win trouble which would fall most direly on others. People's troubles worried him, but again I suspected that he found them identical: the bellow of a trapped elk, cry of an afflicted child, the tearing fall of a tree; Prometheus' vultures, Hercules' poisoned shirt agonized him as much as toothache or hunger, a thought of Gawain lacerating himself wrenched him apart as no *Landsknecht* or hangman would ever do. Only 'the Emperor' shone for him with unique distinction, offering a cause though surely a muddled one.

Each face is a map, a signature, mass of suggestions. Perceval's could be that of a Narcissus believing that he is in love only with the pool beneath him, or a Tiresias of less wisdom and more blindness than the fable alleges. I wished it were capable of a pothouse guffaw, trooper's grin, unpleasant though these almost always were.

Summer, summer. Dusty leaves, bland sun in torrid sky, birds languidly flapping to ponds where gnats clustered in twilight, like netting. Despite, or because of, their new playmate, children grew nervy and quarrelsome in the heat, but their elders continued as ever, working, planning, talking peacefully at communal tables, quietly praying, planting green hopes while, pounded by iron rapists and skull-faced riders, the Empire groaned, and the spotted sickness stalked at will. At Grantz a father, believing the end of the world was imminent, sacrificed his sleeping wife and children with an axe as they slept. He indeed survived, though a nearby abbess, famed for her sanctity, perished, covered with black blains, those footsteps of death.

In evening cool I saw Perceval and Anna crossing a yard. They were always together, inviting but not receiving gossip, rejecting no one but tolerantly left to themselves, walking the field, plying mattock and hoe, talking I knew not what. Displeasure came only from the children, feeling their rights invaded and, believing themselves unobserved, jealously, fretfully, they followed the pair. He was their bearer of delights, which might now be withdrawn. But he noticed nothing, I saw less of him. 'Suppose . . .,' he would begin, then desist, looking round for Anna, so much more easily contented than Kundry. A word from him must seem for her a smattering of silver on smooth, dark water, the sudden bloom of flowers in a pot, and, trying to overcome impatience, I pitied her. She would never have suspected the limits of his gentle love. Deeply, I was convinced that he could love but an absent Kundry, never a devoted Anna, and would furthermore confess agreement with the Milanese genius, that, alone, you belong entirely to yourself, but that even one constant companion halves your being. He reminded me of the youth who, despite ability to walk through glass and overturn mountains, yearned only to know how to shiver and shake. None of these talents would have given happiness to Anna, and Kundry might think them despicable.

Soon I was startled by the voice, subdued, hymnal, of an unseen old woman: 'He should be our king.'

In the material world I acknowledged so sturdily my own, kings were hinges of statecraft, glittering and serious poles of cohesion. I preferred a Gustav, Frederick, even James, to anarchic lords and Hell-struck zealots. They were also sources of comedy, in children's song in Perceval's stories. Swallowing spiders against gout, King Gnama embarrassed all by sprouting a third leg: tawny King Ros the Crumpled so loved himself that he knighted all who resembled him: men, women, a statue, a tree. Perceval told of Alexander unnecessarily harrying Asia aflame with aggrieved gods and outraged sibyls, and, in his pride, seeking Paradise as one more province to dangle. Reaching walls gleaming like apricots in rain, he saw no portals, heard no acclaim. Then the grey old man, always hovering in Perceval's tales, appeared out of a whirl of dust, giving him a dish which, if weighed, would rise not when the counter-scale was loaded with gold, but only when it held but a single feather. The lesson, somewhat cumbersome, was that great Alexander should learn humility. He did not, but, momentarily staring into himself, he acknowledged that his noise and bustle were conceivably lightweight.

In a Manor of Love, kings were objectionable: talk of them was wormy and rotting. Hearing of Alexander a child, hitherto docile and friendly, in sudden, angry tears stamped a duckling to death, leaving everyone aghast. Afterwards, after much soothing and fairweather promises, I heard what at first puzzled me: 'Luck has returned to our good home.' Then I understood. Kremitz was a ship, well stocked, at ease in the calm of a blessed haven. Sails, rudder, the new compass, seasoned crew, were additions for a voyage which need not occur. But, without warning, a breeze had risen, prospects veered. Certainties might vanish and luck, for good, for ill, resume its station.

The August sun was dense, heavy, too yellow, the air trickled, leaves lolled and drooped. Wearily, then insistently, voices began, became a clamour. Curious, I moved out, on to the road, where people had gathered round a stranger, unconscious and bleeding in the white dust. Scarred, black bearded, belt stiff with weaponry, two fingers missing, he was clearly a bandit or deserter. None mentioned Crazy Ritter but all must have thought of him, uncertain what to do. Eventually stirring, opening his eyes, he cursed obscenely, accusing us of robbing him. The women calmed him, produced water, lint, bandages, while Deacon Matthias held council. For once, opinion was divided. The savage mouth, bloodshot, threatening eyes, the knives and pistols, were unprepossessing, no evidence of love, or even of passing goodwill. Some wished to beg him to remain and learn our ways, others

seemed to dissent but were reluctant to admit it. I advised
sending him away, or surrendering him to our guardian nobleman,
but this aroused reproaches, not all of them sincere. Anna flushed
unhappily, Perceval sighed. 'You always foresee trouble, so
trouble comes.'

Heads nodded gravely, Christian charity was besought, but
they awaited his wisdom. The last to speak, he carried the day.
The ruffian was trundled in on a handcart, kissed – not by me –
found bedding, food, clothes. His name we never knew, but the
children, discerningly, swiftly, called him Cow Pat. Their malice
redoubled, for Perceval, with Anna, at once adopted him. Work
he did not, but after their own labours they always joined him
in selfless amity. His sullen, ungiving face, his small eyes, never
relented. Even with his smiling mentors he never spoke, though
I presumed he knew how to. But they were always bringing him
food, repairing his boots, while he glowered at his own feet and,
while perforce accepting their company, glaring at anyone else
who ventured approach. Even in the heat his tanned, riven flesh
looked cold, scaring the indignant children. He ate more than his
allotted share, sprawled day-long under a tree and though, under
persuasion, had at the start given up his weapons, I suspected
that he retained a knife.

The children abandoned my school, or appeared but fitfully,
refusing to study, scowling at older folk, daring me to punish
them and scowling more when I did not. After one session,
dismally futile, they ran out and, seeing Anna alone at the pump,
encircled her, pelting her with weeds and dried mud, chanting
viciously:

'Anna, Anna, wondrous charms,
Finding muck in Cow Pat's arms.'

As I hurried forward, followed in dismay by the grey-beards and
women, they rushed to the sheds. With head lowered, leaves in
her hair, desolate, she was weeping. Smaller, frailer, she then
saw us, shook violently, refused comfort, went away, bowed and
speechless.

Song faltered, discussions were silenced. First a few, then more,
neglected the public meals. Many doors, hitherto always open,
were now truculently closed. The very chimneys seemed out of
shape, voices were distorted. Women said little, but old men
were disposed to blame me for my initial lack of welcome to
whom I could only regard as Crazy Ritter, murderer with hidden
blade. The woodman quoted Jeremiah, Zpanek the charcoal-
burner mentioned unjust stewards and I, appearing more outraged
than I actually felt, meditated my own departure. Yet I lingered,
believing that when crisis came, as it would, I should be needed.

Perceval remained serene as ever, placing an arm round Anna, procuring wine for Cow Pat, conciliating the children whose energy had abruptly wilted, games and spying now replaced by drowsiness and uncertainty.

Could he really not see storms gathering against the sun? His crassness, imperviousness, immunity from proportion and sense, had helped sharpen Cow Pat's knife. Not only he, but all these kindly, self-sacrificial Brothers and Sisters listened to my warnings, disguised as grumbling questions, as they might to a star-eared gypsy whose speech was understood only by horses. To a depleted evening gathering, Matthias, voice shaky but eyes contented, read about Christ's forgiveness of the adulteress, his sardonic gibe at her tormentors. 'A free spirit,' the old man reflected, closing the book, 'he knew the world was loving.' I could have told him that Christ prided Himself in knowing nothing of the sort.

The old were remaining longer abed, the young disputed about trifles, work was more slovenly, sometimes omitted altogether. Cow Pat's silence deepened, but had meaning more menacing than speech. While Perceval performed in his folly, the other man was staring at Anna, not with desire but with muffled tensity in which I could detect hatred. Unflagging charm, played upon such as him, was like a bag of groats offered to a statue, a pout presented as shield from the strangler's cord.

The sky clouded, birds hushed, the heat subsided. One morning we discovered that two founding families had left in the night without warning. Others were preparing to follow. I was soon aware that Anna was no longer seen, and very soon Cow Pat himself had gone, loafing back to whatever stink had bred him. Days of Kremitz, the Moravian isle of Saints, were numbered. Accepting Anna's absence with exemplary forbearance, Perceval was again speaking of the Emperor, a great man becalmed through ignorance of whoever would bring him salvation. I walked with Perceval in a cold evening, past huts silent, perhaps deserted. My impatience left me, he was a child in love with a ceiling moulded with enticing friends – tritons, dolphins, nymphs, but out of reach, always out of reach.

Baffled by my own weakness, wholly disinclined to reform, heal or convert any Emperor, I knew that, like Gawain, I was inextricably pledged to him, though unable to resist the ancient belief that the Devil enjoyed dispatching his creatures to cause grief and disorder in a world already lavishly endowed with both.

5

Grey and wrinkled, the sky was a gigantic nostril afflicted by our passage. High roads, low roads in barbarous disrepair, were crowded, people needing to travel in groups usually led by gilded, lumbering carriages, tightly shuttered, their panes enscrolled with cherubs, mermaids, crossed lances, trumpeting angels. Within must be seated noblemen, prelates, high stewards or envoys, themselves protected by halbadiers, musketeers, huge, dripping boarhounds. Occasionally a window opened, a silver pot was emptied, a cloth dropped on a messy basket, a hand, dried black, fell stiff as a stone. Those trailing behind carried rusted arquebuses, sickles, axes, charred stakes, cut-down pikes, pouches of gunpowder. Stragglers had small chance against wolf and carrion, famine and trooper. Everywhere on tattered landscapes of burnt fields, bells warned of our approach, survivors scuttling to hide from God-haters, plunderers, Germans. With simian grin, a gaunt mendicant had choked out the saying of a renowned Bohemian: 'The German steals, cheats, deceives, like a caterpillar in a cabbage, a snake in the heather, a rat in a granary and a goat in the garden.' A wiseacre in clerk's dress, very soiled, assured us, 'There is no God, no Devil, only their handiwork.' Some had horses, bony nags unlikely to carry them much farther, but, inevitably, Perceval had acquired a well-filled mount. With more initiative than was obvious, an insidious pressure on hearts, he could have sold water at fair profit during a flood without appearing to do so. Smiling, he made others smile with him. He begged me to share the horse, in some hauteur I refused, he implored, I clambered up.

Despite rain, hail, mud, Perceval remained neat in miniver-lined cloak and thick cap, unaware of envious, tatterdemalionly glances. Habitually prudent, I dressed shabbily, though with a stuffed purse bound to my skin, kept secret, for my friend would have borrowed it to admire the embroidery, then carelessly emptied it into distressed or threatening hands. Already he was regarded as singular, separate, special: he who failed to question, and so seldom heeded answers.

Anna had never reappeared, Kremitz collapsed about us, I imagined her skewered by Crazy Ritter's knife. Perceval never spoke of her. Of this I was glad. He would probably have said painful nonsense about her surviving us in one form or another where luck would not fail her. Her fate, I should have had to retort, had not been conditioned by luck.

We were almost the last to leave, for I had searched marsh, ditch, copse for her while Perceval helped cook for the few remaining children. Life, with murder, with joy, streamed past him, because it must: loving water, though unable to swim, he remained on the banks, hoping for a kingfisher, until turning to hear, or thinking he heard, the beseeching cry of an emperor. For him, wickedness was ill health, crime a discourtesy, liable to

194

all. Jesus Himself had, he once told me, blinded someone for stepping ahead of Him at the well. Klansing, a cruel robber, he continued, gave most of his gains to the poor. Character was fluid, little was final, all would be well and, if not, no great matter.

Riding above the dirty procession, fair hair now adrift, he was a free son of the morning mistaken for a leader, perhaps for a deliverer, accepting to the letter the precept, 'Take no thought for tomorrow'.

A legend though false contained some truth. At Nyon he had strayed with a lamb into a lion's den, then halted, amazed to see, of all things, a lion. His bewilderment infected the beast, which unfussily collaborated in a minor miracle by lying down with the pleasantly mannered lamb. At Cremona this is remembered in a painting, at the Signory, of Perceval blessing both animals who kneel before him with quite fulsome admiration.

We were now amongst some six score runaway serfs, Moldavian gypsies, Czech cattle-stealers, preachers mouthing Lutheran absurdities – 'It is a thousand times more important to believe firmly in absolution than to be worthy of it,' reiterated a malodorous do-nothing with the morals of an assassin – renegade monks and nuns avid, rather too late, in lust: go-easy bankrupts, scribes made jobless by printing: dispossessed peasants, outcast retainers all tending grievances and seeking new ones. Roving tax-gatherers spied on petty transactions. Continually driven away with curses and blows, always returning in the night, were wraiths, hideous from famine, from leprosy, clinging to life as if with rotten fingers and merging with the grotesque outgrowths of starved imagination.

Ageing figures strained on ropes, pulling carts and sledges bulging with sacks, their voices, between grunts and cries of pain, lamenting lost infants, belabouring the Trinity, counting their sorrows, denouncing the touts, pimps, thieves. Some Swiss soldiers, having murdered their captain and of uncertain temper, grabbed fiercely painted whores and refused to pay. Here, as elsewhere, petulant scholars clutched books and wine bottles, part of a university without name or building, yet widespread and subversive, with much talk of Galileo, Bruno, new skies. The Catholic Archbishop in the City had subsidized a Protestant round-up of witches, some of whom might be refugees amongst us, and I had glum amusement in trying to identify them. That boy, sweet-faced behind the grime, with ingratiating hands, the broad-hunched virago with eyes seemingly solid as walnuts. All seemed making for the City where, Perceval had told children, the Emperor dwelt in a floating palace which turned so as always to face the sun.

195

Once, from behind a broken mud-and-wattle wall, I heard a call to that other Emperor, Gamalean, genius of the Third Empire, of Last Days, successor to Nebuchadnezzar and Cyrus, riding from forests on a giant wolf to destroy the worthless. A ranter was soon condemning us all, from the great ones in their silent carriages to the leper squatting in the ditch: 'The day of the Lord will come as a thief in the night: then the heavens shall vanish in a roar, and the elements melt with maddened heat, the earth swell and all its works be engulfed.' A prospect less forbidding than the long weeks ahead. Food was diminishing, the mind was invaded by fancies, not all of them fanciful. I began fearing whatever might rise at us like a dust devil: rabid dogs, crouching footpads, a child desperate from want. The bizarre was commonplace. One fellow, dragging a weary cow, had caged his head in a box shaped like a duck's head. Perceval endangered us both by ceaselessly halting for me to give aid, for him to give comforting words, to the fallen, the faltering. When I demurred, he dropped them whatever came to hand, however unsuitable. One wretched scrap of flesh, little more than a ruined nose and eyes as if boiled too long, stumbling along on wispy legs, begged him for food, vainly, as our provisions that day were gone, so received a jewel, which it tried to gnaw.

'How many leagues to Babylon?' Perceval was wistful, though his composure never failed. I fancied that Babylon might be nearer than the City. Of Kundry he never spoke, only of the Emperor, crowned with light but fearfully weakened.

Days shortened, rain fell in gusts from swarthy skies; no benign, ox-eyed goddess waited here, no consoling christs. People staggered aside to perish, or pause, to regain breath, and jeer at a crippled, inert grandam drooling blood under a bush. A voice cackled that the only quiet woman is a headless one. To some solid laughs, a youth smothered her with sacking, removing her strips of ribbon. A burly man, jerkined, gaitered, with tapster's joviality and an eye on our horse, swinging a hedge-bill, accosted us while we rested, then produced from his greasy undershirt a black hunk of bread, some stained biscuits, a dead starling disgustingly dried, then a flagon of wine from a bag. His hands continually touched, as if to still each other. Unblemished by carnal needs, Perceval amiably refused for both of us, though I could have stomached the wine. Offended, the stranger examined me as if for arms (by gross oversight I had none), boasted of raping a bride of Christ in Silesia, of having been sentenced to boiling for adultery. 'No future there, fine sirs. Boiled in my skin, like a chicken. But I knocked the gaoler silly and moved out.' Fearing he might do the same to us, I muttered that Perceval had suspected typhus, and he hurried back into the mass, where

196

people could be imagined sloughing off their souls for a jar of wine or even 'The Riches of the Indies', a compound of pond water, or worse, bark, plantain, dock leaf. Gangs of starving dogs attacked infants, marauders appeared on the skyline but faded before the weapons glinting around the shuttered, grandee coaches ahead. We ourselves never quite starved, and Perceval, accepting both misery and joy as his undoubted due, never once complained. Indeed, the concourse of beggars, monstrosities, the secret rich, the desolate countrysides, held for him some allure, like those trees or boulders which, however often you count them, always yield a different number.

I weakened myself by continually remembering the Duke's lavish roasts and wines, the cushions and apple blossom.

Nights were dangerous. We lay amongst the others, beneath dripping skies, clutching each other for warmth. Perceval would lie down unthinkingly in his fine cloak, and drift into slumbers, undisturbed by groans, scuffles, cries and prowlings surrounding us. I had to train myself to remain awake, feeling my purse solid against me, dozing only on horseback. When I roused him, he would rise obediently, distinct as a dandy amongst the slow, disconsolate, jostling crowd.

At a crossroads, where, my sense impaired, I half-expected to find Gawain awaiting us, a man, hitherto sanguine and reliable, insisted on his gangrened leg being amputated, days too late. Here, too, Perceval dismounted and, oblivious to all, stood as I had seen him at sundown, head bowed, hands folded in absolute stillness, the world turning around him.

At another crossroads we encountered, not Gawain but a mountebank friar, emerging as if from the marsh ground, two urchins shivering beneath him. Spectral in mist he flayed us with words palpably inappropriate: 'Weep and bemoan your fate, for your gorgeous raiment is moth devoured, your treasures rust, which will bear witness and gnaw you like the fire. The wages you denied howl against you, you have condemned the innocent who could give you but empty hands.'

6

So onwards into starveling plains, towards hills now far, now near, in low, unsteady light, itself perforated by chill. People choked, stumbled, reeled away into shades, while others could be seen limping, groaning, but never seen before. Groaning cows and donkeys collapsed in mid-step, few babies survived, milk being poisoned or lacking. Distant villages seemed hulks, stranded, deserted. A coach, inexplicably abandoned by its retinue, was overturned and plundered, its occupants stabbed as they sat with high faces and decorated sticks. We shuffled past a mount, apparently artificial, within which reputedly lurked a hag, once resplendent Great Queen or Venus, now, far from mortal hearts, contriving only a rare hailstorm or crop failure. An old man, however, said that though a voice did sometimes clatter within, the stones blocked no crone but a mouth of Purgatory, guarded by a tufted snake breathing out flame wholly innocuous.

Perceval remembered that at Basle he had supped with Bristle the tailor, who had fallen underground and confronted a being, half-girl, half-serpent, desiring to bind him to her with three kisses. Hesitating to give her the third, he lost her for ever, a loss scarcely tragic.

November sun had its back to the world. Black tempest raged as we reeled on a heath in ice-tipped wings which tore up the clouds, and in its screams some heard the Wild Hunt. A Klingsor region in which, clutching for life, some shouted their names into the swirling hubbub, like poets anxious to be heard for ever throughout the world. Discarded wheels, broken carts, scorched bushes, stiffened corpses with eyes closed, black mouths open, warned of our advance. Crows lumbered above us, unpleasantly swollen. Certain rocks were known to exude sickness over whoever breathed near them; Perceval touched one, addressing it in some outcast jargon, survived, and gave heart to all his followers.

The road narrowed, then ended abruptly at thick woods without obvious pathways and which divided us into smaller groups. What happened to the coaches I never knew. Here, despite branch and swamp, we moved quicker. In these parts, lightning-struck oaks still belonged to Wotan and several of us crossed ourselves when passing one. Perceval never noticed them, and I imagined something shapeless and dispossessed crouching malignantly in a pit.

The City remained uncharted. 'When we reach him. . . .' The Emperor, any emperor, was a fixed star in a dissolving universe. He would succour all. But no, not all, for grumbles started about the Emperor fashioning a maze, then losing himself in it.

'He's only a flowerpot . . .'

'Aye, so empty that the air itself rattles inside it. But he's less, for a flowerpot has uses.'

'Faith, he's fruit of the sun and moon. Strange.'

'We're lost, we all must die.'

Perceval listened, but said nothing.

My hunger was tormenting me, but Perceval was able to thrive on irregular gulps of air. He had the patient serenity of Olympus, where centuries flitted by in an instant. Aloof from personal indignities, he accepted shortages, threats of ambush and cold as he might wages. He may have remembered quelling a riot with a song. Had he a further such feint or trick when the desperadoes encircled us and the barbarous built pyres, when wolves stood stark between trees? I did not rely on it. He was an untrained musician who, incapable of following a melody, improvises a tune, often ineptly, at times movingly. I myself wished for metal about me. I now had a cudgel, filched from a corpse smothered with mud, half lifted by frosty tufts and resembling a blackened, abnormal growth from the earth. By night I reined our horse to my leg. Once an ancient arrow twanged from the dark, transfixing a girl's hand.

I saw no one dependable in crisis. The Duke of Alva had once declared that any sort of soldier can fight a battle but professionals were needed to win a skirmish.

We left the woods, found a pocked, slippery road, the bridges smashed, the toll-houses burnt, a few travellers glad to join us. We were reduced to about twenty: ruined gentry, stalwart ruffians, women scarcely distinguishable from men, one cart and five horses between us. Perceval offered his own too frequently for my comfort, but we made some progress, though the lands were deserted, none knew certain direction, and rations were minute. A mass of aches and sores, unfamiliar pains, inordinate appetites, I cursed my judgement and regretted Kremitz, the lost summer, the loyal, solid faces. Sometimes I cursed Perceval.

The gales worsened. The place was volcanic, lunar in silence and cold: trodden by those now dead, it would never flower. Despair spread. December loomed, our stores were almost gone, the horses lame. Our companions lurched towards us as if their capacity for walk was forgotten. They wanted not me, with my cudgel and florins, but Perceval. In this murk, he gleamed. In utter faith, desperate trust, they implored him to utter some special prayer, even the most educated, a ruined Czech, begging for release, however drastic. Perceval at once agreed, not obsequious but grateful for what he accepted as friendship. He stepped aside, his back to the wind, murmured inaudibly. I closed my eyes against an improvident miracle: sunlight that scalded us to ashes, an angel whisking us to instantaneous and unfavourable judgement, a dish of the most luxuriant though inedible flowers of Palmyra. Yet, before nightfall, the wind slackened, the rain, after initial demur, ceased. Morale rose like a pheasant, hunger was assuaged, even I admitted that we would survive.

We crowded into some desolate barns, hailing blotched straw and derelict roof as if it were Caesar's summer-house. At once a lean apparition in squirrel cap, yellow coat, thrust forward, grabbing Perceval's hands like a blood-brother. His skin was

199

aged, his bright black eyes were young: with curved nose, high coloured lips, he seemed Eastern. He garbled an introduction. Joseph the Shoemaker. I glanced at his feet. They were badly shod.

That night was long, made longer by Joseph's story, told under his own lamp, a Syrian affair of twists and knobs illuminating the intricate colours of his oddly luxuriant blanket.

'Years ago, sirs, so many that I cannot count them, I behaved ill to a good man. He was outside my door, bent under the weight of his own cross, on which he would soon hang. He begged water, I fetched it, then, I never knew why, dashed it to the ground and laughed.'

Perceval was shocked and so, in my own manner, was I, though by no means astonished.

'I still see his disappointed eyes, hear his tired voice. "Friend, did I deserve that? Henceforth, you will follow me." His voice was sad, not for himself but for me.'

Ready to weep, Perceval touched his hand. I myself somewhat withdrew farther into the damp straw fouled by rat's urine, into the jittering rims of darkness. The heavy, alien tones resumed, with unsuitable complacency.

'He was more than a man. Soon I had left my beloved wife, my tender children, going I knew not why to I knew not where, compelled against my will, on my journey to and fro across the earth. Tomorrow I shall be gone.'

I knew without looking at him that Perceval was already prepared to accompany him, carrying his baggage, enduring his professional lament, extracting his thorns, binding his hurts, kissing his blisters. His strangeness – was it ignorance, was it innocence, was it even unconscious guile? – brought him exceptional perils from which his smiling ways ever extricated him.

'How often I have besought death. Rest. But in vain.' Joseph sounded more cunning than contrite, sizing up his new friend. He was also adept at making a short story huge. 'I have prayed for absolution in Rome. The Pope was throned amongst painted catamites and scarlet devils, but gave me only villainy. I helped the Spanish king in his hunt for treasure. But . . .' – his mock-modest, Levantine smile was excruciating in the yellow light, his still eyes were like dabs of tar – 'the treasure I unlocked for him was not what he hoped. I have been farther north than Lithuania, farther east than Tartary, farther south than Tunis, farther west than the Hesperides. I have reached the Garden of Eden, no great matter either . . . a muddy stream, a lot of sand, nine trees needing a lop.'

Sleep would have been easy, but I had to resist. Uneasy at

Perceval's absorbed face, unable to caution him, I could only listen further.

'In Warsaw a quack arrived. A genuine mountebank. An Arab, speaking of women on the moon, the earth hanging in a net suspended from God's forefinger, a few knowing how to cut it loose. He had not yet decided to do so. His turban was oily as a turtle; when I stood up-wind . . . ugh! His mouth, thick as a Pomeranian cut of pork, his face like a walnut. As for his magic, very humdrum. He could make words leave paper and stun the reader, very little more. Myself, believe me or not, he did not like. He repeated, in my hearing, that pernicious Luther's nastiness: that a Jew is as crammed with idolatry and sorcery as have nine cows hairs on their backs. A horrid person. But I could say nothing, at no time have I words, even to you, my dearest young friend, I am dumb as a gatepost. Because I had disgraced myself and my people.'

Evidently this encouraged him, for, with no trace of a gatepost, he continued with vigour, his tongue darting about so rapidly that it seemed a tiny pinkish animal loose in his mouth. 'This Arab . . . covered with jewels, covered with sweat, he looked like the Milky Way. He invited the rich Poles, degenerates all, to a feast. Swilling, gorgings, stinks worse than this polecat den, worse than rotting children and Signor Dry Bone. When all were stuffed full as unbroached vats, he invited them each to lend him a handful of gold, swearing by God's three beards to double its weight. You . . .' – he did not include me, and in profile his hooked face was menacing – 'in your sweetness of nature may not believe his depravity.' Then he did turn at me, in my dim recess,. his fixity of expression suggesting that I both believed and was myself depraved. 'He led them, their feet wobbling, their thoughts like starfish, his servants doubled up under their gold, into a cellar decked up with crucibles, astrolabes, piles of eggs, piles of salts, a furnace. . . . Everything indistinct in the fumes. He swayed his hands, gabbled some nonsense while they gaped in greedy expectation. He dropped the gold into the furnace, it disappeared like a hungry rook. They applauded. Excited as women dreaming of an execution, and feeling as if Hercules is dragging their wombs out with his plug of gristle. However. . . .' He went prim. 'He then poured in salts, swung a brazen censer, intoned more rubbish. Then an explosion shook the building and lost the Mayor his eyebrows. When they all recovered, not much was left, they stood gibbering in the ruins, the Arab had gone, their gold keeping pace with him. The furnace had been dry, with a wide funnel into another cell beneath, where stood a nice cart. . . . Well, well! They beat their wives that night. Weeping eyes make sweet lips. Did you know that the brain is mostly water?' His voice was fat with conceit. 'But that Arab! I heard of him again, where else but in Bremen? He had spent the gold in Constantinople, needed more money, returned West. So what did he do? He studied the doctrine of Purgatory. Some nimble-wits sold maps of it. But our Arab friend sold the Pope a tariff long as Charlemagne's – well, saving your presence, arm. Those in Hell were beyond intercession, rightly so. But Purgatory, quite another matter . . . prayers, masses, at so much a minute . . . indulgences, chantries . . . an outright gift could achieve wonders. No one could lose, all were satisfied. He was made Apostolic Chamberlain to his Eminence of Rivoli. He sold wisdom to the entire College of Cardinals, scraping it off the lips of Hermes himself, who by now was wheezy as a burst bellows. Boils, of course. That Arab', he sighed enviously, 'disproved not the existence of the soul, that's as obvious as half a loaf, but its immortality. Forty thousand years it lasts, not an instant longer. Then it dies like a cabbage. I've picked these things up myself from all over the world, but am not allowed to profit by it. I obey the divine word. I know cures, even for death. Others I can help, but myself,' his groan rolled out as if on wheels, 'no, the Saviour Himself condemned me. Myself, I cannot help.'

His invitation to Perceval to help him could not be clearer, and, in the morning, with snow threatening, Perceval drew me aside, pleading for me to open my purse. He had never before made so open a request, he was always as difficult to refuse as a promising girl who promises, and lack of sleep added to my crassness. While suggesting prudence, I handed over the purse. Very soon Joseph had gone, with all else, save a rhinoceros horn, left in the straw, useful to satisfy women and, in certain circumstances, to foil poison. I was wholly blameworthy, and my reproaches would fall only on air, but Perceval had grace enough to look a little crestfallen.

Nevertheless, Perceval possessed more initiative than I may hitherto have implied. It was never blatant, more a soft exertion on others that made us comply. He now said, 'Later, before the snow ceases, we shall leave. The two of us together.' No command, more a respectful suggestion, but which had only to be stated to ensure prompt acceptance. Moreover, now penniless, I was too dispirited for dissent, even anger, not stoical, merely glum.

We departed, the trees still sagging beneath darkness, Perceval with his customary dignity which lacked all pomposity. I had some shame, flaccid enough, in deserting our sorry crew, but wondered whether he, their adored, had reflected about their consternation, their fear.

With that unnerving sleepwalker's prescience, he was at once

riding along overgrown tracks, through creaking knolls, over
dismal pastures, through hamlets stricken but surviving, where
the hungry, tending our horse with their last oats, welcomed us
as archangels, begging us to eat their meagre rusks, sour milk,
foul cheese, and even their grim dogs licked Perceval as if
recollecting the mild and gracious Orpheus. We were, I judged,
still some hundred leagues from the City, less if we condescended
to use the nearest high road. Perceval, however, was glad to
announce his plan, which was no more than avoidance of any
paths veering leftwards, thus missing all essential roads and
doubtless ensuring death from exhaustion or bandits. Still I
forbore protest. The wind had returned, dulling my resolution, I
had unwillingly put trust in his eyes, mouth, his indefinable
empery. Having long believed he needed my protection, I was
now protected by him.

After frostbound nights and gloomy days we reached a small
dilapidated town, its walls breached, yellowy from the snow,
with a name I can neither spell nor pronounce, which Perceval,
the day before, had correctly foretold would show a pump topped
by a gilded virgin with broken wings. All hills had vanished, as
if flattened by the wind, the place seemed a frontier town hacked
by Turk or Magyar. A vagabond knight warned us from the best
inn, suspected of Plague. Here, Plague was one-eyed, so giving
chances to avoid her. He added that we were in the territory of
the Master of the World, a petty Czech baron noted for protecting
Jews, not out of love but from a current belief that Christ would
appear in judgement only when all Jews were destroyed or
converted. The Master felt in no need of judgement, and gladly
obstructed the blessed arrival. Travellers he protected, taxing
them only a little more harshly than his laws permitted. Doubtless
he was now getting the worst of fiscal argument with our late
friend, Joseph.

'The poor butterfly ravages the grey eagle.' This, typical enough
of Perceval's observations, was unwelcome, inapposite, and false.

We had to sell the horse, almost valueless from hunger and
exposure, to the landlord of the Flying Ram, near the walls.
Wooden, rambling, slanting as if lame, it lowered above cracked
outhouses, yards slippery with dung and aswarm with pack-
mules, dirty hens, geese, some with fly-crusted pails of scourings,
bones, rotted swedes, for which scarecrows tustled and bargained,
single-minded as kites over a dead jawbone. Yesterday a child
had been slashed in a weak, ghostly rush for mouldy pigs'
trotters.

'It's home.' Perceval looked from the window, his expression
light. Gaunt jugglers threw wooden balls they often missed,
gamblers crouched over wind-blotched boards, hands swift as

203

mackerels as they picked up cards, the Devil's picture gallery. Rafters were sketchy with cobwebs, our attic was verminous. I shuddered at a tremor from the floor rushes, through it was only my own shadow. Whores stood boldly in stable and tap-room, ostlers looked murderous, wreathed in tobacco smoke, the landlord was a grinning rogue selling us foul palliasses and, for pillows, logs. Garbage reeked like a badgers' set. Even Perceval was only tentative in his pleasure at carrot and wheat wine, hunks of half-stewed donkey flesh, platters of burnt cabbage, potatoes surely grown in the dropping of New World porcupine. Elsewhere in the town the poor subsisted on bark, acorns and what they could steal. I was too weary to care, and Perceval was content enough in disgusting surroundings, as if claiming, against all evidence, that the path to enlightenment must linger with the horrible. His famed goodness, I thought, twisting amid fleas, derived from the wilful, accidental and the perverse. Worse, even in this cockpit of sores, swindlings, incipient murder, he would succumb to that temptation peculiarly his own, his maladroit welcome to all strangers without discrimination. He was the child for ever excited by mornings, forgetting the tears and penalties at nightfall. The Gospels extort candidates for the Kingdom to revert to childhood, Perceval never had to leave it, but the Kingdom was surely narrow, tortuous, tyrannical, too glibly confused with his casual Other World, of which he never revealed anything of the slightest interest to the intelligent and hard working. To him, the world was a wound needing succour. At the Flying Ram, this was, I suppose, plausible. We would sit amongst snoring drunkards and scared or bestial women. Seeing Perceval gazing at one, quite young, but already toothless, without eyebrows and with a demented expression, fixed as a mask, I dreaded his invitation for her to join us. This, however, was settled by her seeing his eyes, then hastily crossing herself and stumbling away.

Did he have sexual dreams? They were unlikely to be of Babylonian acrobatics, Minoan squirmings. He was imaginable in a brothel, puzzled, or like a bird that has fallen into a house and is alternately frantic and still.

We were far from scented days when Monseigneur chortled about a viscount roused only by dreams of a sharp nail: the lecherous Bishop of Ghent, who could manage only a dream of tortoises. If Perceval dreamed, he might not see Kundry naked as glass, Gawain riding like a tempest, but only dancing butterflies and a rather insipid eagle. My expectations were soon confirmed. 'You see people sadly,' he reproached me, as though concluding a lengthy dispute.

He was always addressing strangers more readily than he did

204

friends; while I slept, he had not. The new recipient, probably not of his favours but certainly of his favour, was an ex-priest, in dark robe, vaguely ecclesiastical, threadbare but of fine cloth, calling himself Count Zebban. He was blind, or claimed to be, black band across his eyes and feeling his way by vibrations through ear-lobes, fingertips and, no doubt, foreskin. True to my distrust of fellow men – I had been, remember, a diplomat – I was sceptical about his blindness, suspected the black band was slitted, and that the vibrations would lead to purses, keys, drug philtres. Only half joking, I suggested that our recent acquaintance, Joseph, had conjured himself into this Zebban. Their voices had some similarity, though the Count was heavily snouted, his eyes seemingly set widely apart between long crops of rusty hair. His hands were too large for the thin arms, strangler's hands.

Perceval disliked any reminder of Joseph, but was soon entranced by the newcomer's description of La Volta, the sorcerers' dance, sinuous, soundless, and, obvious at least to me, lascivious. 'A wondrous man,' Perceval said later. 'Despite his affliction, he sees all.'

Whatever Zebban saw, Perceval saw less. The man was certainly no count, doubtfully a priest, his eyes probably no more than dirty. A stable-boy, with far more perception than Perceval, gibed that whenever the Lord Count coughed, he vomited eels. Our chances of reaching City, Emperor, even a clean bed, again receded.

Yet, as so often with Perceval, I was proved wrong, or if proved right, then in a manner disconcerting and somewhat mocking. The next morning the pair withdrew into a side room. Through the flimsy wall I heard but one voice and many silences. When they emerged, both looked pleased, not with themselves but each other. Later, without speaking, Perceval handed me a stout bag of coins, the nearest to an apology for Joseph he could manage. Taking what was indeed my due I felt foolishly uncomfortable, as though I had taken some unjust advantage of him. I could have been a father, agreeable enough, but besotted with his own son through dislike of his wife.

For two days they were constantly together, with a sequel less remunerative. I would visit 'the Duchess of Five Bankers', tawdry but lively, noisily boasting descent from Artemisia, who captained a Persian ship at Salamis, though she herself sounded Irish. Her wine concerned me more than her person. She had fled besieged Passau; her bold, shrewd face was ravaged, as she had been elsewhere. Perceval she despised as 'a precious gentleman'; at their only meeting he had given her five crowns for wine he did not drink and remained respectfully passive when, uninvited, she allowed him a sight of her leg, glistening like a side of bacon.

205

Count Zebban accosted me, allowing the vibrations to find him a chipped, black settle by a gloomy fire. He shook his head, aggrieved that I was alone. 'She's a fly-by-night. A lapwing. Take more care, esteemed sir. We cannot afford to lose such as you. Myself, I still pray to God, whom you very much resemble.'

Zebbans, Josephs, pseudo-Josephs were wary of me, but nosed out Perceval as surely as a magnet would Achilles. Zebban must be scheming to regain his money and make certain of his prey. Feeling, not for the coins but for my shoulder, he gave a small purr, not of cat but of panther, and instantly I was certain that within the black band, unctuous patter, lurked Joseph, man of wanderings, of travellers' tales. Wheedling, persuasive enough, he began: 'In Thessaly was a lake, and in it, an island. On the island was a girl neither of this world nor out of it.'

A Perceval lake, barely worth retelling. I cursed him for leaving me alone with this charnel-house janitor, now touching his nose-block, yes, artificial, perhaps wooden, signalling to me not to interrupt.

'She promised to remain with me for as long as I loved her, but if I struck her unrighteously three times, I would lose her. We were happy together under the western moon. Did you know that the moon was once square but winds long ago chipped away its corners? But I failed to heed her warning. . . .' Again I seemed to hear the self-reproach of Joseph, self-satisfied beneath the whine. 'Once she refused to come with me to a christening. She was from an older people and shrank from the bestowal of names. Names, she said, sorrowing, detach us from one world, nail us to another. But in anger I struck her. Then at a marriage feast she wept, foreseeing hot love turning cold and, wanting my love to last for ever, I struck her again. My last blow she received at a burial, because she laughed. Sadly, she told me that I had broken my pledge and she must at once leave me. She explained that death is but release into brightness, so that it should yield mirth. At once I shivered violently, as if I had touched a stepmother, a baker's daughter. I had to lie down, she covered me with her own cloak, darkness fell and, when I awoke, I was alone on a stony hill in the hour between dog and wolf, as the Bohemians say. I lamented so long that I wept my eyes away, and am what you see.'

He was cheerful, presumably because I had not rebelled against suffering a tale filched so blatantly from the common stock.

Perceval joined us for supper. Some dozen unprepossessing gamblers were hunched at another table and one, despite his attention on a considerable heap of money, was more aware of the three of us than he pretended. He was thickset in peaked cap fringed with metal and worn low, had a short, well-trimmed, reddish beard, and one cheek rougher and as if slightly higher than the other, mouth and nose crooked.

First Zebban, then Perceval, left me, but interested, even suspicious of this man, I was disinclined to retire. The night was very cold, the wind swung round the ramshackle buildings, I could sense the ground cracking in frost. I demanded plum wine, waited. The gamblers in bad light threw shadows fiercely distorted: the dice fell, mugs emptied, quarrels simmered, I could see red-beard with considerable winnings. He played with lounging, confident insolence that made me certain he would retain them. The others, vicious-looking, increasingly desperate, became louder, less coherent, and red-beard's weapon hand was now sheathed in leather. Yet the violence I expected did not occur. By midnight the other players had slumped, as if from slow poison, while their conqueror, upright, ominous, swept his gains into his pouch as candles guttered. Suddenly I was facing him in the darkness, the air stiff with cold, through which his breathing was just audible, an assassin's whisper. I was unable to move, helpless, and almost screamed as a hand touched me from behind. But no, it was Perceval's. Assuming we were alone he began talking, but clumsily, upsetting a chair, I dragged him out of danger while the unknown sat on, there in the looming depth, motionless, yet, in my mind, around us on all sides.

'I think . . .' – barely imaginable, Perceval was urgent – 'we should leave. Very early. This . . . place.' He shivered, his face pale, his hand on mine, unusually, for almost always he recoiled from physical contact. At first I refused, for this plan must have been Zebban's, but he quickly reassured me. Zebban had already departed, with an unnecessary promise to meet us in the City. I reflected that we were already marked by one more formidable than any Zebban, and that immediate escape was best.

I had already repurchased our horse, a good enough fellow, now restored, and one other. I had also stolen a kitchen knife. The bunch of winter roses at Perceval's belt would give him only fair-weather protection from any red-beard. We rode at fair speed through drizzle and the last shreds of dark down an icy path, Perceval once slowing, taking pleasure I did not share in small black and white clouds above a dead-looking forest. They reminded him of lacework.

I begged him to hasten and, as we neared the forest, my forebodings worsened. The trees, though leafless, were thick, their shadows like threatening antlers, and could conceal an army. Tumbles of frosted gorse covered the path, slowing us. Glancing back, I sensed rather than saw a distant stir, tiny glint. The horses too were now nervous and reluctant. The clouds, in which even Perceval could no longer have seen any reminder of courtly delicacy, had swelled darkly. The forest was only some quarter of a league ahead. The path reappeared, but – his distress maddened me – it led leftwards, skirting the forest which within an instant was behind us, depriving me of any sight of pursuers. My throat was cold and dry, my nerves shivery. Quickly, however, we were halted by a cloaked form, hand raised, apparently alone, Zebban, eyes perfect, a loose grin as if pinned to his flabby mouth. Perceval jumped down to greet him and, so doing, gave the expected sign, for at once a shot sounded from the trees, a hiss, a scurry of earth and stone. Undeterred, he moved towards Zebban, but men were swarming around us, weapons gleaming in dull air, hands at my horse's neck. I dismounted, avoiding slashes at my legs, and was already plying my knife, thrusting off two undersized assailants, gashing a third. Perceval was captured, held by Zebban, standing unresisting, scarcely concerned. I fought on, blood rising, my weapon small but tough, deft against this riff-raff. All were utterly silent. Wary of tree-roots and ice, I managed to twist through the bandits, four of them, and get my back against a solitary tree. Breath steamed from me and, having gained position, I could feel more confident. These cheapjacks would have won no praise from Alva. They were in poor condition and without convincing resolution. They came at me irregularly, I cut one wrist, then a neck. They withdrew, panting, scared, perhaps less of me than of the staring, motionless Zebban. Then, goaded, they were at me again and I heard horses' hoofs. My spirit lost its surge. Hope fell utterly. Zebban wanted Perceval, but would leave me dead where I fell. He shouted at them to finish me. Choking, I felt my arms almost too heavy to thrust further, though I had selected a ruffian to die with me. The horses, or horse, was nearer, they paused again, uncertain, while my gasps tore me and my hand went numb, making the knife weightless, almost imaginary. Zebban cursed, they drew together, poised to ram, but their eyes went huge and pale at the sudden apparition bursting over them on white horse with red-tipped ears, spear aloft in classic pose. The rider charged direct at Perceval and his captor, scattering the others, splitting Zebban's brain-pan into a tumbling mess, then wheeled to me, the rest fleeing.

Perceval, back in life, whistled, the horses trotted up, our champion pushed off his casque. In chased, elegant Milanese breastplate, rich Cordovan gauntlets and golden spurs, grinning at Perceval with tolerant, sardonic forbearance, he was the red-bearded gambler, and, on his wrist, picked out in blacks and greys, was dyed a hawk.

'Come.'

Gawain's voice was unexpectedly quiet against the chipped, untidy face, the sprawling, emblazoned hair. Perceval, neither ostentatiously surprised nor grateful, was embraced, but I had already cried alarm for, despite their leader's fall, perhaps scenting riches and a goodlier share of them, his crew, reinforced, had regrouped at the forest's edge and were advancing on us with muskets and knives.

'They can't shoot,' Gawain said contemptuously, reassuring Perceval, who did not need it, and myself, chagrined at receiving it. He sauntered rather than strode forward, tough, stern, his eyes bog-pools littered with russet leaves. He did not bother to replace the casque, his head flared, vividly opposing the starkness, rime, the pudding sky. Chastened, they drifted to a standstill, uneasily fingering weapons, awaiting a command unlikely to come from amongst themselves. Within easy gunshot, spear in hand, he raised three fingers, made an obscene jest, perfunctorily, as if ordering bread, then, more decorously, softly named them turd-hungry eunuchs, sons of poxed ditch-drabs, bastards of stinking partlets, adding, in careless afterthought: 'Orders have arrived ... I shall manage all. You will kneel.'

Orders! Uttered so indifferently, the word paralysed, until, after a prolonged moment, they obeyed in animal terror, a dozen of the world's misfits, broken, unkempt, useless, less substantial than their pitiful weapons.

'Myself,' Gawain spoke in amused aimability, though Perceval suddenly stepped backwards, his eyes dimming, then closing, 'I respect you as natural men of hardihood, valour, worth. However. . . .' he dropped the spear, pulled out his sword, raised it and, with a gliding deliberation, like a silent sneer, he sliced off the nearest head, which reached the ground before its shoulders, the blood in a torrent, while the remainder pleaded, whimpered, cowered almost into their own bones as the sword lifted again, hung above the man next in line. In repelled fascination I watched. Gawain meticulously strengthened his grip, the victims shrank to mute despair, he slashed downwards but, at the very last, dropped the blade behind his back, the left hand superbly catching it. Turning from them, all fury gone, appeased by his own dark humour, his smile ogrish, teeth vying with eyes, he threw over his shoulder a coin over which to quarrel, allowing them flight and instantly forgetting them as, all at once modest, almost humble, he returned to Perceval, he of the downcast head and drooping stance.

7

'My eyrie.' Gawain's tone gibed at the tall, grey fortress perched on a fierce crag, thickly battlemented, defended by a score of veteran retainers. Rooms were numerous but cramped, narrow spaces concealed between them, Gawain explained, so that he could listen unobserved. Candles flamed erratically in wall-sockets, making the hall in the main tower appear larger, steeper, ringed by dark, labyrinthine tunnels and illusionary columns: the servitors, flitting in and out, lost outline, seemed images tremulously hovering between the obscure and the extinguished. Ceilings were puckered by damp, windows mostly lancets through which light squeezed reluctantly. Clogs echoed on long stone passages. Everywhere, on tiles, mosaics, or carved on balustrades or table, was the flying hawk. All was sterile, wintery. Pines slanted away from us, streams hung frozen, animal and peasant avoided the place as they might a demonic bird subsisting on fear alone.

I would find Gawain, without warning, leaning against a buttress, brooding by a door, sitting over a bare table, intent on the unseen, awarding me the nod due to a guest on sufferance. Patches of youth fretted his lined face, the deep-brown eyes could be hot and challenging, morose and jealous. The redness tinged with grey suggested a sun-god in lean times. Perceval, who beside him looked half-fledged, had once said that though Gawain's body was scarred atrociously, his most fearful wounds were hidden. Despite many braziers, smoking rather than glowing, the castle was raw and cold, and, sheltering no women, comfortless. Its lord must have accepted too readily the saying that to love women is to delve into a sack of snakes in search of an eel. A poet wrote that Lord Gawain's beloved had made sport of his lack of grace and beauty, for her sweetness was mingled with much sourness, her love was honey spread with nettle-rash. In return she told him that he was sunshine eager to be smitten by hail.

The poet continued:

He found her well-salted taunts so much to his taste that he cared not a whit for her marvels, since his first glimpse of her sufficed for a lifetime and cured him of all pain she later inflicted. She had been May outshining brightness itself: she was apple blossom to his eye, gall to his heart. He was at once free and ensnared and thereafter could comfort himself and find mirth at the memory of her infidelities, her malice, and her bitter tongue.

On arrival, Perceval had been presented with a saffron-yellow silk robe, myself with a garment more resembling a sack, though much the warmer. Gawain, usually gloved, capped, fur-mantled, smouldered like the brazier, his eyes missing nothing. Despite

210

his usual show of pleasure at chills, neglect, ill-cooked and carelessly chosen meals, Perceval betrayed nervousness with Gawain, mindful perhaps of the older man's ardours which he could accept but never return. This barbaric chieftain must be as ruthless in these as in all else, insatiable but frustrated, his jagged mouth cruel but apt to tremble, his thoughts caked not with old wrongs but old wretchedness. Gawain's smile, very rare, very sudden, was a ray quivering with young adventure, the rashness of our Duke allured by a new project, or standing at bay: part too of the legend that he was strongest at noon, most tempestuous at midsummer. He would have slain Zebban almost precisely at noon. After that hour he visibly declined into despondency, after nightfall was prone with inertia. He affected a brogue, like a rasping quern, in talk that eschewed dainty bluebells, starlit flower maidens, gardens. He would sit holding a mug, mouth, nose, eyes slightly askew, broken-veined cheeks glowing like his head and beard, his jocularity ambiguous. 'The heaven-sent call to us, to us alone.' He was addressing Perceval. 'Those who leave parents, family, who can despise ourselves. We . . .' – he winked sourly – 'who cast off possessions, yet grab all we can.'

His words recalled another legend, of Gawain's marriage in an Eastern land, an affair of exotic temptations for both himself and the lady. They might share blood with Klingsor, even a Merlin, with flair for the abnormal, bards singing of him misbegotten from a devil's cold sperm, ravaged by passions questionable even in a crude age. Black lust, unexplained bitterness. He hated and despised the Bear Chief but several times rescued him from indignity and death, and all Christendom knew his words to a knight he had twice saved. 'You know the saying that if a man has saved another from death, that other will be his enemy for ever.'

I, for all my suspicions and discomforts, could be moved by red, feverish Gawain. In his conflicts with life, with himself, he could have been he before whom, in a scalding moment, the ghost of Achilles suddenly, overwhelmingly towered. His voice rapid, loud, resounded through the cavernous place, never lighting the melancholy beneath the skin. 'Some Dominican lout told me that, in the Garden, Adam would plough Madam Eve by thought alone, without pleasure, in perfect quietude free from dirt. God alone knew why he bothered. The state of his implement couldn't have done much for her either.'

The heavy eyes, still seldom acknowledging me, glared uncontrollably, but, as it were, at himself. He cooled with equal abruptness. 'Johannes Scotus Erigena suggests we should scatter our seed without impairing virginities or chastity. He's beggarly with details.' His chuckle was mirthless, part of the glooms and depths in which we sat, and against which the few candles scarcely availed. Perceval murmured something, at which Gawain slammed down the mug, then replied in quite another voice, slow, reflective, uncertain: 'Love wrecks us more than the hatreds it should restrain.'

Snowswept days and nights merged in twilit brilliance, through which the two friends moved together until parting at dusk, if part they did. I should have preferred to stay alone, huddled under fur against the cold, but this they were curiously reluctant to allow. So I must slouch behind them, down crepuscular passages, into the abandoned chapel, Gawain always in the lead, talking haphazardly, parodying scholars, pedants, preachers, scornful, alarming, preposterous, though, however, commanding, he was always straining towards Perceval, to charm, captivate, to win some admission. In his way, he too was a follower.

Towards me he had changed, showing not friendliness, certainly not respect, but a gruding recognition, as if I were in some conspiracy known to him and which he would not betray, relishing his own power to do so. I assumed he rated me self-righteous, wily, parasitical. With an ugly grin, he seemed anxious to provoke me, to attack him on his own field to his own order, in some measure of boast confiding that he had lately ambushed a convoy of unarmed Protestant refugees.

'But why?'

The red hair added ferocity to his surprised frown. 'Happen what happens. Happen God's will. I spared the youngsters. Most of them.' He smoothed a ragged eyebrow as if to rub it away. 'Pliny, Aristotle, muddle-headed worm-casts, tell me that God is but nature.' He touched my forearm, perhaps testing its quality. 'Humans may have nature, but don't know what to do with it. They've certainly got behaviour . . . bouts of chaos. Most of them desire to lose. To whip off their own Tom Thumbs and attendant orbs. Wanting to suffer punishments for what they haven't done and don't wish to do.'

He himself seemed one of them. I doubted if the refugees had existed.

'God is really man?'

At this he went cheerful, reaching for words like a gladiator his flail. 'Man at his best, man at his worst. The old God no longer knows the world is still here. Or pretends not to. War, crimes, beastly as a mother-in-law's temper, try to catch his eye, to wake him. For good, for evil.' His hoarse chuckle implied preference for the latter. 'Drunkenness is the nearest most of them get to him. But he's like all of us, getting old, travelling an overgrown road, wondering who created it, where it leads, whether it is even a road, finally whether he ever occurred.

212

Sometimes he meets someone like Jerome, who thought that monks should lament, not teach, and then he lets out a howl. Maybe from guilt.'

He swallowed gustily. Perceval wandered in from an arched patch of invisibility, Gawain plunging on, having motioned him to the stool closest to him. 'Sometimes he's goaded into throwing up someone a bit touched. Most of them are the same. Mischief making. Not poltroons but jokers. Jokes are short cuts, and there's your sermons on mounts. Wanting to make squares from circles, and cursing others when a triangle bobs up. Loving their enemies! Well, they've never met mine.'

The dim mazes and cells echoed him. The hawk on the wall was enlarged and menacing in frayed air from a low, pasty sky. Perceval sat in his own thoughts while gazing, without expression, at Gawain, whose moods swung like a compass finger. 'A Countess of So and So bore three hundred children in a day, yet her reputation was only for laziness.'

He had disguised his feelings, addressing me, apparently flippantly, but with one ear cocked at Perceval, whose full interest he, like poor Anna, could never feel confident in attracting, though he would never plead.

'Two of her children, remember, were tempted by a night queen into a cottage of cake and cherries. They themselves' – his grin was a rictus fixed on the blotched face with its freckles of moisture – 'tasted delicious.'

Thus we would sit, long, often tediously, at a board heaped with brawn, raddled trotters, sausage wrapped in stale dill, Perceval seldom speaking but never nondescript, never without ghostly authority, Gawain boisterous, ruminating, savage, apathetic, always talking, apt to surprise me, which was difficult, and Perceval, all too easily. Once he read aloud from a printed book which, his voice losing its harsh edges in admiration akin to love, he was willing, even needing, to share. The words, though new to me, I knew could only be from Messer Leonardo, incongruous in this remote, monkish fortress in a depopulated province of an empire of dubious future.

'Chiefly, avoid coarse, sharp lines. Shadows on a body, young, delicate, should not be lifeless or stony, but light, dodging, transparent as air: for the body itself is transparent, as you will realize if you stare at the sun through fingers. Light too brilliant yields poor shadows, so beware of it. Notice the softness and charm on the faces of men and women passing down shadowy streets between the darkened walls of houses in twilight when clouds hang. This is light at its most perfect. Your own shadow, gradually merging into it, fades like smoke, like tender music. Remember that between the light and the dark shadow lies

213

something in common with both – a bright shadow or a dark light. Seek it, o painter! For in this is the secret of captivation of charm.'

I was convinced that he felt the passage had significance for his feelings for Perceval, also that he abruptly realized that I had recognized this, for the smile he flashed at me was grateful. 'The waves of light and sound are controlled by the same mechanical law that controls waves of water – the angle of incidence equals the angle of reflection.'

But once again, glancing at Perceval, he knew he had failed. Blundering, disappointed, even hopeless, Gawain attempted to appease him by saying that plovers would risk their lives to contemplate painted walls. He succeeded, Perceval smiled in gentle happiness, then sipped the bad wine after a quick gesture that only Gawain would understand. The brief tension collapsed, we were balanced in our separate stations, making an incongruous unity, until Gawain, his own Lord of Misrule, would spoil it.

At Christmas roads were impassable, rains slopped from cloud which strong winds could not shatter. Trees seethed as if in pain. In Sweden they had whispered many vain promises to the young.

Gawain's fits of animation were rarer. Here the Emperor's city was a traveller's tale. Landscapes and skies closed in further. I felt we had sat here many centuries, would remain for ever, in what Perceval and story-tellers might have termed neither in prison nor out of it. He himself was usually sunk in a trance, scarcely aware of Gawain, now rising, shadow gigantic on the bare flagstones, looking about him for what he did not find, then muttering, 'A happy man is a cemetery.'

8

'But Ho! Across the world I stride
Bedazzling empires in my pride
And challenge all who dare my fame
With splendours flaming from my name,

I, Raynaldo, Magnifico
Under heavens wide.'

Tattered onlookers jostling in dusty lofts, ragamuffin tents, messy inn yards might sporadically cheer Raynaldo ranting and bullying, astrut with flashy rings, green plume and flamboyant cloak, his sword unsleeping, though when his slender, unobtrusive follower, quiet, but clear as a blackbird, uttered his line, ventured a smile, they drew breath, their eyes were ovations, and when he sang he stopped their hearts.

214

From the first, Perceval stepped into place within this mercurial, spurious world where, fallen low, at last gasp, lay Jason the tainted healer, Ulysses, in red wig, with black stratagems, Amlothi the Pure, pranksome Eulenspiegel, Faustus ransacking his own head, Turkish knights avid for the heads of others, Hector defiantly ripping away codpiece, his satyric gigglestick rising like a mace, to howling ribaldry. Gaudy words, spendthrift images wove a toxic fug, in which Perceval became youngest son, innocent victim, opposing trust to craftiness, winning mercy from tyranny and love from the haughty. He worsted Klingsor by the magic of simplicity, overcame by paradox, preserved calm in tumult. In these ragbag dramas, thunderous but empty, he imposed moments of stillness, the stillness of a mirror, a leaf, of a monk reading. It has been said that after he had delivered a verse impressively banal, people at last realized that clouds, horizons, fields, were beautiful. He who to me had so seldom uttered anything of much consequence, now quelled shouts and hoots, sometimes with a grave word, sometimes by merely pausing, or occasionally by interpolating words unscripted, inconsequential, even nonsensical, but arrestingly appropriate. 'Conscience in her dungeon . . .,' he improvised, faltered, failed to continue, yet had intensified a situation hitherto paltry. Once he astonished Raynaldo and probably himself by substituting 'Can he sing?' for 'What is he?' and, though receiving no reply, soothed an audience hitherto mutinous. He was the novice fisherboy who draws up the glittering prize. When he waited, lonely, deserted, he had heraldic appeal, which appeared to infuse the creaking platform with phantoms more convincing than the stolid actors, stalking heavy-footed over painted heaths, graveyards, bridges. His spontaneity, his plangent appeal, made watchers forget the limp banners, tin armour, faded cloths, and see Cathay, the Indies, Other Worlds. 'We die at our own occasion, occasioned by desire. But the nunnery. . . .' He attempted no outstanding role, wandered disarmingly amongst declamations and pleadings, oaths and threats, but with his reticent smile he outsoared them by stroking a cup, holding a flower to the light. Once he had only to cross, nod at two malicious tribunes, depart, but that nod I have always remembered: friendly, slightly teasing, with a hint of authority. On him, paint, false beard, feathers, would have been as absurd as a pike. Armed as he was from within, nakedness might have been his true costume, the small, tawdry theatres displaying his rightful being.

Our sojourn with Gawain had been prolonged until spring, he himself listless, drowsy, at times scarcely conscious, Perceval, the Emperor forgotten, attending him like a squire. All was suspended, the castle a dripping, barren exhalation of winter. At very best,

215

the future was the water rumoured to lurk beneath a desert.

Oppressed, ill-nourished, bored, I sickened, lying many days alternately freezing and scalding beneath worn furs. Unable to close my eyes despite aching lassitude I saw fire encircle mountains, cattle shrivel to their horns, the earth bleed. A table sprouted wings, a helmet melted, reappearing as a chimney, a trembling rose hardened into a manacle. Moonlight became pain, leaves numbers, and, hovering above my wasted body, I peered down sickly white shafts to where abyss and peak were identical. A galley lay wrecked on the moon, a transparent city floated on vapour, green children stood in a twilit meadow withheld from bright lands by a river motionless as if painted.

I felt myself wavering naked on a border between life and death, where lives drained away unnoticed in coughs, rheum, flux. But Perceval now acquired a decisiveness which astonished. From sources unimaginable, he produced fine linen, fresh milk and bread, white meat and latkes, fruits sweetened by honey. From Gawain, the jobbing hero, he brought a quotation from Virgil, probably growled in a tone I should not have relished: 'Surrender not to affliction but stride forward relentlessly, boldly.' Intermittently aware of him through a garish drizzle of colour, I was able, while he coaxed me to eat, to wonder whether he had ever thus tended the Duke, by now as smudged as his head on a coin. His hands, delicate, capable, were at ease with work to do. His need for my safety made me think, ungraciously, of a man seeking sanctuary from his own ugliness. But soon I saw him as a tree, no oak but a birch, luminous, supple, bending to winds but always recovering: he could be cut down but not quickly uprooted. Parched, never quite sane, I loved him, mutely covering forgiveness for moments of exasperation, condescension, contempt.

I recovered slowly. Gawain too revived when a premature spring sun raked the clouds and lit our gloom and was quickly fretting to be back in the world. Perceval was again eager to reach the Emperor, said to be entranced with a top that could spin for ever. Exuberant, shining like a furnace, Gawain kissed Perceval, clasped my arm, with fantastical promises for our next meeting.

Spring was perfunctory, leaves few, tarnished by rain, but exhilarated by release we rode fast. Roads improved, leading through hills beyond which grass stood fresh in milder air, blossom spread white and pink as if on an Isle of Apples, fig groves budded behind intact walls. Villagers waved to us, we were happy together. Sheltering from rain, we found the actors performing in a tavern barn. Their piece was poor, the audience rowdy, and, at a communal supper, with foul meat sold

216

fraudulently as pork, we heard a joke unpleasantly suggestive that the town had a ghetto but no Jewish cemetery.

I had been surprised at Perceval's unblinking attention to the play, following the strident motions, the rantings and murmuring, the songs however lewd. The players, some dozen, were suspicious of me but inevitably charmed by Perceval's lively questions. Soon they were insisting we join them. I tried to demur but Perceval refused to listen. However, they too were travelling to the City, and even a Borgia would not attack impoverished mummers.

All proved better than I had feared: indeed, I began realizing much that, if not important, was interesting. In a noisy English burlesque of authority, Llyr, one of Perceval's childhood deities, had degenerated into a mortal king, very old, discovering through folly the lunacy of irresponsible power, with howls that recalled the Duke outraged by tepid venison, or a gift from the Spider King. Surly audiences wept when Perceval took the hands of two groping old men, the morally blind, the physically blind, and lovingly led them into light and music, in timid parody of his devotion to Kundry.

In such dramas, daughters fed poison to ageing fathers and beheaded their suitors, wandering princes foiled the dark seducer and evil stepmother. Observed more closely, in their patched hose, dilapidated ruffs, trumpery geegaws, the actors became less absurd. Without real talent, each had some small distinction: an unusual break or fall of voice, a curious gesticulation, a humanizing eye, all could defy circumstance with the impervious dignity of mule or camel. And with them moved Perceval as if by right, never laughing, never weeping, but affected by all. When a tumbler missed his footing, an Indian queen flounced off in a tantrum, Ulysses, scratching his head for a scheme, lost his wig, Perceval would retrieve all by a smile, a soft aside, once indeed by a song which none understood but all cheered. His careless sincerity, someone said, would have warmed the moon.

I won no such following. Forced to take part, I was second conspirator, dumb attendant, solemn prelate, my gait and speech devised for diplomatic tables and royal councils, only evoked mirth or groans, my tactful, unrevealing smile always ended in a leer, my least frown was a thunderstorm.

Audiences demanded horseplay, declamation, obscenity, the last occasionally spoken by Perceval though with no sign of comprehension, which added to the juicy hilarity. They were awed by a disembodied voice issued rather creakily, through unseen pipes, strange faces glimmered from steam, thin fairy music filtered from glass rubbed by damp hands; by dirty nymphs changing to hobbledehoy flowers, writhing and lascivious, until, upholding a cracked vase, Perceval with nonchalant improbability

217

transformed them yet again, to nuns or to deaconesses, according to the region's beliefs.

Performance done, we would gather over rye bread and stale cheese, Perceval then being prevailed upon for stories, of which like children these people could never have sufficient.

Now, in some seedy back room or tent, under cheap candle or hanging lamp, would begin a further play, intense as any other, Perceval on a stool while the rest of us lay around him, staring up while he recounted his tales, even the strangest seeming culled from his own wanderings. We forgot to drink, quarrels were lost, the very dogs were hushed, bats forbore from dropping and mice from rustling, he himself as stirred as any of us.

'Macsen was Emperor of Rome, wiser than any before him. One day he summoned nine vassal kings and announced that on the morrow he would go hunting, and that their company would give him greater pleasure than his last victory over Goths. And hunt he did, by the river that flows from Rome, hunted while the sun seemed to stand still, and the nine kings rode furiously to keep pace with him. But . . .' – Perceval paused, his face, all shadows lost, aglow with the prize he was to give us – 'Macsen hunted for no pleasure in killing, but to give those vassals the delight of appearing equal with himself.'

By day, however, on the burdensome journeys, under inclement skies, not all accepted him so willingly. Franta, pitted, ageing, now having to yield a few parts, resenting his attraction for women, threatened him with a duel, obstructed his entrances, jeered at his effects. Once I found them in a muddy stable, Perceval standing modestly while Franta assailed him in the voice usually employed for Herod, Ajax, the Turkish knight.

'You come from nowhere like a meddling gypsy, you turn your nose up at all but yourself, imagining you're high heaven. . . .'

Neither was aware of me, but an aggrieved bird flew out of the rafters, flying blindly around, too scared to see the open door. Franta glared, but Perceval, forgetting him for the darting, erratic scrap of feathers, whistled softly, leaning against a wall, only his eyes moving, until gradually the bird slowed, began another flight, then alighted on a pile of soiled hay and fluttered, acknowledging a guardian presence perched alert and calm. Franta still glowered, but the robin hopped to Perceval's feet, head tilted, inquiring or greedy, then easily flew away into the light.

Like most actors, Franta could be speedily reconciled, his anger seldom far from tears. Subsiding, he inclined, almost bowed, with stately graciousness, and tramped away.

Some such incident must have influenced that Vatican canvas in which Perceval, as Fool on an Isle of Birds, is surrounded by vengeful warriors and lamenting women, yet wholly engrossed with the tiny red-breast on his wrist. A travesty of this is woven on to a cheap scenery cloth in a back-street Neapolitan theatre, isle not of birds but of harpies.

9

The City welcomed us with a rush of sunlight. Heights and depths dazzled, masonry soared into spires, domes, towers, columns jarred the sky. Fountains were shaped like girls, fish, fawns garlanded and indecent, the bridges carved with gods, saints, mythical beasts and swirling foliage. From sombre visages of fortress, guildhall, church, stone patrician faces gazed arrogantly at thoroughfares lined with statues, basins, marbled horses, feet rising, heads outflung and disdainful, manes flowing. Opulent Italianate mansions and arches, continuously rippling with many hues, faced colonnaded avenues, arcaded squares, terraces crowded with stalls, pens, puppet booths, shadow theatres, tents where damaged people wagered on numbers, beads, fighting cocks. Winning, they usually lost very quickly and, beggared, were at once conscripted into an imperial regiment and promised a chance to be martyred by Turks. Dwarfing the ramparts, almost sheer above roofs, belfries, steeples, the palatial hill rendered the City as straining towards it in supplication. Bridges foremost attracted Perceval, always susceptible to passages of contact: the embrace of night and morn, dew and light, the precise and imprecise: the half-seen and dimly apprehended. Across them streamed motley crowds, coaches, imperial messengers in yellow sashes and brocaded coats, priests under tall crucifixes, provision wagons, scholars jabbering in polyglot tongues, and escorted by guards, their visors slitted and cruel, cartloads of silver from the Joachim mines.

We were in no haste to ascend the great hill, content to explore realms of ornate scrolls, bronze lions, eagles, princes, saints; of rich children passing to school, sucking burnt sugar, valets carrying their books; of ruffed, jewelled grandees from Spain and Austria. Perceval also enjoyed venturing beyond the hard, magnificent façades to the cracked, sordid hovels, choked fish-ponds and streams, sick poplars and empty dovecotes, where kites scavenged amongst destitute infants, noseless mendicants and heavy, stinking piles of dung soaked in resin, small flames clambering over them like curls on condemned heads. I was glad to retreat to the ample squares and crescents, libraries, sturdy ancient markets. Elaborate processions were frequent. That of the Serenissima of Venice was a grave affair of greens and silvers. A

219

Spanish embassy paced by, very black, very white, followed by Hungarians with colossal pikemen, dwarfs on stilts, a bear on a scarlet stage masquerading as a general and surrounded by metal birds whirling and humming on strings attached to brilliant poles, a woeful knight in a cart clutching a broken lance and dishevelled rose. At sunset, under clouds like enflamed petals, an imperial barge with ranked shields, standing effigies of Argonauts, leafy prow, slipped through bright-blue Clashing Rocks, twisted past giant Atlas upholding a rainbow-tinted glass globe, then, at a quay arched and flowered, hailed a witch queen on an emerald throne supported by lions. Perceval vainly scanned the shields for a gleaming hawk, then was tricked into buying a falcon painted, very badly, by St Luke.

In a square ringed by warrior statues, before a gigantic backcloth depicting a round table, all seats embroidered with stars save one, empty, velvety black, was enacted the Dance of the Horses in which, to trumpet, clarion, drums, imperial cavalrymen, winged and feathered with snow-white wigs, manoeuvred their mounts like agile galleons before an immense concourse, though not for some years had His Majesty descended to his subjects. The calls and rattle of music, the common blasts, the angles of salutation continued to direct eyes upwards, to Palace and Cathedral, the dance ending with all horses kneeling to a tableau of the Emperor in golden armour embracing Minerva and receiving a sword from a hand thrusting through clouds, a staged vindication, I thought, of recent Catholic persecutions.

Sublimely incautious, Perceval would question any stranger about the Emperor, but answers were ambiguous. All Europe knew of his search for the Elixir of Life, his library of alchemical codices and hermetic texts, his scientific and astrological compendiums, the works of Paracelsus, Albertus, Reginald Scott, his reverence for Dr Dee, interpreter of dreams, numerologist extraordinary intimate with archangels Gabriel, Raphael, Uriel, and who could calculate the size of the universe and commune with the dead, who addressed him in the language of Adam and Eve – bad Latin, his detractors averred. He himself was dogged by an earless Irishman, who had rashly guaranteed the English queen the transmutation of dung – not her own – to gold. A Bohemian bishop, told of his failure, remarked that, to believers, gold actually was dung.

The Emperor himself possessed a bell to summon spirits, had changed lapis lazuli to silver, and ennobled a Silesian child for having been born with a golden tooth. He had manufactured a white clay, which smeared on flesh, induced talk from corpses, if they had anything to impart. People said that he periodically painted himself white, believing himself an ancient god; in

220

mirrors he thus saw an apparent ghost and communed with his former self, mindful of Plato's belief that the truly solitary can be god or beast. Shy, disliking crowds, avoiding his noble councillors, he sought advice not only from a Dee, a Kepler, a Brahe, but from menials and, Perceval nodded happily, from wanderers. Kepler himself was expected, in time for the new century, for which he might pronounce a new law on the properties of light.

At a small table above the river a Castilian gentleman, overhearing our discussion of the Emperor, bowed stiffly to Perceval and smiled familiarly at me. 'At my last audience he received me crowned, quite alone, in that lofty hall, holding a sceptre of the Roman Empire with both hands, as if it were too heavy, or attempting to wrest itself from his grasp.' The dark, spaniel's face above the ruff looked worried, then he shrugged, informing us that His Majesty never uttered his own name and prohibited others from doing so. 'A Saturnian, my friends, thus inclined to meditation, often sad, too sad, under influences best avoided.' He glanced around to avoid being overheard. 'He ordered a Polish lady to laugh, then attempted to trap the giggle' – his dark, trimmed eyebrows rose together in exquisite astonishment – 'in a mechanical machine.'

He bowed again. 'Farewell. Sleep with angels.' But he later recommended us to the Grand Chamberlain, apparently charmed by my companion's graces and leaving him even more anxious to win the imperial trust.

Meanwhile the Emperor was high above us, unseen, and a girl with ringlets like stale straw boldly told us that he did not exist, then conceded that from Palace steps permitted to His Majesty alone was sometimes heard the swish of a cloak, though the steps remained empty. This was surely unpromising. Perceval dissented and kissed the child, though I did not. That night a woman at our lodging pointed up at a star above the Palace haloed in phosphorescence. 'That's our Emperor . . . the real one.'

The magistrature presented a masque, *The Marriage of Heaven and Earth*, for the imperial birthday. A resplendent frontage, columned, porticoed, tasseled, beflowered, collapsed at the sign from a blue and green Merlin, abnormally thin, eerily tall, and instantly a blue and white dome streaked with gold glided up from the ruins, then, to songs and stringed music, was reversed into an immense cauldron emitting black mist slashed by lighting which formed a goddess in snake-haired mask, staring and very cold, nine maidens dancing before her until fading into rainbow sky where, in languid nuptials seen as if through gauze, reclined sun and moon, beneath them darting satyrs, imps, elves, exhalations of an antique subterranean order that might survive our own. Yellow-robed monkeys performed a ballet, an impious hunter was changed

221

to a stag by naked nymphs weaving invisible spirals, a dazzling lord was abruptly strangled by ropes of vine leaves and ivy. Neapolitan fireworks spread archers, unicorns, galleons across a sky changing from blue to scarlet and purple, deepening to moonlit black, until flat, fierce, supreme, the sun reappeared with flaring, extended arms, rousing thousands of many-coloured flowers from the singing earth, overwhelming all with torrents of radiance, paean to the wisdom of supreme majesty.

We had parted from the small troupe, outside the City walls. To proceed farther they needed a licence, which Perceval and I did not. Improvident, impulsive, they lived as it were in tragedies with happy endings, and could not believe that Perceval would leave them. My announcement they first considered an illusion or jest, then they threatened us, desisting only at Perceval's own sadness, which led to a heavily staged and tearful reconciliation.

In the City he at once encountered Minou, pallid, round-shouldered, straggly haired student who begged us to inspect the books and prisms in his small riverside cabin. Structures of light, he chattered, unlocked the universe. Copernicus, Kepler, motion and density, fibres and atoms, possessed existence more comprehensively than love. Despite worn clothes and mouldy bread, he had the confidence of spring. 'Do you know . . .' – he was certain we did not – 'that a straight line has more curves than the River Meander? That I can reveal you seven worlds in a fish's eye? The earth is a magnet, spinning like that top of the Emperor's. God hates knowledge, He governs by fear and mystery, shrinks from the new light hiding in the tallest skies. But to us who are ready, there are no longer mysteries. We shall renew life, you can call us the Knights of Hell, for what is Hell?' He allowed no time for me to inform him. 'Hell is independence, so damned by old and rotten authority. We are the true Ascension. The head contains two cups, one bright, one black. We drink from one, we drink from the other, and create a third. There is the real Trinity. Just that. Quite sufficient.'

I yawned, Perceval smiled apologetically. The Knight of Hell, not noticing, forgot his prisms in his haste to uncover a lambskin parchment, but had to listen briefly to Perceval's quiet babble about the gates of Hell being seen in Persia on the Elburz Mountains where a queen – her name sounded like 'seamstress' – burnt seven children yearly to renew her youth. But Minou, sensibly, was not listening. 'When gods descended to earth, it was to win salvation for themselves. If worlds must be created, why do it so badly?' He laughed grittily, stroked his hair as he

222

might a pet, then looked important. 'I can show you worlds more wonderful.' Unstopping a pale-green flask, we had first to sniff it, then dab in one finger and faintly anoint our eyes and tongues. 'Look at two vertical lines, so-called straight. One goes up, the other goes down. Now!'

He kept part of his promise, for he and Perceval swiftly swelled into giants outsoaring the twin spires of Zagreb, a snail broadened wider than the Dome of Muhammad Abdin, wall cracks opened huge ravines, lines impeccably rigid rained down, my ring was a raft pulling me sweating to a sea-blue pit where white Titans fondled then tore apart an eyeless child. With his usual acceptance of the unusual as habitual, Perceval said later that he had seen no more than smudged air, though I suspected that he had partaken of queer drugs and scents so often that he no longer noticed their effects: inhaling fumes from the Bear Chief's cauldron, sipping Kundry's syrup of roses, truffles, unicorn horn, he had regularly seen hands rising from lakes, green men hanging by their hair, dwarfs stamping so that trees bounded up at their feet.

Finally climbing the hill we saw between towers and trees, ramparts and steeples, aflicker with sparkling wings, aviaries above the stables housing the renowned stud from Araby, Spain, Hungary. Our Spanish friend had done us well, Gawain too might have scattered our praises. Gates, doors, opened to us unrequested; carvers, confectioners, hound-masters, lackeys were deferential, the Prime Steward extended welcome. Sumptuous apartments of gilded panels, damask cushioning, filigreed arches, were prepared, and we were speedily receiving ladies, gallants, leading courtiers, together with savants, artists, architects, chief gardeners, hangers-on. Poets in flowered caps wide as arum lilies tiptoed towards us with pinched lips and shrewd eyes, netting phrases, sighing at music unheard by others. A Moorish mirror framed with arabesques was ceremoniously presented but, as mirrors could symbolize prudence, my own gratitude was qualified.

Nevertheless, I was more at home in a palace than in a manor of love, and immediately sent a courier to the Swedish court. I had no disposition to consider myself some barbarian trooper stabling his horse in a venerable church, and I desired some official post. The Grand Chamberlain, with a nebulous salute to Perceval, made much of me, showed me a few diplomatic dispatches, and escorted me on a visit to the Hall of the Imperial Gaze which exhibited the skull, still flecked with gold, of Postumus, Consul of Rome, beheaded by the Boi who, casing it with precious metals, used it for tribal rites.

223

The hill was an Olympian jumble of palaces, fortress, basilica, Cathedral, streets, gardens. Within the Imperial Palace incessant motion was reflected in Venetian convex mirrors fixed at all levels, not least from tame, exotic birds flopping between the great, painted spaces. I sensed that courtiers, gazing protractedly at their own reflections, were, however uncertainly, beginning to delve, or imagine, novel reaches of themselves, testing new poses and grimaces when thinking they were unobserved. Here was a live tapestry of satins of Nicosia and Cordova, roseate sheen, lacquered cheeks, coxcomb hair, toy weapons. On distant ceilings, languorous deities preserved immaculate calm, while beneath, stewards with white rods manipulated suppliants, inventors, envoys, notables, as if disposing troops for battle. Court ladies passed like huge bells. Few faces possessed what artists were calling 'finish'. Details of eye, mouth, skin, were blurred by sagging muskiness, sickly perfumes; grotesque shadows from New World plants sprouted in a gallery, closet, passage. I could not now conceive Gawain here save as uncouth invasion, a Scythian parting the stiff air like a curtain though he might indeed be roaming nearby, ready to pounce and rape, impelled by what he refused to tell.

When haze covered the City, we were suspended above. Protruding from it were spires and weather-vanes – golden cockerels and ships, silver griffins, floating on an amorphous sea dividing the Emperor from the multitudinous lives beneath.

Throughout the Palace were images of a naked youth, David, or Dionysus, on wood, canvas, tapestry, the last, sometimes designed by the Emperor himself, apt to display victories in Hungary, Wallachia, Moldavia, unrecorded in chronicles but testifying his leadership of Europe, to which he had addressed a Letter of Majesty to establish universal peace. Everywhere too were circles, on floor and wall, the Emperor holding them emblems of unity, fusion of opposites, the Aristotelian concept that eternity is circular, though His Majesty was being disturbed by Kepler's revelation that planets move not in circles but ellipses. The Monarch believed, furthermore, that the universe was a knot, tightened or loosened by mortal behaviour, and he was supposedly working on a grand design to reduce knots, labyrinths, spirals to simple circles, enclosing and explaining the All, he himself ruling from the exact centre of a circle, explaining that the Round Table was a model of time and the cosmos.

Befitting his habitation, the Emperor loved representations of clouds and horizons, illusions of what was, yet what was not. He had mortgaged a year's Czech revenue for cloud paintings,

Orphic and Christian, from Venice and the Netherlands. Clouds symbolized transcendence, yet also, I had to believe, his own foreign policy.

Much repeated in court sermons was Christ's 'God is Spirit'. Preachers were as frequent as poets, the latter rather too candidly needing cash and praise. Occasionally a verse was heard praising Kundry: eyes chips of an emerald, arms like ivory and so on, but Perceval seemed to hear nothing.

All nations met on the hill. Greek, Hebrew, Latin, Arabic strove against French, Czech, Magyar, Spanish, Italian, even English. Seeking unity within diversity, the Emperor tirelessly collected plants, artefacts, coins, shells, letters from Galilee, rings from Crete, from which insights and dogma were stupendously entangled, seeking new forms, potencies, functions. Colours could impregnate shapes, numbers engender music, metals create mind, dream divulge fate. A single formula could cover all knowledge, were it to be rediscovered. All is truth, declared His Sovereign and Apostolic Majesty, making me wonder not what he meant but how he would end. The court was now gaping at some oblong paintings he had commissioned, normal enough to Perceval, of grinning basins, naked lovers with animal heads and feathered genitals on lawns where trees sang and beasts talked. Mineralogists, metallurgists, cartographers, numerologists were assured of bounty. A weather expert from Palermo was hired for fees which demanded a poll-tax: he made the Palace so tropical at Christmas that many had to flee to the frozen gardens. The Emperor was intoxicated by a Cracow sage who, until a massive rebuke from Kepler, convinced him that Paradise was a 'spherical quadrilateral', supported by 3 and 9, 40 and 30. A new species of tulip, costing the Treasury forty thousand ducats, was escorted up the hill with honours befitting the Pope, the Emperor not rejoicing in its gaudy stripes but revering its shape, which expressed both the chalice of creation and the clasped hands of an initiate.

Between Palace and Cathedral lay the Golden Street of the Phoenix, a vaporous avenue of laboratories mostly dedicated to manufacturing gold, which must then theoretically crumble into the ether of the quickened soul, the climax of mind and spirit. Such was the imperial wish. I glimpsed alembics, distilleries, retorts, young men and wrinkled magi slanted over crushers, phials, scales, pots and glowing balsam and hellebane while, behind bronze screens and simmering vats, sounded incantations and consorts, music profoundly affecting chemicals, bodily acids, broomflower, belladonna, Saturn. Mandrakes floated in jars of alcoholic juices, fungus white speckled with purple: eggs were piled in warmed dung alongside the dried testicles of a lion and some gleaming asterides. In all, I considered, a college of mountebanks imperilled by Galileo and Copernicus, Kepler, Brahe, more genuine conjurers of space and identity, yet whose works I remained rash enough to ignore. I was more concerned in dissuading Perceval from purchasing a voyage to the moon, an interview with Isis, and the spectacle, in itself expensive, of an Afghan levitating over a maypole.

The custom of hiring lunatics to enliven funerals and weddings had allowed them to infiltrate the court, and we soon saw a figure arrayed as a nobleman walking on his hands, everyone feigning not to notice. Perceval went ashen at the sight of an expressionless mechanical man moving stiffly in silver armour designed by the Architect General to herald the new century, which was already forcing the nervous to hasten to witches and soothsayers in efforts to obstruct it. The fashionable, top-heavy with learning, stood in ante-rooms hoping to be overheard by the Emperor as they discoursed ponderously on the speed of planets, magnetic propensities of squares and cones, electric particles within water and wood, while minions praised, courtesans giggled, scaramouches swayed and mouthed in imitation. Newly installed was a zodiacal dome, purple by night, golden by day, through which rode a radiant sun, illuminating the mobile constellations, each crafted with neat heraldic skills. Here a Viennese doctor reminded me that my head was protected by Aries, my arms by the Gemini, my neck by Taurus, that when battling for His Majesty against Turks I should follow the precepts of Gentleman Clowes against touching metal when the wound approached the celestial sign of any of my wounded parts. Finally, he told me that I already owed him five ducats.

His Majesty, fervently awaiting Johannes Kepler, master of all secrets, had no interest in Turks, indeed had queried their existence but, I learnt, hated the human mouth, whatever its guardian emblem. Too often greedy and unloving, it enclosed ugly teeth, ulcerous skin, tongues furred and malicious, furthermore uttering nonsense. Perceval wholeheartedly agreed. His face, however, always a little apart even in crowds, was downcast and rather solitary. Despite our instantaneous welcome, no request had yet come from the Emperor for his company. Also, save for a few pages and kitchen girls, no children roamed the Palace, their absence making everything heavier, slower, more predictable. The summer breeze would not blow Perceval's stories so that they alighted on some boy and girl dreaming in woods, indeed stories such as his were here pushed aside by the latest wonders and speculations. Perhaps the ending of the century would be the superannuation of all stories.

Absence of children was not wholly remedied by the prevalence of animals. A recent tract had denounced the world as a fenceless menagerie and, on this glittering summit between earth and sky, it smacked of some truth. Student of the organic, the Emperor regarded animals as brothers and sisters of humanity, albeit superior. He had favourites, not Buckinghams and Concinis, but two eagles. Wandering at will in garden, apartment, passage, beneath the flurrying birds, muzzled by jewels, were Barbary apes festooned in velvet with cloth of gold collars, court sashes, heavy sandals too big for them, and apt to be mistaken for Albanians; a lion with the Litany tied to its forepaw, a leopard, usually slumped though watchful, in a latrine, a panther which had usurped the Ivory Pavilion. Emerging from dusk or unlit rooms, a mass of queer stars and shadows, they seemed live cousins to the weathercock animals hovering above the City below us, and nights were accompanied by flutterings, growls, shufflings, even, I feared, slitherings. One gallery was haunted by a unicorn, of which the Emperor had commissioned a likeness; in another, the parrot, Ovid, gave utterance sharp, laconic and repetitive.

His Majesty was also a botanist, collecting flowers for their medicinal properties, symmetries, symbolisms, combining as hermetic embryos of the soul. Injury to plant or animal, an imperfect drawing or incantation, the careless bestowal of names, could entail misfortune, set princes awry. This did not ingratiate me, but through loving flowers less purposefully Perceval applauded, revering the Emperor as a universal genius to whom encouragement, service, devotion could never be sufficiently yielded. A daisy, he instructed me, as though to a child of wanton rebelliousness and stupidity, was eye of day, related to the sun, so that wisely, punctually at noon, the Emperor anointed his eyes with a drug distilled from daisies.

Rooms were lumbered with flower miniatures from Utrecht, Antwerp, Nuremberg, London, the artists often present, quarelling with botanists, physicians, alchemists, ignoring the gardens in haste to get paid, while the Emperor, absorbed in his florilegium, would forget conference, audience, banquet. He had his portrait composed entirely of flowers: sunflower hair, violet eyes, peony lips, nuts and berries everywhere, roses and lilies entwined irregularly, signifying his quest for the lost part of his soul, though malcontents affirmed that his soul was complete, though female.

Debarred from their natural focus, courtiers drifted in haphazard patterns as if in the slow, disordered aftermath of a dance, sometimes re-forming in small, tight groups, holding hands or embracing as if to keep each other from falling, never quite sure that great doors might, without fanfare, swing open and reveal,

227

solitary and rigid, faintly glowing against the darkness behind him, staring at them as though through paint, an eagle on each shoulder and leading a tiger cub on a green chain, the crowned and breathing power of the August House.

11

The gardens, terraced so subtly that they disguised the slant of the hill, absorbed Perceval while he awaited the Emperor's summons like a disciple his messiah. He was ever hurrying me out to his latest discovery, though I was frequently intrigued by my own findings.

Amongst the scented Fountains of Paradise, twinkling with lustres, Merlin rode a stag, goldfish darted between blue, circular leaves on crimson stems, ranged like ethereal stepping-stones to a pavilion where there might, at very least, hover a Chinese butterfly or transparent angelic wing. Reaching, apparently, to infinity, was a birch hedge labyrinth from which Perceval had to rescue me, finding me somewhat over-engrossed with a mosaic of a splendidly tumescent Bacchus. Carved parterres were laden with aramanth, crown imperial, Mexican marigolds, steepling hollyhocks, the summer air bulging with colour. Pallid Diana smoothed her hair on a green wall. Summer-houses – of all words the most beautiful, Perceval declared – crested small, bland knolls, one known to shelter a phoenix. Flowers were known to yield ghosts so that the gardens, he felt, were luxuriantly haunted. Nor was this entirely implausible, for the sharpest light melted to a deceptive shimmer – I never discovered the actual bounds – and, at his most solemn when joking, Perceval suggested that they altered with the sun. Blossom haze trembled into a peacock: tree and flower were motionless, their shadows were not. One statue of god or emperor possessed no shadow, all seemed breathing. I suspected that, when alone, he told them his stories of Merlin and Morganeuse, Gawain and Kai, and, when they yawned, he transferred them to squirrels and carp. Sylvanus was glimpsed in thickets, tangled with flower and leaf, delighting Perceval, who always sought the half-seen, inconclusive, barely imagined. Music lulled grotto, arbour, grove, though played less for these presences and courtiers than for the flowers; since, His Majesty asserted, flowers appreciated the waverings of lute and viol. Often impatient with Perceval's musings, I understood them better in these untroubled spaces. Artificial breezes wafted rose petals, distances revealed the lion, the panther, at once gone. Oblique lights disclosed a lawn, but no, a flat green pool, Hermes receded into a birch, a path lured us towards a tree bright with birds, strangely

228

silent, then seen painted on a trellis. No gardeners were seen but beds were forever dainty and weedless. A secret organ trilled birdsong, grottoes of mothy twilight moved to successive regions on concealed wheels, large green eyes glaring from within, no face seeming to lie behind them. Low aqueducts of Tuscan stone, covered by clumps of myrtle, bleached apple trees, cypresses, refreshed pools so fashioned that sprites seemed lurking under the surface. Voices murmured but always too far ahead, inveigling us to bridges and paths that ended only at hedges cut into minotaurs, satyrs, gorgons. The more we hastened, the less we reached. From unexpected vents issued coloured steam which, dissolving, appeared to have altered the prospect ahead, now littered with lakelets that vanished at our approach, or remote pinnacles stretched through air unnaturally bright but fading when a cloud or bird crossed the sun. On a mossy plinth Janus looked both ways, sometimes with tongue extended. At noon a flame always appeared on a stone altar carved with butterflies, scallop shells, a pregnant dancer. A small meadow, guarded by renegade Turkish mutes with scimitars, was blurred with pale hellebore, fiery poppy, henbane yellowy-white as a duck's egg, the many-fingered hemp, broom's rash yellow, blue verbane, from which licensed chemists collected petals, leaves, stamens. One of these was seeking a mixture with which to transform sunlight to the hues of copper. I demanded the benefits of this, but he at once looked so astonished, then petulant, that Perceval, ever commiserating at others' expense, took all my thalers to compensate him.

Once, unaccompanied, I descended a shaded avenue and found, beyond an artificial hill, Parnassus, reserved for invisible beings, though we once saw a head revolving in constantly changing lights, a white, polygonal temple on a circular island, reached by a tiny blue boat with silver oars. Entering, I saw mirrors deftly aligned to windows to give illusions of spaciousness, a low bed covered with smooth red pall, and at once felt strange dryness on the air, making me breathe so fast that I was soon choking, bemused with echoes of sounds I had not heard, feeling tremors against my feet, and thinking derangedly of a cellar imprisoning a violent bull or children missing from the Palace.

Later I described it to Perceval. He did not seem surprised but asked me to show him the temple, which, mortified, I failed to do. However often we passed Parnassus, to the left of the arboreal clock, to the right of the lichened Hadrian, I could never find it and my inquiries elicited only sceptical or suspicious shrugs. Perceval then inquired whether the place had held any spear or pot, but already I could not remember. He merely smiled with some secretive knowingness. This was more his domain than

229

mine, convincing him that tree, water, flower masses, effigies, were stationed to be comprehended only from the sky; those with bridges, mazes, basins, had zodiacal counterparts. He sounded assured, professional, though privately, unwilling to spoil his moment, I had long believed the zodiac was invented by ambitious and monopolistic priests, but managed to assume gravity as with boyish zest he related a curved brook to Virgo, roses to the Lyre, five oaks to Arthur's Wain. Roses planted in shape of a cross represented the merging of life and death. He added, with apparent inconsequence, that, calling herself Margaret, the Great Queen had lately ruled in England.

Though I had received no response from Sweden, the Emperor was known to have said that he had heard much of Perceval and was making ready to greet him. Perceval, very happily, seeing me intent on a new Aldine text, shook his head with unusual, though unnecessary, superiority, remarking that in Egypt the Princess had spoken of Thoth being God not only of writing but of death. I was surprised, not by the over-gifted Thoth but by mention of Kundry, so long unspoken between us that she could have been a once-favoured toy now forgotten in a chest.

The atmosphere of the gardens increasingly pervaded the Palace, which we now penetrated more deeply, owing not only to the nomadic animals and transitory birds but to more paintings, chosen by the Emperor and hanging in the most distant quarters, and in which landscapes, vegetables, boulders, mule-heads, if reversed, or seen in mirrors, became priests, a wild king, clouds, a smile.

Invited by the Grand Chamberlain, accompanied by new friends, inquisitive officials, spies, libertine buffoons with dazed eyes and elongated noses, we visited the domed planetarium, rounded, constructed on rails so as to be easily swung to confront particular areas of sky. Beneath tall, rearing telescopes, glassy floors, within which fish seemed to move, were decorated with star patterns, and a golden circle on a black screen was attributed to the renowned Arnold of Villanova. A Neoplatonist was pleased to inform us that the dome expressed Ideal Form in which the All became the One, though Perceval did not hear him and I was more interested in a third eye, painted in blue and yellow on the forehead of a stone magus.

Perceval, indeed, was more anxious to be initiated into the Emperor's House of Mystery. He already knew that in it seven rooms unfolded successive degrees of understanding, each heralded by secret tests, obstructed by riddles, so that few candidates passed farther than the third. In every room, save the last, presided imagery from planets, numbers, trees, animals – salmon, stag, horse, bear, raven, serpent. For myself, disliking mystery, disbelieving most of it, even the first offered no temptation, and I understood that the floors, though flat, gave swaying effects of ascent, which I should have found displeasing. Perceval, of course, chattered incessantly about it, and I fancied that its secrets were ill-kept, as such matters generally are, people always hinting importantly at what others had long known. We heard of sprawling decorations: a wraith rising from a bowl, a snake encircling a tree, Scythian queens, twelve youths spattered with blood, a head half-white, half-black, with bandaged mouth, an inscription beneath it: *If any Lord of the Grail should by divine grace be ruling an outlandish people, he must divulge not his race or his name, and devote himself to securing their rights.*

Few such lords were to hand.

The symbols of the first six rooms were mostly of Grail and redemption, the old matter of bleeding lance, pierced ring and fish, old men, young women with curved, cruel mouths, Death rebuked by a singer. Darkness and light, lonely valleys, specks of grain, a pomegranate, a tangle of flowers shaped like a dish or the womb of a love goddess. Snake, wrens, peacocks.

Infinite bliss, perfect understanding, Earthly Paradise, dying in order to live, to me were less preferable than worldly wisdom and the prospect of employment. Perceval rebuked me, eyes and mouth pleasant, almost affectionate. 'You are a scoffer. You make simple things difficult.'

I envisaged his reaching the seventh room, Heaven itself, by no means from strict exercises and arduous meditation but by accident, stumbling into it in pursuit of a damaged rat or wounded bird. From him, remember, originated the phrase 'In all innocence'.

We agreed that Heaven, so often imagined but nowhere very plausibly described, was here quite empty, without tricksome mirror, intricate signs: a dazzling Other World with white purity of light corroding the ephemeral, exalting the imponderable. 'If only. . . .' He brought his hands together, bright face clouding. To myself I conceived austere thoughts of God inspiring the search for light, which then revealed that no God exists. The absence of the Grail meant that it was now within one, completing all souls but my own. I had long noticed that the word *soul*, like *truth*, is invariably followed by something foolish.

12

A new star sparkled in the distant constellation of the Serpent, apparently heralding the new century and demonstrating the fluidity of matter.

My letter arrived, ordering me to replace the Swedish envoy, retiring through pox and bad conscience, and for some weeks I was far from gardens and spiritual prolixity, immersing myself in the political rivalries. Two predominated. One, derisively called the Mystics, supported the Emperor, affected Spanish dress, for the Spanish professed to explore evil and darkness in order to reveal goodness and light. A favourite Mystic text was: 'Rise, you sleeper, arise from the dead, and Christ shall enlighten you.' With Jesuits watching and waiting, the Mystics were opposed by the Realists, a branch of the Viennese 'Custodians of the August House', intriguing for the Emperor's replacement, in face of Turkish invasions, Protestant unrest, approaching bankruptcy.

All agreed that the crisis would not occur until after the ceremonies for the new century, only a month ahead.

Perceval, of course, though devoted to the Emperor, was immune from political understanding or interest, and kept his own path and indeed almost all encouraged him to do no more. As ever, he was one of those before whom grand personages bow, doors open as if of themselves, beasts lick their hands, rub dangerous heads against their legs, and servants beg to assist without waiting for payment. Ladies were calling him Serenella, the Serene; all agreed that he was one the Emperor would be delighted to honour. On his wall he now had the Emperor's portrait, sent by the monarch himself; sad eyed, pearls in his ears, a jewel in his beard – had it, I joked, lodged there accidentally or did he suck it for its abstruse powers? Perceval's sigh merely made me sound crassly irreverent.

Away from the gardens, Perceval, despite invitations and popularity, was again inwardly troubled. Needing children as Gawain needed sun, he must feel his stories dying within him. The ladies and gentlemen in their boudoirs and arbours desired not his stories but his charm. Simultaneously, the Realists suspected him: his obscure origins, secretive ambitions, designated him as one more baleful influence within the parvenu imperial entourage. There were whispers abroad, saying he wore a green hat, suggesting the reincarnation of Merlin, even Wotan.

I was not expecting ever to see the Emperor and present my credentials. Kepler had arrived, vanishing at once into the sanctum, then seldom seen. The monarch was always about to appear: small processions would form, ladies rehearse curtsies, lords prepare their grimaces, petitioners finger their scrolls, but the massive, eagled doors remained fast. Long awaiting audience had been Signor Colorni, with his new gun that shot twenty thousand bullets in one burst. After a fruitless month he departed for Constantinople. Perceval admired him, not for the deplorable gun but for his dexterity. He requested a card – a queen. Perceval handed him one and received it back – an ace! His Majesty, I soon reported, believed that an inspired ruler need not in fact rule; he has to do more, he has to *be*. Most laws were enforced by the wicked and ignorant: true law should be expressed in verse, song, incantatory prayer, to move the heart and reach the soul. Perceval was perplexed that any of us should demur. For him, the more we strive, the less we achieve. Pausing from my dispatches, I envisaged the Roman Emperor, Lord of the West, on his lonely terrace, gazing over the mountains, real or imaginary, towards infinite freedoms in boundless space, while harvests failed, disease roamed, tax gatherers were assaulted and laws ignored. The future, I advised, lay not with the Mystics. Nature, I continued, tends towards confusion and violence, to be remedied, however briefly, by authority. The Emperor, before Kepler's arrival, had been absorbed with an unfinished epic in which Prometheus liberates humanity but surrenders to vicious, vulture-like self-doubts, and wanders the suffering world in self-imposed silence. The Emperor himself, as a seeker, descends to the underworld for mysterious teachings, then climbs back to earth robed in sunlit wisdom.

My dispatches were warnings, increasingly urgent. I had always preferred to respect strangers rather than love enemies, to obey laws weak or unjust rather than rejoice in the overthrow of all law. No emperor or deliverer would save the world, but if each of us controlled himself the world would slightly improve. The Emperor was continually dismayed by those who failed his expectations, and, privately, I considered that after initial and excited intimacy, Perceval would do likewise.

My misgivings were confirmed by a Holsteiner banker, Friedrich von Epp, dour, complaining, whose criticisms derived from evidence that too few people resembled himself. He was, however, well informed, telling me that the Realists were determined to keep Perceval from the Emperor, and I at once had a vision of him lying strangled in the fierce light of the seventh room. Himself possessing what the Emperor called a divided soul, he said drily, ambiguously, that even a sensible man could learn from Perceval, though I noticed that he showed small inclination to do so. He was influential and respected, though, at home, cultivating a singularity more appreciated by Perceval than by me. He introduced us to his family, a collection of dolls inhabiting model byres, farmsteads, salons, castles, churches. To add to these he travelled far, returning with a Pomeranian grenadier, Lorraine chevalier, Jutland pastor. Pouring us rare wine, he would reveal the latest price of Lithuanian timber, Lübeck honey, Münster cloth, and, in the same tone, the activities of his toy ménage. Fondling an indifferent manikin, he introduced him as Jan

Dombruski, Jagellan bravo, tempted to saw off his own head. Another, Mynheer van Rafte, was Perceval's favourite, to be addressed with meticulous kindness. Friedrich, severe, humourless, expected by the Realists to help revive the Empire, lowered his voice before Mynheer van Rafte. 'The good man has one failing. He calls himself Lord Leicester', and indicated another doll, some seven inches high, in large farthingale, leaning on an exquisite balustrade. 'He calls that worthy lady, Madame Elizabeth, whereas, you may observe, she's only a miller's wench.'

Perceval, pensive, suggested that untruths were not always lies. He had once mistaken a common sycamore surrounded by stones for the World Tree, but the error had served him better than medicine.

The value of the last word can be disputable, though he could see more than I did, occasionally receiving less than medicine. When I once saw a plain fountain, he insisted it was an image of Isis, then approached it with deference, trod on some hidden pedal and was promptly drenched. 'Yet', he remained imperturbable, 'I was scarcely mistaken.'

He would see grass ripple on a windless day, stars in daytime skies, gifts less important to me than glass roses from a rich heiress, commendation of any kind, report of a weavers' plot – though when were weavers not plotting?

Far more frequently than I did, Perceval attracted the outlandish, the dubious, the deranged, now gathering in multitudes to wreak their will on the new century, one indeed guaranteeing to postpone it, for a title and cash payment, an offer kept secret from the Emperor. Perceval had to arrange a supper for 'the Assistant of God', an itinerant fakir who later made the company drink a yellowy liquid of some potency, poured from wine-skins of improbable antiquity. Then, donning black cape, red cap, he gestured, throwing on the air the outline of a bleeding corpse dangling from a tree. A boy sprang as if from nowhere, knelt, gathered the blood in a cup, drank it, fell senseless, recovering three days later. His master rather spoilt the trick by adding one already familiar: pulling a goat from the air, then by elaborate passes shrivelling it into a pair of horns which floated away through the window. The fakir had recently escaped burning at Millein for claiming that magic is finite and Jesus had wasted much of it for future generations by performing trifling miracles. The Ascension had been no great matter, an affair of catalepsy involving the tongue; he himself could teach it but at a prohibitive cost. Historians have claimed that he was subsequently swallowed by a great fish of his own invention. Jesus, he told us, had not died on a cross, itself only an emblem of despair, but years later, in India. The fakir had left that country after accidentally eating

234

beef, thus polluting Brahmins at sixty-four paces. His masterpiece, changing solid gold into a black cloud, I thought unlikely to improve the imperial finances, and the Realists soon hustled him down the hill.

Perceval never seemed much interested in Jesus, far less than in Gawain, and of course Kundry, and God he seldom mentioned, though in a tavern once, to the players, who so loved words and names and riddles, he did suggest that Satan too was part of life. They applauded when he continued, probably quoting some wordy fraud, 'The Straight leads less directly to the Centre than the Crooked.' Scarcely tavern talk, and the landlord had looked anxious.

I suspect that, if he ever thought about it, Perceval in pity rated God not the cause of Creation but the result, dying with each death, returning with uncertain prospects, at each birth.

The old century was gasping its last, the Emperor remaining invisible with Kepler, discussing spatial orbits, discussing Dürer, examining his many clocks, fondling erotic illustrations of goddesses screaming as they coupled with animals, impaling themselves on a horn; of old gods crouching to suck the boys they had stripped. He enjoyed, I had learnt, handling coins, for a coin was more than currency: in shape it was the world in miniature; its superscription was his own head, crowned and laurelled; its numerals linked him with gods and Caesars, stars and elements, past and future.

My few glimpses of him were very late at night: a half-figure cowled in shadows, beneath an arch, beside a pillar, head averted.

Despite the collapse of a century, the world continued. The Sultan sent a team of Arab mares, at which the Emperor never glanced, though their slender grooms attracted him. A Spanish deputation offered him a stupendous bribe against France, which, to the Treasury's distress, he refused. From the Tsar, an ice palace of dramatic writhings, breathless taperings, debonair turrets, ornate domes, occupying seventeen wagons though melting before it had left Poland. German and Bohemian states were being wrecked by religious outbreaks, but still the Emperor conferred with valets, locked himself in with Kepler, while great councillors paraded with gleaming panoply, and without direction. The Mystics were enraptured by solemn verses about a candle: its virgin form born from innocent flowers, the flame a birth into higher being ... voices outside chattering about rebellion, a town in flames, soldiers dragging Lutherans into Romish churches ... rapine, Plague, threats from Vienna. ... But see, the candle is slowly consumed: the soul will escape, the last twitch of flame will light a new wick, a further illumination.

Good events, bad events, the Emperor rebuked the Realists, were but bubbles on the sea.

I looked to my ciphers and confidential Swiss couriers, my missives reporting mortars, culverins, bombards covertly assembled: some Palace and Cathedral windows, on flimsy pretext, being replaced by oiled cloth. Pack-horses were limping beneath loads heavier than flax, wheat, apples. In cellar and cloister, mill and stall, was muttered 'new lamps for old' and, to wild applause, a Czech nobleman cried aloud, 'They get hold of an owl, get a cheap mob to admire it, and call it government.'

The new century was upon us: the frontier, the brink, the unknown, so that some may have dreamt of the sea monster, the virgin chained to the rock, the dazzling saviour from the sky.

13

By Emperor's order, a ceremony, devised by Jesuits, was held in the Cathedral square to exorcize the baleful old century. The whole court flocked beneath a throne, huge and canopied, propped on gilded dragon's legs. Politically, it was essential for His Majesty to show himself at his most effulgent, but the throne remained isolated in tragic emptiness, the people murmuring, the rest of us speechless. An historian of a later era did suggest that the Emperor had indeed been present, enthroned, but invisible, owing to his white clay.

On the vast black and white paving we must have resembled exotic chessmen. Heavily wigged, ruffed, cloaked, the four great State Councillors led the procession, moving slowly as if under water, to salute the throne, followed by the mitred and plumed, the sashed and jewelled, ladies with tall hair enclosed in tinted nets, sprinkled with stars, silver droplets and sprays, necks and shoulders thick with cypress powder, some faces as if dazed by their own finery. Foreign guests were stiffly important, noses high; also botanists, librarians, geomancers, astronomers, ringed by guards in slashed capes and high green boots with golden spurs. Marshalled by the Grand Chamberlain performing like an archangelic sheepdog, we listened not to the parrot Ovid, but to a bishop from a marble pulpit reading a prayer written by the Emperor for the restoration of harmonies and the Rod of Nourishment, commended by Cicero as requisite to liberate mankind from grossness, on behalf of true knowledge and science. Needful too was the settlement of correspondencies, the recovery of vital memory lost since Pythagoras. Hanging from twin towers were the rival clocks of Ptolemy and Copernicus, the former strung with crystal globes moving in constant dance round a golden earth.

To chanting of a *Dies irae*, a pole tall as a mast, flower-wreathed, carved with demonic faces, suddenly blazed with blue and yellow flames, emitting impish, explosive sparks. Goaded by an air pump a plywood Augustus raised one arm, and, behind him, an eagle was expected to swoop from a festooned dome but failed to do so. A banner shaped like a hand was unfurled, pointing in the breeze away from charred remains of the pole towards the future, suddenly manifest in a pyramid of spades, sickles, sheaves. Across the Cathedral steps, ghosts, probably students disguised, danced lugubriously, monotonously, until routed by a monk upholding a Gospel of St John, then throwing black beans over his shoulder, bowing to an epicene representative of Peace, and consigning to a sulphurous pit abruptly opening on the tessellated stone a bearded, grinning Turk. Trumpets sounded and arrows at once plunged into the Ptolemaic clock, shattering it, to the clang of Cathedral bells.

The tableaux were adequate, the singing well drilled, the sermons brief, but during a pause, as if from the blue, soft sky, an unrehearsed noise sounded. Thunder? Could it be cannon? Had the Emperor, Illustrious and Universal, stamped his God-given foot? Consternation started, faces lost blood, were suddenly stained white, until music resumed, blasting somewhat too loud.

The festival allayed none of the certainties and suspicions. The century shuffled in, as if shamefacedly. Surreptitious too was Kepler's departure, to the Emperor's desolation. With precipitate energy he summoned a cardinal from Vienna, who raised tithes, borrowed from Jews, hired spectacular equipages and escorts, arrived in state, to find that His Majesty had already forgotten him, was receiving no one, in grief for a Protestant general whom, over-impulsively, he had beheaded.

Then it was, and, despite ostensible secrecy, known immediately throughout the Palace and the City beneath, that Perceval received the famous letter borne by six attendants under a scarlet awning, in which the Emperor, Supreme, Apostolic and Thrice Blessed, begged his son and brother to visit him at the seventh midnight from this date. Enclosed were golden keys of the House of Mystery. Were Perceval admitted to the first six rooms, into the seventh he would be escorted by the Emperor himself. The Realists were confounded. His fits of lassitude vanished, he was light as June, almost dapper, though dangers were now so threatening; yet so complex, that I was unable to make him acknowledge them. Very quiet, he was never unobtrusive, his personality, difficult to delineate, still teased. The Realists spoke

237

louder, maintaining that with his disputable origins, alien, perhaps from far East, far West, he was a spy of the Persians or their Turkish allies, or sent by France to exploit the monarch's fears and beliefs, and undermine the August House.

Revealing my sources, witnesses, dispatches, I urged him to leave the Palace, forgo the Emperor, disregard Heaven. Delay might be fatal. But his smile, ever simple, contrived to make me unconvincing and pompous. He had total trust, not in me, not in any government, sect, regiment, but in himself. Nor could I ever disdain such trust. The oft-told tale of his contact with Remingen is, I can promise, true. Remingen of Utrecht was famous for his unpublished treatise, *Concerning Universals*. He promised to outline people's characters and prospects, if permitted to hold one of their intimate possessions – ruff, codpiece, towel. Asking him to tell me about myself, I unfairly handed him a ring borrowed from Perceval, given him long ago by the Princess and deeply cherished. Holding it, Remingen postured theatrically, eyes racing, mouth opening, eyes staring at me in unflattering disbelief, before telling me that my soul was illimitable, my death would be secret, that I would be remembered in poetry and song by all save Chinese and Mexicans. Meanwhile, Perceval giggled happily at my warning, and declared some nonsense about my forcing him to return to himself. Shrugging, I desisted, swiftly to learn more, this time from Friedrich, who claimed it came from Magister Böll, most percipient of his dolls.

A belief had long existed that, from the beginning, the Church had contained a small and secret group, a second Church, with knowledge older than Jesus' own. This group had been founded by John, the beloved disciple, on the Saviour's command after disappointment with Peter. His own teachings, still imperfect, couched in obscure or contradictory parables, neat maxims simplistic or untranslatable, over-facile hermeticism, he bequeathed to John. More tolerant, less mercurial, more clear-thinking, John taught that man is capable of moments of rapture and insight, glimpses of the Kingdom vulgarly misunderstood as the Other World beyond death, moments to be prolonged by physical, intellectual and moral rigours. By a last, though considerable miracle, Jesus rendered John immune from death until the end of the world. The inner Church would replace the Papacy and establish the true Kingdom, moral dominion in this world.

At first barely mentionable, yet now filtering down into the City, was the suggestion, originating in Perceval's mild countenance, generous mien, rumours of his easy access to the House of Mystery – he had indeed passed the first six ordeals though disclosing no more – that he was John himself, fated for spiritual marriage with the Emperor, and, in this century, a harbinger of the Last Days. Some added that John and Gamalean were identical. This was breath-taking blasphemy and heresy, uniting Jesuit and Black Brother, Papalist and Lutheran, noble and peasant in horror, in demands for Perceval's consignment to wailing, gnashing of teeth, outer darkness, promised by Jesus at his most explicit. Perceval and the Emperor would surely drag each other to doom.

Perceval visited the Emperor several times, and a day had been appointed for their entry to the Seventh Room. Reports were fattening accusation, rumours of conspiracy, forebodings. His Majesty, in a gush of delight, was declaring to all within hearing – not, in truth, very many save, of course, the eagles – that his new friend's soul shone through his eyes, blue for fortune, blue for life, that his hair contained gold of eternity, casting rings of light, and showing that the pure in heart had already seen God. Meister Eckhardt, His Majesty would say, had declared that even God cannot frustrate the humble soul with supreme ambition.

The imperial confessor, unlikely to be pleased, surely reported all this to Mystic and Realist alike.

Three days after Perceval's second audience the Emperor's lion was found poisoned. All recognized this as a deliberate political act. Following his third, a hasty summons from the distraught monarch, I awaited him in his apartment, where he returned only long after dawn. I need not have come. Neither markedly secretive nor devious, he was silent, very troubled and, ashamed of my questions, I left him.

Thenceforward he kept much alone, probably freeing himself from his few worldly preoccupations, in training for the Seventh Room, his Thule, his distant castle. That the Emperor was to accompany him had given him not pride but comfort, though I realized that he was purposely delaying, perhaps from humility, perhaps from something more disturbing. Certainly his earlier elation had evaporated. Wearily disregarding covert threats and unmistakable growlings, closing his door to affectionate ladies, downright toadies, he seemed paralysed by a revelation from the Emperor, an intimation from Klingsor, or by agonizing doubts. I wondered too whether the House of Mystery had hitherto disappointed him, setting lifelong hopes at naught, or overstimulated him, leaving him unnerved.

Yet, as the City clamoured with news of a rebellion of serfs, typhus on the Danube, his obduracy broke, and, in the last despair, he came to me, making me, in my turn, dumb. He had seen Kundry.

In the House of Mystery he had witnessed a ritual in which within fumes rising from a cauldron, an apparition of the Princess had implored his help. He could think of nothing else. No spears would now lift for her; her dewy chalice had dried, her hair was white and sparse, her face and body ravaged, in the hideous travesty which he had, in his callow blindness and fears, first seen her: eyelids, nose, chin, monstrously fleshy, only her pleading eyes fully her own.

His distress was such that I could not state my disbelief. Cabalistic tricks were commonplace, the Realists could be behind this, but I merely sat with him as his head drooped, heavy with tears, weakened in loss of colour. On the next day, he and the Emperor, twin souls, were to enter Heaven. They did not.

I was reading early in a favourite arbour where roses, myrtle, a stone boy in a pool were concealed by tall, neat hedges. Sparkle of dewy leaves gave illusions of movement so that I continually glanced up from the page. Once a tiger, toothless, almost blind, limped past me, drank a little, wandered away. Then, from the Palace, its columns and balustrades still hazed, I saw Perceval, pack on shoulders, leading an unimpressive horse, walking towards a gate. I called out and, after hesitation, he turned aside to me. We looked at each other, the stone boy mediating between us, wistful, lonely, a little apprehensive. Sky, trees, our reflections in the water, were numbed. He would have left me without farewell, not from coldness but from our belief that endings do not exist, only a reliable pattern of withdrawal and renewal. He had withdrawn from his cherished Emperor, forgone the seventh room, anxious only for Kundry, now needing protection and love. In fresh sunlight he looked resolute, armed in his own way for new adventure. Neither of us spoke, words crumbling within us. With manly effort he kissed me, then, under my embrace, trembled, his face transfigured into small planes of light. A moment later he had gone, draining the cup of selflessness, the true Grail, a poet who had never written, seeking a princess dispossessed and perhaps long dead.

The Emperor, no phantom but a lord wounded anew, lamented him so much that he forgot what little appetite for government he still retained. The eagles deserted him or were destroyed, he wailed a little, then, in the smallest room in the Palace, settled himself to wait. Soon a coach arrived from Vienna, soldiers marched, the Crown was taken elsewhere, and he too wandered away.

Five

As the fire mounteth of itself, upward, and is carried round with the heavens, so the soul of man is led upward . . . by the senses, and doth many things in and out of the body without them.

Sir Walter Raleigh

I have built my religion out of *Parsifal*. One can serve Providence only in the guise of the Hero.

Adolf Hitler

The eternal life bestowed by the Grail is the truly pure and noble.

Adolf Hitler

I confess that I do not know how to finish this memoir. Several alternatives offer themselves. I select what follows partly because of what I must call the commonplace singularity of the chief personage, partly because it concerns the only influence, hideously ironic, wielded in our own time by Parsifal.

Trees, turrets, were perfunctory scrawls on grey, damp air, the vagueness exaggerating the heights and depths of this castle which villagers named 'The Middle of the World', though its real name derived from a robber knight who had resisted the Huns. From a high room I looked down at the wide courtyard where black, uniformed spectres drilled, drilled, almost soundlessly, automatons stalking in four circles, two evolving clockwise, two in reverse, wheels of some uncanny machine designed to produce nothing save stupefaction. All figures were abnormally tall and slender, as if bred from some monstrous experiment, and indeed they themselves were encouraged to copulate with carefully selected girls on the grave of some warrior, to imbue the child with heroic virtues. On the nearest edge of the courtyard a silver gong glinted from a solitary pine, dully reflected in the pool beneath.

Despite my companion I felt unpleasantly alone, bemused by the revolving circles, the mists, the dreamy flow of sensations. Our business was concluded, I had no wish to talk further. I knew of microphones beneath floorboards, within pipes, the advisability of keeping close to the wall on staircases, the danger even to neutrals. Behind me was the circular, overheated room, one wall red and black with shelved files, at which the owner would periodically glance like a complacent father. I was glad not to be shown their contents, despite a professional interest in all that pertained to this place, somewhere within which was reputed a collection of skulls gathered from Eastern captives in evidence of his genetic beliefs. The room, smaller than I had expected, was meticulously tidy, dusted and varnished like a spinster's parlour. The desk was broad, on which lay gloves and cap, startling black on the white, polished surface, the black strap and silver death's head badge sharply reflected on a small, bronze cauldron engraved with leaves and horns. A table, another circle, was crowded with artificial roses, glistening as if washed, dainty chocolate boxes, cardboard animals, tin trumpets, cushions embroidered with initials. These were presents, for he enjoyed standing godfather to babies of the Black Guards, born in what he termed the special orchards. At several levels but scrupulously in balance hung neatly framed pictures: a bloodied spear poised over a purple bed, burning pyres, a nude but discreet woman by a lake, a warrior, fair-haired as those stationed without, galloping naked with lance raised towards the dawn, a girl with flowing, straw-coloured hair, cornflower blue eyes, Greek nose in white robe. Others, of birds, harvests, trees, were so crude and garish that I wondered whether my host had himself committed them.

Too warm, breathing hard, nerves not quite steady, I turned to confront the puffy, faintly Mongoloid face, expressionless as a tennis-ball, lumped behind thick, rimless pince-nez. The small blue-grey eyes blinked too frequently, one hand had a tendency to tremble. Mediocre, with receding chin, thin, drab hair smoothed flat, he too was uniformed: black riding breeches and high boots, black tunic, belt, buttons, a mysterious flurry of oak leaves, silver stars and threads on collar and lapels, his ring emblazoned with two lightning flashes, Thor's mark, stamped over a Gothic 3. They yet seemed unwarlike, a mere defence against ridicule.

At the start, sententious as a pastor, he had required my pedigree, titles, credentials, his tone mild, somewhat ingratiating. Though our business had ended inconclusively, he was reluctant to release me, while sensing my anxiety to depart. Noting my gaze at the black cap and gloves on the pale table, he sighed lightly though markedly. 'I am a soldier of fortune, destined, I could say doomed, to be one of the lonely. The revolutionary

. . .' – pride gleamed within the dull skin – 'is always a stricken being, I should say man. Misunderstood. Not least in your country.'

Stricken he was, one of many whose minds had bypassed the eighteenth century. Popularly, at times sardonically, he was called Faithful Henry, and once, though not recently, the Russian leader had applauded him as Guarantor of Order. He admitted hopes of being exalted to be Duke of an autonomous Burgundy-Lotharingia. I also knew his membership of the Thule Society, renowned for political murders and defamation of posters of its enemies with paste moistened by the sweat of bitches on heat. I had data of his study of Nordic runes, his belief in himself as avatar of Henry the Fowler, medieval conqueror of Slavs, reputed founder of tournaments, before whose tomb he had knelt to promise conquest of the East. Likewise, he was convinced that his own leader, Wolf, had returned to earth after several previous incarnations, a belief disregarded by my Swedish government.

His prim courtesy fitted his neatness, his fear of dirt, of smoking, disease, abnormality. His noiselessness reminded me of a fish. Reputedly, when telephoned by Wolf, he listened standing to attention.

Inwardly, I too sighed. After a bath heated by oat straw, I had breakfasted on leeks and mineral water, and, though I was now being offered drink, the choice was between barley water, cold herbal tea, or pure water with a petal in it.

As before, with embarrassing respect, even obsequiousness, he questioned me about Parsifal. Was his aura visible? Faint yellow, perhaps, tinged with violet? Ineffable gold or gentle white?

'I see him as a creature of air and fire. The thought of him eases my stomach cramps.'

From his desk he pulled a reproduction of the Venoux *Parsifal the Redeemer*, a sickly arrangement of a haloed youth with blue, wondering eyes adrift on a cloud of pallid gold. While light glimmered from glass, wood, metal, the flabby hand stroked Parsifal's idiot face as if to elicit admiration from it.

'*From Bohemia's woods and fields* . . . the beauty of those words always makes me weep.' I did not observe him doing so. Replacing the picture, he stared at me, the light on his spectacles momentarily giving an effect of blindness. 'I believe he would have appreciated my own simplicity of regimen, and indeed I have the temerity to style myself a Grail Knight, one of those through whom we deliver ourselves from class and complexity, the blight of modern man.'

The words were snipped off, dry and worn smooth by repetition. He lectured, perhaps seeing not me but an amorphous mass of initiates. 'The stars, the seasons, the fields, are smothered by steel and glass. The cleanliness of leaf and wave, the hardness of stone, innocence of beast and bird, the sublime essence of reaper and smith, of mother and child, need restoring. In his devotion to ravens, our leader sets an example to the world. I myself . . .' – the monotonous voice slightly altered, charged with curious pride – 'have a university degree in agronomy. Even as a boy, I was entranced by blossom and harvest, snows and brooks. I could have been a poet. Indeed . . .' – though he was irredeemably humourless, he contrived a small, pinched smile – 'in certain respects I believe I actually am. Still . . . I recognize it is the significance, the very point of my existence, I salute Parsifal as the perfection of chivalry, the spirit of the countryside tilting against mongrel towns, lawyers and clerks. The blood feud, trial by combat, is more life imbued than dusty law. Inspired by him, we are the first to respect, even reverence, the peasant. We must recover our aegis as a farming race. Conquest of Eastern soil will replenish our rural disposition. Our land will be the everlasting, I should say eternal, fountain of youth and blood inspiring the Folk, ever mindful of our ancestors. It is never easy . . .' – he sounded reproachful – 'my, so to speak, friend, the Grand Huntsman. . . .' He hesitated, probably doubting my own youth and blood, sensing my incipient yawn, my scepticism about Parsifal's reverence for peasants, his pudgy nose crinkling as though uncertain where to breathe. 'He, overlord of our forests and animals . . . you will not believe, credit, this, but he cannot tolerate dogs. Dogs! Well. . . .' Another thin smile wavered, quivered, the small, dull head lifting as if to prevent it dropping off. 'True . . .' – he was disposed to be fair – 'there's mess, dropped hairs of course, and worse. . . .' Glancing about him, he was reassured by the cleanliness. 'But not to waste your time, we are the only people with wholesome respect for animals. A few Buddhists, perhaps. . . .' He paused, then smoothed away Buddhists with a gesture vaguely appeasing, then regarded me more fixedly, even pleadingly. He who was not with him was against him. 'Pristine!'

He tasted the world approvingly, as though he had invented it and seemed tempted to explain its meaning. Instead, he said, 'You are aware, sir, that I have founded the Ancestral Heritage Institute! For racial research, for physical and moral hygiene.' The dense, round glasses gleamed with sudden menace, a reminder not of moral hygiene but of the armed men revolving beneath the windows. 'We have proved, proved systematically, that our peasants are biologically superior.' He did not offer a definition of what he meant, but continued, his terminology smacking of bad journalism, opting for 'portals' rather than

244

'doors'. 'Our movement is organized initiative. We are preventing Eastern drugs, breath of devils, noxious plants, inorganic materials, from spoiling our sacred farmsteads, where we cleave to clean soil, tender foliage, the oak's strong roots. We are pledged to destroy diseased cells. After victory I shall personally superintend the Duchy, foster a green land of art and science, animals, the tall and sunburnt. The French kings debased it for cheap wine. The world will look on us with astonishment. I have already ordered herb gardens to embellish our villages for the sick and retired.'

A chill flickered along my skin. All embassies knew of those villages, the hellish camps. Earlier, he had used 'disinfecting' for those 275,000 children and old people deemed unfit to live.

Faithful Henry was standing slightly closer to me, oppressively so. 'My good heart will ruin me. Yet sometimes I feel a denizen of Olympus, beyond life itself. Bound by mystical kinship not only with my Leader, with Parsifal himself, but with spirits of unknown living and dead, with the woods and grasses. What all of us can learn from these wonderful souls is the insignificance of conventional morality. Enlightenment, racial insight, comes as easily to the wicked as to the good. Even Wagner would not be admitted to the company of saints. I myself am chiefly to be considered not as a conscientious minister but as a scientist with a conscience. That will be my place in history.'

I retained composure. The head, while speaking, in fervid anxiety to convince, had remained absolutely still, as though in a surgical collar. The voice moistened somewhat, describing a recent command performance of *Parsifal* attended by the Party hierarchy.

The hands rubbed together, never quite mastering that small, stubborn tremble. 'My researches reveal that each Tuesday, Elizabeth, Empress of Russia, would, with all her courtiers, exchange costumes. Men dressing as women, women as men. To deceive spirits!'

His manner was condescending. 'There is more in that than ordinary people can imagine. As for Elizabeth, well, woman is function, but man is will.' He sighed again. Could he have recalled the wife of the Propaganda Minister, who would certainly have disputed it?

He continued, inexorable, boring, yet with the unpleasant allure of the nonentity in power. 'A demon once posed as Brahmin and begged a peasant to surrender his children. The peasant agreed to do so and the demon at once ate them. The peasant, feeling no sorrow, only marvellous delight, was transformed into Buddha.'

The story baffled me and, disappointed, he withdrew somewhat

245

to the safety of the military cap and gloves. He was subtly altering, seemed drugged, speaking from memory, his words as though recorded. 'Curiosity is not inherent in man. I have discovered cave-dwellers in Tunisia still ignorant of pottery, spinning, almost unaware of fire, with no desire to learn anything at all!'

His disapproval contained the pathos of one with unbounded ambition and no talent.

That evening I witnessed the ritual through which Faithful Henry periodically rallied his paladins. From a high gallery in the Great Hall, itself lit by torches flaring from walls and making the scene tremble within gigantic, ever-moving shadows, I sat with neutral diplomats, looking down on a huge round table. Here, on high, pig-skinned chairs, twelve black-uniformed leaders feasted with their commander, each sporting a newly presented silver ring and dagger of honour. The hard, young faces under harvest locks were suitably scarred, duelling being obligatory. The meal, wholly vegetarian, with cold broth instead of wine, was at odds with their animal appearance, and I suspected that, earlier, they must have surreptitiously gnawed fine roasts, swigged expensive liquor.

Damp perforated the air, much was opaque, like those distant towers and underwater cities that had obsessed Parsifal.

Before this session we had descended various levels of the castle, some steps perilously slippery, to Valhalla, crypt of the illustrious dead, where funeral urns rested on stone pedestals, each holed to allow escape to any lingering spirit.

Here was a Night of the Gods, on the frontier between real and unreal, world and underworld. I myself was midway between roseate, raftered ceiling and submerged darkness, surrounded by swords and spears crossed between flames, sculptured shields and armorials, and the metallic Party emblem.

Faithful Henry was at his most parsonical, doubtless fresh from communions with Henry the Fowler, as he addressed the knights, conviction unable to galvanize his monotonous delivery. He could have been dictating to a secretary.

'For thousands of years you have battled against wizards flitting from evil Asia. You are steadfast Rome and Sparta withstanding corrupt Carthage and Troy. Today you triumph against subhuman Tartars. Great days are restored. This hallowed place has always endured miracles of valour and sacrifice, and I can entrust you with knowledge of an ancient rune, promising that in this region a castle will bear alone an onslaught from the East.'

He paused for applause, which did not come. From my colleagues covert somnolence was starting. I detected no scepticism or protest from below, at a revelation surely ominous for them.

'Destiny is awarding you the great chance. My loyal ones, you will inherit a world you yourselves have made happy and beautiful. You will destroy, even exterminate, the last ape leading the last Mongol. You are handed the shield of wisdom, the whip of power, some of your hands will touch the Grail itself. Remember you have the duty, the moral right, to overcome our foe, but no right to enrich yourselves by as much as a cigarette, which, as the truly cultured, you abhor. Your task is to rebuild a Europe rotting from perversion and racial laxity, yet to keep intact your souls. You are harsh at times to others, you are always harsh to yourselves. Hardness, decency, courage, poverty, belief, obedience, struggle. The Castle, not the University. Our leader has taught us, imbued us, with the glorious knowledge that ours is a doctrine of conflict, not of inertia. Happiness, fortune, personal survival, are nothing. We survive in the All. Sacrifice befits nobility. What did the mighty Richard Wagner teach us? Purification of blood and being, contempt for greed, for gold, elimination of dross. The simplicity of Parsifal, unaffected as a cowbell in the mountains.'

My own information about current traffic in black-market food, jewels, purloined real estate, drugs, convinced me that the youths' contempt for gold and personal survival was less thorough than their commander assumed, though they would not jib at the elimination of dross. That the Australian blackfellow perhaps best expresses racial purity might not have amused him.

My associates drowsed. A few torches now languished; night, pouring over us, was ready to crush even the preacher. Through the dimming tissue of air I discerned a puny strut masquerading as the Duke's stride.

'The impossible is a mere word. We are promised victory or destruction. There can be no other.'

But heads were moving forward, cocked to something else. Further blood pledges, more nonsense, or. . . . I was suddenly convinced that from the East I could hear the distant pounding of guns.

The world, wounded chief, seemed dying. The great spear, sought as a healer throughout the West, was simultaneously dreaded for its poisoned tip. Klingsor commanded, a tortured face on the murky horizon, self-maimed and scornful, wielding a black grail, spurious magic, for world power. We inhabited a terrain of huge shouts, baked towns, scalded fields. People marched, though the more they tramped, the less they progressed. Parsifal could have inspired a march but was inconceivable as part of it, booted,

247

helmeted: unwittingly, he would have transformed it to a procession, leading it to some fresh meadow where all would demand a story, or perchance over a cliff, himself but no others growing wings in the process.

In Provence Faithful Henry had ordered a search for the buried Grail, by soldiers with hazel rods and steel detectors, so far in vain. No more than Parsifal had I been much concerned with this enigmatic object. We knew, of course, legends of a god tilting the blue cup of the sky, showering mortals with random and often inappropriate gifts. To him, the Grail symbolized a bright, distant gleam, a path to fulfilment. For him, Hell was stagnation, walls closing in. Heaven was always movement. The Grail, Heaven itself, he might now locate not in the centre of the world but in the centre of the mind where light and darkness meet.

Today the Great Queen had finally evaporated. In Italy Hercules had achieved a brutal return, bestriding the ancient peninsula, his shouts scaring all save Wolf and Steel Boss. I once had witnessed Wolf's visit to Rome which, shabby and impoverished, had to be embellished with vast, sham-classical cardboard frontages hired from film studios to conceal slums and decrepit tenements.

Few leaders survived the test of light. Wolf ruled the core of the old Empire, sacrificing to an imaginary past, while, in the north, the Steel Boss sacrificed to a future of his own devising. Briefly, the triumvirs clasped hands, renewing universal war. Like Parsifal, they not only dreamt but enacted their dreams.

My mind, logical in professional dealings, is elsewhere oblique, snatching, often too late, at passing colours, sensations, shapes, striving to relate them to patterns continually elusive. The past is no Roman road but more often a maze, sometimes a shadow within which I seek instants of reality. Sometimes a tressed, sumptuous lady in light-green velvet stands on grass flowered white and scarlet, stroking a pale unicorn and watched by a golden, slightly aggrieved lion: pyramids fade as the world turns: a ruler, amid wild plaudits, advances to frozen doom: song stills a multitude.

I had few beliefs, only some apprehension of a rich texture of life, now glowing, now dulled: my existence is now a torrent, then jammed.

Gawain's chapped face and raw, bitter eyes I saw no more and I heard some rumour that he had perished violently at a well or ford. Only poets were certain, but they all disagreed, tending, moreover, to choose words best suited not for truth but for rhyme.

Parsifal I have, inevitably, failed fully to realize, less because he was, or seemed to be, unfinished and over-passive but from my own lack of subtle candour that might have induced more

248

confidences from him. Incapable of deceit, he had degrees of silence, spreading a blank page which I have inscribed as best I can. A poet, a musician, could give more direct access, as they can when imagining the deaf. Had I the skills, I should contrive not music drama but a viola sonata, to convey the smile within his smiles, the masks under his face, the unheard laugh, the pain or desire beneath his stories.

He too I never spoke to again, though on my diplomatic missions I occasionally fancied a glimpse of him in a youthful form giving florins to a beggar, helping a woman drag a heavy cart, or seated wide-eyed in a theatre accompanied by ladies agog not with the play but with him.

For a time rumours flitted about his name: he had been haunted, in misery and wonder, by the words of Jeanne d'Arc – 'The Light comes in the name of the Voice' – and dismayed by a long-lost rebuke from 'a creature in woman's form. . . . God alone knows what it was'. Most agree that he devoted himself wholly to ravaged and penniless Kundry and that together they discovered a sublime peace. That she was abject and pleading I cannot believe.

Popular memories of him, however, if not wholly crushed, were dispersed in the inferno of the Thirty Years' War when again the cauldron boiled over, scalding the West. Later, when his image revived, it was distorted, more so even that that of Jesus. Nor was this surprising. Uninterested in preaching or founding a group, he was of those who write only in dust. He left no message: for the virtuous he was a token, somewhat epicene, a youthful innocence and love, embracing whomever he met and indeed, in some legend, he invented the kiss. He has no shrine in Transylvania, is never evoked by drooling or foul-mouthed Californian drug-idiots.

Perhaps that curious 'Knight of the Centre' tag denoted some principle of balance, reinforced by his 'sereneta' poise, his left in harmony with his right. In ballad and woodcut, however, he achieved no place: carnival and puppet theatre ignored him, only a few scholars and poets cherished his name. And Wagner. In the atrocious regimes of Wolf and Steel Boss certain saints and messiahs retained power, but not Parsifal. No rescuing hawk swooped from the sky, no polite saviour performed a casual miracle, helpful dwarfs were promptly gassed.

Jesus, though often as inexplicit, was the more astringent and powerful, wielding irony, anger, knowledge. Parsifal did not. Both had pity, both contrived life on their own terms, Jesus convinced of his own mission, a word that may have meant nothing to Parsifal. He was not a poet carving profiles of moments and silence; he had no talent but conceivably some genius, growing the third eye of self-scrutiny, and sensing that he that loseth his life shall save it. Within himself he enjoyed long moments and brief, exquisite hours. I cannot imagine him screaming under torture, or betraying friends. Professing no absolute beliefs, he demanded no homage. In bed he probably slept, soundly and at once, entering his Other World at will. I imagine him and Kundry sleeping naked, hand in hand, gliding not into each other's bodies but into each other's dreams.

Much of his allure derives from misreadings. People read of his poverty without understanding that this meant not penury – he never lacked subsidies – but political impotence, in affairs with which he was unconcerned.

What did I learn from him? Very little. That in a totally brutal society his smile would be insufficient, that a youth who can neither shiver nor shake is inhuman. In siege and death camp people sustained themselves through stoicism, fear of death, desire for revenge, seldom to imitate a Parsifal. His belief, shared with Jesus and Socrates, that wickedness derives from ignorance, is demonstrably untrue. Faithful Henry knew very well what he did, and gloried in it, from positions if not of scholarship, then at least from research. Gawain could have given important answers.

I did learn to fear charm, sugary amiability, more than I did frank savagery. Often my irritation with Parsifal outbid my affection. Save towards Kundry, his feelings were too perplexing. He appeared all of a piece, but I was never certain. In his desires, or lack of them, in his undoubted curiosity, he may have seen life as towering extremes, or as a bland flow towards nowhere in particular.

Wagner alone preserves him. Him I first met parading amongst devotees in dark, floppy cap and cloth-of-gold trousers, soon praising vegetarianism while gulping hunks of venison. Braying the necessity for chastity, he had nevertheless booked a double room.

Experience has warned me that major artists, generous in flourishing their talents, are often mean with their personalities. Wagner was an uncomfortable presence, noisily overbearing, though I was glad of his account, delivered with self-satisfied winks and chuckles, of the origins of his marvellous *Rheingold*. In Genoa he had been awarded what he called the Order of Dysentery, First Class, through overeating ice-cream. On the boat home he lay very sick, barely conscious, sleepless. In rocking haze he felt as if buried in water. Then a rushing turmoil, real or imagined, resolved itself into E Flat Minor, echoing in chords, repeated, fragmented, which ultimately steadied into prolonged melodic structure still resounding with undulating intimations of water.

To me he was initially civil, perhaps scenting from my attire the chance of further royal patronage, but when I mentioned, albeit casually, that I had known Parsifal and might perhaps be able to assist his great work, he was offended and turned his back.

The work itself, for all its sonorous splendours, seldom recalled my friend, who would never have exclaimed, 'The Saviour's cry is stealing through me.' That he 'was chosen by God as a Saviour' he would have received in silence, impossible to interpret, but would not have besought Kundry to have faith in the Redeemer and then baptized her. I never heard him commend any orthodox belief, though he might have recognized Wagner's insight when, kissing Kundry, his hero cries what Klingsor had long known, 'The pain of loving!' Platitudinous but telling.

I was always coarsely determined to survive, not from fear of death – itself probably an inconvenient blind alley – but from a need to bear witness, however unsatisfactory, of certain events. When the malodorous pact between Wolf and Steel Boss collapsed, I was twice invited by the Swedish Red Cross to deal with Faithful Henry in the matter of prisoners of war, Scandinavian hostages, and those unknown millions in camps.

'Imagine it – London, New York, in an ocean of flame. The skyscrapers alight, toppling, groaning. A huge pyre of diseased intellect, free thought, bad breeding. Destroyed, my dear sir, by the new weapon. And by the crusader's soul, the refined outlook and bearing of the true soldier. The triumph of the Grail, the real enlightenment, the real ascension.'

The war was ending, with Wolf's bitter, despairing promises of secret weapons, dedicated, irresistible cubs defending his mountain lair, star-insured miracles. Then, with Eastern hordes at the gate, his capital reeling under titanic blows, he killed himself underground. 'I have been Europe's last hope. She has shown herself impervious to love and persuasion. My own people are unworthy, they have no right to survive.' He denounced even Faithful Henry, for attempts on the succession. A new government was being formed. The Black Guards, however, still held thousands of prisoners, for whom I was again negotiating. Faithful Henry himself, with gambler's assurance, had attempted contact with international Jewry, admitting 'past unpleasantness and mis-understanding'.

I had driven to north Schleswig in a car painted with white stripes and red crosses, moving very cautiously along mined roads, through bombed streets and burning suburbs. A pall of dust and rubble obscured the sun, dim people stood mutely waiting for news. From a tavern sign hung a uniformed body, placarded *I dangle here because I left my unit without permission.*

Now 'Lord of the Upper Rhine', Faithful Henry had twice been defeated in battle, to the satisfaction of his rivals. Reaching his HQ I had expected to be searched, but the guards were listless, allowing me inside with perfunctory shrugs and nods seemingly distilled from drugs or fear. Artillery was audible, some ten miles away, flames crackled nearby, occasional wails lifted from the sulphuric gloom. HQ was a damaged, unostentatious villa, and I at once noticed that guards and clerks were no longer glistening Nordics: amongst them were slanted eyes, squat bodies, bowed shoulders, imperfect eyes and teeth. Their predecessors were long dead, or at the front, always retreating, and lurching back, and delayed by frantic orders to exhume and burn thousands of bodies from mass graves.

Faithful Henry was soon guaranteeing me a spectacular triumph, in which my country would be fortunate to be allowed to exist. His uniform, like his spectacles, like the ramshackle office, was soiled, his stomach cramps had evidently worsened, for his pallid face was tight with pain even amid his boasts and promises. Behind him hung a wide, astrological map.

He continued, but momentarily my attention lapsed. A month previously, his country ripped apart, the enemy's tanks but two days away, the Grand Huntsman had invited me to a gala on his estates. The banquet must have made millionaires of the black-market barons. Boards were stacked with steaming haunches of venison and boar, platters of goose, capon, sucking pig, gleaming backs of spiced ham whose resemblance to our host almost infringed copyright. Roasted peacocks, stuffed swans, baskets of quails, recalled the Duke's last ceremonial appearance, and the brazen, jangling eagles borne aloft as the invaders held triumph in Paris a few years back.

Nevertheless, in the courtyards behind, being shoved into lorries, vans, rustic carts, were European art masterpieces, antiques, bric-à-brac, thrust together indiscriminately for hasty removal. I saw a Tintoretto, a Tiepolo, enticing Bouchers, even Van Duelph's celebrated, if inaccurate rendering of Parsifal standing dejected, in a grove, bow in hand, a dead swan at his feet. Books in ornate, crested bindings were heaped like stooks.

Amid a retinue of tailors, barbers, jewellers, art dealers, theatrical maestros and designers, the Grand Huntsman, outsize as ever, dominated his guests, the scornful diplomats, uneasy Party officials, puzzled journalists, wavering toadies, ambling between the groups in a violet kimono draped over showy white uniform, rows of medals, broad, jewelled belt, red socks and

252

shoes. A bluish paste covered the massive, porcine face, through which blue eyes stared like glass. Around us some hundred foresters stood clutching boar spears in green leather jackets, medieval peasant hats, curled antique horns at their shoulders, slavering hounds leashed to their wrists.

He was cordial to me, for his first wife had been Swedish. He spoke confidently of opera, his daughter, his rebuilding projects, movies about Napoleon, Suss Oppenheimer, Frederick the Great, flushing irritably at my ignorance of these. To be unaware of the magnificent, he growled, was a great crime, then unexpectedly he grinned like a schoolboy over a bag of sweets. Of the war he said nothing, though twice a mass flotilla of bombers darkened the landscape, racing to pound Wolf's last army.

Parsifal would have greeted him, as he would Wolf, with a friendliness that I now find supine. Again I reflected that such a jovial freebooter, intelligent but ruthless, could be the most dangerous of all. Nevertheless, within a month, he had crumbled, was blown away into dust or legend.

I forced myself back to Faithful Henry, and now saw that his ceremonial dagger was replaced by a small pistol. We were alone. Throughout the house was a tight atmosphere in which a shuffle, a cough, in the improvised ante-room reverberated as menacingly as the barrage farther off. I also realized that my brief was already outdated. I was dealing with a phantom, petty lord of an Other World no larger than a burial mound, which in truth it was, and still shrinking.

'You must know that I have made a discovery of the utmost importance. The historical saviour was never Jesus. A vile conspiracy transferred to him the teachings and miracles of a much-travelled man who died at a great age. I speak of Apollonius of Tyana, the forgotten Master. I intend to take the utmost steps to remedy this misapprehension. He is on a level with Parsifal himself. The two together . . .' – the unctuous smile suggested the likelihood of a third – 'could correct the whole world. I have given orders for a temple to be built in my future capital of Burgundy-Lotharingia. Christianity I shall ban, you remember its weakening the Vandals and Ostrogoths, and the traditional reverence for dead heroes.'

I was seeing the ending of a drama, which was to make me feel that I should have centred this book not on Parsifal but on Gawain and Klingsor.

My mission being useless, I attempted a few moments of reasonable converse. 'Minister, do you regret nothing?'

'Ah!' His small wince was involuntary, followed by a strange, sliding smile which almost suggested a moral seriousness, then he gazed at me in puzzled wonder. 'Yes, I too have sinned!'

253

He stood very still, as if to receive orders, and indeed his next words sounded as though learnt from a stern teacher.

'In such times, I can term them abnormal – my boys dying appalling deaths, forty degrees below zero – the bravest of the brave, first into battle, last to die. In the Honest Labour camps, too, the instructors have suffered strains, headaches, which move me enormously. Clouds of smoke, repulsive ashes – unbecoming to men of chivalry. It is the curse of greatness that to create new life it must step over the dead.'

He swallowed, lost concentration, hesitated, tried again, the unsteadiness of his hand more pronounced. 'Such times . . . they forced me to disobey the first rule of my Order.' He was abject, ashamed, shoulders dwindling, mouth drooping, a mere incision on a decaying face, eyes as if pleading forgiveness. 'You will have noticed, I had to recruit racial dirt. Balts, Ukrainians, Tartars, Galician gypsies . . . Muslims . . .' – he listed them in methodical need for accuracy – 'into brigades bearing the most hallowed names in Europe. How your friend would have grieved! He, supreme embodiment of purity!'

He had been forcing out words against tears and self-disgust, but now said briskly, 'You will convey my plans to the Swedish government. In this I shall be acting on my own responsibility, for the present authorities remain incomplete and, when I have time, I shall join them, then disperse them without discussion. You will also include the Americans and British, who must be allowed some part in the reconstruction. I must tell you that the late American President lacked racial and political gravity. He was a proof that Latin and polyglot civilization and culture are matters of people pretending to be what they are not. His death was an act of Providence, Providence itself. I shall form a Party of Union. As guaranteed.' At my perplexity, he gestured, with surprising force, even arrogance, at the wall map. 'Most favourable stars have been plotted by Herr Wolf, of Hamburg. The West . . .' – he spoke as if to a fellow conspirator, not of the first rank – 'cannot dispense with me, the guardian of order.'

His speech was a complacent purr, belied only by the disobedient hand. 'After an hour's talk, which you will arrange, the American generals will admit that without me they will face chaos. Twenty millions are on the move. The British too will concur. They will salute the wisdom of our dead leader, that readiness to forgo freedom is the mark of true culture. Survival is what now matters, for all of us, against the barbarians. Our recent Minister of Information showed intelligence by remarking that Shakespeare made Lear insufficiently cunning. Together we can withstand the verminous East, can overcome all, save perhaps the temptations of overwhelming victory. Here too mine will be the restraining hand.

'But I have secret information that the Russian advance is spent. They cannot risk further attack. Their new offensive is nothing but a gigantic, I go so far as to say stupendous, bluff. Staff officers declare we have no more troops, but that is lying, bald-faced treason. To counter this, I have revived Frederick the Great's personal order, that cowards be publicly thrashed. I am visiting the law's ultimate penalty on even the relatives of those who surrender without having been wounded. But there is a matter on which you can advise me.' The dry voice softened again, its earnestness childish but for the repellent eyes.

He then astonished me further. Could he be serious? But he was incapable of humour.

'I intend to conduct negotiations myself. In person, who else? But you can inform me, versed as you are in bourgeois protocol, on a matter of very considerable moment. Do you recommend that I greet their supreme commander with a bow or a handshake? On such niceties . . .' – he paused, as he had done before, savouring a word he could never have used previously – 'matters of the utmost urgency may depend.'

I was soon watching his departure 'to the temporary seat of power', offering himself to the new government. Leading some thirty glossy automobiles, he at once rammed his own into a barbed-wire fence, from which an hour was needed to extricate it. The rest you know. The eerie drive, his arrival at Government House, greeting the new leader with willingness to serve under him, his immediate dismissal as politically questionable, proscribed by the victors. With a cavalcade always diminishing he drove in endlessly constricting circles with no coherent goal, until, wholly deserted, with false papers and rudimentary disguise, he joined thousands of refugees, and, about to cross water, inviting arrest by, pedant to the last, unnecessarily proffering those forged identity papers to an indifferent British sentry. But a suspicious officer ordered his arrest. His suicide followed, preceded perhaps by a yearning thought of Parisfal, now left to Wagner alone.

I too may be a sentimentalist. On the first evening of peace, avoiding raucous celebrations, I stood beneath stones made colossal by moon glimmer, lined as if by runes and expertly sited for purposes not wholly proven. Lost powerhouses of spirit. All was still, though clamour and music trailed far off. Green light seemed woven between the dim, silvery stones and stiff trees. I awaited the witching moment, the boundary between one day and the next, expecting what would never come: not Faithful Henry engulfed in silliness, not the Duke in mercurial folly and ardours, not Monseigneur's chatter or a lecture from Kepler, not

255

Wagner in his pomp, not a savant denying the existence of opposites, but the moan of old Gawain, red gambler, as he searched for Parsifal.